CHECKPOINT CHARLIE

A NOVEL BY
TOM ARNOLD

Checkpoint Charlie is a work of fiction, although it is based on events that occurred in Europe in the summer of 1966, of which I was a part. It is as historically accurate as research and memory allow. All the names have been changed.

First printing: August 2006
Second printing: January 2014

ISBN 978-0-9849954-1-7

Author's websites:
        www.bleugenepress.com
        www.tomarnold.us

Published by:

Bleugene Press
3471 Timberline Drive
Eugene, Oregon, 97405
U.S.A.

Text set in Dutch801 Rm BT
Book layout by Skye Blaine, skyeblaine@comcast.net
Cover design by Jennifer Andrews, jennifer@helioscreative.com

Printed in the United States of America

For Carolyn

I am indebted to the following people whose support and help were invaluable to me in writing *Checkpoint Charlie*: Dan Armstrong, Mary Arnold, Linda Clare, Wayne Harrison, Bredan Marsh, Jeanie Planck, John Reed, and Mark Schroeder.

I would like to thank Boris Bulatovic, Wolfgang Epple, Dorothee Hoffmann, Giulietta Kneidel, Lenka Lopuchovska, Sebastian Oarcea, Monika Rauch, and Christian Tanggård, who helped me with translations into Danish, German, Czech, Slovakian, Hungarian, and Serbian. The English I pretty much handled on my own. Please see the final pages for direct translations.

I am grateful to Alexandra Hildebrandt of the Mauermuseum—*Museum Haus am Checkpoint Charlie*—and to the museum itself, for providing details regarding escape attempts.

The map of east Europe as it existed in 1966 is the work of Jennifer Andrews. Her picture is worth at least a thousand of my words.

Finally, I owe a special thanks to Shelton Leslie for his infinite patience in keeping this stubborn Luddite and his computers harmoniously functioning.

Tom Arnold
January 13, 2006

Author's Note

Much has been written about the Cold War, that half century of global tension following the end of World War Two. It is not my intention in this forward to provide you with a detailed history lesson, but rather to refresh your memory with a few pertinent facts regarding the political climate of that period with the hope of enhancing your enjoyment and appreciation of *Checkpoint Charlie*.

After World War Two, Europe was divided into two parts: Countries on the western part of the continent, (Belgium, Denmark, France, Iceland, Italy, Luxembourg, The Netherlands, Norway, Portugal, and the United Kingdom), fell under the influence of the United States. The North Atlantic Treaty Organization, NATO, was the military alliance of these nations, which also included Canada. In subsequent years, NATO expanded to include Greece, West Germany, Turkey, and Spain. The countries of east Europe, (Albania, Bulgaria, Czechoslovakia, East Germany, Hungary, Poland, and Romania), became satellite nations of the Soviet Union. Their military alliance was the Warsaw Pact. Greece, lying at the far southeastern edge of Europe, was not allied with the East Block as you might think looking at a map, but with the west. By a strange quirk of political and geographical fate the most repressive Communist regime, neo-Stalinist Albania, and the most open, friendly-to-the-west Communist state, freewheeling Yugoslavia, each shared a border with Greece, and with each other. Albania, under the rigid dictatorship of Enver Hoxha, was closed both to tourism from outside and emigration from within. By contrast the president of Yugoslavia, Marshall Tito, permitted almost unrestricted movement by both Yugoslav nationals and foreigners across his borders.

For all Europeans, however, no matter where they lived, the Iron Curtain was both a physical and a psychological barrier between east and west.

With a desire to both punish the Germans for their past sins and to prevent them from regaining political and military power and perhaps perpetrating yet another world war, defeated Germany was severed into two states, East and West Germany, the *Deutsche Demokratische Republik* (DDR) and the *Bundesrepublik Deutschland* (BRD), respectively. Although they shared a common heritage, language, and culture, (in contrast with the Yugoslavs, who did not), the German people also had a collective responsibility for the war itself and for the atrocities committed by Adolph Hitler on the Jews, Catholics, homosexuals, Gypsies, and the other groups whom his Nazi death squads sought to eliminate.

Nowhere in Germany, indeed in all of Europe, was the Iron Curtain partition experienced more dramatically than in Berlin, which was controlled by the victorious World War Two allies: Russia, France, Great Britain, and the United States. The ancient city of Berlin had been the capital of Germany before the War, remained so during Hitler's Third Reich, and was the seat of government for the new state of East Germany. (Bonn, six hundred kilometers to the west, became the capital of West Germany.)

As postwar relations between the Soviet Union and its former wartime comrades-in-arms chilled into the Cold War, Moscow's grip on its satellite republics tightened and the city of Berlin became a pawn between the US and the USSR. Tens of thousands of East Germans, including many East Berliners, fled west, seeking a higher standard of living and greater political freedom. Finally on August 13, 1961, the president of the DDR, Walter Ulbricht, with the approval of Moscow, physically divided the city itself. Overnight, government workers constructed a barrier through Berlin. At first only a temporary barricade of wood and barbed wire, it was soon replaced with a permanent concrete wall, topped with a round casing and razor wire. This almost insurmountable structure, which became known simply as *die Mauer*, or the Wall, was a miniature version of the Iron Curtain that divided Europe. Nowhere else were the armies of NATO and the Warsaw Pact stationed in such close proximity to one another, 'eyeball to eyeball' in the words of one observer. With the possible exception of Cuba during the missile crisis in the fall of 1962, Berlin was the most likely flash point for yet another worldwide, armed conflict.

A wide, featureless strip of ground flanked the 3.5 meter high Wall. This barren buffer zone, widely known as the 'death strip', was booby-trapped with mines and trip wires. The dirt was regularly raked so the footprints of anyone who ventured in could be easily spotted and followed. Cruelly named border guards, *Volkspolizei*, patrolled the entire area. The People's Police were under strict orders to shoot to kill anybody who tried to escape.

After a while, as it became more and more difficult for the East German regime to recruit enough border guards willing to gun down their fellow citizens trying to escape along the 300 kilometer border between East and West Germany, the government found it expedient to install stationary, unmanned motion-sensitive guns. *Selbstschussgeräte* automatically fired deadly shrapnel designed to maim as well as to kill. Originally, these weapons had been developed during World War Two for use in Nazi concentration camps, but were not actually deployed until the postwar division of Germany. (Presumably it had been easier for Hitler to find Germans willing to kill Jews than for Ulbricht to find Germans willing to shoot other Germans.) Beginning in 1971, some 45,000 of these obscene weapons were installed along the border. Along with unlucky would-be escapers, *Selbstschussgeräte* slaughtered more than a few wayward dogs and cats that strayed into the barren swath of no man's land. Although they were never actually deployed inside the city limits of Berlin, the installation of these unmanned, automatic guns in the countryside freed up the manpower necessary to fully militarize the Wall. (It is illustrative that in a society plagued with chronic unemployment, the socialist regime was unable to recruit, train, and arm sufficient numbers of young men and women willing to fire on their own countrymen.)

Die Mauer divided Berliners and prevented almost all contact between German citizens fortunate enough to live in the western part of the city and those trapped in the East Sector. Families were divided, lovers were separated, and workers were cut off from their places of employment. The main bridge over the Spree River, which meanders through Berlin, was closed, further isolating east from west. Subway stations in East Berlin, known as *Geisterbahnhöfe*, or ghost stations, were closed and patrolled by armed *Vopos* ready to shoot anyone who tried to jump on or off a train.

Before the Wall was built, movement throughout Berlin was tolerated by the East German regime, if not encouraged. Once the construction of *die Mauer* was complete, however, leaving the East Sector was next to impossible for a resident of East Berlin, unless one had a large amount of hard currency, or possessed an extraordinary capacity for risk and danger. With 'real money', one could bribe one's way to freedom in the west. Without West German marks or French franks or American dollars, however, the only remaining option for someone determined to 'go west' was a daring exploit of some kind. Such desperate attempts to escape usually ended in failure and failure often meant being shot by the *Vopos* or, if one were lucky, captured and imprisoned in a bleak penitentiary or asylum.

Between the end of World War Two in 1945 and the early 1960s, the West Sector was largely reconstructed. Buildings which had been bombed into rubble were removed and in their places sleek new apartments, business centers, shops, factories, restaurants, and parks were built. Trees were planted, streets repaved. All aspects of civic infrastructure were renewed until it was almost impossible to see any trace of the War. Free market capitalism transformed West Berlin into an island of bright lights, stores overflowing with merchandise, and smartly dressed people. This first-world enclave was completely surrounded by the dull, gray, dimly-lit socialist state of the *Deutsche Demokratische Republik*. From a propaganda perspective, it could not have been better planned. What better way of demonstrating the superiority of western capitalism over Soviet socialism than by creating a sparkling jewel of the former in the belly of the latter? For this very reason, West Berlin was an ever-increasing irritant to the East German government.

By 1966 precious little civic rehabilitation had been undertaken in the East Sector. Although such official sites as the Communist Party headquarters, the seat of the East German government, the infamous 'Palace of Tears' border control on Friedrichstrasse, and the offices of the hated State Police, the *Staatssicherheit*, featured newly constructed—if architecturally tedious—buildings, most of East Berlin had changed little in the intervening years since the end of the War. A few shoddily built apartment buildings, similar to low-income projects in many large eastern American cities, rose from the landscape of wartime destruction. In some areas, the rubble of bombed buildings lay where it had fallen more than twenty years earlier. One can easily understand how West Berlin became a glittering beacon, beckoning to anyone wishing to escape East Germany for a better life in the west.

While leaving East Berlin was strictly forbidden and access into the East Sector by West German nationals was almost as difficult, other westerners could enter and leave as tourists. There were, as one might expect, strict guidelines and conditions: All visitors had to be out of the East Sector by 6:00 PM. Photography was discouraged and in many areas prohibited. Every tourist was required to exchange a minimum amount of hard, western currency for East German marks, ostensibly for use while a guest in East Berlin. However, consumer goods were in short supply so there wasn't much to buy and *Ostmark* were completely worthless anywhere else. Furthermore, any unspent *Ostmark* had to be surrendered at the border upon returning to West Berlin; they couldn't be exchanged back into western currency or saved for another visit.

Travelers wishing to see the splendor of socialism, East German style, passed through one main portal: a heavily-armed border crossing on Friedrichstrasse known as Checkpoint Charlie.

(Many people have asked me where the name Checkpoint Charlie came from. Travelers going from west Europe to East Berlin passed through three checkpoints: Checkpoint Alpha at Helmstedt on the East German Border, Checkpoint Bravo at Dreilinden at the Berlin city limit, and Checkpoint Charlie between West and East Berlin.)

A sign warned all those who chose to cross into East Berlin at Checkpoint Charlie: YOU ARE LEAVING THE AMERICAN SECTOR. Ostensibly to recognize the four nations governing Berlin, but more to eliminate any possibility of misunderstanding, the warning was repeated in French, Russian, and German. Another sign, primarily intended for American tourists and not as easily seen, warned that there were no diplomatic relations between the US and the DDR and travel into East Berlin was highly unadvisable. Anyone running afoul of the authorities in the East Sector could expect no help from the embassy.

Between the construction of *die Mauer* in 1963 and its destruction when Germany was reunified in 1989, twenty-six years later, approximately five thousand East Berliners escaped to the west and thousands more surely contemplated doing so. According to official records, several hundred wall jumpers, *Mauerspringer*, were wounded or injured trying to climb the Wall. Estimates vary, but somewhere between 190 and 240 more died for their dreams of freedom.

——✶—✶—✶—✶——

"*Gallia est omnis divisa in partes tres...*" 50 BC (approx.)
— Rome.

Julius Caesar, addressing the Roman Senate upon his triumphant return from the Gallic wars, explaining his division of Gaul into three regions to prevent its resurgence as a world power.

——✶—✶—✶—✶——

22 June, 1966 —
Berlin

Was ist das hier?" shouted the huge East German policewoman, standing mere inches away from me. Her fetid spittle sprayed on my face, chest and arms. I was completely naked and had no idea where my clothes, or for that matter, my friends were. The soldiers had separated us soon after we'd entered the concrete building at the Wall. My passport was also missing, although it would have been worthless there, anyway.

The fat guard's broad Teutonic face was flushed with anger. She had coarse, short-cropped blonde hair and wore little, if any, makeup. I couldn't tell. A deep, ugly red gash slashed through her right eyebrow like a misplaced Heidelberg scar. This woman's thick body was stuffed into a uniform of the *Volkspolizei*, the border police of the East German Republic. The buttons on her dull-green tunic pulled at the buttonholes, revealing a tan blouse underneath. Each buckle on her Sam Browne belt was clasped at the last hole. Blondie trembled with rage. In spite of my terror, an incongruent, funny image splashed across my mind: If she got any madder, she would explode and smother me in an avalanche of blubber. I struggled to suppress a smile, which only enraged her further.

"What is this?" she repeated, slapping me on the chest. I stood in front of her, my back pressed against the cinderblock wall, my fingers laced together on top of my head. A single, overhead floodlight illuminated the smoky room. I was alone, wet from fear and heat, in a small, windowless cellblock with this big enraged guard and her two smaller, younger male subordinates. She had a pistol in a holster and carried a riding crop. Blondie was a caricature of a Nazi SS officer straight out of a Hollywood 'B' movie, except that it was 1966, twenty years after the end of the war.

The two young men, also in *Vopo* uniforms, alternated between aiming their Kalashnikov AK-47 automatic guns directly at my groin and smoking cigarette after cigarette. I would have liked a smoke myself, but they didn't offer me one, and I didn't dare ask.

Blondie's supremacy filled the small room like a stench; the two other guards were closed-mouth, rigid, and silent. Were they as petrified of her as I was?

"You will turn around with face to the wall!"

As I obeyed her order, the last thing I saw was her picking up a pair of rubber surgical gloves from her grey steel desk.

"You will separate your legs and put your hands upon your feet!" Every word from Blondie was a shouted command and I wondered if she was even capable of normal speech.

Over my shoulder, I watched in horror as she pulled the gloves onto her sausage fingers, slowly and deliberately, one casing at a time.

"*Achtung!* Follow the order immediately!"

The two male guards moved toward me. I spread my legs and bent over, grasping my ankles with my hands. With a guard on each side of me, blocking my view, I heard Blondie's boots clack as she crossed the bare cement floor in a solid, measured cadence. I felt her latex paws on my quivering butt cheeks, spreading me open. My anus puckered, knowing what was coming next.

"Yeaooowww!" I shrieked as she thrust two thick, meaty fingers deep inside my rectum. I involuntarily clenched my sphincter muscles, which only made the pain even more excruciating. Forgetting Blondie's command, I reached back and grabbed at her hand. The two *Vopo* guards seized my wrists and yanked my arms away. Still holding their AK-47s, they leaned backwards until I thought my shoulders would separate. I was completely immobile, powerless to resist. Slowly, Blondie raised her arm, lifting me off the floor. I could feel her sadistic grin like a burning iron on my back. I was being torn apart and I was about to pass out. Finally, after what seemed like hours, she jerked her fingers out with a corkscrew-like twist. Her knuckles tore at my anus. I fell back on my feet.

"Ayyyeeee," I screamed again, straightening up, desperately wanting to clutch my backside, which was on fire. I didn't know what she expected to find, what she suspected I might be smuggling out of her People's Republic; if she had wanted to intimidate me, though, she had been one hundred percent successful. Along with the searing pain in my anus, I felt completely humiliated and vulnerable.

"Your hands will be upon your head!" the blonde *Vopo* shouted. "Your back will be to the wall!"

The guards let loose of my wrists and I struggled to clasp my hands over my head. I turned and faced my tormentor. As I pressed my raging backside against the rough cinderblock surface, I wondered if Blondie realized that obeying her order was providing me with a slight amount of relief. Blondie snapped the rubber gloves as she peeled them off her hands and dropped them into a wastebasket. Her thin lips formed into a cruel smile as she picked up the riding crop.

"Ich nicht sprechen Deutsch," I lied, for what must have been the hundredth time. "I do not speak German." Although I did, in fact, speak a little German, I was terrified and not about to let her know. Naked and alone, the language barrier was the only defense I had left. *Was I being detained? Under arrest?* Although the Wall sliced through Berlin less than a hundred meters from where I stood, the four of us were light-years from freedom. I had no idea when, or even if, we would be released, or why we were being held. I wondered if they had lawyers in East Germany. *Would I be taken to court and forced to defend myself in a language I barely understood? And against what charges?* Maybe I would simply be taken to some remote location and shot. *Who would ever know?* Sweat dripped off my face and down my back.

All day long, while the four of us had wandered the desolate, nearly deserted streets of East Berlin, the thick concrete walls of the detention bunker had been soaking up mid-summer Teutonic heat. It might have been cooling down outside, maybe even turning to dusk, but I had no way of knowing. The tiny interrogation cell was stuffy and hot. Blondie's hostility contaminated the air; I inhaled her bile with every breath. Nothing from outside came in; no light, no breeze, no sound, nothing. In between Blondie's rants, a wall clock ticked in the silence. Other than large black-and-white framed photographs of Nikita Khrushchev and Erich Honecker, the clock was the only adornment in this stark chamber. Never had I seen a red hand move so slowly. Perspiration drained down the crack between my buttocks, intensifying the pain Blondie's thick fingers had inflicted. Under these dire circumstances, I knew playing dumb was my only option. I wished I were anywhere else, even back in California. Time passed slowly. I had a grim opportunity to contemplate.

I had fled the Golden State almost two years earlier, less than a month out of high school. The country seethed with political and racial discontent. Race riots battled anti-war demonstrations for headline space. Less than three years earlier, the Ku Klux Klan had firebombed a black church in a city we called Bombingham, killing four little girls, and things were only getting worse. The Draft Board was demanding my presence for a physical in Berkeley, with my subsequent induction into the United States Army a certainty. Two of my friends had already been killed in action in Viet Nam. Every night on television, Walter Cronkite told the nation how many more lives had been lost in the twenty-four hours since his last report; the maimed were beyond counting. Ho Chi Minh and Malcolm X were in every American living room.

I had no intention of being shipped off to Southeast Asia. The cold war in Europe had been on the periphery of my adolescent attention, competing against what, for me, were much bigger issues. Until that afternoon in Berlin.

"I believe you speak German. But I will question you in English. Explain, *bitte*, these marks." Blondie whacked my chest and legs with her riding crop, not hard enough to cut into my flesh, but with enough force to sting painfully. Wide, horizontal strips of hair were missing. My body hair was thick to begin with and the bands made me look like a striped convict. A fitting image, I thought: Did Blondie know about traditional American prison garb? I wondered what German prisoners wore. My skin, already tender from the torn-off tape, reddened into welts under her abuse.

"I do not speak German. I do not understand German. I am an American citizen. I want to return to the other side." I considered myself an expatriate and the irony of uttering the words 'I am an American citizen' was not lost on me. The two young *Vopo* guards fidgeted. They didn't look much older than I was. Had they been drafted? Was there a draft in East Germany? Their Kalashnikov AK-47s remained aimed directly at my groin.

"Explain why you have not hair here." Blondie smacked her crop against a tender red furrow on my chest. I winced and gritted my teeth.

I was not about to tell her that yesterday we'd smuggled copies of *Der Stern, Die Welt, Newsweek*, and *Time* magazines across the border, taped to our bodies under our clothing, for our new friends in the East Sector. These weeklies were all forbidden, *verboten,* anywhere behind the Iron Curtain, but especially in East Germany. Why had we done this? I didn't know, except that it hadn't seemed so unreasonable, no more than a minor infraction of the rules. I didn't think it was a big deal, and I certainly didn't think we would get caught. Even if the border cops searched us at the Wall and discovered the contraband, how bad could the punishment possibly be? What more could they do to us besides confiscate the magazines and deny us entry? I was young and demonstrably foolish, as you will see. I often did things because they appeared to be good ideas at the time, without thinking of the consequences. Like hooking up with

Mara, which had felt right, at the beginning. Or, at least, it hadn't felt wrong.

I wondered how she was holding up. There wasn't much doubt about where she was; she would be enduring the same grilling, the same painful, intimate examination that I'd suffered through. Being a girl, it would be much worse for her. What I really wanted to know was; would she ever speak to me again?

"I demand to be taken to the American Embassy." This was a futile request; there *was* no American Embassy in East Berlin.

"You will tell me what I wish to know." Blondie's voice, for the first time, was now quiet, and consequently even more menacing. She returned to her desk and the massive wooden chair creaked beneath her bulk. The leaders of the Communist world scowled down at me in stoic disapproval while the clock ticked, marking the passing of my life. I had been held in this interrogation room for almost three hours. My arms ached, my back was sore, and my backside felt like it'd been torn open. The cement floor was wet with dripped sweat, and I badly needed to piss. So far, at least, I had not been beaten or tortured. Other than the painful, degrading full-body search and the whacks with Blondie's leather whip on my thighs and chest, I hadn't been touched at all. Nevertheless, standing naked with machine guns pointed at my genitals for so long terrified me. I'd never even been arrested before. It was only a matter of time before these thugs got serious.

A sign on the free side of Checkpoint Charlie advised tourists that they could expect no help whatsoever from the American Embassy in West Berlin if they got into trouble in the East Sector of the city. And we were in deep trouble. Louisa, Mara, and I were U.S. citizens. Simon was English and I assumed he was beyond the reach of the British Embassy. There would be no rescue.

"I demand you take me to my embassy." I tried to make my voice sound forceful but it came out a pathetic bleat. The entire might of the United States Army, that very same military machine I was doing my damnedest to stay out of, would be of no help in extracting a single American hippie from the forceful embrace of the *Volkspolizei*.

Eventually, the telephone on Blondie's desk rang, breaking the stillness. I jumped. The phone disappeared into her gigantic hand as she leapt to attention. The two young guards, who had slowly relaxed into inattention, sprang back into combat stance with their AK-47s again aimed at me. Looking at her fingers wrapped around the receiver and their fingers around the triggers sent chills up my spine.

"*Ja, mein Kommandant,*" she squeaked into the mouthpiece in a submissive tone of voice I had not yet heard. Slamming down the receiver, she shouted an order to her underlings, who saluted and left the room. Here it comes, I thought with a shudder; they would return any moment with handcuffs and rubber hoses. I tried to mentally prepare myself for the beating I knew was coming, knowing full well that I would crumble. My bladder would be the first part of my body to fail. I also felt pressure in my gut; Blondie's fingers had excited my bowels. I had a horrible vision of myself writhing in pain on the floor in a filthy soup of blood, piss, and shit.

The guards returned with a cardboard box and set it on Blondie's desk. They saluted without saying a word and resumed their positions at my sides. *This is it, this is where things get rough.*

Instead, the blonde *Vopo* opened the box and dumped the contents— my shoes, clothes, and wallet—onto the floor. Everything but my passport.

"You will dress now. Quickly! *Schnell! Schnell!*" She slapped her whip on the table. Even the other two guards jumped.

I was stunned at this sudden change, of course, but I didn't need her to order me a second time. I had no idea what was coming next, but it couldn't get any worse than what I'd already been through. Or could it? Was this tiny room only a temporary stop on my way to a permanent prison cell? *Where was my passport?*

Once I'd gotten dressed, I was marched at gunpoint down a short, narrow hallway. Blondie led the way and the two guards followed behind me, jabbing the barrels of their Kalashnikovs into the small of my back. The metallic clack of jack-boots echoed against the concrete walls.

Soon, I was reunited with Mara, Louisa, and Simon. I took several deep breaths. We were in the same large room we had passed through on our way into East Berlin, where we had submitted our passports to the *Volkspolizei* for inspection and purchased the required East German marks earlier that day. Through the steel-reinforced windows, we could see the concrete maze, illuminated by gigantic overhead floodlights, and beyond that, *die Mauer*. Checkpoint Charlie, our gateway to freedom, was tantalizingly close. I could almost feel the throbbing pulse of West Berlin, just beyond that hole in the wall. The reflection in the dark sky over the Wall reminded me of the Northern Lights. I wanted more than anything to be there, on the other side.

"Are you guys OK?" I asked. "How about you, sweetheart, you don't look so good." We waited, guarded by the young *Vopos*, on a hard, backless wooden bench. Mara quivered. Her face was pale, her thick, curly hair damp and stringy, her eyes glazed and red. She looked straight ahead without answering. Was she ignoring me or couldn't she hear me? I put my arm around her and she collapsed into my shoulder, sniffling softly. When I smoothed back her hair, she began sobbing.

By comparison, Louisa appeared much more composed. She sat with her arms straight and her palms flat on the bench next to her hips, raising herself slightly. Her eyes were closed as if she were meditating. I admired her stoicism. I could almost hear her say, 'and this, too, shall pass'. My blue work shirt was wet with sweat, and now with Mara's tears as well. I wished Mara were stronger, more like Louisa.

Simon nodded and muttered something hard and unintelligible. His eyes scanned the room through slits. His shirt was partially unbuttoned. I remembered Simon's naked body from the communal shower at the youth hostel, how little body hair he had. Maybe he hadn't aroused as much suspicion as I had.

Are you guys OK?" I repeated. "Did they make you—strip-search you completely—like they did me?"

The redness around Mara's eyes flooded the rest of her face as she nodded. She sat curled in an upright fetal position on the bench, her arms clenched around her knees.

Louisa said nothing; her contorted position was answer enough.

"Those bloody bastards had me bent over like I was some sort of flaming—" Simon growled through clenched jaws.

"*Seid still!*" Blondie shouted at us. I jumped away from Mara.

Mara was the most shaken up of the four of us. She'd shifted into a ball with her arms wrapped around her chest; her eyes scrunched shut, swaying slowly back and forth, as if in a trance. In one hand she held some white material crumpled up that might have been a handkerchief. Mara hadn't said a word. I felt closer to her than I had in months. I wanted to put my arms around her again, comfort her, but I didn't dare move. I felt guilty about getting her into this mess. In many ways, I had become Mara's protector as well as her lover and it was my fault she was here now. She hadn't wanted to come back into East Berlin this morning, but I'd insisted.

Mara and I had knocked around in Europe together for several months so I knew how traumatic this afternoon had been for her. This is not to say that three hours of degrading interrogation at gunpoint was easy for any of us, especially since we were completely naked the entire time. I couldn't imagine how Mara, who was so modest she had trouble peeing behind a tree, had endured her intimate ordeal.

"I'm so sorry, sweetheart," I whispered, "I had no idea this was going to happen."

Mara just trembled, her large breasts quivered freely inside her tee shirt. Her red cheeks were wet with tears. Strands of hair stuck to her forehead. I was afraid she'd gone into shock.

"Are you all right? Can you just hang on a little longer? I think we'll be out of here pretty soon." I tried to inject a note of hopefulness into my voice.

"It hurts everywhere," she mumbled, now glowering at me with shiny eyes. "You *know* what they did to my—to me."

A menacing glare from Blondie shut us up. I could envision her curling her lip and snarling. If it were true that people came to resemble their dogs, Blondie owned a Rottweiler.

We sat motionless and silent while an animated discussion began between the blonde *Vopo* and a shorter man who acted like her superior.

"*Du hast es nicht gefunden,*" the *Kommandant* said, his voice steady and quiet.

"*Ich traue denen nicht!*" Blondie answered. She had reverted to the same squeaky tone she had used when the phone rang. She pointed to us and glared.

"*Wir müssen sie gehen lassen. Wir dürfen keinen internationalen Zwischenfall riskieren.*" His tone remained firm and cold.

I couldn't fully understand what they were saying, but I surmised that Blondie wanted to continue interrogating us while her boss, the *Kommandant*, wanted to let us go. Since they hadn't found anything suspicious, there was no justification to detain us. I glanced at Louisa, who *could* understand everything they were saying, and she didn't look very worried. She hadn't twitched a muscle since they'd brought us together here. A dozen or so younger guards silently stood at attention. They all held AK-47s. They were all male and I realized with a jolt that Blondie was the only female guard I'd seen. Had Mara's inquisitor been a man or a woman? Would it have mattered to her? Was he in this room with us? *Did that matter to me?* How could it be that after all the months we had known each other, all the kilometers we had traveled together, all the nights we had spent in each others arms in youthful, exuberant coupling, I didn't know her well enough to answer these questions?

Blondie was losing the argument with her short superior officer. The familiar pink color crept up through her neck and into her face like a sunrise as she became more and more agitated. Her voice had been getting higher and louder while his tone remained quietly stark, dangerous with detached superiority. The *Kommandant* took a step backward, straightened to formal attention, and said something that sounded like a direct order. Blondie paused and turned her head toward us before answering, her eyes drilling through us with palpable antagonism. The blonde *Vopo's* face was crimson. She opened her mouth and then, wordlessly shut it and turned back to the *Kommandant.*

"*Jawohl, mein Kommandant!*" They both saluted, and then the big blonde *Vopo* turned on her heel and marched out of the room. I hoped I would never see her again.

The short *Volkspolizei Kommandant* stood in front of us with a handful of passports. I took a deep breath. His fingers were pale and delicate; I wished he had been my 'examiner'.

"You will go now. Do not return to the *Deutsche Demokratische Republik.*" His English, although heavily accented, was flawless. "You have been lucky this time. It has been decided that you are free to leave. You four, do not come back to the DDR. *Auf Wiedersehen.*" One at a time, he handed us our passports and then turned to his desk.

"I bloody well better be free to leave," Simon hissed, stuffing his passport into his jeans. "You've no right to hold us here."

The *Kommandant* whirled around and settled an icy stare on Simon with clear, blue eyes. He took one short step back toward us. Maybe he was thinking we *were* worth an international incident.

"Goddammit, Simon, shut up." Mara suddenly became animated. "Let's get the hell out of here. You're going to get us into more trouble if you don't keep your big mouth closed." She started toward the door.

"You're damn right," I agreed. "Let's get out while we can." Presumably, the *Vopos* could change their minds and decide to keep us longer. We'd been given a reprieve. The situation could have ended in any number of ways; 'You will go now' being the best one. Absolutely nothing could be gained by arguing.

Louisa still hadn't uttered a single word. Had the guards discovered she spoke fluent German? Had her last name, 'Braun', raised any eyebrows?

"I'm with you, mate." Simon's words dripped with sarcasm. "I reckon I've enjoyed as much of this bloody workers' paradise as I can stand."

Gripping our precious passports tightly in our sweaty hands, we left the *Volkspolizei* bunker and scurried through the concrete block maze toward Checkpoint Charlie. I could scarcely believe we were finally free and I kept looking back over my shoulder. I half expected to see jack-booted *Vopos* running after us, firing bursts of bullets from their Kalashnikovs over our heads and then into our backs. I remembered the photos of would-be escapist Peter Fechter, as he lay badly wounded in the dirt strip of no-man's-land between east and west. The *Volkspolizei* had shot him after he'd run across the bare ground and tried to jump the Wall and, less than a hundred and fifty meters from where we now hurried toward our own freedom. Neither the *Vopos* nor the soldiers of the American army had dared to come to his aid. Eventually his screams for help became moans, and then he was quiet, and finally he had died, his blood soaking into the thirsty German earth.

We were alone, though, weaving our way through the cement barricades. The harsh, cold glare from the enormous overhead floodlights twisted our shadows into grotesque shapes that danced around us in a macabre mockery of our fear. The Wall wasn't getting any closer. I took Mara's hand and pulled her along, trying to keep up with Louisa and Simon. I could hear Friedrichstrasse, on the other side, vibrant with noise and motion, in sharp contrast to the dark and lifeless East Sector that we were leaving behind us. Beyond the well-lighted area in the immediate vicinity of *die Mauer*, East Berlin faded behind us into shadows with just occasional dim streetlights and tavern lamps breaking the gloom.

Suddenly, we were out of the maze into open space. Checkpoint Charlie was only a few feet away. A searchlight scraped along the top of the Wall, sparkling the razor wire. Two American Army soldiers holding rifles with fixed bayonets stood at attention a few feet on the other side, facing each other. We darted through the portal.

"You're getting out late," one of the soldiers said without turning his head. "Curfew was hours ago."

"We got arrested, or detained, or whatever you call it," I said. "The *Vopos* kept us there for hours."

"Is that a fact?" The soldier's interest was obviously aroused and now he looked us over more carefully.

"We were strip-searched. They stripped us naked and—"

"Just shut up. He gets the picture." Mara clutched her sketchbook to her chest.

"Y'all need to come back here tomorrow and make a full report 'bout that." The other soldier pointed across the street to a whitewashed wooden building. In front of the squat, temporary-looking structure a massive, tall flagpole flew the American Flag and beneath it the colors of the infantry of the U.S. Army, illuminated by a mega-watt floodlight. "There won't be nobody there at this hour."

"I'll do that." I had no intention of going inside any U.S. Army headquarters anywhere at any time for any reason. "What time do they open?"

"Oh-six-hundred hours the civilian liaison'll be there."

"Where's the nearest place with toilets?"

"Just walk straight down F-Street. There's lots a bars. You can't miss 'em."

"Thanks," I said. "See you tomorrow."

"Y'all got your passports back, right?" the soldier asked as we walked away.

I took several more steps before I turned. "Yeah, they gave 'em back." Now, no longer facing the immediate threat of being shot, I noticed how painfully itchy walking was.

I was overwhelmed by the sheer exuberance of the West Berlin, the stunning contrast between the two sectors. We stopped at the first *Gaststätte* we came to and hurried straight for the restrooms. None of us had been allowed to relieve ourselves for the entire interrogation.

"I don't half have to spend a penny," Simon said as we walked through the kitchen to the men's room.

"My mom used to call it 'feeling your back teeth float'," I said.

"'Tis that and more, mate." We stood side by side at the single urinal, listening to the long-overdue splash of piss against porcelain.

"So, what do you make of it?" Simon asked, once we were back outside waiting for the girls.

"I think I need a drink to unwind, calm down a little bit." I looked at my hand and realized it was still shaking. Fishing my pack of Drum from my pocket, I tried to roll a cigarette, but the thin paper tore in half and the shag tobacco ended up on the sidewalk. I ground it into powder, and then into nothing at all.

"No Drum roll for you." Simon produced his pack of Player's Navy Cut cigarettes and lit a couple. The flame from his match pointed straight up in the windless, Berlin night. Simon's hands were a lot steadier than mine as he handed me one.

"What do *you* think about all that?"

Simon's eyes narrowed as he looked back down Friedrichstrasse toward the Wall and the darkness beyond it. "What do I think? Fuck those buggers!" Simon spat into the gutter.

"I couldn't agree more," I said. "Things used to be so simple—"

"Simple. Right. Not going to be so bleeding simple any more."

"I feel like I've been … violated. Raped."

Simon looked back inside the bar, where Louisa and Mara were weaving through the tables toward us.

"Imagine what *they* must feel like."

"Think about Johann and Liesl," Simon said. "They have to *live* there."

The girls had rejoined us. "What do you suppose we do now?" I asked.

"Won't do any good to file a complaint with the embassy," Louisa said. "No diplomatic relations, remember?"

"I'd like to figure out some way to shove something up *their* butts." I looked back in the direction of the Wall. "Revenge would help sooth the pain."

"You're going to exact vengeance on East Germany?" Louisa's tone was a blend of mockery and curiosity.

"The hell with that. Let's get a bus back to the hostel," Mara said. "I don't feel like walking all that way." Mara had slipped her bra back on in the WC; her breasts were once again in their familiar shape and location.

Simon jabbed me in the ribs with his elbow and raised his eyebrows. "How about supper? I rather fancy that Italian place we found the other night." Simon was hungry; maybe, just maybe, our world was returning to normal. If anything in Berlin could be considered normal in the long, hot summer of 1966.

"Food's OK with me as long as it's quick and doesn't take all night," Mara said. "I'm a lot more tired than hungry. Frankly, I don't know how you can eat."

"Tired and hungry? That's all? Blimey, what about your bum? Aren't you sore?" Simon asked.

"Just shut the fuck up, OK Simon? Of course I'm sore. We don't need to talk about it."

Louisa's eyes were connected to us, but she hadn't spoken a word.

"What was that Italian place called?" I asked. "Luigi's or something like that."

"Italian would be fine." Mara fumbled in her backpack for her Marlboros. "As far from Germany as we can get."

"Think it was Guido's," Louisa said. "Taxi'll be faster." She stepped off the curb and waved down a cab. Soon we were speeding through Friedrichstrasse traffic toward the Charlottenburg section of town. According to the huge clock on the wall of the Deutsche Bank, it was about eight o'clock.

Guido's Authentic Italian Bistro was packed with people, but we finally found a table. We ate pasta cafeteria-style until we couldn't eat any more, and then we just sat smoking and drinking beer, and tried to put the horrendous events of the afternoon behind us.

"So," I said to Louisa, "you never let on that you speak German, huh?"

"*Nein.*"

"They weren't suspicious of your last name? You'd think 'Braun' would be a dead giveaway."

"Sure they're used to seeing all sorts of names on American passports like Braun, Sanchez, Goulet, Kaminski, Goldman, and so on. After all, we're a nation of immigrants."

"What do you suppose makes Guido's Authentic Italian Bistro so authentic, anyway?" Mara asked, sullen, oblivious to a faint mustache of foam on her lip.

"Well, its gotta be the lighting." I picked up Chianti-bottle candelabra and held it over my head gazing up at it with a somber, reverential look on my face. "Give me your tired, your hungry, your huddled masses, yearning to eat free— "

"No, mate, don't be daft; it's the checkered tablecloths."

"How about the music?" I said. "Can't get much more authentic than violins."

"What about the waiters in the toreador pants?" I put the candle back on the table, spilling wax down the rattan sheath onto my fingers.

"No, its—"

"Alright already, I'm sorry I asked. Can we just finish up and get out of here? I can't stand to sit around much longer."

"I reckon we could have found some place with padded chairs," Simon said. "Give your bum a—"

"That's not what I meant." Mara turned red. "I just want to be alone for a while. I don't want to be around so goddam many people."

Simon stood up and disappeared in the direction of the WC and Louisa went to the counter to pay the bill.

"It's a good thing the hostel is around the corner. We won't have far to go." I didn't want to walk any further than I had to, either.

"I don't want to stay in those dorm rooms tonight." Mara blew a flume of smoke from her mouth as she spoke. "Let's go find some pension or hotel or something. I just can't be around a crowd. Today's been way too fucking much."

"What a terrific idea. Wish I'd thought of it."

"Well, you probably did, if I know you."

Regrouped outside, we told Simon and Louisa we'd meet them in the morning in the common room and left Guido's in search of a cheap place to stay.

About six blocks from the hostel, down a narrow side street, we saw an open doorway under an illuminated white sign that read: ZIMMER FREI.

"What do you think, sweetheart?" I asked. "Looks OK to me."

"Its gonna have to do. I'm done walking for the day."

We brushed past a woman wearing too much makeup and too little clothing to be anything other than a prostitute and crossed the sticky lobby floor to the weathered reception counter. The place reeked of perfume and stale tobacco. The clerk stubbed out his cigarette, put down his football magazine and looked up at us wordlessly through thick-lensed, wire-rimmed glasses. There wasn't a single hair anywhere on his head.

"*Wieful cost eine Zimmer?*" I asked in my best street German.

"Don't worry about how much it is, just take it. As long as it's got a shower."

"*Ein Zimmer mit Dusche,*" I added. And to Mara, "one bed, right?"

"Fine. Yes. One bed. I don't care."

"Do you wish the room for the whole night?" The clerk's English was as perfect, and as accented, as the *Kommandant's* had been. It was like they'd gone to the same school, had the same teacher.

"Yes, of course. We'll leave in the morning."

"Twenty marks, please. Room 204 is just upstairs and to the left."

"This room *does* have a shower, right?" Mara asked.

The desk clerk turned his shiny head toward her. "Naturally. The WC is just down the hall."

I paid the twenty marks and we climbed the stairs to the second floor. I let Mara gain a couple of steps on me and then leaned forward and kissed her right buttock.

"Ummm … now I remember why I love you so much."

"Christ, you never stop, do you?" Mara pushed my head away.

"You want me to?"

"I want you should leave me alone."

As soon as we were inside, Mara pulled the gauzy curtains shut and disappeared into the tiny bathroom. I heard the water running and soon steam billowed out from the wide crack under the door. I took off my shoes and socks, lay back on the bed, and checked out the dingy room. Along with the lumpy double bed, there was a rickety dresser with one drawer missing, a print of some deer in a clearing in a forest, and a worn Persian rug on the wooden floor. A stack of white towels, neatly folded, sat on the dresser. Otherwise, the room was bare. A single light, a dirty, white globe with a graveyard of dead flies inside, hung from the ceiling. Room 204 didn't smell much better than the lobby had. Through the thin wall, I could hear muffled words punctuated with laughter and then the squeak of bedsprings and a soft thud against the wall.

Ten minutes later, Mara emerged from the shower wearing her tee shirt and a hotel towel, knotted below her belly button. As she crossed the room, the towel flashed open.

"Did you manage to wash off all the *Vopo* fingerprints?"

"I sure as hell hope so."

"Did you leave me any hot water?"

"You'll have to go find out for yourself. It wasn't cold when I turned it off."

The shower was wonderful. I let the hot water run down my face and over my body and when it started to turn cool I turned my back and bent over. I was still sore from the body search, but at least I was now clean. The cold water felt good and I gingerly spread my buttocks open. A tasty, filling meal with plenty of beer, a long, soothing shower, a private hotel room with Mara; the day was ending up a lot better than I'd expected it would a few hours earlier.

When I came out of the bathroom, Mara had already turned out the light and was waiting in bed. The harsh glare from the vacancy sign outside lit the room. I climbed in next to her, bringing the towel with me. After the traumatic events of the afternoon, Mara's plump body felt familiar and comforting. The variety of sounds from the next room had distilled into a wordless rhythm of squeaks and knocks. I stroked my hands down her neck to her back, tracing the bumps along her spine with my fingers. In spite of everything we'd been through that day, I couldn't help becoming aroused. I started to nuzzle her colossal breasts, searching for a nipple like a newborn puppy .

Mara pushed at the top of my head. "Cut it out. Not tonight. Just hold me, all right?"

"Just hold you?"

"Yeah, just put your arms around me." She paused for a moment, gathering steam. "Christ, think about it, David. I just had some dirty bastard's fingers...." she broke off and choked back a sob. "The last thing I wanna do is fuck."

"OK, OK, I'm sorry."

"Tomorrow night. Soon. I promise." Mara turned over and spooned her ample buttocks into my groin, flattening my erection against my stomach. Almost immediately her deep, regular breathing told me that she was drifting off. I laced my fingers across her belly, gently kneading her plump flesh in unison with her snoring. The last thing Mara saw before she shut her eyes and fell asleep was the sign outside the window: ZIMMER FREI.

"*Frei* means freedom, right?" she asked, slumber slurring her words.

"Yeah," I mumbled after a moment, "*frei* means free." But she was already gone.

23 June —
Berlin

I lay awake long past midnight, listening to the nocturnal sounds of West Berlin, unable to calm my seething mind. Negotiations on the street followed by the clump of footsteps on the hotel stairway and then the squeak of bedsprings became a repetitious pattern of sound as the hours passed. But it wasn't the noisy consummation of bartered sex or the incessant glare of the ZIMMER FREI sign that kept me awake. Such intrusions had never bothered me before, but while Mara was able to insulate herself from the ugliness of the previous afternoon by curling up in a ball with a pillow over her head, my emotions swirled and bubbled. Our arrest by the *Volkspolizei* felt, in some as yet undefined way, incomplete. Mara reacted to adversity, discomfort, and almost anything she regarded as unpleasant by withdrawing from it, but I was far more confrontational. Tired as I was, my brain refused to shut down. I had been invaded, assaulted, and although I had no idea what I could do about it, I could not do nothing.

Finally I gave up on sleep altogether, gently rolled out of bed, and fumbled in my pant's pocket for my Drum and papers. The rhythmic rise and fall of the bundle of covers and the snoring from inside them assured me that my presence in bed was not missed. I stood at the window, the smoke from my cigarette drifting slowly eastward through the lights toward the darkness beyond.

While Mara slept, I reflected on how we'd gotten ourselves into such a predicament. Or, more accurately, how *I* had gotten *us* arrested at the Wall. The previous morning, Mara, Simon, Louisa and I had crossed into East Berlin for the fourth day in a row. (Mara hadn't wanted to come with us, but she was even less inclined to stay behind by herself, so, reluctantly, she'd come along). When we returned to Checkpoint Charlie a few hours later, a suspicious *Vopo* noticed us and detained us for questioning.

Blondie was the same border cop we had seen every day as we left East Berlin. We didn't know it at the time, but we found out later that *Vopos* were trained to look for repeat tourists.

Why? Any visitor to Berlin might be curious about the East Sector. Cold war tensions were very high. Almost three years to the day had passed since John Kennedy had visited Berlin and declared himself a citizen of that beleaguered city, with his famous '*Ich bin ein Berliner*' speech. Thousands of people had crowded into Rudolf Wilde Platz and cheered wildly, not caring as the popular American president fractured their language with his Boston accent, just grateful for his promise that they would not be forgotten in the ongoing convulsions of east/west politics.

East Germany, like most of east Europe, was difficult for westerners to visit. Visas for travel anywhere behind the Iron Curtain were laborious to get on short notice. Often the requirements changed without warning or even reason, according to the whim of some bureaucrat in Budapest or Prague or Warsaw or somewhere else. Berlin was a western enclave surrounded by the stormy state of East Germany and connected by a single, paved umbilical cord to the mother country. All entrance and exit ramps along the autobahn between Helmstedt and Berlin were barricaded and guarded as it passed through the *Deutsche Demokratische Republik*. Since West Berlin was connected to West Germany politically, if not geographically, no visa was required for travel from West Germany across East Germany to West Berlin.

Berlin was also unique for this reason: An ugly concrete wall, some three-and-a-half meters high, flanked on one side by a barren strip of no man's land, physically divided the city. *Die Mauer*, a tangible embodiment of the Iron Curtain that divided Europe, not only brought the armed forces of the North Atlantic Treaty Organization and the Warsaw Pact into the closest possible proximity short of hand-to-hand combat, it also afforded the easiest access for tourists to get a glimpse of Communism. For some arcane diplomatic reason, visas were not required to travel between the east and west sectors of the city. Getting into or out of East Berlin was relatively easy, as long as you had a free-world passport. For someone to venture inside for a few hours or even a day to get a firsthand look behind the Iron Curtain was understandable, but multiple visits aroused suspicion on the part of the *Volkspolizei*. After all, why would anyone want to return a fourth, third, or even a second time? There wasn't much that would interest a typical vacationer. In a society that struggled to produce the barest necessities of life, shopping, as a westerner understood the concept, was a cruel joke. Monotonous food, clothing, and other merchandise had little more than souvenir value. Socialism, at least the version by which Walter Ulbricht ruled East Germany, was not much to look at. The radio tower, which reminded me of the Space Needle in Seattle, was in the East Sector, but it wasn't open to the public. To the average sightseer, the glitz and glitter of West Berlin was certainly more appealing than the dreary colorlessness of the Communist side. The West Sector was lively; full of movie theaters, sidewalk cafes, singles bars, museums, art galleries, and shops well supplied with consumer goods. The sounds of traffic mixed with the music that flowed out of open windows and doorways. In short, West Berlin exemplified mid-Sixties capitalist culture in full bloom. Who would want to revisit the drab, lifeless failure of East Berlin once their curiosity about Communism had been assuaged? For most tourists, one single day was plenty of time. It should have been for us, too. Our fourth day was about three too many for Mara, and I knew she'd never let me forget it. I flicked my cigarette out the window and crawled back into bed. Mara's noisy breathing didn't change.

I had first noticed Miriam Liebowitz, who preferred to be called Mara, several months earlier, wandering around the *Reijksmuseum* in Amsterdam, renowned as the home of some of the greatest works of art in Europe. She had a rucksack on her back, and a leather case of some sort under her arm. She had a small American flag sewed onto her pack. Our paths crossed and recrossed many times in the cavernous rooms until we were standing side by side in front of Vermeer's seventeenth century masterpiece, 'The Love Letter'. We exchanged smiles and a few words and I trailed after her for a while before I lost her in the crowd. Later that afternoon, as I returned to the hostel, I saw her sitting at an outside bar on the edge of Dam Square, a pack of Marlboros and a nearly empty glass of beer on the table. Parked on the chair next to her were her oversized leather briefcase and her backpack.

"Hey. I saw you at the museum, right?"

"Yeah. In front of the Vermeer." She blew a flume of smoke out of the side of her mouth and half-smiled at me. "You're American, right?"

"Nothing I'm proud of. Mind if I join you for a beer?"

"Might as well. It's a table for two and it's that time of day." She shifted her gear from the chair to the ground.

I motioned to the waiter, pointed to Mara's glass and held up two fingers.

"You wanna cigarette? By the way, my name's Mara."

"Thanks, I got these." Mara cocked her head and watched as I twisted up a nearly perfect cigarette from a fresh pack of Drum shag tobacco.

"What's your name, anyway?"

"Sorry. David."

"Well, David, you do that pretty well."

"Too much practice." I lit the cigarette.

"Me, I gotta have a filter."

"It's all a matter of taste, I guess. So, what's in the briefcase?"

"It's a sketchpad and some pastels."

"You're an artist?"

"Sometimes." Mara scooted the case closer to the table and looked out across Dam Square. The waiter arrived with two tall schooners of Heineken.

"Great. Show me some of your stuff."

"Some other time. I'm not in the mood."

"That's a new one on me. I know you've gotta be in the mood to paint or draw something, but I didn't know you had to be in the right frame of mind—"

"Don't push it, OK?" Mara reached down for the sketchpad with one hand and gathered up her Marlboros and matches with the other as she stood up.

"Hey, I'm sorry. Don't go away mad." I put my hand on her arm. "Besides, we haven't finished our beer."

The girl looked at me for several seconds, little creases forming around her mouth and eyes, like she was trying to make up her mind about something. Finally, she eased herself back down into her chair. "OK, well, I'm sorry, too. I guess I'm over-sensitive. Can we talk about something else, though?" Mara tilted her head back and combed her fingers through her thick, curly hair. I took the opportunity to scan her ample anatomy.

We sat there for well over an hour, exchanging our life stories, which were really more like explanations of how we had come to be in Amsterdam, smoking and drinking Dutch beer on Dam Square. After a while, it was almost as if the spat over her sketchbook had never happened. Eventually, I started to get hungry.

"You staying at the hostel?" I asked.

"Yeah, I've been there for almost a week."

"Funny, I haven't seen you around."

"I don't hang around there much when I'm awake."

I took a last drag and snuffed out my cigarette. "Well, I'm starved. What do you say we wander back and maybe find some chow along the way?"

"I could definitely eat."

I fished in my pocket and found a few Dutch guilders mixed in with Danish kroner and German marks and left enough on the table to cover all of our beers. Road etiquette would have been for each of us to pay our own way, but I did it anyway. *Who knows*, I thought, *where this might lead*. We shouldered our packs and started walking across Dam Square, weaving through smartly dressed office workers, tourists gawking at the immense palace, hippies, and drug dealers in the general direction of the hostel. At the edge of the square, a streetcar suddenly emerged from the snarl of cars, mopeds, bicycles, and pedestrians and screeched around the corner. I grabbed Mara's hand and pulled her back from the curb.

"Thanks." Mara looked at me with a big smile. "I wasn't paying attention."

I smiled back, but didn't turn loose of her hand. "We Yankees have to watch out for each other."

"Yeah, I guess." She rearranged our fingers until they were zippered together.

Later we sat around the common room at the hostel, her with her Marlboros and me with my pack of Drum. We'd stopped at a little, hole-in-the-wall Indonesian café and filled up from a Ristaffel buffet. Buffet's were great places to eat, especially if you adjusted your metabolism to survive on one main meal a day. You could get your money's worth and then some.

"So, how long have you been over here?" Mara asked.

"A little over a year. Closer to two, actually. How about you?"

"Two years in September. Where all have you been?"

"Copenhagen, Paris, a few weeks in Flanders, the usual. It's all here." I slid my passport across the table. "Let's see yours."

"OK." She fished her neck wallet out from the deep crevice in her full bosom and extracted her passport. "Just don't look at the picture."

I opened her passport.

"Miriam? I thought you said your name was Mara."

"Shit! I told you to skip that page. I fucking hate the name Miriam." She reached across the table and tried to snatch her passport back.

"OK, cool down. Mara is fine." I watched her light another cigarette, surprised by her outbreak. So, the content of her sketchbook was a touchy subject and she didn't like her real name. A minute or two of silence followed, while I rolled a Drum and we let the tiff evaporate and traced each other's travels by the visas and border stamps we'd collected. I noted the French stamp from Orly Airport.

"So, how did you like the Louvre?"

"I never got in. The line was way too long. I went up to the Rodin museum instead."

This one I had to digest for a moment: *An art student, in Paris for the first time, unwilling to wait in a line at the most famous museum in the world?*

"So, where are you gonna go next?" Mara asked. "I don't imagine you plan to stay here forever."

"I'm not sure." I slid her passport back to her and retrieved my own. "But I think somewhere in east Europe."

"Behind the Iron Curtain?"

"Yeah, I'm dying to see what it's like back there. Maybe Czechoslovakia. Or Hungary. They say Budapest is the Paris of the east. How about you?"

"No particular plans. I'd like to go back to the real Paris."

I took a deep drag from my cigarette and blew the smoke toward the ceiling. And then, because I was nineteen, because we were two country-men bumming around Europe, because I was beginning to find Mara attractive, in spite of the three or four personality quirks she had already exposed and, well, just *because*, I issued the invitation: "You want to go with me?"

Mara leaned back in her chair, mashed her half-smoked, filtered American cigarette out under her foot and frowned. "I don't know. You sure its safe?" She arranged her passport wallet back down inside her blouse and twisted a curly strand of hair around her finger.

"People travel behind the Curtain every day. We could most likely find some kids around here who've been to Czechoslovakia or Romania or Yugoslavia or somewhere."

Mara clasped her hands behind her neck, closed her eyes, and stretched her neck back until her face was nearly parallel to the table. After a few moments lost in thought, she snapped back to the present. "OK. What the hell. You gotta die sometime, right?"

"Die? Nobody's going to die. Look, you don't have to go, if you don't want to."

Mara looked at me for a long moment, brushed the ringlet away from her eye, and smiled. "No, I think I wanna go. I like you, or rather, I trust you, or something." There was a long pause and then she added, "Oh, shit."

I was feeling exactly what she was saying: Oh, shit. "Quick trip. It'll be interesting to see something different."

"Can I think about it and tell you in the morning?"

I was pretty sure she'd already made up her mind in spite of wanting a night to think it over. "Sure. We get visas, go have a look around for a couple of weeks, and then come back."

"Let's just hope it's all that easy."

The next morning, Mara met me in the common room. I'd already had a roll and some Gouda for breakfast and was enjoying my first Drum of the day.

"OK. I'll go with you. But no more than two weeks, OK? Two weeks absolute maximum."

I stuck out my hand. "Two weeks, tops. You have my word." It had taken us less than twenty-four hours to go from walking down the street holding hands to shaking hands on a negotiated plan. And we weren't even lovers.

So, decision made and freshly-minted agreement in place, we went to the Czech embassy and applied for tourist visas. We were told it would take overnight to process our applications, so Mara and I spent the rest of the day doing laundry, checking American Express for mail, buying a roadmap of Czechoslovakia and some emergency rations in case we got stranded between rides, and otherwise preparing for our trip into east Europe. We finished up back at the same pub on Dam Square where we'd met the day before. Mara was walked-out from trekking around Amsterdam, so we decided to just stay there for dinner.

"You want to go back to the hostel or should we look for a cheap hotel?" I asked after dinner and a couple of beers.

"Hotel? You think you're pretty slick, don't you?"

"I just thought we could get an earlier start in the morning if we didn't have the whole hostel scene to put up with." I could feel my neck warming.

"And that's all you had on your mind, am I right?"

"Cross my heart and hope—"

"Just shut up. We better get back before curfew."

We left Amsterdam the next morning under a dark sky that threatened to rain on us. Standing by the freeway, we managed to flag down a ride just as the first fat raindrops hit the windshield. I was glad to be inside a car, still dry. It was much more difficult to hitchhike once you were wet.

Late in the afternoon, our ride dropped us off and we watched the taillights disappear down a narrow, country road away from the autobahn. Although it was still overcast, the rain had stopped several hours earlier. We were deep in the Bavarian countryside, close to the German/Czech border and, thankfully, still dry.

The next town we would come to would be Cheb, inside Czechoslovakia. By sundown, however, we were still standing in the same spot, the likelihood of getting another ride fading with the light. I was tired and ready to call it quits for the day. While I'd tried to keep up a conversation, in German and English, with the guys who had picked us up, Mara had napped, her head resting on my shoulder. If it started raining again, I wanted to be in some sort of shelter in the trees, not standing by the side of the road.

"I think we're done for the day. We should find a place to camp out."

"You mean we're gonna just sleep outside somewhere?"

"Sure, come on. Follow me."

"Well, shit. Where're we gonna, you know, wash up and, oh, never mind."

Could it be, I asked myself, *that in two years of bumming around Europe, Mara had never camped out?*

We hiked down the unpaved lane away from the autobahn, trying to stay out of the ruts and keep our feet dry, until we could no longer hear traffic. A gentle breeze made the branches sway and the shadows shift. We found a wide spot in the thicket, rigged up a makeshift rain shelter with our ponchos, and unrolled our sleeping bags. Mara disappeared far into the trees while I stood by the edge of the clearing and peed.

As the daylight finally melted into a dark, moonlit night, Mara snuggled up against me and didn't resist when I tentatively began exploring her body. I worked my hand down between her legs and began massaging. She was already warm and wet and slippery. Suddenly she clenched her knees together and covered my hand with hers.

"I don't know about this. We're outside, for Christ sakes."

"Sweetheart, outside is the only place we have. There's nobody for miles." I wrapped her hand around my erection. "Besides, you're as excited as I am."

"OK, but pull your sleeping bag over us." I don't know how she managed it, but the tone of her voice was a combination of both resignation and excitement.

I rolled over on top of her and slid inside before she could change her mind.

"Oh, God," she whispered, sucking in her breath. "You're so big."

"That's not it, it's just been a while for both of us, right? We've both got a lot of pent up—"

"Can't we just shut up and do it?"

"Sure."

And we did.

Czechoslovakia was our first road trip. I was entranced; Mara hated most of it. Exchanging American dollars on the black market allowed us to stay in modest hotels for about the same amount of money we were used to paying for youth hostels in the west. I knew this was risky; the moneychangers were furtive and seemed to disappear as quickly as they appeared. Often they would mumble 'change dollars?' without even breaking stride as they passed us on the street. Mara was a much more enthusiastic lover indoors than she had been the first night in that grove and her voracious appetite for sex made exchanging money on the black market a risk worth taking. At least as far as I was concerned.

"You know, Slick, one of these days you're going to get caught dealing with these creepy people and we're going to be in deep shit." Mara was positive we'd get arrested and spend the rest of our lives in some frozen Gulag somewhere, living on bread and thawed-out snow. For her, every moneychanger was an undercover cop just waiting to entrap us and haul us to prison. Furthermore, it didn't help her sense of security any that we frequently had to present our passports when we went into museums or other public places.

"You want to start staying in hostels again? Men's and women's separate dorms and all that crap?" I put my arms around her. "I like sleeping with you."

"What *I* want is to be out of Czechoslovakia." Mara pushed my hand off her butt and wiggled out of my embrace.

One night as we came out of a bar about nine o'clock, we were stopped by two patrolling policemen who demanded that we show our passports. Of course, we didn't have them with us; we'd already turned them in at the pension. (Mara disliked hotels the most since the law required that passports be surrendered to the proprietor upon check-in at night and were not returned until departure the following morning.) The cops should have been satisfied with our overnight registration, but instead they walked us back to the hotel and demanded our passports from the concierge. Then they checked the desk register to confirm that our names and passport numbers had been entered correctly. I got the impression the cops were checking up on the desk clerk as well as on us. Mara spent many restless nights convinced that by dawn our passports would be in the hands of the criminal underworld, never to be seen by us again, stranding us behind the Iron Curtain for all eternity.

"Nobody ever asked for my passport at a bar in Amsterdam or Paris," Mara said. That onerous detail of east European tourism really scared her and I had to admit it was a little unnerving to me as well, though not enough to deter me or dampen my enthusiasm. She could hardly wait to get back across the border into Germany but I wanted to stay and see more. Reluctantly, Mara agreed to stick with our original schedule, and I promised her we would leave when we had planned and not one day later. Our visas were only good for fourteen days, anyway, and my curiosity didn't extend to finding out what happened when tourists overstayed their invitations.

Czechoslovakia was our first opportunity to spend a protracted amount of time together without the segregated dormitory-style sleeping arrangements we were used to in the hostels. For almost two weeks, we spent every waking minute together, not to mention all those nights. I loved every minute exploring a landscape and culture far different from anything I had encountered so far, even in west Europe. But Mara couldn't lose her fear that something would go wrong; we'd lose our passports, get arrested exchanging money, anything that would ruin our lives forever.

"You know, I seriously doubt they're going to lock us up together in prison. It's going to be just like a hostel; segregated cellblocks." My feeble attempt at humor went unappreciated.

By the time we arrived back in Amsterdam, I wasn't sure how much more traveling together we would be doing. We'd met, discovered a few things we shared in common, such as art, beer, sex, and disillusionment with everything American, and started sleeping together in less than a week. Now I was getting to know her and our differences were beginning to emerge and swamp our similarities. The sex was wonderful, as all sex is when you're a teenager, and I didn't want to give that up. Mara liked sex, too, especially after a couple of drinks and with the lights out. But, she was cautious where I was reckless, fussy where I was easy-going. Fortunately, she had a diaphragm, which meant that at least we didn't have pregnancy to worry about. So, we stuck together in a state of libidinous limbo, having plenty of energy to screw, but not much motivation to develop much more. Sooner or later, something that would either bind us closer together or make us go our separate ways would happen, but until then I was willing to tiptoe around her hot spots and enjoy the sex.

It was hard work being aimless and dissipated! Not to mention horny.

But I digress. The look and the feel of the old cities, especially Prague, took me aback. Where I had grown up, in Northern California, everything had a patina of newness around it; there was not much sense of history. You couldn't walk where, say, the Huns had rampaged or the Crusaders had spread Christianity at the point of a sword or Caesar had extended the Roman Empire, although you could buy replicas of the weapons they used in shopping mall cubicles. The closest comparison I could make between east Europe and California was the string of Catholic missions established in the eighteenth century by Father Junipero Serra, each one a days' donkey-ride away from the last. Christianity had been established as the state religion in Prague for over a thousand years before Spaniards brought it to the New World. The ancient castles and churches scattered throughout the Czech hinterlands made it feel that old.

Many of the streets in the small Czechoslovakian towns we passed through had been built of cobblestone long before automobiles were invented and were too narrow for vehicles. People, especially in the rural parts of the country, still relied more on non-motorized carts than on cars and trucks. In the fields, old women raked and pitch forked hay into huge piles that were then hauled away on long, flat ox- or horse-drawn wagons. It was as if the industrial revolution, with both its benefits and its drawbacks, had never happened here.

In the cities, there was little neon. There were no junk food restaurants and most of the stores seemed very short on consumer goods of any kind. Sometimes we would stumble across an open-air market with makeshift tables and baskets of potatoes, onions, cabbages, carrots, and so on. Always there was bread, and sometimes we found cheese and salami.

Billboards were nonexistent. In fact, there was a minimum of any kind of signage at all, including street signs. This made it challenging to find lodging, ascertain directions, or locate public toilets.

For all these reasons, Czechoslovakia offered a fascinating and completely different landscape from California or even the west European places I'd been. A fascinating world lay hidden behind the Iron Curtain.

The People's Republic of Czechoslovakia was an unlikely political organization of two distinct ethnic populations, Czechs and Slovaks. The country struggled to survive as a rural, proletariat state and had little to offer visitors except itself and its history. For a typical westerner, it wasn't a vacation destination.

In public, the Czechs seemed quiet, subdued, almost defeated. In the privacy of their own homes, however, they tended to be more open and gregarious. On several occasions, we were the guests of local families for lunch or dinner, and once for an overnight stay. I was enthralled. The commercialism I hated in America was absent. Whatever it was I was looking for, I felt was close. The pace of life was slower; the food tasted better, life seemed simpler.

We often found people who spoke German, occasionally even an English-speaking student, and by using a combination of sign language, English, German, and facial expression, we were able to buy cheese, bread, salami, beer, wine, and so on. (Speaking German was risky. You had to establish right away that German was not your mother tongue and was being used only as a matter of convenience. In the mid-sixties, anti-German sentiment was still strong throughout Europe, and especially in the East Block countries. Czechoslovakia had been one of Hitler's first conquests, and the Czechs blamed Hitler and the subsequent Allied victory over the Axis powers for the oppression they now lived under, courtesy of the USSR.) The one thing I found in common with the Czech families and students we met was a distrust and dislike of government. Two weeks in Czechoslovakia merely whetted my appetite for Romania, Bulgaria, Yugoslavia, and especially Berlin. Berlin had been in the news a lot recently, and I was eager to see it.

Thus it was that in June of 1966 four of us walked through Checkpoint Charlie into East Berlin for a day of sightseeing. Simon, who was English, was my new traveling companion. I'd met him on an autobahn cross-road hitchhiking down to Amsterdam from Copenhagen. Simon was tall and lanky, with fine blond hair almost to his shoulders, and he was trying hard to grow a beard. He'd come very close to being shipped to Northern Ireland as a soldier to fight the Irish Republican Army. I wasn't clear as to his exact legal status vis-à-vis the British Army, and I think he preferred it that way. On the few occasions when I did try to pry information out of him, he deflected my questions, and after a while I gave up. I suspected Simon's situation had similarities with my own draft status. His attitude ranged from sardonic to aloof with a strong dose of disillusionment thrown in. In another place, in another time, I could envision my new friend in khakis, a pith helmet and gaiters. I particularly enjoyed his accent and his English slang. He had a dry, almost brittle sense of humor that you could miss if you weren't paying attention.

Simon and I enjoyed traveling together. I discovered I much preferred his company on the road to Mara's, if you left sex out of the question, which at our age was almost impossible. When he and I were on the road, usually hitchhiking, I had the sense that we were not only going somewhere, but leaving something behind us as well. For me, it was America; the world's Mecca for consumption, waste, fraud, and social corruption of one sort or another. Not to mention the ever-increasing escalation of the war in Viet Nam and the bombing in Laos and Cambodia. As for Simon, I never did really learn what he was running from. He wouldn't let me see that far into him. He mentioned a mother in Liverpool, but he was evasive about the rest of his family and his life.

Mara had been an art major at Boston College before she dropped out, after only one year. I never did understand why she quit. Mara carried a sketchpad and was always on the verge of drawing scenes and buildings, which I was content to merely photograph. She claimed she could draw pretty well and although I rarely actually saw anything she'd sketched, I concluded she was wasting her talent. But asking to see some of her sketches or venturing an opinion that she could do something with her ability usually upset her and caused a squabble. The space between complimenting her and saying nothing was slim. The only truly 'safe' time to bring up art was when we were in a museum somewhere.

Mara had short brown hair that my father would have described as 'mousy' and she spent a fair amount of time fussing with it, twisting a clump around her finger or tucking it behind her ear. She was a nervous person by nature, a chronic fingernail biter, and a worrier. Mara could be trusted to find and dwell on the downside to any given situation. She was probably the least appropriate person to travel into east Europe with; my vision of two young lovers exploring romantic castles and quaint little villages soon collided with her tendency to constantly look over her shoulder to see if we were being followed.

As I said before, Mara and I didn't do as well on the road together as Simon and I. Perhaps if our first road trip had been somewhere other than into Communist Europe, things might have been different. In addition, it wasn't her style to skip a meal when we were in the middle of nowhere or to sleep under a bridge because we were miles from a hostel or a cheap hotel. Youth hostels were at the lower end of her comfort scale as far as overnight accommodations went. She wanted at least one hot meal and one hot shower a day, along with clean underwear— Simon would say *knickers*—which was something of a luxury when you were bumming around the way we were. Mara was always on the lookout for a laundromat. Still, she'd lasted nearly two years in Europe, alone, without returning to the States. That by itself was an achievement for anyone. I had to give her credit for sticking it out.

The first year living abroad was always the most difficult, when your family and familiar surroundings pulled at you the hardest. It was tough being so far away from home as a teenager. Home was still home, no matter how unsatisfactory it might be. Being thousands of miles away could get awfully lonely at times. I had known lots of other kids who'd returned to the States after just a few months, once their Eurail pass expired or their money ran out and life on the Continent was no longer a vacation. Faced with the prospect of a temporary nomadic lifestyle morphing into something more permanent involving a job and a room, many gave up and went home, often on non-negotiable, one-way tickets sent by their parents. I admired Mara for her strength of character, for not going back to Boston. She had actually been in Europe several months longer than I had.

Mara, of course, didn't have the draft hanging over her head. She didn't face the prospect of being inducted into the army and being sent off to Southeast Asia to kill or be killed. No matter how much she might agree that the war was wrong, it could never be the same for her. Anyone could volunteer for the army or navy, but only men could be drafted.

Louisa was the fourth member of our impromptu Berlin touring party. She'd been born in Munich and had immigrated to the United States with her parents in 1950, when she was eight years old. Her father had found a good job teaching German language and European history in a high school in Chevy Chase, just outside of Washington, D.C. Louisa was pragmatic, a practical nuts and bolts sort of person. She was more reserved and didn't often express much emotion. Louisa was fluent in both English and German and held an American passport, as did Mara and I. (Simon's passport was British, of course.) Since Louisa had been born in Germany and spent the first few years of her life there, of the four of us she seemed to be the most at home in Europe. I didn't know how long she had been in Europe this time, but I knew she had been back and forth several times already in her life. She and her parents had taken many European vacations while she was still in high school.

We'd all hooked up one early evening in Amsterdam at the youth hostel, in the common room. Simon and I had just gotten off the 'bahn. I guessed correctly that my brand new girlfriend Mara would be there; it was too early to go out for a night on the town and too late in the day for museums. The kitchen was vibrant with activity; dinners being cooked, sandwiches being built, almost everyone smoking. I caught phrases in lots of languages, some of which I recognized, many I didn't. A pretty blonde girl I'd seen once or twice was stirring some homemade soup, filling the room with the smell of onions and garlic. Mara was sitting at a table writing a letter, Marlboro in her other hand. I was hungry. Simon and I hadn't eaten a real meal since breakfast in Denmark early that morning. One of the rides we'd gotten had crackers and schnapps, but that didn't count, according to the growling in my stomach. After saying 'hi' to Mara and catching up with her for a minute, I wandered over to the cooking area. I leaned over the stove and sniffed at a pot of boiling vegetables.

"Smells good. Do you speak English?"

"Hi, I'm Louisa." The blonde soup maker offered me her hand.

"I'm David. Looks like more than one person can eat. My friend and I just got in from Germany. Feel like sharing?"

"Just like that? Bit brash, don't you think?"

"Sorry." I could feel my face heating up. "Shouldn't have bothered you." Sometimes, in a hostel common room, you could invite yourself to share a meal, maybe contribute from your own rucksack larder like you would at a potluck, and things would work out fine. Other times the only thing you ended up putting in your mouth was your own foot.

Louisa looked at me and dimples slowly formed above the corners of her mouth.

"Bread," she said.

"Bread?"

"Have plenty of soup, but kind of short on bread. If you traipse around to the bakery down the street, *then* we'd have enough for a meal."

"I take it that's an invitation?"

"Silly boy."

"There's three of us."

"Get a big loaf." The late afternoon sun coming through the window illuminated tiny gold flecks in the girl's clear blue eyes. "Better get going, before they close."

"I'll be right back." I went back to where Simon and Mara were sitting. "That blonde chick's name is Lisa or something. She said if I went and got some bread, she'd share her stew with us."

Mara scowled over toward the stove. "Who is she, anyway?"

"I haven't a clue, sweetheart, but she's got hot soup and she invited us to join her."

"Good on you, mate, I'm starving." Simon stood up and stretched. "Reckon I'll go with you and fetch some beer."

As we passed Louisa on our way out the door, she put her hand on my arm.

"Rye," she said.

"And would that be your sense of humor or your choice of bread?" I asked.

Louisa smiled fully now. "Hurry up. Soup's ready."

The four of us spent a few days sightseeing together, (although we wouldn't have called it that), walking around the huge outdoor markets, the *Rijksmuseum*, (where I'd first met Mara), the Van Gogh Museum, and Dam Square. We were in Amsterdam long enough for both Mara and Louisa to receive money from home at American Express. Mara got a money order for two hundred dollars, but I didn't know how much Louisa got. It must have been a lot more though, because that night she offered to treat us all to dinner.

And, naturally, we all accepted. Without hesitation.

13 June —
Amsterdam

$-\!\!\star\!\!-\!\!\star\!\!-\!\!\star\!\!-\!\!\star\!\!-\!\!\star\!\!-\!\!\star\!\!-\!\!\star\!\!-$

How about a canal tour of the city?" Louisa suggested one morning at breakfast. "Probably see lots of stuff we'd miss on foot."

It sounded like a good idea, and since we had no other plans for the day (we seldom had any plans at all) we agreed. After we cleaned up our table in the common room, we walked down to the central railway station where the tourist cruises departed.

Downtown Amsterdam was an amalgam of various forms of transportation; trains arrived and departed from the station, busses and trams jockeyed for road space with taxis and delivery trucks. The canals, crowded with motorboats, tour boats, delivery barges and other watercraft, carried people and goods throughout the city. There were also houseboats tied up to makeshift docks on some of the side streets. These reminded me of mobile homes with the wheels long since removed. Simon claimed there were even floating brothels.

"You know," I said, "I think I've seen every kind of boat there is here."

"Everything except gondolas," Simon said.

"What do you mean, gondolas?" Mara asked.

"In Venice. They use them as a kind of water taxi. I'm surprised you haven't heard of them."

"I haven't been to Venice yet, so how would I know about gondolas?"

"Mom, paintings, or books, perhaps," I said. "I thought everyone knew about gondolas."

"Very romantic and all, they are. Care for a cigarette?" Simon offered his pack of Player's around.

"I rather fancy I'll have one of my own." Mara faked a British accent.

"Well, at home, anyway, they are quite well known. Can't fathom why word hasn't reached the colonies."

There were hundreds of bicycles as well, almost all of them black, stacked up in long rows against lampposts, benches, and advertising marquees. Many had flat tires, bent wheels, rusted chains, and looked like they hadn't been ridden in years. There were at least as many bikes in motion, weaving in and out of traffic. I stopped counting the near misses I saw. The only thing lacking was an airport.

The wide flat tourist boats were covered with benches and all looked about the same. According to the placards, they cost about the same as well. We watched a workman, cigarette dangling from his lips, wheel a handcart loaded with several cases of Heinekens into the cabin of one of the boats.

Simon nodded his head in the direction of the beer. "That one looks good to me. I reckon we'll be well set if we're lost at sea."

"Suppose we should have bought some limes at the market this morning?" I asked.

Simon laughed. "Not to worry, mate, I've got these." He produced several oranges and a couple of hard bread rolls from his backpack.

Louisa bought four tickets and we walked down the gangplank onto the gently undulating deck.

"I sure hope this boat is seaworthy." Mara peered over the edge down to the murky water a few feet below. A sheen of oil floated on the surface.

Louisa didn't say anything, but looked at me and winked.

We floated around for most of the day, listening to the guide describe Amsterdam in Dutch, English, and German. About mid afternoon, a pretty girl dressed in traditional Dutch garb and yellow, wooden shoes passed out cardboard boxes with sandwiches, lukewarm French fries, and paper dishes of mayonnaise. Simon sliced his oranges and rolls and divided the pieces among us.

"Meager fare, this," Simon said. "I'll be bloody well ready for a proper meal come suppertime."

"I imagine you'll fill in the void with some beer," Mara suggested.

"Capital idea. Anybody else?" Not waiting for an answer, Simon slid off the seat and lurched up toward the cabin with the exaggerated sway of a sailor too new for sea legs. Soon he returned with four frosty green bottles, each topped with an inverted glass.

"I didn't say *I* wanted one," Mara said.

"Not to worry," he said, "I'm sure it won't go begging."

And it didn't.

That night, Simon took us on a walking tour around Amsterdam's famous red light neighborhoods. As in much of Europe, prostitution was legal in Holland.

"Hamburg's got the *Reeperbahn*, Paris has its *Place Pigalle*, and in Amsterdam you'll find the ladies of the night in *de wallen*." Our tour guide, it seemed, had a wide-ranging knowledge of the subject.

"I think it's disgusting," Mara said as we wandered up and down the streets of the sex district. Shop after shop displayed sex toys, pornography, risqué post cards, and so on. These stores alternated with bars offering Heineken and Amstel beer. And of course, there were enough prostitutes to service the crew of a destroyer.

The whores were exhibited like so much merchandise in tiny cubicles behind plate glass windows that faced directly onto the street. A few of the girls were completely naked, the rest nearly so. Lest there be any doubt as to the nature of the commerce, there were red lights everywhere and many of the rooms themselves had a pinkish glow to them. Some of the girls stood, some sat, a few boldly fondled themselves or pressed their breasts against the glass.

In one window a woman wearing only crotchless black leather chaps and matching gloves crouched on her knees and elbows on a blood red hassock. She had heavy metal rings dangling from both nipples and a tattoo of a black leopard on her arm. A pair of handcuffs bound her wrists and a black leather riding crop was clamped in her thick, crimson lips. The whole bizarre scene was bathed in an eerie purple light. Mara quickly pulled me away, her eyes wide, as she looked back over her shoulder, speechless.

The streets were crowded with people, tourists like ourselves, would be customers, occasionally uniformed policemen. Every so often we passed a window with drawn curtains....

"Well, mate," I joked to Simon, "d'you see anything you fancy here?" We had stopped in front of a set of five or six adjoining windows and Simon was blowing kisses through the glass at a pretty redhead who looked to be about sixteen years old. She had firm tits and a thick patch of equally red pubic hair and stood out by comparison with the predominately black-haired, olive-skinned Asian girls beckoning from the nearby windows.

"Appears to be an Irish tart by the looks of her." Simon cocked his head to one side.

"Tart? Don't you have another word you use? Pastry, or wicket or some such?"

"*Crumpet*, mate. The term you want is crumpet." Simon pursed his lips and blew another kiss toward the window.

"Crumpet, strumpet, whatever you want to call them, I'm ready to go," Mara said.

"Come on, sweetheart, we're just window-shopping." I was getting a kick out of watching Simon and the Irish.

Louisa didn't say anything, but she seemed to be paying closer attention to us than to the fleshy landscape around us. I winked at her. There was a hint of a grin on her face.

"Well, I've seen enough of this crap to last me a lifetime. If you and Simon want to keep wallowing in sleaze, fine, but I'm going back to the hostel." Mara took Louisa's arm and started walking across the canal.

"Hold fast, we'll go with you," Simon called out. He put his fingers to his lips one last time and waved to the redhead behind the glass, who was cupping her breasts and thrusting them toward him. Simon pulled his hankie from his hip pocket, daubed his eyes, and shook his head sadly. We caught up to the girls. I tried to take Mara's hand, but she jerked it away and stuffed it in her pocket. We marched back downtown.

At an outdoor pub at the edge of Dam Square we ordered four Heinekens and four shots of *Genever*. I rolled myself a cigarette and offered the pack to Simon, who shook his head. Mara fished a Marlboro out of her knapsack without bothering to take the box out.

"Thanks for the offer mate, but I believe I'll have one of these." Simon tapped the end of a Player's Navy Cut against his thumbnail.

I threw back the Dutch gin and washed it down with half the schooner of beer. "Mara, my sweet, what do you say we skip the hostel tonight and go back to that little pension we stayed at the other night?"

"Oh, you've read the menu and now you're ready to order, is that it?"

There was that grin on Louisa's face again, just the slightest upturning at the corners of her mouth. Simon's attention was focused on the district we'd just toured.

"Well, yes, the smells from the kitchen have aroused the appetite, so to speak."

"So to speak," Louisa said.

"Don't you two ever get enough?" Simon said. "Consider the plight of a poor bloke going without—"

"How could I ever get enough of this?" I put my arm around Mara and squeezing her up against me, accentuating her cleavage.

"Cut it out!" Mara pulled away for a moment, then leaned over and whispered, "At least save it for later, OK?"

"Ah, the promise of delights to come." I rubbed my hands together.

"Just shut up, alright?" Mara said.

We all walked back to the youth hostel, where Mara and I retrieved our rucksacks.

"We're going to skip the group scene tonight and find a pension somewhere."

"Dam Square tomorrow, then?" Simon asked.

"American Express," Louisa said. "Expecting another check."

"American Express it is, then. Say ten?"

Mara and I checked in to a fourth floor room close enough to the railway station to hear train traffic through the window. Streetlights from below reflected onto the ceiling. I stood at the window smoking a nice, tightly rolled Drum while Mara brushed her teeth and took a sponge bath at the sink. Soon I smelled Woodhue, the only perfume she ever wore. That scent was a clear, wordless signal that she was as horny as I was. I flicked the cigarette through the window and watched it arc out of sight into the canal, too far below to hear the hiss. I turned just in time to see Mara pulling the sheet over her.

I waited for a moment and then jerked the sheet away. Mara crossed her legs and tried unsuccessfully to hide her breasts with her hands. I could feel myself hardening.

"*Nude reclining in cheap hotel by moonlight,*" I said, framing her with my thumbs and forefingers. "Where is Rubens when we need him?"

"Fuck Rubens. You'd better get in here before I change my mind." Mara pulled the bedding from the floor and rolled herself up in it. "And quit calling me plump."

"Fat chance of that. I know you too well."

"You just *think* you know me too well."

I got under the covers and fumbled around, pulling sheets and comforters away until we were skin against skin, and began fondling her back.

"Think you could close the curtains?"

"What on earth for? We're on the fourth floor, remember?" But I got up and did it anyway.

I stood next to the bed, holding my full erection with both hands. "Anything else you want? I'm not getting up again."

"Don't be that way, Slick. Stop pointing that damned thing at me and just get back in here."

Mara pushed my head between her colossal boobs and wiggled around until she'd filled my mouth with a thick, erect nipple. I played with it, sucking it deep into my mouth, feeling the tiny bumps against my tongue. After a few minutes, I moved toward the other one, pausing along the way to nuzzle my face into her deep, perfumed valley. Oh, that Woodhue! I breathed in deeply and knew I would never again catch a whiff of that unique scent without thinking of Mara. Woodhue was connected to Mara the way the odor of freshly ground beans was connected to a cup of espresso. How she wore it, and *where* she wore it.... Could anything else ever smell so exquisite?

I opened my mouth as wide as I could until I got the end of her nipple back to my molars. I bit gently, feeling her flesh swell between my wisdom teeth. She sucked in her breath sharply and grabbed the hair on the back of my head.

"Oh, my god, David, you know I love it when you do that," Mara whispered. I rolled her on top of me and, with my hands in her armpits, began swaying her torso from side to side, dragging her dark, damp nipples back and forth across my face, through my mouth. This little part of our routine we called 'catch-and-release' and it never failed to drive her crazy. Mara reached both hands down between us and, in one fluid stroke, spread herself open and slid me inside.

"Oh, yeah, home again at last." I sunk my fingers deep into her buttocks and began pumping her up and down on top of me. Before long, I felt the tingle of her fragrant juices draining off me into the towel. She squealed when I spread my arms, venting her backside.

"Jesus, take it easy." Mara grabbed my forearms. "I've told you a million times not to mess around with me there."

"Sorry," I whispered. I shifted my hands to her hips and continued the rhythm, gently pushing down as I thrust myself up into her.

Mara leaned forward and took hold of my shoulder blades. "You don't have to ... to take it ... *that* easy!" Mara was close now; this was one part of her I knew very, very well. Our bodies had memorized these moves. When we fucked, she said it was like being on an Italian railroad train; we never left the track and always arrived at the station on time. In the dim light, I could see her face, head thrust back, eyes closed, mouth open.

"Oh, holy shit. Harder. Harder!" The ancient Dutch bedsprings whined and groaned under our onslaught and for a long moment I was afraid we would crash through onto the third floor below. And then, with a final spasm of ferocious bucking, she collapsed on top of me, sucking my lips into her mouth along with her hair, her orgasm still quivering through her supple, sweaty body like water simmering in a spaghetti pot.

"Come on," she mumbled, once she'd begun to catch her breath. "Your turn now."

And it was.

Mara was like that. Behind closed doors, in the privacy of a darkened hotel room, something inside her escaped. In bed, a clandestine, hidden Mara came alive and she was consumed by an almost insatiable physical hunger. She was not partial to gentle stroking and extended foreplay; she liked her sex fast, hard and rough. How could I complain if she chose to keep that lusty side of herself deeply concealed the rest of the time? Wasn't it, after all, the best sex I'd ever had? It was certainly the *most* sex. So what if Mara had erected a concrete wall between her outward image and her secret carnal cravings. So what if for me, the line between what she called a 'public display of affection' and our personal intimacy was a little blurrier? I was getting laid plenty and that was enough.

Anyway, Mara's obstreperous attitude aside, the four of us got along quite well. Soon, we were cooking most of our meals together in the communal kitchen, when we weren't eating out in some café or pub somewhere, going out for a few beers at night, becoming friends. There was a lot to see in Amsterdam and we were in no hurry. We had our whole lives to live.

———✳✳✳———

14 June —

Madurodam

━━━━━━━━━━━━━━━━━━━

W e'd heard of a miniature city called Madurodam so one day we decided to go see it. At breakfast that morning, I spread out a map of Holland and began plotting out a route on the public transportation system.

"Let's just rent a car." Louisa stood behind me, her hand on my shoulder, looking at the pastiche of connections I had figured out on the busses, trains, and tramlines. "That way, we can go to Delft as well. Like to see where that famous blue porcelain comes from."

"It's going to be quite a ways away. Almost to the Hague."

"Don't worry. Just got that money from home. I'll pay for the car and the gas."

Soon we were headed north in a rented Peugeot.

Madurodam, 'Holland in a nutshell' as the brochure said, was laid out over about five acres and had dollhouse-sized replicas of every major building in Holland. KLM airplanes taxied around Schipol, the main Dutch airport, and ships and barges floated on little canals. Toy soldiers stood at attention, guarding the Queen as she arrived in her horse-drawn carriage. Tiny windmills dotted the farmlands, their vanes turning lazily in the dappled sunlight. Bells tinkled as you walked past the churches. We spent several hours wandering around, crossing and recrossing our earlier paths, noticing details we missed the first or even second time through, calling each other to 'come see this!'

"Says here if you only have a day or two in The Netherlands, you can see everything you need to see here." Louisa read from a guidebook she'd bought at the gift shop.

"I'm glad we're bums and not tourists," I said.

"Everything except the Van Goghs, the Vermeers, and the Pieters."

"Well, sweetheart, you can buy those on postcards if you want."

"Everything's here except for the red light district, mate," Simon said. "Haven't seen a single working girl."

"Alas, lad, Madurodam is a Christian town." I gestured to the miniature Westerkerk Church, which at that moment was chiming its tiny bells.

"Christ, you're both hopeless." Mara shook her head. "Postcard art and whores. Europe is wasted on you both."

"Hold on, there, lassie, I *am* a European. Always have been."

"Getting late," Louisa said. "Let's go see Delft while there's still some light."

"I imagine," Mara said, "that's exactly what Vincent Van Gogh used to say."

We drove up to Delft and walked around narrow streets looking at blue porcelain in shop windows. Louisa bought a set of demitasse coffee cups she thought her mother would like and arranged for the shop to ship them back to the States. Simon announced it was teatime, which for him meant he was ready for his afternoon beer.

"What luck. Is that an AMSTEL sign I see before me?" I framed the sign with my hand like the prince holding the skull. "Alas, poor Heineken, we knew you well."

We'd come to the town square, lined with several outdoor pubs and thick with people. We spent the rest of the fading afternoon drinking beer and people watching before driving back to Amsterdam.

Amsterdam was a city well laid out for walking or bicycling. It was flat. In an effort to reduce car traffic, the city provided free bicycles for anyone to use. If you wanted to go anywhere, you just jumped on one of the ubiquitous white bikes, pedaled to your destination, and left the bike leaning up against a lamppost or canal guardrail for someone who wanted to go somewhere else. The theory was that if there were bikes everywhere, nobody would steal them. This system worked well enough to foil thieves, but not vandals. Unfortunately, many of the bicycles ended up in the canals. Since we didn't often find four vacant, functional bikes in one place, we walked or took the streetcars most everywhere we wanted to go. Every few days we checked our mail at American Express.

We all got along well together. Simon and Louisa settled into an easygoing friendship apparently not destined for anything more intimate. I sensed in her a need for something deeper and more complex than Simon could or would provide, and as far as he was concerned, brief encounters were preferable to long time commitments. Although Mara and I were lovers, always on the lookout for chances and places to get it on, we didn't think of ourselves as a couple. Somehow, there just wasn't enough *us* for that.

When one of us came up with an idea, like Louisa wanting to see Madurodam or Mara discovering yet another museum crammed full of old Dutch masters, our casual lifestyle made it easy for the rest of us to tag along. Even Mara went along with the flow most of the time and, with the exception of the evening we'd spent wandering around the red light district with Simon, was pretty good-natured.

Sometimes for dinner, we would just keep roaming until we came across what promised to be a good eatery. Restaurants with English translations of their menus tended to be more expensive and so we avoided them. Most places had either outdoor tables or large plate-glass windows; we often ordered dinner by pointing at someone else's plate and nodding enthusiastically.

There was a large population of Asians in Amsterdam, a legacy of the Dutch colonial empire and we soon discovered that the best places to eat were Indonesian. It occurred to me that there were probably as many Thai restaurants in Holland as there were Mexican restaurants in California. That was fine with us; we considered ourselves citizens of the planet, as stateless as Gypsies. We were just four kids bumming around Europe, without a timetable or itinerary, aimless and willing to go anywhere at all, except back home. Ristaffel was as appropriate in Holland as pasta was in Germany or curry in England.

✴✴✴✴

15 June —
Amsterdam

L et's go to Berlin," Louisa suggested the next afternoon as we were all sitting at a sidewalk café eating lamb gyros and French fries with thick, sweet mayonnaise.

"Just like that? Out of the blue? Berlin?" Mara said.

"Why not? Never been there. Any of you?"

None of us had been to Berlin. Because we were so compatible, and had no other plans at the moment, it sounded like a good idea. By now, we'd seen quite a bit of Amsterdam. It was time to move on.

"Well, I suppose I've had my fill of Van Gogh and Rembrandt, for the time being. I could stand a change." This was a good omen because it meant that maybe the four of us would stick together for a while. "You're talking about *West* Berlin, right?"

I wondered if Mara was thinking back to our two-week tour of Czechoslovakia and how unsettling it had been for her and so I decided to finesse the 'West Berlin' part. We had become like a small family, learning where each other's edges were, giving and taking in easy ambience. I rolled myself a cigarette, spilling a little shag tobacco on the glass tabletop.

"Yes, West Berlin." I remembered the cold sweaty feel of Mara's hand in mine after I bought koruny on a dark side street in Prague, the cops marching us back to the hotel, the soldiers who seemed to be everywhere we went. "I don't know if you can even get into East Berlin."

That wasn't quite true; I'd had friends in Copenhagen the previous winter who'd crossed the Wall into the East Sector at a place called Checkpoint Charlie. I didn't mention this to Mara, however. There would be plenty of time to ease her into another foray into Communist Europe once we got there.

Simon just shrugged. "It's all about the same to me, I reckon. We should hitchhike there in pairs. You mustn't stop on the autobahn once you leave Helmstedt and enter East Germany. When we get rides, it's certain to be for the whole go."

I'm not sure exactly how he knew this. We were always absorbing bits of information about life on the road in Europe, arcane tips that might or might not ever come in useful. It was a habit of mine to make mental notes of everything I heard. We lived a rootless existence; since we never knew where we would be a year, six months, or even a week in the future, we tended to remember everything we overhead in youth hostels, cafes, train stations, American Express mail lines, and anywhere else our no-madic population temporarily congregated. For example:

Mental Note: You could live cheaply on the beach at Ibiza, so long as you liked seafood and could afford the expensive ferry ticket to get there.

Note: In Greece, you could support yourself selling your blood at the hospitals, since the Greeks wouldn't sell theirs.

Note: Work permits were easy to get in Germany, which never had enough Germans to fill its many factory jobs.

Note: Behind the Iron Curtain, western money was always worth more on the black market than in official, state banks.

Note: Denmark had the best health care system for indigents, which was free if you said you had no money.

And, Note: There was no stopping on the autobahn between Helmstedt and Berlin. God help you if your car broke down or you had to take a leak.

So it was agreed that Mara and I would go together and Simon would hitchhike with Louisa. We'd rendezvous at the youth hostel. My youth hostel guidebook listed several hostels in Berlin, so after examining a street map, we chose one in Charlottenburg, more or less at the center of the map. The Charlottenburg hostel was as close to downtown as a youth hostel in a large city could afford to be. It was also the closest hostel to the fat, pink line zigzagging through the city, a fact I didn't mention to Mara.

Mara looked directly at Simon. "I think we should skip going out drinking tonight and get a good night's sleep for the trip tomorrow. I don't want to stay out late and hit the road tired in the morning."

I knew this wouldn't sit well with Simon, who liked 'a wee pint in the evening' as he put it, to help him sleep, but I said, "Right-o, see you at breakfast."

I waited until Louisa and Mara had disappeared down the hall to the girls' dorm. "A quick one before we turn in?"

Simon grinned. "You read my mind, mate. Lead on."

16 June —
On the Road to Berlin

The next morning, we all met in the cafeteria. I recognized Mara and Louisa's backpacks by the door; they'd gotten up earlier and were already almost finished with breakfast. Simon and I ate quickly to catch up and then we left the hostel and walked to the big, open-air market, where we bought cheese and bread for the road. It was the earliest we had ever been to the Albert Cuyp Street market, but already the place was mobbed with shoppers.

"Look at this," Mara said, "everything's already open."

"Lots of people get up a lot earlier than we do," I said.

"That's the bloody truth." Simon's 'wee pint' last night turned into at least four that I'd counted, plus a *Genever*, and it hadn't been easy to rouse him.

"Did you guys go out drinking last night after we went to bed?" Mara's voice was not quite accusatory but still had a 'boys will be boys' tone to it.

I smiled. "Why, darling, whatever would give you that idea?"

"Maybe you and Simon should ride together and I'll go with Louisa."

"Nonsense, Mara me love," Simon said. "I reckon we'll stick with the plan."

Louisa was quiet, but her smirk told me she was following everything.

"You know, Lou, you should consider taking up bantering." Simon caught the look on her face.

Louisa just looked at him with her blue eyes wide open and a straight, dimple-less face. "Anything like rugby?"

"There, see?" Simon chuckled. "By Jove, you're getting it already."

We took a streetcar to the last stop at the edge of town, shouldered our backpacks, and stepped down onto the pavement. The freeway entrance was already crowded with several clusters of hitchhikers waiting for rides. Road etiquette required that we take our place furthest down the onramp, so we started walking.

"If you guys had gone to bed when we did, instead of staying up half the night boozing, maybe we would have gotten here sooner," Mara said.

I knew Mara well enough to know I should keep my mouth shut. Louisa was several paces ahead. Simon just grunted. He was blessed with a constitution that allowed him to drink as much beer as he liked and never suffer a hangover the next day. Unlike me.

"It's you bloody Americans and what you call beer," he explained one morning when I was complaining about a headache. "I'm quite certain I'd waken with a hangover if I'd grown up drinking that piss."

"It's probably just the lime that keeps you from getting hangovers."

"You've got it all wrong, mate. That protects us from getting *scurvy*, not hangovers." Simon laughed. "Can't teach you Yanks a bloody thing."

Simon's strategy of splitting up worked well. We got rides easily; shortly after he and Louisa climbed into an Audi, Mara and I caught a ride with some kids in a VW Microbus. (Louisa and Simon got to Berlin long before we did, but the hippies who picked us up had just come up from Marrakech and we probably had a lot more fun on the way!) We met that night, as we'd planned, at the Charlottenburg youth hostel.

17 June —
Berlin

✦✦✦✦✦✦✦✦✦✦✦✦

That first day, we just roamed around West Berlin, taking in as much as we could. Even in its current, truncated configuration, I estimated that you wouldn't run out of places to go and things to see for at least a month. The Zoological Garden required most of a morning to see it all. We managed to fit in a brief visit to the state art museum and the Museum of Science and Industry that afternoon after a quick, stand-up lunch in an open-air cafeteria.

I was fascinated by some of the technical achievements the Germans were responsible for. (My father had once told me this story: Just before the outbreak of World War II, some American scientists at MIT had sent their counterparts in some German university a few inches of steel wire several times smaller in diameter than a human hair. The Germans returned the wire a few weeks later with no comment. At first, the Americans had assumed that the Germans were impressed with Yankee technological prowess, until a closer examination of the thin steel wire revealed that a hole had been bored right down the center.)

Tiergarten reminded me of Golden Gate Park, through which I'd wandered a couple of times on family outings to San Francisco. Demonstrations against the war in Viet Nam were happening in Golden Gate Park and Tiergarten brought up feelings of both guilt, for not being there, and—surprisingly—homesickness.

That night we searched out a singles bar Simon had heard about. This joint had telephones at every table and table numbers hanging overhead. When you saw someone you wanted to talk to, you just picked up the phone and dialed the number over their table. I'd never been to a place quite like it and it was standing room only. We waited half an hour for a table, had one overpriced beer, and left. Our telephone hadn't rung once. Around midnight, we headed back toward Charlottenburg. Neon flashed, music blared, hookers beckoned and the smell of sauerkraut and wurst permeated the air. Berlin was a party town; it showed no signs of slowing down for the night.

18 June —
Berlin

We quickly learned that Berlin was much larger than Amsterdam and more expensive as well. But where Amsterdam was continually growing, pushing westward into the sea by constructing dikes and thereby creating new real estate, West Berlin was as large as it could get, being bordered on all sides by the hostile *Deutsche Demokratische Republik*. This proved, in some contorted way, that politics was a stronger force than nature: It might be possible to push back an ocean, but when you bumped up against Communism, well, you were stuck.

I was considering working in Berlin the upcoming winter to replenish my finances, so Simon and I toured the vast Osram light bulb factory while Mara and Louisa went shopping on the Kurfurstendamm. Simon had mentioned a few times that he missed his family, especially his mother, but he wasn't sure he was ready to return to Liverpool, even for a visit. I knew exactly how he felt.

Fortunately, the Charlottenburg youth hostel served breakfast, and we used supermarkets more often than restaurants for our other meals. Some of the things we wanted to see were too far away for walking, but Louisa navigated the bus system like she'd lived in Berlin her whole life. Even using public transportation, we still ended up trekking for miles. Eventually, Mara's feet gave out. She sat down on a bench and fumbled in her rucksack for a Marlboro.

"OK, I've had it. It's time to quit walking and ride something."

I looked around but didn't see any busses or streetcars. Across the street, though, I saw a stairwell leading underground that I assumed was a subway entrance.

"We can hop on the subway and see where that takes us." I unfolded my map of Berlin. "They call it the U-Bahn."

"Won't see much of the city if we're underneath it," Louisa said.

"I don't care about seeing any more of Berlin right now. My feet are killing me."

"Right, then, let's have a go at it." Simon flicked his cigarette into the gutter.

"Think you can make it across the street?" I asked.

"I don't know. You might have to carry me."

A blue and white enameled sign over the entrance announced LEOPOLDPLATZ. I figured I would find it on my map once we were on-board. I ground out my half smoked Drum as we descended underground.

The subway was built before the war and did not observe the east/west border overhead. In several places, the tunnel passed under the Wall. Entering the U-Bahn from a West Berlin station was much like walking down into a subway station in New York or London or Paris; there were newsstands, kiosks selling hot dogs and soda, illuminated billboards advertising cameras, travel destinations, and so on, musicians with open guitar cases in front of them playing songs for donations, and lots of people. The platform was crowded with students and commuters and tourists getting on and off the trains.

As we left the station and entered the tunnel, the light faded to darkness behind us. After a few seconds of darkness, we slowed for the next stop. This station was named WEDDING, and was the same as the first: Crowded, bright, noisy, and busy. I wondered what the word meant in German.

"Pretty ironic, in the most divided city in the world, they go and name a station 'Wedding'."

"Was WEDDING long before they split the city up." Louisa had a way of saying things like that, correcting my thoughts as it were, without making me feel stupid. She assumed the identity of an immigrant whose second or even third language was English and said, in some fake dialect, "You are making, how do you say it, a 'poon'."

"A pun. Poon is a completely different thing." I smiled at her; she knew what she was doing.

"You should have been able to figure that one out yourself, Slick." Mara said.

Again the train zoomed into the dim tunnel but then it slowed down until it barely moved. We emerged less than a minute later at another station: REINICKENDORFER STRASSE. Next to the station sign was another sign, in German, which I couldn't read in the dim yellow light, except for the words Deutsche Demokratische Republik.

The next several stations were another world. The train slowed until it barely moved as it crawled past darkened, vacant platforms. There was just enough light to see that the stations were not completely deserted, however. Soldiers stood motionless in combat stance with their guns pointed at us as we slowly rolled past them. The headlight from the train glinted off the gun barrels and on one hand I was sure I saw the sparkle of a gold ring. Mara was terrified and almost pushed me off the bench. The subway never came to a complete stop and the doors never opened; nobody got on or off. In fact, other than the armed soldiers, these stations were deserted. The shadowy faces on the young guards were blank and unsmiling. Then the train left the last darkened station and picked up speed as it roared into the murky tunnel. For a few seconds we were in total darkness. Finally, we screeched into KOCHSTRASSE and were once again in West Berlin, all bright and busy. It was surreal and so unnerving that I didn't have the heart to extract the obvious multi-lingual pun.

The stark contrast between the two sectors of Berlin was nowhere more apparent than in those few kilometers of the underground transportation system.

"Think what it must be like for a Berliner to take the tube to work every day and see what we just saw," Simon said as we walked up the stairs out of the underground.

"If that's East Berlin," Mara said, "I've seen as much as I want to."

I had just the opposite reaction. I wanted to see more, to see it all. I could barely wait. Beyond the traffic of the busy intersection, I could see the graffiti-covered Wall.

"Jeez, Mara, come on. We've come all this way."

"I'm sure there is lots to see without having an army pointing guns at you."

"They were just on duty, watching the trains."

"Don't push her," Louisa said. "She can stay behind if she wants. Three of us will go." Then, to Mara, "There's a lot more of West Berlin to see."

Mara looked at me, and then at Louisa, and a funny expression came over her face. "Nah, I'll go. I don't want to stay behind alone."

Louisa turned to me with a grin and winked.

"Right-o, then, that's settled. Tomorrow we'll see how the other half lives."

"So to speak," Louisa said.

"Indeed," Simon shot back.

"I just hope it doesn't get any weirder than those stations," Mara said.

19 June —
Berlin

★—★—★—★—★—★—★—★—★—★—★—★

The warning on the large sign next to Checkpoint Charlie was unmistakable: YOU ARE LEAVING THE AMERICAN SECTOR. Lest there be any doubt about the dangers to which we were about to expose ourselves, the text was repeated in French, German, and Russian. There were several other signs in the vicinity, which, in my haste to enter the East Sector, I didn't bother to read.

"You know, Slick, I'm not sure I wanna do this," Mara said. "I don't want to get into any trouble. There's no American Embassy."

"What kind of trouble do you think we'll get into?" I asked. "Lots of people go into East Berlin for a look around." As if on cue, a Gray Line Tour bus pulled up to the Wall and about a dozen people unloaded. After reading the signs and taking photos, they passed between the sentries and through the checkpoint. "See, tourists. It'll be fine."

"Well," Simon said, "its not exactly on the Cook's Tour, now, is it?"

"Neither is Liverpool, far as I know," I said.

"You wouldn't bloody want to go there, either, mate." Simon laughed.

"Come on, you guys, it'll be OK. We'll go take a quick look around and come back and that'll be the end of it."

We followed the Gray Liners through a series of concrete blocks until we reached the custom's office, where we were each required to exchange about forty Deutsche marks for *Ostmark* and submit our passports for inspection. Fortunately, the guy who ran the hostel had advised us to bring cash, since the border cops wouldn't take traveler's checks, so we were prepared. The whole procedure took less than fifteen minutes and seemed fairly routine, if you didn't mind having AK-47 machine guns pointed at you.

We left the concrete bunker and began walking east, across a broad swath of litter-strewn pavement, into East Berlin. Eerie quiet replaced the noisy activity we had just left on the other side of the Wall.

Simon, Louisa, Mara and I spent most of our third day in Berlin walking around the East Sector. We passed block after block of tenant-like apartment buildings, a few of which had crudely painted graffiti pictures and slogans in German. Most were unadorned multi-storied cubes with row upon row of identical windows. Shirts and pants hung from clothes lines, drying in the hot German sun. A few stores offered bread and canned goods and we saw one butcher shop catering to a long line of customers. The one department store we found was closed and had a steel grate in front of the glass doors, one of which was broken. Although the hot, humid German summer day made us feel like we had walked for miles, a look at the map showed that we had never strayed more than a few blocks from *die Mauer*.

On our way back out, we stopped to eat lunch in a dusty, run down cafeteria-style restaurant near Checkpoint Charlie. From our sidewalk table, we could see the Stars and Stripes waving from a high flagpole just over the Wall. Slavic choral music drifted in from the kitchen. The few other patrons were also westerners, eating a late lunch before returning to the West Sector of the city. Although there wasn't much to choose from, the portions were plentiful. As we slid our trays down the counter, a woman on the other side dished food onto our plates until we said '*halt!*'

Lunch was a large pile of sauerkraut, a large sausage of some kind, (two for Simon), and several thick slices of hard, black bread. There was no butter, but we were provided with a big pot of spicy, seeded mustard. And beer.

"This beer is terrible. I can't believe we're in the middle of Germany drinking stuff this bad." The beer had a flat, watery taste to it that I didn't like at all.

"Look around you," Louisa said. "Lots more wrong with this place than the beer."

A few stools down the counter I noticed a pitcher of greenish syrup. I nodded to the waitress and pointed at the pitcher. She poured our beer glasses full.

"*Das ist Berliner Weisse*," she said, looking us over.

"At home, we call this lager and lime," Simon said. "Although this isn't really lager."

"I don't care much for it. I liked the beer in Amsterdam better." The addition of the sweet, green syrup had not improved the flavor, in my opinion.

Mara, who was not much of a beer drinker to begin with, took one more sip and quit.

"I wouldn't mind having a Coke or something. Do you know the word for 'water'?"

"*Wasser*," I said. And then, to the waitress, "*ein Glas Wasser, bitte.*"

Louisa was the only one who liked the beer. She'd finished her stein and was working on Mara's. Somehow, Louisa had gotten to it before Simon, a rare feat. I pushed my almost-full stein down the counter to him. "No sense letting this go to waste. If you can drink it, you're welcome to it."

We sat and talked for a while, smoking, watching people on foot and bicycles outside. The few cars mixed in withthe bikes were noisy and belched smoke. One had **TRABANT AUTOWERKS** painted on the side. So, those were the infamous *Trabbies* we'd heard about. Although they were technically automobiles, and moreover the pride of post-war East German industry, they shared more in common with a two-stroke American riding lawnmower than with, say, a Porsche or an Audi.

Finally, we were ready to leave. The food was cheap; after we paid, we still had East German marks left over. I had no idea what we could spend them on since most of the shops we'd seen had so little to offer. As it was getting late in the afternoon and we had to be out of the East Sector by six o'clock, we headed toward the sun. Mara slipped her hand into mine and squeezed my fingers gently, silently thanking me for the water.

"You're welcome," I said.

Walking along a deserted side street, we saw a man with what appeared to be a sketchpad sitting in front of a ruined building. The building looked as if it might once have been a church; still standing at one end was something that could have been its steeple. The man, who I guessed was about our age, was drawing the church with colored pencils. We watched for a few moments before he suddenly noticed us and tried to cover the sketchpad with his hands. I could tell from my brief glimpse that he knew how to draw.

"*Was möchtest du?* Why are you here?" He looked agitated, his eyes bored into me for several seconds before he turned his head and looked up and down the street. It was a look I shall never forget. Eyes may be windows to the soul, but the look on that man's face and his nervous scanning of the area both frightened and challenged me. Whatever had intrigued me about east Europe was crystallized in the cold stare of the artist as he returned his attention to me. Louisa was dead right in her assessment of East Berlin: There was *lots* more wrong here than the beer.

"We are tourists. We came to see East Berlin. What are you drawing?" I spoke in English. Mara, who was carrying her own sketchpad, appeared particularly interested.

"*Nichts*," he said. "I make nothing here. There is nothing to see here."

"You were drawing. I saw your picture. You are a good artist."

"*Ich bin kein Künstler*. I make no art. I will go now." He gathered up his pencils and pad and began walking swiftly down the street.

"*Warte!*" Louisa called out after him. "*Warte, bitte!*"

Hearing Louisa shout at him in German just made the guy run faster. We stood in the street and watched him disappear down a side alley.

"Maybe using German wasn't such a hot idea," I said.

"We're in Germany," Louisa answered.

"Let's get the hell outta here." Mara picked up her sketchbook. " I don't wanna get stuck here after they close the gate. This is spooky."

Consensus was easy. Hours spent wandering around the desolate, lifeless neighborhoods behind the Wall had undermined the feeling of adventure and bravado we'd started with in the bright sunshine of morning in the youth hostel. Our chance encounter with the artist had not reassured any of us about the hospitality of East Germany. With curfew approaching, we began walking toward the Wall, toward Checkpoint Charlie. Mara was practically pulling me. Simon checked his watch: five-thirty.

At the border, a very large, grim, stern-looking woman in a dull green *Volkspolizei* uniform ordered us to produce our passports and East German marks. She was obviously the senior officer in charge and in command of the two younger male soldiers with her.

"*Ostmark? Haben Sie Ostmark?*" The fat, blonde guard didn't smile.

Simon, who'd been in charge of the money, put the rest of the East German marks on the counter. "*Deutsche marks, bitte*," he said.

"*NEIN!*" Blondie said in a loud tone of voice that forbade argument and slid our money from the counter into a drawer that she shut with a slam. Apparently, there was no reverse exchange. After scrutinizing our passports and faces for several minutes, she finally laid the passports on the counter, said something in German, and pointed to the door leading to the maze and, beyond that, the Wall.

We were free to go. For the first time, it occurred to me that we might *not* have been free to go, that there might have been some minor glitch in the system, some political point to be made, which could have prevented us from crossing back through Checkpoint Charlie. I'd always taken my freedom of movement for granted, much like my freedom of speech or any other freedom I was used to. That was the

American in me, for what it was worth. Outside of civics class, I'd never spent much time in my nineteen years thinking about it. My liberty being in the pudgy hands of a frowning, overweight East German border guard, however briefly, was a sobering thought.

"It's a tax, a bloody tax. That's all it is. They are taxing us for the privilege of seeing their rotten little workers' paradise." Simon came from a country where some homes still had coin-fed heaters in the bedrooms, and he had a decidedly bitter attitude about extortion.

"Imagine what it's like," he'd once told me, "to have the bleeding gas blokes poking about in your flat. It's akin to having a parking meter in your bedroom."

"Must be quite an impediment to conjugal bliss." I glanced at Mara, who blushed and smiled. Mara was really quite pretty, even more so when she smiled or blushed. She was not as quick to smile as she was to blush, and very seldom was I treated to this double whammy. The night felt full of promise.

The four of us scampered through the concrete maze leading up to the Wall. Suddenly we were through Checkpoint Charlie and we emerged, as if from a dimly lit trench, into the bright, gaudy traffic-clogged streets of the West Sector. I hardly noticed the American soldiers, one black and one white, standing guard at the gate. We took a streetcar back to Charlottenburg.

"I can't get the image of that artist out of my head," I said. We were sitting several floors above street level in a little bar near the youth hostel. "Why do you suppose he ran off so suddenly?"

"You got me." Mara shook her head. "I wish I could've seen what he was drawing. Something scared the shit out of him, though."

"Yeah, but what?" My question floated there in the smoky haze, unanswered. Beyond the manifest considerations of life in a politically and socially repressive country, none of us had any explanation. "I don't think we look that intimidating. We're just four tourists having a look around. What could be threatening about that?"

"Think about the hassle of getting in and out of East Berlin." Louisa sat close to the open window and every so often a puff of breeze fluttered her hair. "Maybe he wasn't frightened, exactly. Could be he just didn't want to be around strangers who were free to leave when they wanted to."

"You may have a point there," Simon said. "It must be bloody tough to be in a jail cell having visitors who can walk out of the place when they damned well please."

"Well, yeah, maybe." I wasn't completely convinced. "But did you get a look at his face? I think it was more than that. He looked scared."

We sat around for a while, mulling over the possibilities. Mostly, we were quiet, thinking about the events of the day; the gargantuan, blonde *Vopo*, the terrifying feeling of isolation and despair on the other side of the Wall, the strange artist who had bolted the minute we tried to talk to him, and the stark contrast between the life we enjoyed and the existence they were forced to endure just a short distance away.

"I wouldn't half like to have gotten my money back." Simon dumped the few East German coins he hadn't given to Blondie into his empty glass and shook it around.

"Less than two dollars," Louisa said. "Forget it."

"That's kind of annoying." Mara scowled at Simon. "Do you mind?"

I said, "It's getting late. It's been a long day and I, for one, am kind of tired. Ready to call it a day?"

"Right, we'll meet for breakfast in the morning?" Simon said. "We'll plan out tomorrow tomorrow. I'm ready for a good sleep as well." He didn't bother to retrieve his change.

In some deep and subtle way, my view of the world was changing. I can't tell you exactly how, any more than I could look at a rainbow and tell you precisely where the line between yellow and green was. Some transformations are abrupt: You don't always see them coming, but you know when they hit you. Other changes are transitions that you only vaguely perceive and have to wait to see what they are later, in their entirety. How I was feeling right then, in that bistro in Berlin, was one of the gradual, not-so-sudden kind.

As we walked toward the stairwell, I looked out the window, eastward down Friedrichstrasse toward the Wall. Illuminated by spotlights against the darkness beyond, the red, white and blue fluttered gently in the midnight breeze.

20 June —

Berlin

I t was easy to imagine that the activity in the street had continued un-interrupted while we slept. Shopkeepers swept clear the night's debris of cigarette butts and scraps of paper from the patches of sidewalk in front of their stores into the gutter. Waiters served coffee and pastries in place of beer and pretzels. A variety of both open and closed trucks, haul-ing box upon box of shoes, clothes, appliances, toys, and food from some apparently endless supply, clogged the streets. The contrast between East and West Berlin was stupefying; as I looked at the bumper-to-bumper snarl of delivery vans with impatient drivers waiting to unload their cargo, I couldn't help remembering their poorly-dressed comrades just a few blocks away standing in similar lines for a chance to buy a ration of potatoes or cabbage, a few slices of ham, perhaps a shirt or a pair of shoes. Where, I wondered, was the balance?

After a mid-morning meal of coffee, fruit, and pastries, we set off walking toward the Wall. There wasn't much discussion about it; we just knew we were going back to the East Sector for another look. Or, as Simon put it, a walkabout.

"I don't know what draws you back there," Mara said. "There's lots to see on this side of the Wall. This side of the *continent*, for that matter."

"I wish I knew, Mara, but I really don't." I couldn't answer that ques-tion even for myself, much less for anyone else. "There was something about that artist's face, his eyes, before he ran away."

"So you want to go back there because of a look in some guy's eyes?"

"You can stay here if you want."

Mara's shoulders slumped, and then she took a deep breath. "No, what the hell, I'll go back with you once more, and then that's it. No more East Berlin, no more East Germany, no more east anything."

"OK, I promise."

A lot of our existence was like that: Spontaneous. As much as possible, we avoided having any kind of schedule or itinerary. Coming to Berlin in the first place had been a spur-of-the-moment idea. We could stay as long as we felt like it, and then we could move on. Furthermore, we might not all move on together. This was a fluidity that we cultivated. We craved aimlessness and worked harder to achieve it than we might have wanted to admit.

When we got to the Wall, we found a small museum, *Haus am Checkpoint Charlie*, which had somehow escaped our attention the previous day. Maybe our heightened awareness of the stark difference between the two Berlins made us notice this little place less than fifty meters from the Wall itself.

"What say we have a look inside?" Simon said.

"Fine with me," Mara said. "We didn't get to a single museum yesterday. And I still haven't made up for the day we spent on the road getting here."

That was a good sign. Mara poking fun at herself meant we were likely to have a good day. Or at least an OK day, considering where we were. Of the four of us, Mara was the most emotionally volatile, and it bothered me that her moods could have such an effect on the rest of us. Because she was my girlfriend, more or less, I felt responsible.

Haus am Checkpoint Charlie was unlike any museum I had ever seen. There were no breath-taking works of art, no chronicles of natural history, no icons of any great religions. This museum, a converted two-story house, was devoted entirely to documenting the history of *die Mauer* and to the many escape attempts from East Berlin that disillusioned but courageous citizens had tried. The rooms, connected with narrow stairwells, were crowded with everything from various getaway vehicles such as a homemade submarine, the remnants of a hot-air balloon, and a tiny Isetta car, to fake Soviet uniforms, documents, digging tools, and so on. Hundreds of photographs, some enlarged to poster size, lined even the staircase walls. They couldn't have crammed in a single additional exhibit. This history of protest bulged at the seams, as if the collective will of the people to be free could not be contained.

Haus am Checkpoint Charlie had the disorganized, haphazard feel of a museum in the making, a depository still collecting specimens rather than a true museum like we were accustomed to seeing. This museum, open-ended, and unfinished, reflected the struggle between east and west. Little did I suspect that my friends and I would soon be playing bit parts in the very same drama we saw documented on the walls of the *Haus am Checkpoint Charlie*.

We spent most of the morning exploring the cluttered rooms, piecing together the desperation of people who had risked their lives to escape from the reality of what we'd seen the day before in the East Sector. Some had tried to leave by actually scaling the Wall, while others devised subtler plans involving fake passports, identity cards, travel documents and the like.

Dominating one wall hung a huge black and white photograph of a bullet-ridden body, bleeding to death in the dirt, while armed East German soldiers watched, frightened looks on their faces. Under the photo was a single line: Peter Fechter 1944 – 1962. A placard on the wall next to the photo explained that Fechter had been mortally wounded as he ran across the barren buffer zone toward West Berlin. This brave but unlucky kid had been eighteen years old the day he died, twelve days before my own sixteenth birthday. I stood staring at the image, mesmerized, until Louisa, without uttering a single word, finally took my hand and led me down the stairs.

The idea that someone could feel so imprisoned, so repressed by the government that he would try to dig a tunnel under the wall, construct a tiny submarine in his living room, or sew together a makeshift balloon and hang a cobbled-together basket underneath it so he could crawl or dive or float with his family to freedom was astonishing. It was one thing to read about 'oppressed masses of people' behind the Iron Curtain, distant, faceless, and anonymous, but another thing entirely to actually feel and smell the fabric of a homemade hot air balloon or to put your hand on a pitifully small trowel and touch the same worn handle that some desperate refugee had grasped as he scraped at the dirt, night after night, in a narrow tunnel. The evidence of these escapes, and many other less successful attempts, were all on display in the *Haus am Checkpoint Charlie*. By the time we emerged several hours later into the sunlight of Friedrichstrasse, we were considerably subdued. Even Simon was quiet, and it was getting close to lunchtime.

We walked the remaining few paces to the Wall, past the American army sentries, through Checkpoint Charlie, and into the East German bunker, where we exchanged money and were sternly ordered to be out by six o'clock.

"We are leaving the American Sector," Mara said. That was the first time any of us had spoken since leaving the *Haus am Checkpoint Charlie*.

I put my hand on Mara's neck. "Sweetheart, I left the American Sector years ago."

It was nearly one o'clock by the time we reached the church where we saw the man drawing yesterday. Sure enough, there he was, sitting on the same bench he'd been on yesterday, drawing on a large white pad.

"*Guten Tag,*" I said.

Startled, the man turned around and started to get up.

"Wait. We just want to talk to you for a minute." I had an inspiration and held out my passport. "We are Americans."

Simon grimaced and fumbled for his own passport. "I am British."

To my ears, his voice was a dead giveaway as to his nationality; there was no confusing his English accent for an American one. But then, maybe the subtle differences between English and American would be lost on a foreigner. After all, I wouldn't have been able to hear any difference between a Berliner and a Bavarian.

"*Ich bin Johann.*" The man looked to be about our age, certainly not more than a few years older. He clasped his sketchpad against his chest with both arms. His blue eyes slid from side to side, scanning the street, before they settled on my face. "What do you wish to speak about?"

I held out my hand. "My name is David. We are tourists here. We came to see East Berlin."

The artist's brow furrowed into the universal sign that meant, 'why?' Finally, warily, Johann took my hand. "As you can see, there is not much here which can interest you." He retrieved his hand from my enthusiastic grasp and waved it around at the pot-holed street, strewn with rubble and litter. The debris was a sharp contrast to the almost sterile cleanliness of the West Sector.

"It is quite different from West Berlin," I said.

"You are coming to this place from Checkpoint Charlie? From Friedrichstrasse?"

"Yeah," Mara said. "We walked here this morning."

"That is a long walk. And from where you came in West Berlin?"

"The youth hostel in Charlottenburg."

"'Tis indeed," Simon said. "One can work up an appetite."

"Not to mention a thirst," I added.

Louisa spoke, for the first time, in German. "*Wir sahen dich gestern hier. Du bist weg gelaufen. Gestern Abend unterhielten wir uns darüber und wollten zurüch kommen um dich zu finden.*"

"*Ah, Sie sprechen Deutsch.*" A wary smile crossed Johann's face. "But for what reason do you seek for me?" I detected a shadow of suspicion, either in his voice or on his face.

"*Ich bin in München geboren, bin aber nun ein amerikanischer Bürger.*"

Louisa explained that she had been born in Munich but was now an American citizen. The artist looked doubtful. In English, Louisa said to the rest of us, "Maybe it wasn't such a hot idea to speak German after all." Then, again in German, to Johann, "*Willst du meinen Ausweis sehen?*" She fumbled in her rucksack for her passport.

"No, no, that is not necessary. But I do prefer we can speak English."

"That's fine with me," I said. "I don't speak much German."

"I don't speak any German at all." Mara fidgeted and looked in the direction of the Wall. She liked knowing what's going on, what was being said. Her only experience trying to learn a foreign language had been a few years of high school Spanish, which, so far, hadn't been of any use to her at all. She hadn't been to Spain and didn't seem much inclined to go there, Prado Museum or no Prado Museum.

Mara couldn't be bothered with even the rudimentary rules of international travel, as we on the road understood them. Rule One: When you crossed a border, you immediately learned to count from one to ten as well as how to say 'please', 'thank you', 'left', 'right', 'youth hostel', 'toilet', and a few other words in the lingo du jour. Mara always assumed that no matter where she was, sooner or later she would meet someone who spoke English, hopefully before she got hungry or tired. Or had to pee. So far, she'd been pretty lucky. I often wondered how she got along before we started traveling together.

"I have studied some English in school," Johann said, slowly, laboring in English. "But I am not having much opportunity to practice." The artist seemed to be relaxing his guard. Was he finally convinced that we were genuine tourists and not some kind of East German undercover agents?

"So, you are an artist." I quickly felt foolish for stating the obvious.

"I wish to be an artist, but such is not permitted to me."

"Not permitted?" Mara asked. "What do you mean?"

"The government it say what you will be, what work you will do. My legal profession is to be a painter of houses. I must paint upon the graffiti. Do you know this word—graffiti?

"Same word in English," Mara said.

"The government they decide what you best can do to help the state, and that must be your work."

"Have I got this straight, then?" Simon asked. "You want to be an artist, but your official job is to cover over the decorations people put on buildings?"

"Exactly! It is exactly as you say." Johann almost laughed.

Mara looked perplexed. I wondered if the juxtaposition of her having dropped out of art school in Boston and Johann being forbidden to pursue his passion registered with her. She said nothing.

"That's bloody bizarre." Simon shook his head incredulously. "You don't get to choose your own job?"

"I am liking to be an artist, but the government say there are enough artists but not enough painters of buildings. And so, that is what I must do. I draw and paint art when I can." Johann used the word '*Künstler*' to describe himself as an artist.

"Can we see your drawings?" Mara had been an art student since she was in junior high school and now at the ripe old age of twenty considered herself a failed artist. I thought of her more as a failed student, since she continued to carry her sketchpad around with her all the time. I didn't know how anyone could consider themselves a failure at twenty, but it was a popular notion with her. There was a huge difference between being a failure and being a drop out. We were all dropouts from something; it was part of the ethos of being on the road in Europe in the mid-sixties. But Mara was the only person I knew of who thought of herself as a failure.

Johann handed Mara his sketchpad and she gave him her leather case. As she slowly turned the pages, Johann's talent was self-evident. There was clarity of line and form. Subtle shadings of pastel color emphasized the predominant use of black and gray.

"Everything what you see here are coming from Berlin." Most, he explained, were within walking distance from where he lived. Some of the pictures depicted country themes; fields, rivers, and trees. Mara looked impressed. Johann had not opened her sketchbook.

"These are very beautiful." I had never taken any art courses in high school and I was no connoisseur, but both my mother and father were collectors, so I'd been around art most of my life. Carmel, where I grew up, was supposedly an artist's colony, too, although to me it was mostly a tourist town with too many art galleries peddling what I considered to be 'hotel art'. I could see that Johann was good; he had the eye and the stroke of a painter.

"Where are these scenes from?" Louisa asked. "We haven't been to East Germany, except for now, in East Berlin. These country scenes—?"

"They are all coming from inside the boundaries of the city. All from the East part of Berlin. I have not been outside from Berlin since it became closed, from since *die Mauer*, the Wall was built. From that time, I have been here."

"How is that?" Mara asked.

"It is, how would you say it—" Johann reverted to his native language, speaking to Louisa. When he was finished, she explained that there wasn't much freedom of movement in East Germany. Visas were required for not only travel outside the *Deutsche Democratic Republik*, but for travel within the country as well. The authorities refused to grant Johann an exit visa to leave East Berlin.

This piece of information surprised me. I knew that passage through the Iron Curtain from west Europe to east Europe required visas that took weeks or even months to obtain, depending on the requirements of each individual country. (Going from east to west was, of course, almost impossible. There was virtually no legal emigration from Iron Curtain countries and the borders were all well guarded to prevent escape.) But I had naïvely assumed that between the various socialist republics travel would be unrestricted, that it wouldn't be difficult to go from, say, Berlin to Budapest. And it was even more bizarre that a government would control and limit travel *inside it's own territory*. What would it be like to live in Carmel and have to apply for a permit to drive one hundred miles to San Francisco? Or maybe to go from Manhattan, where my father used to live, over the East River to Brooklyn, to visit his sister. Would there be some sort of official kiosk on the Brooklyn Bridge?

"Some times I try to have permission to visit my mother in Dresden. My mother is very old and ill. The war was difficult time for her. Each time I am told no. They say that I am needed here, in Berlin, to do my work of painting houses. I believe the reason they do not say is that I might escape." Johann laughed. "To escape from East Berlin to East Germany is not a real escape, do you not agree? That is, how do you say in English, from the cooker to the fire."

"Out of the frying pan into the fire," Mara said.

"*Ya*, that is it. Out of the frying pan into the fire. Here we say '*Er kam vom Regen in die Traufe*'. It mean he came from the rain into the tub."

"I think it's about time we go from the east to the west," Mara said.

I ignored her comment. "Listen. Why don't we all go get a beer somewhere? Will you come and drink a beer with us?" The hot, summer sun had fatigued me and I thought a cool beer in a shady place would be the perfect antidote.

"And maybe a bite to eat," Simon said.

"Do you think you must ask a German two times if he will drink a beer?" Johann smiled wide. It was the first time I had seen him smile. "I know a little place where we will not be seen."

"I hope it is better than the café we had lunch in yesterday." I said. "The food was OK but I didn't like the beer much."

"You maybe ate in a *gaststätte near die Mauer*, yes? These places are for tourists only. We Germans do not go there. It is too close to the Wall, and, as you say, the beer is not so good."

"Lead on, McDuff," Simon said.

"McDuff? What is this McDuff?" Johann asked.

"Not to worry, mate, its just a joke," Simon said.

Louisa explained the Shakespearean allusion as best she could. We shouldered our rucksacks, Johann packed up his sketchpad and pencils and we followed him down the street.

Mara frowned. "Can't we just leave? I really don't want to be here any longer."

"Just one beer, one quick beer, and we'll head back," I said. "Promise."

"There's no such thing as 'one quick beer' with Simon," Mara said. "Or you, either, for that matter. Besides which, Slick, your promises don't mean shit."

"Just watch. We'll be out of here so fast it'll make your head spin."

Louisa followed this without comment, but I thought I could see a trace of annoyance on her face. Or was that a smile in disguise?

"You see, it is difficult to live here if you are not a member of the Communist Party. The state is in every place. You must be very careful of the *Staatssicherheit*. The *Stasi* is like your American FBI but much bigger. There are *Stasi* in every place. You cannot always know who is *Stasi* and who is not. Sometimes, yes, but not every time. They must know everything about every people all the time."

"Bloody hell." Simon was scanning the room for a waitress. I could tell he was ready for a beer.

Johann glanced over at the bartender. "I do not know this man but I do not believe he is *Stasi*. But it can never be sure."

We were in a small, dimly lit *gaststätte*, sitting at a table in the back of the room, away from the windows. More light came in from the smoke-grimed windows than from the three low-wattage light bulbs hanging from the ceiling. There were a few posters on the walls, which depicted silhouettes of factory workers and farmers. The writing on the posters was not in English or German, but Cyrillic Russian.

I nodded to the nearest poster. "Do you speak Russian?"

A sly smile crossed Johann's face. "*Nyet*."

At another table, some laborers in overalls looked us over and then continued eating. Hearing the word '*nyet*', the man sitting closest to us twisted in his seat and stared for a moment, and then turned back to his companions. It sounded like they were telling jokes; one would speak for a while and then they would all laugh, and then another would talk followed by more laughter. Otherwise, except for the hired help the café was empty. A bluish haze of tobacco smoke clouded the room. The bartender had a broad face, straight black hair cut in bangs across his forehead, and a droopy black mustache which hung over a short, unlit cigar. His thick eyebrows formed a bridge above his dark eyes and wide, flat nose.

After watching us take our seats, the barkeep barked something toward the kitchen and resumed reading a newspaper at his station by the cash register. The workmen laughed among themselves, drinking their beer from liter steins. Soon a hefty barmaid with a thick plait of blond hair brought us our own steins of beer, three in her right fist and two in her left. As I lifted the heavy mug to my lips, it occurred to me that this joint wouldn't need a bouncer. Anyone who could carry five liters of beer at a time could probably handle someone who had drunk five liters. The bartender looked over as we paid the waitress for the beers. Johann fished in his pocket, produced his pack of cigarettes and offered them around. I took one and offered him my pouch of Drum in return, which he took with a smile. Mara lit one of her own Marlboros. Louisa didn't smoke, although she might just as well have.

"How can you know who your friends are here, then?" Mara asked.

"This you cannot know always. Sometimes someone is trapped in a small crime, in a small deception against the authorities, and then he is told that his crime will be forgiven if he helps to catch bigger criminals. It is not possible to know all who work this way for the *Stasi*."

"We have the same thing in America," I said. "The cops will often try to get a minor criminal to incriminate bigger crooks."

"Yes, I believe it is the same in all places. *Polizei* are *polizei, ya?*"

"Bleeding coppers are coppers, same everywhere." Simon wiped the foam from his mouth with the back of his hand and then wiped his hand on his pants.

"But here the crimes are different. Many things which are not crimes in America, I think, are crimes here."

"What do you mean," Mara asked. "Do you mean like stealing something or robbing someone? That will land your ass in jail anywhere, I imagine."

"*Nein, nein.* Of course, we have also those offenses. I am speaking of other things. As example we have a crime called *Republikflucht*. This is the crime of trying to leave the country without the proper visa. Those who escape, who swim the river or try to climb over the Wall, are guilty of *Republikflucht.* If a man will return to the DDR," here Johann laughed, "if a man will return to the *Deutsche Demokratische Republik* after escaping, he will go to prison for the crime of *Republikflucht!*"

"If someone goes to the bother and risk of escaping," Simon said, "I shouldn't think he would return, crime or not."

"That's exactly right. But some do come back if they have family here."

"And it is still illegal?" Mara asked.

"Yes. And sometimes if a man escapes which has children here, the children are taken from the mother for, how do you say it, *die Kindesannahme.*"

"Put up for adoption," Louisa said.

"Like suicide," I said.

"*Bitte?*"

"Suicide," I repeated. "If you try to kill yourself and fail, you can be put in jail for trying."

"Here it is like that, like a slow death. But why can anyone want to die in America, where there is everything?"

"Well, that's a damned good question." I couldn't come up with anything else, any answer that would have made sense. How could I explain why a person would want to commit suicide in the richest nation on earth to someone trapped in East Berlin? Couldn't wealth buy mental health?

I looked at my watch: Five-fifteen. We had less than an hour to get back to the West Sector before curfew.

"We must go now. Checkpoint Charlie closes in forty-five minutes. We have to get through the Wall before they lock the gate."

"*Ya, ya*, you must go now." Johann looked around the room, fixing his eyes for a moment on the Slavic proprietor, still sitting on his stool by the till.

"I would like to come back tomorrow to see you." I lowered my voice. "I would like to talk with you some more. Can you meet us?"

"Yes, perhaps such a thing is possible," Johann leaned his shoulders in toward us. The workers had already gone. I wouldn't have noticed, except that Johann's eyes had immediately looked in their direction when he heard the scraping of chair legs against the wooden floor. We were the only people left, besides the bartender, who was still smoking his cigar and reading his newspaper. I noticed him looking at us a few times after checking us out when we first came in.

"Where can we find you?" I asked.

Johann tore the corner off a page from his sketchpad and wrote something on it. "This is my address. I am home tomorrow. You will come to see me, but if there are people in my street, pass by and do not stop at my door. You will then come back another time." After glancing again at the bartender, he passed the scrap of paper to me.

"Bloody ironic, don't you think?" Simon laughed.

"What's funny?" Louisa asked.

"If we don't get going, we could be arrested for being here in the East Sector after curfew. Johann would be committing a crime if he were *not* in the East Sector."

"*Bitte?*" Johann asked, not understanding Simon's point. Louisa explained it to him in German. When she was through, Johann grinned.

"I believe you have a way of saying, ah, hanging humor or death humor."

"Gallows humor," I said. "We call it gallows humor."

"I am leaving a few minutes behind you." Johann stood up. "I am hoping to see you in the morning."

"Yes," I said. "We will come tomorrow. *Auf Wiedersehen.*"

Mara took my hand and tried to pull me along. "I'm ready to get outta here. This place gives me the creeps."

---

21 June —
Berlin

"Here is the street you are looking for, and the number must be about here." The proprietor of the Charlottenburg youth hostel indicated a spot with his finger. I started to circle the area with a ballpoint pen, but the tall man grabbed my hand.

"*Nein, nein!* You must not mark this *Stadtplan* in such a way. You do not know these people, these East Germans. If the *Volkspolizei* will stop you, and they find this map, it can mean much problems for that person living at that address. You must, how do you say it, *abspeichern,* remember—"

" Memorize?" I guessed.

"*Ya, ya,* that is right. You must memorize the address and the streets you will take to get there. And you must be careful always there."

"Careful?"

"Very much careful. How do you say it—spies to the State Police are in every place."

"You mean informants?"

"*Ya, ya*, that is it. You must be careful to say nothing by anyone. The Stasi —"

"I know all about the *Stasi*. I will be very careful," I said. "*Danke vielmals.*"

I had awakened that morning with a feeling of excitement. We now had a purpose, a sense of direction. We were going to visit a new friend in East Berlin. As always, the enthusiasm of going to a fresh city, country, or region was enhanced once I made a personal connection. I liked meeting local people wherever I traveled; such contact added depth and texture to the landscape. Just as a photograph is much more interesting with a person standing in front of the castle or waterfall, a memory of a place is enhanced if it is connected to a specific face and name. I'd often been a guest for lunch, dinner, or even gotten overnight lodging in a strange city, simply because I started a conversation. Perhaps I was a better judge of character than I realized at the time, or maybe people were just friendlier. Then again, it was probably my brazen personality.

For us on the road, language differences were seldom a barrier. I had studied Latin in high school; most of the languages we encountered were derived from Latin. In the past year and a half, I'd picked up enough street-German, *strassen Deutsche*, to get by. I looked forward to visiting Johann at his apartment.

Because it was close to eleven o'clock when we left the hostel, we decided to take a bus rather than walk. Friedrichstrasse had once been one of the main boulevards through Berlin; now the Wall cut across it, separating prosperous, brightly glittering West Berlin from the sad, lifeless electricity-starved Communist part of the city.

Passing through Checkpoint Charlie was no less a culture shock that morning than it had been the first time. So much rubble still remained from the Allied bombing that it was hard to believe almost twenty years had passed since the end of World War Two. It didn't look like any progress had been made since the previous day either.

"I don't know if this was such a great idea." Mara wrapped a coil of hair behind her ear. "We saw East Berlin, or all that I wanna see of it, yesterday."

"Well, Miriam, my dear, sweetheart, light of my life, you don't have to go with us." My fingers ached from her squeezing my hand. "You can stay on this side and explore around on your own. You liked the Kurfurstendamm. You could go back there. Or find a museum somewhere."

"Besides, the Nazis were great art collectors. Sure to be a stash of treasures around somewhere you haven't discovered yet." Did I detect a slight sneer in Louisa's voice?

Mara scowled. "I don't want to hang around on the K-dam and I don't want to go to any more museums. Can't we find something else to do? And don't call me Miriam, Slick."

"Why don't you search around and see if you can locate a public swimming pool?" I asked. "We could all get together later for a swim. I think we'll all need to cool off."

"Rubbish," Simon said. "Johann invited us to visit him and I think we ought to make good on that. In any case, we should stick together."

I glared at him. If Mara wanted to stay behind, that was fine with me. I didn't want her along pissing and moaning and ruining the day for the rest of us. A break for a while might be just the ticket. I was too late, though. Simon had her talked into going back with us.

"All right, I'll go with you. But this is it. This is the last day for me, going in there."

"OK. But couldn't you just try to be a little more positive?"

"Fuck off. I'll be any damned way I want to be."

"In England, we would say 'piss off'." Simon grinned.

"You, too." Mara glared at him. "You can fuck off or piss off or jerk off, for all I care."

Nothing I wanted to say to that. Nothing I *could* say to that.

There was already a line at the *Haus am Checkpoint Charlie Museum* when we got off the bus.

"It's funny," I said. "They've already built a museum for a few hundred East German escapees, but I can't remember seeing one for the millions of slaughtered Jews."

"That's funny?" Mara said.

Louisa didn't say anything.

After we passed through Checkpoint Charlie and wound our way through the concrete maze, we once again exchanged the required amount of West German marks for East German marks and took off on foot in the direction of the church where we'd first seen Johann. I found it annoying that we couldn't just reuse the left over *Ostmark* we'd neglected to surrender from the previous day rather than exchange even more western currency, but the rules were the rules.

"Not all that much money," Louisa said.

"I know, it's the principal behind it."

Close to the Wall, the streets were deserted, just as they had been before. The further into East Berlin we walked, the more people we saw, mostly on foot or bicycling. Occasionally a small, dilapidated car coughed by, belching black smoke behind it. The thin, high radio tower dominated the skyline. We passed block after block of dull, graffiti-decorated apartments and office buildings, the monotony broken only by the appearance of the shiny new Communist Party Headquarters building. A dark statue of a somber Karl Marx guarded the entrance. As always, Mara had her leather-covered sketchpad. Today she'd remembered her bitchy attitude as well.

"Have you got the map, then?" Simon asked.

"Of course." We were several blocks into East Berlin, out of sight of the border, so I unfolded the map. We had a healthy hike ahead of us.

"We should get a taxi." Mara was already sweating. "It looks like a hell of a long way to walk to me."

I would have preferred a cab or a bus to a long walk in the humid midday sun myself, but given Mara's frame of mind, I wasn't about to give her the satisfaction of agreeing. Louisa resolved it neatly.

"Oh, sure." I could tell from Louisa's tone I wasn't the only one becoming annoyed with Mara's whining. "That'd put Johann in even more jeopardy, having a taxicab show up at his front door with four western tourists. I think we'd better walk."

Mara glared at Louisa's receding back, but didn't say anything. She knew better than to mess around with Louisa.

It took us almost an hour moving along at a brisk pace with intermittent pauses to check the map to get to the address Johann had given us. His apartment was in a drab residential neighborhood of shabby, identical buildings. The street looked deserted, so we knocked on the door. Soon, we heard heavy footsteps on the stairs.

Johann opened the door and looked carefully up and down the street. "Ah, you did come." He sounded mildly surprised. "This is my home. Come in quickly."

"I don't know about this," Mara said.

I didn't bother to argue with her, but grabbed her by the forearm and pulled her inside. With a last glance, Johann shut the door behind us.

Johann's apartment was at the top of the building, on the fourth floor. We followed him up a windowless staircase that spiraled around a lifeless elevator. Judging from its dirty windows and cobwebs, the elevator hadn't functioned for years. The illumination on each flight came from a single dim bulb controlled by a timer that Johann slapped with his hand as he went by. The light stayed on barely long enough for us to reach the next landing.

"We have great electricity problems. Sometimes the lights are not strong. Sometimes the electricity do not come at all." Johann laughed. "In the *Deutsche Demokratische Republik* all comrades must share what we have, even if it is nothing!"

"I got plenty of nothing, and nothing is plenty for me," Mara sang between gasped breaths. She probably didn't think she was being funny, but I had to chuckle. Just when you least expect it, Mara could come up with something completely off the wall, but, somehow, relevant.

The paint on the walls was old and chipped and in many places, bare cement showed through the faded yellow surface. The edges of the creaky stairs were curved into their centers, adding to the well-worn appearance of the building. I wondered if it had been built before or after the war. And then, as we ascended, I wondered *which* war.

"Tell me, Johann," I asked, "how is it a housepainter lives in a building with peeling paint?"

"Socialism at it's finest," Simon said.

"Exactly!" Johann grinned. "The children of the shoemaker have not shoes!"

"Now that you mention it, I can't remember seeing a single shoe store," Mara said.

At the top of the staircase, we walked down a narrow hallway to a door at the very end. Johann opened the door and ushered us inside.

"You coming from the west can see much of what we are here living with. But for us to see the west, this is not possible. They do not want us to know of the west. This example, I cannot travel to see my mother in Dresden, so I certainly cannot travel to West Berlin. It is also forbidden for us to have any magazine or newspaper from the west."

The front door opened, and a girl came in with a large cloth bag. She had short, dark hair and wore no makeup. She looked about our age, maybe mid-twenties. Her only jewelry was a Jewish Star that hung from a slender gold chain around her neck.

"This is Liesl, my girlfriend." Johann put his arm around the slim girl's waist. "*Liebchen,* these are the people I met yesterday."

The girl covered Johann's hand with hers, smiled, but didn't say anything. I wondered if she spoke English.

"Liesl is a teacher."

Louisa said something to Liesl in German and they both giggled. Mara, who spoke no German whatsoever, frowned.

After introductions were made, Liesl opened several bottles of beer from the bag she'd brought in.

"Well, I suppose, a bag of beer is as good as a basket of Champagne," I said.

"What means 'a basket of Champagne'?" Johann asked.

I explained Hemmingway's Count Mippipopolous to them.

"We *are* in Berlin, not Paris," Mara said. "And your hero has been dead going on five years now."

Soon we were all drinking beer, smoking and chattering away in German and English, mostly the latter. Johann preferred to keep the conversation in English, for practice he said. Liesl still hadn't said anything and I was convinced that she didn't speak English.

"I would like to see your artwork," I said. "You must have a big collection."

"Yes, right at this time I am having many pieces. Maybe tomorrow I will have nothing."

"Why is that?" Mara asked.

"It is this. I did explain to you that I am not permitted to be artist. I must be a housepainter, the job given to me by the authorities. When I draw or paint, it is *verboten,* and so sometimes the *polizei* will come and take all I have made and take it into the street and make a fire. They do come and burn everything I have made." Johann laughed out loud. "They also give me, how do you say it—" At this point he switched into German.

"A ticket, a citation," Louisa translated.

"Yes, that is it! And I am to pay a fine! But since I have been making paintings and not working, I have no money for this fine." Johann laughed again. "It is, how do you say it, *die Scherzfrage.*" He looked at Louisa.

"A conundrum."

Johann slid a large suitcase out from under the bed and opened it. It was crammed full of sketches, drawings, paintings, block prints, and so on.

"You can see," Liesl said, "all what money he get he spend on paper and pencils and oils."

So, Liesl did speak English. I smiled at her and began looking through the trunk. I could see why the East German government didn't approve of Johann; his style was about as far from Socialist Realism, the official style to which all Communist art was supposed to conform, as you could get. Socialist Realism displayed the strength of the worker and his relationship to the state. There were no determined-looking blue-collar workers standing in front of gargantuan factories here, no brawny farmers hauling produce out of lush fields to hungry proletariats, not a single battleship or bomber with a red star, like the posters we had seen in the café the day before. Instead, there was scene after scene of East Berlin, captured in pastel and ink as a city of desolate beauty. A few of the places I recognized from our walks over the past few days. Johann also had some portraits, face and figures, also drawn in pen and ink over pastel shading, harsh black lines against only a suggestion of color. The faces were unsmiling, anguished, lost. In sharp contrast to the landscapes and bleak portraits were a scattering of oil abstracts, vivid splotches of paint on small bits of cloth, some of which were squares of denim. I set a few of these aside so that I could examine them more closely. One was a black and white image of a naked, slender girl; the only touch of color a single blood-red tear dripping down her cheek from her dark, right eye. Another was of a river with several bodies floating face down, pale and lifeless against the black water. In a third watercolor, a young woman stood in a river or lake, water rippling away from her knees, a sad smile on her face.

"These are wonderful, Johann." I was gushing a little, but I thought we were all impressed with Johann's ability. I knew I was. We were also making sizable inroads into the bag of beer. "I can't believe you are not allowed to pursue your career. You clearly have passion for what you do."

We spent over an hour looking at Johann's work. There was a bleakness to his style, something shadowy and depressing. I was reminded of the darkened, guarded subway stops. The few figures he had drawn were hunched over as if in pain, the faces sad. Although some of his abstract works were in bright colors, most of Johann's drawings were black and white with little more than the pastel wash.

"I am sorry, but it is true. By the law, I must be painting across the graffiti put on buildings and not pictures. This word—graffiti—it is the same in English, yes?"

"Same thing," Mara said.

"So your work will never be in an art gallery?" I thought of all the museums I'd been in, the street vendors with sketches hanging below clothespins from lines strung between lampposts, the chalk drawings on the sidewalks in Paris and Amsterdam and Copenhagen with plates and hats of coins. I realized that in my world, 'art', stretching the gamut from museum masterpieces to pavement sketches, was not just all around, but allowed to be so. Good or bad, it was *permitted*. Not hidden in a trunk, under a bed. Not burned in the street like a Ray Bradbury nightmare.

Johann laughed. "Such a thing can never happen." He paused for a minute and then continued. "Can you like to take some of my work with you?"

"Are you sure?" I asked. "These must mean a lot to you. Do you want to give them away?"

"Exactly correct." Johann began to spread some of his favorites on the bed. "These have much meaning for me. It will be better if you will take some. Some you take will not be burned in the street. I have lost many paintings that way. If you will take some with you, they will escape that ending."

"Bloody hell." So far, Simon had been uncharacteristically quiet, but inside, he must have been boiling. "For all that, I think I should like to have a few myself as well."

We'd passed the afternoon quickly, looking at Johann's work, visiting and drinking beer, but we did have the six o'clock curfew to consider. I stood up to go.

"Please. You must now choose." Johann spread more of his paintings around on the floor.

We each selected some favorites from Johann's large collection. I picked two abstracts and one pen and ink portrait with a pale blue and pink background.

"This must be Liesl." I picked up the picture of the beautiful girl standing knee-deep in the river, her head tilted to one side, her eyes focused across the water. This time, I noticed an abandoned bathing suit hung over the branch of a tree. I looked back and forth from Liesl to the painting. She *was* beautiful. My eyes lingered on her, perhaps a moment too long.

Johann nodded. "Yes, from by the Spree."

I put the portrait of Liesl on the three pictures I had already selected. Looking up, I saw Mara glaring at me through a haze of Marlboro smoke, slowly shaking her head from side to side. I handed it back to Johann. Even if I could sneak it past the *Volkspolizei*, I knew Mara would turn it into confetti if she got her hands on it.

Simon chose some abstracts and a haunting sketch of the same church where we first saw Johann. Louisa had drifted into the kitchen corner of the main room and was talking with Liesl in German.

"You must be careful passing through the border control." Johann explained that it was illegal to export works of art from the DDR without the proper permits. Obtaining such permits was out of the question. Forms would have to be obtained and filled out. Bureaucrats placated. Instead, we'd have to devise a way of sneaking the pieces by the *Vopos* without arousing any suspicion.

"I'm sure as hell not going to get caught smuggling stuff out of here." Mara twisted a thick strand of hair around her forefinger. I was certain she'd caught me staring at Liesl.

"It is a joke, do you not agree?" Johann had a quizzical expression on his face. "I am forbidden to be an artist and so these paintings are forbidden as well. They are not art because I am not an artist. But if the *Volkspolizei* will stop you at Checkpoint Charlie and discover them, then suddenly, by some magic, they become art!" He laughed.

"And so that makes you an artist, correct?" I raised my pant leg and wrapped three of Johann's pieces around my calf. Then I pulled my sock up over them and lowered the faded denim. Simon was wearing shorts, which he rarely did, so I hid his pictures on my other leg.

"You're going to get us all arrested. I can see right now that I am gonna spend years in Spandau Prison for smuggling." Mara began packing her own sketches that Johann had been looking at while we went through his trunk.

"Got a better idea," Louisa said. "Why don't you put Johann's pieces in with Mara's in her case? That way they'd stay flat and not get crumpled."

"Absolutely not! If you wanna go to jail for smuggling, that's your business. But I don't want any part of it." Mara snapped the clasp of her fancy sketchbook shut with her fist.

Johann laughed again. "It shall not be Spandau Prison. This place is reserved for old Nazis. Only Hess remains. Another prison, perhaps, but it shall not be Spandau."

"Small fucking comfort," Mara said. "Maybe we should go through Checkpoint Charlie separately."

"*Nein.*" Liesl's voice radiated disapproval. "This you must not do. The *Vopos* they do watch. They know you have come in together and they will be aroused if you do not come back out the same. You must all go out together, the way you came in. It is the safest way." She leaned forward for emphasis and again my attention was drawn to the gold chain with the Mogen David dangling an inch away from her milky-white neck.

"So. You are Jewish." The words were hardly out of my mouth before I felt foolish for stating something so obvious.

Liesl didn't answer. She stood up and began moving full ashtrays and empty beer bottles to the kitchen sink.

"I am half Jewish by birth," I said.

Liesl either didn't hear me or chose to ignore me. She didn't say anything. There was an awkward silence for a moment or two and I wondered if I'd said something wrong.

"Right, then," Simon said. "We had best be shoving off as we have a long trek ahead of us."

"I wish we could stay longer. It seems like we just got here." I stole another glance at Liesl. I couldn't get the image out of my mind of her standing naked in the river.

"Yes, the time has passed quickly." Johann began shaking our hands. "I am happy at this time to speak English with my new friends."

Finally, Liesl turned from the sink and spoke. "If you will come tomorrow, I can make a meal for us. It can be nice to have a lunch together." Liesl looked directly at me. Her star glittered on her pale skin. Her stare lingered on me until I turned away.

Simon and Louisa nodded agreement, but Mara rolled her eyes. For me, this chance encounter was becoming an adventure but I knew Mara well enough to know that she was not at all enthusiastic. She'd had enough of East Berlin and wouldn't want to come back yet another day. We'd had to drag her along this time. How was it that I was hanging around with somebody whose concept of travel, exploration, and curiosity was so far divergent from my own? She would be much happier in the safety of Amsterdam, Paris, or Copenhagen than she was here in East Berlin. I remembered our brief trip to Prague and how anxious she had been to leave, how two weeks in Czechoslovakia had been barely enough time for me but about a week and a half too long for her.

"I would like that," I said. "But don't you have to work?"

"I will tell them that I am sick. I do this many times and so it is familiar for them to hear that I am sick. It is summertime, so Liesl she have not school."

"Right, then. We'll be back tomorrow," Simon said. "Can we bring you anything?"

Johann laughed. "From the west you can bring nothing. From here we can have enough."

"At least some of us will be back tomorrow." I looked at Mara, who scowled but didn't say anything.

Johann walked down the four flights of stairs ahead of us, slapping the light timers on each landing. When we got to the ground level, he looked out at the street before he let us leave.

"*AufWiedersehen.*" Johann quickly closed the door behind us. We set off walking toward the Wall.

A few blocks before we got to the border crossing and Checkpoint Charlie, I pulled my socks up and Simon gave me a visual once over. Mara's face was pale, her jaw clenched, her knuckles white from gripping her sketchbook. Louisa appeared relaxed, almost nonchalant. Although my stomach was churning, outwardly I must have looked normal, because the *Vopos* passed us through without incident. Once we were safely on the west side of the Wall, I took the paintings out of my pants.

"*Now* can I please store them in your attaché case?"

Mara didn't answer me, nor did she offer to open her sketchbook.

"Jeez, Mara, it's not like you use that damned thing for anything anyway."

"Fuck off. It's none of your business what I use it for."

I carefully rolled Johann's artwork up. We stopped at a newsstand and I bought a Newsweek and wrapped it around the artwork for protection from my sweaty palms. There were already a few damp stains around the edges. Martin Luther King was on the cover of the magazine next to a banner proclaiming 'Black Power!'

That evening, instead of bringing food back to the hostel from a grocery store, the four of us went out for dinner. We were all very hungry, both from the amount of walking we'd done and from having had only a couple of beers for lunch at Johann's apartment. We found an Italian restaurant with outdoor tables a few blocks from the youth hostel. Guido's Authentic Italian Bistro turned out to be the perfect choice since it had an all-you-can-eat pasta bar. That day had been the longest 'between meals' time I'd seen Simon survive since I'd met him.

"You know," I said, "I'd like to take them something tomorrow when we go back in."

"What do you mean?" Simon asked, his voice thick through an oversized coil of fettuccine.

"Oh, maybe newspapers or magazines or something. That sort of thing." I forked another meatball into my mouth, still chewing on the last one. I was hungrier than I realized.

Mara's knife and fork clattered onto her plate. "Jesus, Slick, are you out of your fucking mind? I'm not going back into commieland with you carrying some sort of contraband. I'm not one to tempt fate. You know me well enough to know that, right? I don't want to go back there at all, anyway. It freaks me out."

"Look how easy it was with the pictures. They never even searched us. It'd be a snap."

"That was coming *out*. You're talking about going *in*."

"We've been in twice so far and we haven't been searched yet." I tried to be nonchalant as I spun my fork in my spaghetti.

"How do you propose to get past the *Volkspolizei* with a bunch of magazines?" Louisa didn't seem to be questioning whether or not it was a good idea, only how we might possibly go about doing it.

"Under our clothes, Lou, same way we got the paintings out. We'll get some tape. Nobody's searched us yet."

"*We* will not do any such thing. *You* can do any goddam thing you want. Spend the rest of your life in some fucking prison. I'm not having any part of it." Mara crumpled her napkin and threw it onto her unfinished cannelloni.

"Fine." I was getting more than a little exasperated with her. The way I saw it, Mara was way too cautious and lacked a sense of adventure, while I was prone to doing things because they seemed like good ideas, without thinking of the consequences. "You don't have to go back if you don't want to, Miriam." I turned to Simon. "How about you?"

Simon had deftly switched his empty plate with Mara's and he was attacking the remaining cannelloni as if he hadn't already finished his own dinner.

"Call me Mara. I hate Miriam. You know that."

"Well, that's your real name. Miriam." I suppressed a chortle at a fleck of marinara sauce she'd inadvertently trapped in her hair.

"Mara!" She glared at me through narrowed eyes.

Simon finished the last swallow of his beer and laid the heavy glass stein flat on the table, a signal to the waitress that more beer was needed. I wasn't far behind. He'd already finished off the bread and butter; I hoped the waitress would bring more, along with another round. I was reminded of the old story about the kid who gobbled his food down fast because he had lots of brothers and sisters and if he doddled, he wouldn't get his fair share. Simon ate like that.

"Tell me, mate, how many brothers and sisters did you say you had?"

Simon glanced up but didn't answer.

"How is it you always ask him that when we're eating?" Mara asked.

Simon gave me a long, hard stare. Finally, he said, "Right. Just tell me, if you would, how far you want to go with this. What is it you want to prove? You must have some idea or other up your sleeve. Or up your trouser leg, as it were."

"I don't know. I just wish there were some way we could help them, do something for them. They've been so nice to us." I opened the Newsweek and flattened Johann's artwork out on the table next to Martin Luther King. What *was* it I wanted to prove?

Mara pulled a strand of hair out of her eye, playing with it a while before letting it go. "What do you suppose will happen to you when you get caught? Notice I didn't say *if*, but *when*. I don't even want to guess. I don't think trying to sneak magazines into East Berlin for some people we don't even know is a very smart idea."

"Of course it isn't a smart idea. That's a plenty good enough reason for me to do it. I don't think we'll get caught, and if we do, what is the worst that can happen? They'll get confiscated."

"No, the absolute worst thing that can happen will be when you get locked up in some forgotten hell-hole of a prison in East Germany and they throw away the key and no one will ever see you again."

"Mara, it isn't right that they can't read whatever they want. That they can't travel wherever they want. Think about it. We bop around here and there and don't think twice about it. Just a few days ago, we were in Amsterdam. A month ago, Paris. Johann can't even visit his mother in Dresden. And Dresden is in the same stupid country." I didn't care much for the government running people's lives. I hated it at home, and that is why I'd left. It was starting to rub me the wrong way here, too.

"That may all be true, but there isn't a damned thing you can do about it."

"Only thing you could do for them would be to get them out of East Berlin." Louisa hadn't said much up to this point. "Of course, that would be impossible. No idea how you would do it—"

"Or why," Mara interrupted her.

"Like Mara says, this whole thing is tricky. Visiting them. Even going into East Berlin. Remember how Johann looked up and down the street before he let us out?"

"It's a police state, David," Mara said. "You forget about little details like that."

"Well, I don't know either. Besides, no one said anything about getting them out of East Berlin. All I said was I wanted to take them some magazines as a small gift." My sense of excitement was building. We'd just sashay in through Checkpoint Charlie with a load of contraband, right under their noses! I tried to keep my enthusiasm out of my voice.

But Louisa's comment did get me thinking, brought me back to earth. Lots of people had tried to escape, as we'd seen in the *Haus am Checkpoint Charlie* by the Wall. Although some attempts had been successful, many more had failed. It had only been four years since Peter Fechter had bled to death in the dirt after being shot trying to jump the Wall. He had made it almost all the way across the barren warning strip of ground before being hit in the back and then the stomach with machine-gun fire. As he lay screaming and slowly bleeding to death in the dirt, neither the American soldiers nor the *Volkspolizei* dared to help him. Crowds had gathered on both sides of the wall to witness the incident; Peter Fechter had died under a lingering cloud of teargas the *Vopos* had used to cool things down. That photo from the staircase wall in the museum was etched in my memory.

Tunneling under the Wall had been tried, as had running across the no man's land strip of ground and jumping over it. Someone had even built a hot-air balloon in his living room and floated with his family to freedom. One resourceful man had let the air out of the tires and removed the windshield of an already low-slung sports car and then raced under the semaphore. He was successful but his daring stunt would never be repeated; within days, the *Volkspolizei* constructed the concrete maze so there was no longer a direct path from the bunkers to the Wall.

Would-be escapees who failed ended up in prison cells or coffins.

My 'escape' from California had been simple by comparison. All I had to do was get a passport and plan my trip. My mother bought me a train ticket to New York and my dad paid for one-way passage on a tramp steamer to Le Havre. Nobody shot at me as I stepped off that dock in New York onto the gritty deck of the *Aqua Serene*. I couldn't even really call leaving California an escape when I compared it to some of the heroic exploits chronicled in the *Haus am Checkpoint Charlie*. What was it I had run away from, anyway? Had all I'd really accomplished by exchanging California for Europe been a change of scenery? But East Berlin was clearly no utopia, either. I could not imagine living in there, which was as unappealing in its way as Carmel had been. There was something subtler than landscape happening, and I was determined to figure out exactly what it was. My world was getting bigger and I found it deeply unnerving that I was no longer sure where the boundaries were.

22 June —
Berlin

━┿━┿━┿━┿━┿━┿━┿━┿━┿━┿━

In the morning, Simon and I purchased half a dozen magazines at a newsstand near the youth hostel. *Time* had a cover story on the increasing carnage in Viet Nam. Lyndon Baines Johnson, all jowls and scowls, peered out at his countrymen against a background of angry anti-war demonstrators. ('Hey, Hey, LBJ, how many babies did you kill today?') *Die Welt* and *Der Stern* both featured German events so far as I could tell; although my *strassen Deutsch* got me by, I could read far less German than I could speak. I added my Newsweek, with King looking only slightly happier than the President, to the collection. We gathered up a few more German magazines from the common room at the hostel. All in all, we would have a nice gift for Johann and Liesl, assuming that Mara's dire predictions of discovery and imprisonment didn't come true. Louisa went in search of duct tape. I wasn't sure if duct tape was even available in Germany or how you would ask for it in German. Our wandering around Berlin had been focused on museums and people watching and other touristy pursuits, not looking for hardware stores. Louisa's fluency made her the obvious candidate. Mara stayed in the common room, smoking her Marlboros, writing letters, and looking through her sketchbook, mostly fretting.

"Let's see." Mara laid her pen down and closed her spiral binder. "You want to smuggle these magazines past those guards by taping them to your legs. You expect to stand at that counter, hand over your passport, fumble around in your pants for cash, and keep a straight face. You must be fucking nuts. Haven't you read the signs? Nobody's gonna be able to help you if they search you and find them. You are talking about the Iron fucking Curtain here, Slick, not taking a crib sheet into a final exam. *This is serious shit*. Those Nazis are gonna lock you up and throw away the key and there won't be a damned thing anybody can do to get you out." Her fingers crept up toward her hairline. I missed the piece of pasta.

"We won't get caught, Mara." I didn't bother pointing out that technically, the border guards were *Volkspolizei*, not Nazis. What would be the point? "We'll hang around by Checkpoint Charlie and wait 'till a bunch of people are going through and they're too busy to pay any attention to us." I was nineteen seasoned years old and if not immortal, certainly above and beyond the grasp of some pimply-faced border cops who didn't look much older than I. Also, I was an American, and although I was an expatriate, it didn't say that on my passport. Being American might just carry some weight.

Furthermore, I didn't really believe the warning sign posted on the west side of the Wall, the *Haus am Checkpoint Charlie* and its somber displays notwithstanding. Growing up with a left-leaning, politically active mother and a screenwriting father who had barely managed to survive the McCarthy era and continue working in spite of his many suspicious friendships had taught me to take a jaundiced view of the pronouncements from the government. Any government. The idea that the good old USA didn't want me to visit the big, bad DDR and would exaggerate the danger of doing so seemed like just so much propaganda; I didn't believe the warnings were based on reliable information.

In the men's room of a restaurant near Checkpoint Charlie, Simon and I taped the magazines to our legs and chests under our shirts and pants. Louisa had found some clear postal-strapping tape somewhere. LBJ kissed my left calf; Martin Luther King snuggled up to my right. Those few magazines seemed to sum up home for us: Race riots and the war in Viet Nam. The very issues that had made so many of us leave America in the first place were turning up in German-language editions of American magazines. Even here in the divided city of Berlin, where the cold war was most likely to heat up, people seemed preoccupied with domestic problems in the United States. You couldn't get away from it.

After considering the idea, Louisa decided to forgo carrying any magazines into East Berlin, but for Mara, it was completely out of the question. She was petrified with fear by the whole idea, and Louisa, I guess, felt a sense of solidarity with her. In fact, Mara almost didn't go with us at all. I don't know why she did, and I wished she hadn't. Considering what happened later, it would have been better if she *had* stayed behind.

Walking stiff-legged was awkward, but within a few blocks we had mastered the technique of bending our knees just enough to keep moving. The edges of the magazines chaffed at the backs of my calves and into my armpits, and the tape itched and pulled at my hair. Simon looked like he was just as uncomfortable. I could hardly wait to get to Johann's apartment. I hoped we looked more or less normal. Thankfully, it was a hot, muggy day because by the time we got to the border, we were overheated. When was the last time I had been grateful for humidity? As a rule, I preferred cooler weather. Carmel was often chilly and foggy, even in the summer. On that fateful day in 1966, however, hot and muggy suited us just fine; everybody was sweating and we fit right in with the hoards of shoppers and sightseers on the Kurfurstendamm.

Shortly after we arrived at the Wall, a tour bus arrived, and we mingled in with the air-conditioned tourists as they lined up at the checkpoint. A few stood next to the stony-faced American soldiers and had friends take their photographs. By the time we got through the now familiar routine of passport inspection and mandatory money changing, the tour bus sightseers were perspiring as much as we were.

Finally, we were back again in East Berlin. We had not been searched. Passing through was nerve-wracking, but without incident. Mara and Louisa, who had melded into the tour bus line at the other end, joined us a few blocks later, once we were out of sight of the border shack. This time, instead of walking, we took a bus and got off a few stops before Johann's block. As it had been the day before, the street he lived on was deserted. We hurried to his door and knocked.

Johann greeted us with a big smile and quickly shut the door to the street behind us. "So, I am happy you have returned. You are hungry, yes?"

Simon nodded. "Quite famished, actually."

Johann scrunched his face. "What means 'famished'?"

"It means he'll eat whatever you put in front of him." Mara jumped in before Louisa had a chance to translate.

"Excellent! Liesl is making for us a fine meal."

Walking up the stairs was difficult, encumbered as we were. Johann led the way, smacking the light switches as he went. When we were only about half way up the first flight, the dim bulb timed out and we were in darkness.

"Johann wait," I said. "You have to go slower. We can't move so quickly today."

Johann paused at the landing, slapping the timer again. Eventually, we arrived at the fourth floor.

"I can not understand," Johann said, once we were inside his apartment. "The climb is the same as before. My apartment is in the same place." He laughed. "Perhaps you are tired from the walk in the sun?"

I didn't say anything, but took his hand and put it on my pant leg. A big smile replaced his quizzical expression as he ran his hand over the smuggled magazines. I began to unbuckle my belt, but Johann shook his head. Glancing at the window, he switched on the radio and led me to the sleeping alcove. The living room windows had a nice view into the living room windows of the identical apartment building next door, which meant we were equally exposed to the neighbors. The alcove was more private; there were no windows in that end of the apartment. Simon came with us and Johann pulled the curtain across the doorway. Mara and Louisa stayed in the kitchen with Liesl. I could smell something cooking and figured she was busy making lunch.

"What have you done?" Johann's eyes widened as I lowered my pants. "*Mein Gott*, look at this!" He suppressed a shout.

I yelped in pain as we stripped the tape from our legs and torsos and laid the magazines on the bed. Simon gritted his teeth. Johann picked up one of the magazines and started turning the pages, carefully, as if he were afraid of creasing them. He was clearly impressed. Yanking the sticky cellophane away from my skin hurt and stripped away swaths of hair. I looked—and felt—like I had been spanked.

"What you have done is very dangerous and forbidden. Do you have one idea of what will happen if you are discovered?" Johann's scolding could not mask his excitement at seeing the West German magazines now displayed on his bed. "I have not seen such papers for a long time. This ... *Druckerzeugnisse* ... is completely forbidden. I am not remembering the word in English. Liesl, come now and see this."

Simon just managed to get his pants up before the girls came in. I was a little slower, pulling my Levi's over my chaffed skin. I was glad I had worn clean underwear, which was not always possible living on the road like we did. Liesl just shook her head in amazement.

"That's exactly how I felt." Mara shoved back a renegade strand of hair. "I was sure we were all gonna end up in jail. Or worse."

"What you have done for us...." Liesl's voice trailed off. Her eyes were shiny. "This is a fantastic thing. But why? Why would you take such risk?"

"Well, you invited us for lunch," Simon said. "It seemed only courteous for us to bring something. What the *Volkspolizei* don't know won't hurt them, right?"

"The *Vopos* can make big trouble for you if they find out what you do." Liesl's voice was quiet. "And also for us."

"No kidding," Mara said. "I tried to tell them that, but they wouldn't listen."

"We just mixed in with a busload of sightseers and crossed over without a problem," I explained.

Johann was reading a story in Newsweek, his fingers moving slowly under the lines.

"Come, let us eat." Liesl slid the curtains across the window as she led us to the dining table. "*Liebchen*, you will have much time to read after our guests will go."

Our hostess had made a tasty lunch of bratwurst, sauerkraut, and fried potatoes. Johann opened the small refrigerator, which he had filled with bottles of beer.

"I must, how can I explain—," he switched to German, speaking directly to Louisa.

"Johann wants to correct your poor impression of East German beer."

"Ya, that is right. I have for you a selection of many fine beers."

"Jolly good show." Simon was already seated, poised to pounce on the steaming plates Louisa was serving. "I would welcome such a correction."

We sat around the round, wooden table on four chairs and a backless bench, which looked incomplete without a piano. I wondered how often Johann and Liesl had guests, or if they had ever had four westerners for lunch. We were all pretty hungry, I guess, because we devoured everything Liesl served.

"So, you are enjoying your holiday in Berlin?" Johann asked. "You are having an automobile?"

"No, no car," I said. "We pretty much travel by hitchhiking and using the bus or subway."

"Ah, yes, the U-Bahn. Upon standing near the stairs, we can hear below the trains pass. Of course, the entrance is blocked."

"Tell me, Johann, why are there so many soldiers on the platforms on this side?"

Johann laughed for a moment, and then his face got serious. "When first the Wall was built, it could happen that people from the West Sector would cast out *Druckerzeugnisse* upon the platform as the U-Bahn did pass. They did not want those trapped here behind *die Mauer* to be forgotten. Now such is impossible. Even to slide open a window on the U-Bahn is now *verboten*."

"I tried to tell him bringing that shit in was a dumb-assed idea." Mara looked at Johann. "All those soldiers with all those guns."

"Of course you are most correct. I am thanking you one thousand times for taking such a risk."

We continued on with lunch, complimenting Liesl on her efforts. Soon the table was cluttered with dirty plates and empty beer bottles. When we were finished, not a single shred of cabbage or sliver of potato remained. Simon saw to that.

"So," I said, after we had finished the food and were working our way through the beer. "Is it really that difficult for you to leave East Berlin? If you wanted to go somewhere, say West Germany, isn't there some way you could do it?"

"It is like this." Johann formed a sphere with his fingers, touching his thumbs and fingertips together. It looked like a rough approximation of a globe. "To go anyplace, a person must first get an exit visa from East Berlin. Even to go to some other place in East Germany, a person must first get a visa. This, as I have said, I cannot have from the authorities."

Johann's beer selections were having the expected effect. Each bottle tasted better than the watery stuff we had drunk in the tourist trap near the Wall on our initial visit.

"Suppose that you could go to the west. Would you want to do it? Would you wish to escape to West Germany?"

There was a sudden silence around the table. My question, blurted out, was a true conversation stopper. Liesl began clearing away plates and empty bottles. Frowning, Mara got up to help. I don't think she liked the direction my questions were leading us in.

"Johann have spoken many times about going to the west." Liesl's voice was barely audible. Again, there were tears in her eyes. "Such idea, it is a dream. A dream only. There can be no passage for us past the border to the west. We have no money."

"Why do you say you have no money?" Louisa asked. "What's that got to do with it?"

Johann answered. "It is possible, for those with much money, to pay certain people for secret passage to the west. It is also dangerous and can be failure or success. There are people who make a business of such escapes."

"Even to leave Berlin is forbidden for us. Johann have tried many times to get a permission to visit his mother in Dresden. Every time he ask, they say no."

"Yes, my mother is very old and not well since the war. When I left Dresden to come to Berlin, it was not then so difficult. That was before the Wall. Here have I met Liesl and so I stay one long time. Now it is too much difficult to go to back to Dresden. Also, I am an artist and not a painter of houses and that makes more trouble for me."

"What would happen if you could get permission to go to Dresden?" I asked.

"If I could get such permission it would still be difficult to go to the west. Dresden lies close to Czechoslovakia but it would not be easy to get there. Not impossible, but also not easy. But to cross from Czechoslovakia to Austria, this must be very impossible. This border is well guarded."

"Yes," Louisa said. "Dresden is still East Germany and Czechoslovakia is still east Europe. But Austria is the west."

Mara just stood there with a dazed look on her face, fidgeting with a strand of hair. She was beyond words and I was more certain than ever that she should have stayed on the other side.

"Come on, Mara, it's OK. We're just talking." I tried to take her hand, but she jerked it away.

Perhaps it was the tears in Liesl's eyes, perhaps the image of Johann's artwork being burned in the street in front of his home, or perhaps it was only the effects of a few too many beers on a hot afternoon in a stuffy East German apartment, but I began to wonder how you might escape from such a place. I could picture Johann and Liesl living somewhere in the west, at liberty to pursue whatever careers they chose, free of the stifling authoritarian regime of East Germany. Johann having exhibitions in galleries in Paris or Amsterdam or Copenhagen. Or New York. Liesl maybe teaching. Anything, as long as it was what they wanted to do, and moreover, where they wanted to do it. It was a nebulous idea, but I thought, what the hell, it couldn't hurt to sit around and talk about it. Intriguing and impossible. It would never get past the speculation stage. There was no way four teenagers, three from America and one from England, could outwit the *Volkspolizei* and the *Staatssicherheit*. Besides, the whole day, starting with our smuggling in the magazines, then making sure that Johann's street was empty before we knocked on his door, and now talking about Liesl and Johann escaping from East Germany, was getting to Mara. For some perverse reason, I found this amusing. I could imagine her bald before the afternoon was over.

Someone knocking at the door interrupted my daydreams. We all froze in place; nobody moved a muscle or said a word. In a moment, there was more knocking, more emphatic. Johann rose and silently motioned us to sit still and be quiet. He went to the door and opened it a crack. We heard him exchange a few words in German with a woman in the hallway, after which he shut the door.

"It is, how do you say it, one who is too much curious."

"A nosy neighbor," Mara said.

"She heard voices speaking English, so she must come to see." Johann laughed. "She is a harmless old woman."

"So now even the neighbors are spying on us?" Mara walked over to the window and peeked out the curtains. "I think it's time we were leaving."

"For you, it is so easy." Liesl's voice had no trace of recrimination. She was simply stating the facts we all knew were true. "You have only to show your passport and you are free."

I looked up at Liesl, meeting her steady gaze for what felt like hours.

"You coming or not?" Mara asked.

I ignored her. My mind was racing in high gear. "Suppose an escape route did not go through Austria?"

"How do you mean?" Johann asked. He got up and closed the window, stopping the lazy breeze from floating in and, perhaps, our words from floating out.

"Listen," I said. "East Germany shares a border with Czechoslovakia. Czechoslovakia has a border with Hungary. And Hungary has a southern border with Yugoslavia."

Liesl had a blank look on her face as she slid her hand into Johann's.

I could see Johann's eyes light up. "It is not so difficult to get visas for travel in these countries. Many people do travel inside these countries for holiday. Some peoples will go to the Black Sea. But to cross to the west—"

"I think it could be done, if someone wanted to do it." My legs and belly itched. "I have been down to Greece, to the border between Greece and Yugoslavia. There's a lot of construction going on there right now. At least, there was last summer. They were building roads, making detours, and so on. Everything looked pretty temporary. Dirt roads, plywood shacks, like that. I think at the right time, with some luck, a crossing could be made there. Into Greece. Then you would be free."

Nobody said anything. Louisa's face was impassive, expressionless, her eyes switching from speaker to speaker as she followed the conversation. Mara just looked down, shaking her head. Liesl looked at Johann. Simon brought some more beers from the refrigerator and passed them around. The only sound was 'pfisst' as bottles were opened. It was like we were old friends already, and yet we barely knew these people. I fumbled for my pouch of Drum and started to roll a cigarette. My fingers were trembling and I spilled tobacco from both ends of the rolled paper.

"Don't you see? We could use the bureaucracy in our favor. *For* us rather than *against* us."

Simon took a long drink from his beer, lit a Navy cut and tossed the pack on the table. Eventually, I finished building a bumpy replica of a cigarette and lit it. Simon broke the long silence with a deep burp from his belly.

"You could excuse yourself, you know," Mara said.

Simon didn't say anything, but I could almost hear the words in his mouth: *She's your bloody burden, mate, you deal with her.*

I took my roadmap of Europe from my knapsack and spread it out. The map was well worn and beginning to tear at the folds and had blue lines where I had drawn my previous travels on it with a marking pen. Now Johann closed the curtains. We all clustered around the dining room table looking at the map. Simon's box of Players made a hill under France. Cigarette smoke settled like fog over Europe. It was Mara who broke the silence.

"I think you're fucking nuts, David. It was enough of a crazy-assed idea for you to sneak those magazines in, and if you really think you're gonna smuggle two people out, it will be ten times worse. A hundred times worse. Those mags could've landed you in prison. What you're talking about now is gonna get you shot."

"I don't think so. Suppose we did it legally?"

"You can definitely count me out," Mara said. "Legally or not, I don't want any fucking part of this."

"Legally?" Simon asked. "How the bloody hell do you think you can sneak two people across the Iron Curtain legally?"

"You can't." Mara paced back and forth from the table to the door. "You're asking for trouble. I'm ready to get out of here."

"Damn it, Miriam, can't you just shut up for a while?"

"Damn it yourself. You could probably get busted for even talking about this shit. And don't call me Miriam. You know I hate that name."

"Well, act like Mara then."

"Fuck you, Slick." Mara went into the bathroom and slammed the door. She was certainly making it easy for me if I wanted to break up with her. I looked at Louisa, who was staring at me, into me it felt like, with those clear blue eyes. A smile crinkled the corners of her mouth. *What was going on?*

A few things were falling into place in my mind. A plan was beginning to gel. I was beginning to see how it could be done. At least in theory. Risky, but maybe doable. Just maybe possible. Liesl brought more beer to the table. Taking the bottle caps, I put one on East Germany, one on Czechoslovakia, one on Hungary, one on Yugoslavia, and one on Greece. I took Mara's pack of Marlboros from her backpack, shook out a handful, and connected the bottle caps, forming a bold, white tube from Berlin to Athens.

My imagination was in overdrive, undoubtedly fueled by the effects of cold beer on a hot afternoon. My chest and belly and legs itched where the sticky tape had ripped the hair away. My mind was racing forward with ideas. I felt a little dizzy. *Was Mara right? Was it time to come out of lala land? Where had she disappeared to, anyway? What was that look Lou had given me?*

That I had never even contemplated such an endeavor was no doubt fueling my fantasy. If I had been older, maybe been more experienced, possibly even spent any time in jail, the foolhardiness of the whole idea of helping two political dissidents escape would have been overwhelming. Reason would surely have prevailed. But I was young and invincible and predisposed against common sense. The possibility of failure seemed remote, the consequences unlikely, Mara's nervous skittishness aside. The image of *Vopos* making bonfires out of Johann's art in the street burned in my brain. I couldn't imagine a beautiful young girl, a Jewess, no less, standing in a river, going up in flames. Hadn't they burned Joan of Arc at the stake? I took a lengthy swig from yet another bottle of beer from Johann's endless supply. Looking back at the map, I struggled to focus.

"Suppose Johann and Liesl were able to get exit visas to visit his sick mother in Dresden?" I wondered what Mara was doing so long in the bathroom.

"Where does that get us?" Simon picked up the Berlin-to-Dresden segment and struck a match.

"Right across the border is Karlovy Vary, where the mineral baths are." I pointed on the map where less than an inch and a thin pink line separated Dresden from Karlovy Vary.

"Ah, yes, Carlsbad," Johann sighed, using the German name. "To take the waters at Carlsbad, that is a popular thing. A doctor will sometime make a recommendation to take a cure at Carlsbad."

"And suppose you were to tell the *Stasi*, or whoever, that your mother is very ill, which you say she is, and that you have to visit her and take her to Karlovy Vary—Carlsbad—for the waters. Suppose a doctor makes this order for her health. If the *Stasi* knows everything about everybody, then they probably already know she is not in good health. Or, they could easily check and find out."

"My mother she get a pension from the state which is more money because she cannot work. They will know she is sick."

"And does she go to the doctor often?"

"Yes. I believe her doctor will make such a recommendation for her to take the waters at Carlsbad. It is not a hard thing. Many old Germans go there."

Mara reappeared but there was no sound of a toilet flushing.

"Do you think they would grant you a visa to leave Berlin?" I asked. "I mean, they have told you 'no' already, correct?"

"Yes, that is right. But perhaps with the help of a doctor they will now permit me such a visa."

Liesl spoke. "Yes, but Carlsbad is not an escape. It is still east Europe."

"You don't have to worry about it," Mara said. "You'll all be in prison long before you get to Karlovy Vary." She lit a Marlboro and started to put the pack back in her pocket. I took the package and offered it around. "When you're done with this bullshit, I want my smokes back."

"Shut up, Miriam," I said. And then to Johann, "once we are in Karlovy Vary, you go to Prague instead of returning to East Germany. From Prague you travel through Hungary to Yugoslavia."

"It's Mara, goddammit."

"And my mother? How will my mother come to Praha?" Again, the German rendition. "Do you have an idea for this, also?"

I stared hard at Johann. Finally, I said, "Your mother would have to return to Dresden. I don't see how she could come with us. Perhaps, sometime later—"

We all sat in silence for a while. I didn't envy Johann. I was offering up an unconscionable dilemma, which, when reduced to the basics, was this: To possibly escape to the west, but at the cost of maybe never seeing his mother again. But then, so far he had not been allowed to leave East Berlin to visit her anyway. I thought of my own mother, back in California. I hadn't been very close to her at the time I left, but it hadn't occurred to me that I might never see her again. Leaving the States on a one-way ticket wasn't as final or irrevocable as Johann defecting from East Germany. I wondered how close Johann was to his mother. Did the love, or at least the bond, between a son and his mother trump politics and the quest for political freedom? More specifically, between *this* son and *his* mother. Many German families had already been separated by the partition of Germany; we had seen ample documentation of that in the museum. Was I perpetrating yet another heartbreaking story like the ones we had seen on the walls of the *Haus am Checkpoint Charlie*? Or did I have some crazy notion of being a hero, of being part of a successful adventure destined to be detailed on those very same walls? Was this all just reckless nonsense lent credibility by too many bottles of strong beer?

In the stillness of that drab East Berlin apartment, the enormity of Johann's dilemma crushed me: A long-odds chance of freedom in the west at the cost of leaving his mother behind. This time, I made the trip to the refrigerator.

"What you are talking about is bloody dangerous," Simon said.

"That's the understatement of the year," Mara said.

And I had no idea about Liesl. We had just met these people. Johann and Liesl might be dissidents, with spirits kindred to our own discontent, but they likely had very different worldviews. Where for me America was a land of conspicuous consumption and waste, a place where a reverence for material possessions had replaced respect and love of nature, our new friends would probably regard supermarket shelves overstocked with choices as a big improvement over their own standard of living. Just as Simon, Louisa, Mara, and I had been formed by our society, our political system, our cultural heritage, so had the beliefs of Johann and Liesl's been molded by where and how they lived. This realization, in and of itself, was not all that surprising; what was startling to me was the thought that those aspects of America I found so abhorrent would be the very things to which they might be drawn. But was it really so, or was I projecting some out-of-focus assumptions which, under closer scrutiny, might prove to be askew?

I knew only that Johann's mother was old and ill and lived in Dresden and that his father was dead. All I knew about Liesl was that she was beautiful and Jewish. And that she loved Johann. Johann had left Dresden for a visit to Berlin and had met Liesl and they had fallen in love and now they were living together. That wasn't very much information, but it was still a whole lot. *How much more did I need to know?*

"What about you, Liesl," I asked. "What do you think about this idea?" I couldn't take my eyes off her. I watched her lips form around her words.

"I am frightened by this talk." Liesl's voice was low and quiet, barely above a whisper. "It is a thing we have thought about. Even, I can say, dreamed about. It is a thing we can speak about only with the soft voice. But never do we believe there can be a way. The cost is so dear. The danger is so big." Liesl walked to the kitchen sink and found a Kleenex. She blew her nose, folded the tissue and blotted her eyes. "But I go where Johann goes."

"And your family?" Mara asked. "Are you ready to leave them behind?" There was a lilt in her voice that made me think she was hopeful that Liesl might have family ties that would be strong enough to derail the whole scheme.

Liesl had tears on her cheeks. She tried to light a cigarette but her fingers were trembling. Lou, the only non-smoker in the room, struck a match for her.

"Liesl, she have no family no more," Johann said. "She is the only one. She have no brothers and no sisters. Her mother and father were taken to Flossenbuerg by the Nazis."

"Johann, *bitte*, no—"

"Sush, *liebchen*." Johann got up and put his arms around Liesl who by this time was weeping. "We do not speak of this. It is too much for her. She was very young when they were taken away. She never did know them." After a pause, Johann continued. "Liesl was at the home of some friends on this night. Perhaps her father did think something terrible can happen and many times he did put Liesl with these friends. In the morning she found at home nothing. No one. Not mother not father. A broken door only with the black mark of a boot upon it. After the Nazis took them away, she became a daughter to these friends."

"Flossenbuerg? I've never heard of Flossenbuerg."

Johann turned to me. "This was a prison, a camp, for politicals. Many have died there. Those who tried to kill Hitler were hanged at Flossenbuerg."

For once in my life, I didn't know what to say. Nobody else did, either. We hardly knew these people and already one of them was in tears. I am half Jewish by birth, on my father's side. This meant that from a *Jewish* perspective, I was not Jewish at all, since it is a matrilineal religion. In Nazi Germany, on the other hand, being half Jewish by birth was more than enough to get you deported to a concentration camp. I'd never practiced the religion, although my grandmother kept a kosher kitchen in Brooklyn, complete with four sets of dishes.

I just sat there; silent, stunned at the depths of emotion being shared between almost total strangers. I felt guilty for having made Liesl cry and Mara lose her temper. I was playing God. Who had granted me the right to raise Johann and Liesl's hopes by dangling a paradise in front of them that I wasn't sure I even believed in myself? And if we failed, if *I* failed….

My breathing was shallow and my stomach tightened into a knot. I tried to roll a cigarette, but the paper blotted the sweat from my fingers and the dark shag tobacco fell to the floor.

Simon cocked his forefinger behind his thumb and propelled the Prague-to-Budapest segment toward me. It rolled off the edge of the map onto the floor.

Finally, Liesl's sobs subsided; she slid out of Johann's embrace, went to the kitchen sink, and began washing her face. Louisa sprang up and followed her. Mara waited too long to go with them, and so she was stuck with the boys.

Simon slid his pack of Navy Cut cigarettes from under the map and lit one and then passed the pack over to Johann and me. Soon the room was again hazy with smoke. Johann opened the window but left the curtain alone. He turned up the volume on the radio.

Mara sat frowning, clutching her leather sketchbook in one hand and a few thick, brown curls in the other. I knew that if we were actually to try to help Liesl and Johann get out of East Berlin, she would have no part of it. Nor would I encourage her to do so. Dropping out of Boston College and running off to Europe was probably the most rebellious thing she had ever done. Getting her to cross Checkpoint Charlie with a couple of magazine smugglers had been a major effort. For Mara, what we were discussing now would be completely out of the question.

Liesl, now somewhat composed, asked, "How are we leaving Yugoslavia? It is still Communist country. We surely cannot get exit visa from Yugoslavia."

"Our passports will be good only for travel to Carlsbad," Johann said. "Not farther."

"I don't know what we would do at that point," I said. No frontier crossing would allow them to pass with East German passports and no visas.

And then, in a flash of terrible clarity I will remember until I die, an idea came to me and in that same instant I knew we could only go forward. Up to that minute, we had been talking about escape to the west as a daydream, an impossible fantasy. But in my mind I now saw a pathway to freedom, a plausible way to make it happen. And with that inspiration came a burden of commitment: How could I back away from a scheme that might well be viable? *Would* be viable. After all, sneaking the magazines through the Wall had been a cinch. Obviously, in spite of the AK-47s, the rigmarole, the attitude of the border guards, the *Volkspolizei* weren't all that observant. How could I say, *I have an idea for getting you out of this dump, but I'm too chickenshit to give it a try*? It was a volatile brew of immortality, arrogance, desire for revenge, with alcohol as an accelerant. There was also this: In some mysterious way, answers to questions about the *how* had made dubiousness about the *why* evaporate.

"Your *East* German passports," I said. I couldn't contain the excitement in my voice. "What if you had *West* German passports?"

"I do not understand," Johann said.

"What if we were able to get you West German passports?"

"*Bundesrepublik* passports?" Louisa asked.

"How would you manage that?" So far, Simon had been pretty quiet. But while Mara was nervous even talking about such a bizarre idea, let alone participating, he seemed eager. Or, at least curious enough to continue talking about it.

"Listen to me. When I lived in Copenhagen last winter, I knew some people who were into all kinds of shady activities. Cigarette smuggling, untaxed whisky, some drugs. I know someone who could probably point me in the right direction to buy counterfeit passports." I thought of Lars wandering around the cold, wet streets of the Danish capital, his guitar case filled with cartons of Marlboros, Pall-Malls, Camels, and mentholated Salems.

"I'm sure as hell glad I was in France for the winter," Mara said. "I wouldn't have wanted to be with you then."

"You don't have to be with me now, if you don't want to."

"I'll remember you said that."

"What do you think would be involved getting fake passports?" Louisa asked. "And, how good would they be? Do you think they would fool border guards?"

"Well, I don't know, Louisa," I said. "But I would think they would have to be pretty good. I mean, why else would you want a passport other than to cross a border? I suppose we wouldn't know unless we tried."

"That kind of a test would have pretty high stakes." Simon fidgeted with his pack of cigarettes, flipping the top open and shut with his thumb.

"No shit, Sherlock!" said Mara.

A car backfired in the street below, sounding like a gunshot. My sphincter tightened. Mara jumped.

Johann laughed out loud. "It is just a *Trabbie!*"

Finally, Liesl looked at me and said, "This escape. Why? Why will you do such a dangerous thing?" Her slender fingers wrapped around my forearm. A shiver went up my spine.

"*Ya,*" Johann said. "You do not even know us. For what reason will you think to do such a thing? We have no money, we cannot pay you."

"That is exactly what I want to know, too," Mara said. "Why on God's green earth do you wanna take a chance on spending the rest of your life in prison? I think you're out of your mind, if you ask me."

"You've given us your opinion often enough," I said. "I didn't ask you. You don't have to stick around with me if you don't want to."

"Damn right. I'm *not* going to stick around for this nonsense."

"You two need to calm down," Louisa said. Liesl loosened her grip and her hand slid into her lap. My arm was on fire.

Johann just looked at me, his face a blend of wariness and excitement.

I turned to Liesl. "I don't know. Honestly, I can't tell you. It just seems like the right thing to do. Sometimes I believe in the west we have too much. Here you have so little. I never thought much about freedom, but now that I can see how little you have, it makes me think."

"Freedom, my ass." Mara said. "It may be 'the right thing for you to do' but I don't want any part of it. I don't want to get killed or go to jail. Or you either, David. This is a fucking stupid idea and it's going to fail and you're going to end up dead or in prison."

"Like I said, Mara, you can just butt out; you don't have to get involved if you don't want to. Besides, all we are doing is talking about it. Nobody's said we are going to *do* anything yet." I wished she would just shut up and keep her negativity to herself. Why, oh why, had Simon insisted on her coming along? She could have been happily touring some garden or museum in the West Sector, enjoying herself a lot more than she was here.

Johann and Liesl may not have understood every word that flew between us, but the anger in our voices could not have left any doubt that we were having a fight. I didn't care so much about Simon and Louisa being there; they were used to our spats.

The conversation died. I felt like Mara had painted herself, maybe us, into a corner. If I hadn't even mentioned helping get Johann and Liesl to the west, the four of us could have left them there, thanked them for a nice lunch, maybe exchanged addresses, and that would have been the end of it. But Mara had challenged me, and an idle thought had turned into a full-blown discussion, and now instead, we had raised their hopes, waved a flag in front of them, some blurry vision of freedom, but a vision nonetheless. Smuggling in the magazines under the noses of the *Volkspolizei* had not only been daring, but it had demonstrated to Johann and Liesl that we were willing to do dangerous things for no apparent reason. I felt the enormous weight of Walter Ulbricht, the East German Republic, the *Stasi*, and the *Volkspolizei* crushing us down. I suspect we all felt that burden.

Finally Simon spoke, smashing out his cigarette in the overflowing bowl on the table. "We had better leave straight-away. We haven't much time to tarry before the curfew."

I looked at my watch. "Its only two o'clock. We don't have to be in any big hurry." Simon kicked me under the table. He probably thought we all needed some breathing room to reconsider my crazy idea. It was stifling in the tiny apartment, anyway, and thick with smoke. I wasn't ready to leave, but Simon and Louisa were already up and moving, so I started gathering my stuff up as well. Mara carefully repacked her cigarettes and I folded my map.

"I've never cared for anyone telling me what I could or couldn't do," I said. "That's why I left America in the first place. Now that I have been in here, East Berlin, for a couple of days, I can see you have it even worse than what we have to put up with in the west. It is very different in some ways; we have lots more crap we can buy and so on. But not so different when it comes to someone running your life."

"What is your work in the west?" Johann asked.

There it was, I thought. There was the difference. I didn't have a job because I didn't *want* one. I could afford to bum around Europe taking temporary jobs only when I needed to. Some things were the same and some were miles apart.

"I don't have a job," I said. I couldn't look at anyone. I didn't feel embarrassed because I was unemployed, but because I could afford to be.

"I imagine you will be making license plates or breaking rocks soon enough," Mara said.

Louisa explained these references to prison life to Johann, who laughed.

"We will come back tomorrow and talk about this some more," I said. I wasn't ready to leave yet; I wanted to stay and fantasize about daring escapes and dashes to freedom and so on. The strong German beer was working against my better judgment. Simon was right, though, it was time for us to go.

"You must wait maybe one more day before you come back," Liesl said. "Do not forget how carefully they watch you at the border." I wouldn't be able to forget how *she* was looking at *me* as she grasped my hand.

"OK, then," I said. "We will see you in two or three days' time."

We all said our good-byes and thank-yous and so on. Mara shook hands with both of them, and I sensed finality in her, like she didn't expect to see Liesl or Johann again.

It was about four o'clock when we reached Checkpoint Charlie. My legs burned and itched where the tape had skinned me and the long walk in the sun from Johann's apartment had intensified my discomfort. I was eager to get back to the youth hostel, take a shower, change into some shorts, and maybe try to find a swimming pool somewhere to cool off. I also wanted to take a nap; the tipsiness I had felt from the afternoon drinking beer had given way to drowsiness.

Mara, Louisa, Simon and I entered the brightly lit border shack. Even though it was mid-afternoon, the overhead floodlights were on. Ironic, I thought; the only place the East Germans squandered their scarce electricity was at the Wall, right next to energy-rich West Berlin.

"*Kommen Sie mit mir.*" The huge *Vopo* beckoned us to follow her into a back room. She had our passports firmly clenched in her fleshy hand. A roll of fat bulged over her tight collar. In fact, her entire uniform appeared barely capable of containing her body, which had to be at least six-feet-two or six-feet-three and over two-hundred-fifty pounds. The fabric of her pants stretched tautly across her wide ass and massive thighs. (There is no way she could have smuggled anything anywhere like we had done!) Her glossy black boots appeared too small to support her, and yet she balanced perfectly. A pair of young *Vopos* with Kalashnikovs guarded the exit from the room to the concrete maze leading to the Wall. We had no choice but to follow her orders.

They separated the four of us; Mara, Louisa, and Simon were herded elsewhere by other gun-toting *Vopos* and I was left alone with the fat guard and her two underlings.

"*Ausziehen!*" She shouted. When I failed to respond, she began to unbutton my shirt. I understood that I'd been ordered to undress. As I lowered my jeans, her piggish eyes widened at the sight of my striped legs. She tapped at the hairless bands on my naked body with her riding crop.

"*Was ist das hier?*" She pulled a rubber glove over her hand, her fingers like sausages in casings. It is strange how inappropriate thoughts can creep into your mind at inopportune times: I would not have thought surgical gloves came in sizes large enough to fit this woman's hands.

━━━━

24 June —
Berlin

━━━━━━━━━━━━━━━

Here is how I think we can pull it off," I said. Simon and I were back in Johann's apartment. We had given him and Liesl a detailed account of our lengthy detention at Checkpoint Charlie two days before. Mara and Louisa had stayed in the West Sector. Mara had been so terrified by the strip search and interrogation on our last exit that she didn't want to ever come back. It had been difficult to get her to even leave the hotel room the next morning. When we finally did return to the hostel around noon, she'd holed up in the common room with her Marlboros and a book and demanded to be left alone. She was finished with East Berlin, East Germany, and had sworn never to travel behind the Iron Curtain again. For Mara, the misgivings and uneasiness she had felt in Czechoslovakia now had a concrete basis. Our arrest had moved the specter of danger from speculation to reality.

Honestly, I couldn't blame her. The experience we'd all gone through a couple of days before had been painful and humiliating, not to mention thoroughly terrifying. But where her reaction to the gross invasion of her body to which the *Vopos* had subjected her had been to vow never to return behind the Iron Curtain, my response had been exactly the opposite. I wanted to get even with the fat bitch who'd abused me and, by extension, the system that had put her in the position to do it.

Louisa had stayed in the West Sector, too, on that day, not wanting to leave Mara alone. The four of us were still traveling as a group, with the plan being that we would travel to Amsterdam as we had come, hitchhiking in pairs. We hadn't yet set a date for leaving Berlin, but for the time being, Louisa wanted to stay with Mara, partially out of a sense of sisterly compassion, and partly because she didn't feel like risking any more misadventures, at least for the time being.

"I don't think she should be alone; she's still pretty shaken up. Why don't you guys just go ahead and leave us behind."

"You're probably right—"

"Besides," Louisa continued, "we're going to have to get out of here by ten. You know, they don't let you just loiter inside for the day."

Even though the girls had not achieved the level of friendship that Simon and I had, Louisa stayed with Mara to lend whatever moral support and comfort she might want. Also, Louisa wanted to check for mail at American Express and send some letters from the Post Office. And, although she didn't come right out and admit it, Louisa probably felt a little nervous about going back into East Berlin. I couldn't blame her; I wasn't completely at ease with the idea myself. But then, I was reckless and invincible, more willing to tempt fate than common sense and prudence would suggest.

Simon had been indignant at what he felt was an invasion of his person, which he described as a 'near buggering' by the *Vopos*. His reaction was similar to mine; it was preposterous to consider getting even or fighting back, but we couldn't just let our degrading arrest pass. Neither of us could see any point in contacting the embassy or filing a complaint. It was clear to me that nothing useful would come of it, other than being reprimanded ourselves with an official 'we told you so' lecture by some embassy flunky.

"We'll be taking quite a chance, I reckon, what with that little Commie bastard warning us never to come back," Simon had said as we walked down Friedrichstrasse toward Checkpoint Charlie.

"Yeah, well, there's only two of us now. If you remember, he said 'you *four* do not return to the DDR'. We could argue that we are not four, but two."

"It's a sticky wicket, mate; I doubt the *Vopos* would agree with that logic."

"You coming with me or staying with the girls?"

"With you, mate, to be sure. Somebody's got to cover your arse."

"So to speak. You didn't do such a great job of covering it last time we were here."

Simon grinned. "Nor you mine."

We left Louisa and Mara on the Kurfurstendamm and took an eastbound bus down Friedrichstrasse to the Wall. None of the *Vopos* looked familiar to me; there was no sign of either Blondie or the short *Kommandant* at Checkpoint Charlie and soon we were walking toward Johann's apartment. Maybe they had days off, too. Somehow, we'd gotten lucky.

I doubt I could have talked Simon out of a role in my plan. In fact, my plan had really become our plan and as chancy as it might have seemed, the various elements were falling into place.

The one thing we would need, besides plain old blind luck, was money. We were all more or less indigent, itinerant bums who only stopped and worked in one place long enough to save up enough money to move on. We certainly didn't have the wherewithal to do what it was we wanted to do. Louisa Braun was an exception; she always seemed to have plenty of cash and never mentioned having worked anyplace. She had been in Europe for seven months, bumming around like the rest of us, except for once when she had flown home for her father's birthday. She had only stayed in D.C. for a week before flying back to Amsterdam. She frequently received wire transfers of cash at American Express; none of us resented her apparent wealth since not only was she more than willing to share her good fortunes with us, she never let it set her apart as a person. She was just another expat wandering around Europe, only richer.

I explained to Johann and Liesl that Louisa would ask her dad to send us some money. To 'fund our operation' as she put it.

"I'm going to Copenhagen," I continued. "There is a place there where I can purchase passports for you and Liesl. I will need to take some photographs. I will get the passports and then get visas for you to travel through Czechoslovakia and Hungary to Yugoslavia. That's going to be the most difficult part of the whole journey."

"*Nein,*" Johann said. "I believe the hardest thing is to get the permission to travel from East Berlin to Dresden."

"Yes. Well, that is the part *you* have to do." I said. "The whole plan begins with this. You must get an internal visa for travel from here to Dresden and then a Czech visa to get from East Germany into Czechoslovakia. In Karlovy Vary, you will become West German tourists with West German passports, and the rest of the trip should be easy."

"You do not yet understand," Johann muttered. "Nothing in our world is easy."

"OK, well, easier then."

"Until we get to the Yugoslav/Greek border," Simon said.

"Yes, that may be difficult," I said. "That will be the last border crossing. That's where we go from east to west and the customs officials and border guards are likely to be more vigilant."

"And what then?" Liesl didn't say much, but now she was staring at me with unblinking attention. She didn't speak English as well as Johann and he occasionally translated for her. They had developed a subtle code; when she didn't understand something, she would tap his arm or wrist with her fingers and he would explain in German. Several times, I wished that Louisa had been with us on that particular visit. Our escape plan would be problematical enough without the added uncertainties caused by language barriers and inevitable misunderstandings. There would be plenty of communication problems as it was since none of us spoke Czech, Hungarian, Greek, or any of the various Yugoslavian dialects.

Yugoslavia was not a country like most other European countries. It was really not much more than just a loose federation of six semi-autonomous regions bound together mostly by allegiance to Marshall Tito. The brutal but well-loved World War Two partisan leader had united the people of Croatia, Bosnia, Herzegovina, Serbia, Montenegro, and Macedonia into one cohesive anti-Hitler coalition of guerilla fighters. Yugoslavia had no national language, just regional languages and wide cultural divisions. The states comprising Yugoslavia didn't even all use the same alphabet; some regions used English letters and some Cyrillic. Fortunately, for our purposes, there were no internal borders in Yugoslavia, nor were internal visas required for city-to-city travel, as in East Germany. Once we entered Yugoslavia from Czechoslovakia in the north, we would not have to present our passports to any border officials until we got to the southern border with Greece.

"I was there last year." I went over the details I vaguely remembered having told them about previously. "The border between Yugoslavia and Greece was complete chaos. There was a lot of construction going on and the whole area was a fucked up mess. We'll choose a lesser-used route, somewhere off the beaten track, where maybe the guards are not as diligent or well trained. Also, if they decide to come after us, I expect the major border crossings will be alerted first and the back road places will hear about it later. At least, I hope that's what happens."

"D'you really think they will care a fig about two teenagers running away?" Simon asked.

"Yes, they will care," Johann said. "Not so much because it is me and Liesl. The most important thing is, how can one say it, a bad publicity."

"Bad press," I said. "Another failure for them, another success story for the *Haus am Checkpoint Charlie*."

"What is this ... this *Haus am Checkpoint Charlie*?" Johann asked.

"You've never heard of it?" I was incredulous. "It is a museum just over the Wall dedicated to those who escape and those who die trying." I described the place as best I could.

"*Mein Gott*. A museum...." Liesl's voice trailed off. She walked over to the window and stood there, staring at the building next door and the slender patch of blue sky between them. Johann started to follow her, then changed his mind and returned his attention to Simon and me.

"How are we to know what is the situation on the border at this time?" Johann wanted to know.

"I'm going down there to have a look for myself," Simon said. "I'll check it out and see what's what."

"Right," I said. "Simon is leaving in the morning."

"You will take a train to this place?" Johann asked.

"No, mate," Simon answered. "I met a bloke at the youth hostel who fancies a road trip. He has a new BMW motorcycle but he's a little short of cash at the moment. He offered to take me down there if I'd pay for the petrol."

"How long time will it take to drive a motorcycle so far?"

"It will take us at least a week or more since we have to get back out to West Germany and go from there. We shan't be able to get visas from here."

Johann brought a round of beers from the refrigerator, pausing to look out the window for a moment with Liesl.

"So, all we need now are photographs." I brought out my camera and removed the color film and loaded a fresh roll of black and white. Finding suitable film had been a little difficult but passport photos were black and white and so we'd searched camera stores until we found a roll. "We'll need several so we can get visas, too."

Liesl disappeared into the bathroom, the only room in their apartment place that had a door. I looked around the walls for a suitable background. After all, we could hardly look around East Berlin for a photo kiosk and ask for passport photos. A plain white wall, if I could find one, would be the best. Every surface in the studio was covered, almost cluttered, with Johann's art. The wall by the door had the best indirect light and the added advantage of being on the opposite side of the room from the window. I began taking down the paintings and drawings and stacking them on the table.

"I hope you will take more pieces with you." Johann watched me clear the wall.

"I don't think so," I said. "Too dangerous. When you are free in the west, you can give me many more. I don't want to risk taking more now."

I looked at the bare wall and at my passport and Simon's as well, and the color and texture looked fine. "I wish we had a genuine West German passport to see what the background really looks like."

Liesl emerged from the bathroom with her hair carefully combed and her lips painted red. That was the first time I had seen her with any makeup at all. Where Liesl had been pretty yesterday, a little hairspray, some lipstick, perhaps a little mascara had transformed her into a true beauty. I felt my face flush warmly as I found myself staring at her and I averted my gaze to Johann. Maybe it was because she didn't speak fluent English, maybe it was because she was naturally shy and tended to defer to Johann in conversations, but I had less insight into Liesl that I did Johann. Johann was open, laughed a lot, and even though we had only recently met, I was already thinking of him as a friend, someone it felt like I'd known a long time. Liesl was more hidden, shy and quiet. Sometimes I imagined she was flirting with me, but that was more likely my age and vanity than anything else. She and Louisa, who wasn't with us on this, our fourth foray into the East Sector, had hit it off well, though, yakking away in German.

Anyway, I was encouraged by Liesl's freshening up for the photos. She smoothed Johann's hair and straightened up his shirt. I wanted to take several pictures of each of them, hoping that at least a few would be of passport quality. We would need extras for each visa application. I shot most of the roll. It was hard to get Johann to look serious; I don't know how he could smirk at a time like this, but he did. Liesl had the opposite problem. She looked frightened, like a trapped animal, and Johann was able to elicit only a faint smile.

There didn't seem to be much else to do once we'd taken the photos and rehung the art, so after another beer and some more studying of the map of Europe, we were ready to leave. I wanted to get the film developed right away to be sure we had suitable pictures. If not, we would have to come back to the East Sector for another try. Simon intended to leave in the morning for Bonn, the capital of West Germany, to start getting the visas for his scouting trip to the Greek border.

"How can we contact you in the meantime?" I asked. "Can we write to you?"

"*Nein,*" Johann said. "You cannot write to us. The *Stasi* reads every letter."

"Every letter?" Simon shook his head. "They can't possibly read every bloody letter."

"You do not understand, yet, the DDR. They read each and every letter. Hundreds of people work for the *Staatssicherheit*. They are terrified of escapes from this perfect workers' paradise." Johann laughed. "Can you imagine such a thing? We must be crazy to leave."

"Crazy is right," Simon said. "I reckon that is why in the Soviet Union they put dissidents in insane asylums rather than in prison. If you want to leave heaven, you must be bonkers, right?"

"Also here, it is the same. The asylums have many who are not crazy, but who are political. So, we must wait for your return."

Liesl was quiet, but she was paying close attention.

"Give us two or three weeks," I said. "That should be plenty of time for you to get the visas you need and for us to do the things we must do."

"You will come back to Berlin in this time?" Johann asked.

"Yes," I answered. "When we have finished with all our preparations, I will come back. By that time, with luck you will have the permits to go to Dresden and Czechoslovakia."

"Maybe you should show your good faith to the Commies and paint a few apartments. Prove your good intentions." That was Simon.

"That would be, how do you say it, a misunderstanding, a question, what is the word, *liebe?*" Liesl tapped Johann's arm. *Why hadn't Mara ever looked at me the way Liesl was looking at Johann?*

Johann smiled, almost a laugh. "A dilemma. What you mean is a dilemma. I do not want to make the *Stasi* suspicious. Perhaps to begin working as they wish I must and to ask for visas to Dresden at the same time—"

"This you must decide," I said. "You know the system here better than we do. We will return in two or three weeks' time. Unless the photos are not good enough for passports."

Johann walked us downstairs and checked the street, a routine that was becoming familiar. With his all-clear signal, we slipped out the door and were on our way back to the Wall.

I was sweating by the time we got to Checkpoint Charlie. We were 'clean' and had nothing to hide. Our passports were in order. We had receipts for the currency we had exchanged on our way in. Nonetheless, I was certain the guilty looks on our faces would give us away. We were going to go to prison for what we were thinking, what we were planning to do. The guard who had taken our passports was taking forever, while the sweat was soaking into the raw spots on my body and driving me crazy. I briefly thought about running out the door toward the Wall, wondering how far I would get before being shot in the back. What could be taking them so long?

Eventually, the *Vopo* reappeared, confiscated our *Ostmark*, and handed us our passports. Without so much as an *AufWiedersehen*, he waved us toward the Wall and turned his attention to the people in line behind us. I took a deep breath and we left the bunker and entered the maze.

* * * *

1– 6 July —
Copenhagen

━┿━┿━┿━┿━┿━┿━┿━┿━┿━┿━┿━

According to Lars, the going rate for a counterfeit passport was two-hundred-fifty American dollars, in cash. I didn't know how he knew this; just one more tidbit of arcane information destined to be filed away in my burgeoning 'road-knowledge' file. But I had to trust him because I had no other options. And, since I had to trust Lars, I would be forced to extend that trust to someone else. Someone who I had never met.

I walked along the canal, casually but intensely paying attention to each person I passed. The dull blue-black water undulated under a tepid breeze coming off the sound. Ironic, I thought, to be more apprehensive, or at least as cautious, in Copenhagen as I had been in East Berlin. As the daylight faded, the lights in the bars and apartment buildings gradually came on and reflected off the oily surface. In spite of the warm summer evening, I had my jacket zipped up to my neck and wore dark sunglasses. I didn't want to be recognized, or remembered, if something were to go wrong with my plan. What would I say if a cop, or worse, an Interpol stopped me? How would I explain five hundred dollars in cash and some passport-type photos? I had no experience with such schemes as the four of us were trying to pull off, and I knew it.

The only frames of reference I had regarding people crossing borders for a supposedly better life in greener pastures were the migrant laborers in California where I had grown up and Louisa coming to the States when she was a child. I'd never really thought much about the Mexicans who picked the lettuce and artichokes in the Salinas Valley, and Louisa's immigration had been perfectly legal; no fake passports or other subterfuge had been involved. Anyway, I was taking extra precautions, which I believed were necessary and at the same time perhaps, a little silly. Windbreaker zipped to the neck and dark glasses at dusk? *Who did I think I was kidding?* I didn't know, but the zipper stayed up and the glasses stayed on as I meandered down the street. I was not taking any chances even though what we were doing was the riskiest thing I'd ever been involved in. I was nineteen years old, with a lot more daring than common sense. We were in over our heads, way beyond reason, and I was both scared and excited.

Trash littered the street; the city maintenance workers who spent countless hours keeping the city's touristy areas swept clean hadn't been here for months. Empty *Aquavit* bottles, hot dog wrappers, used condoms, scraps of paper and other evidence of life lived cheaply on the street clogged the gutters and floated against the walls of the canal. Pages of *Politiken*, the daily newspaper, with help from gusts of soft, fetid air, were making their final descent into the murky waterway below. The 'walking street', only a few blocks away, never looked like this.

As I approached a *Pölser* stand, the unique aroma of cooking hot dogs, mixed with the other smells, added a greasy quality to the air. I passed open doorways of taverns and heard music—a few bars of *It's A Hard Day's Night* and then a few paces later Mick Jagger complaining loudly: 'I can't get no … satisfaction' 'Can't get no … girly action'. He just wasn't in the right place; he should've been in Copenhagen.

Without warning, Louisa's face flashed into my mind, and I made a valiant effort to blot her out and picture Mara instead. I wondered what Mara was doing at this particular moment, back in Amsterdam. Same time zone, evening there, too. Maybe she was on Dam Square, perhaps even sketching, although that seemed like an unlikely possibility, or having a beer and *Genever* at one of our favorite bars. I thought I missed her. I *wanted* to miss her. But at the same time, I was glad she was there and not here, doing what I was doing. Counterfeit passports would be way beyond her limits. I wondered if she missed me and I was annoyed at myself for not knowing us well enough to have that answer. It occurred to me that I had more guts than brains.

My armpits were damp and felt both cool and warm as my arms swung in cadence with my footsteps. My skin had almost completely recovered from the magazine-smuggling escapade, and it had been over a week since I last saw drops of blood in the toilet bowl. At least the physical damage I'd suffered in Berlin was repaired.

I was tempted to slip into one of the dives that lined the canal for a beer, which I badly wanted. I envisioned Simon, somewhere on the road to southern Yugoslavia, no doubt in some pub or café, well into his second or even third beer, and dinner. Simon was as regular as a Timex about food. But I had to keep a clear head and I didn't need alcohol for that. Moreover, I didn't want to do anything that would mark my presence after I left. I didn't want anyone to remember a sweating American kid in a zippered windbreaker wearing dark glasses—at dusk.

From a side street, two uniformed policemen turned the corner and walked in my direction. They were looking at me; checking me out with the precision of cops everywhere. Their ominous black nightsticks swung by their sides like third legs as they marched toward me. Their eyes focused on the bulge in my jacket; someone from one of the banks had tipped them off to watch for an American kid dressed funny with a pocketful of hundred dollar bills. No one could be up to any good changing money *from* kroner *into* dollars. As the distance between us narrowed, I prepared to run, wondering if I could disappear into the shadows or down an alley without being caught. I sized them up: One was fat and didn't look like he could move fast, but the other cop was taller and leaner. And then they passed me, one on each side, with hardly any notice. I realized that I was no longer breathing and sucked the tainted air deep into my lungs.

That area of Copenhagen was off the tourist circuit. It was a nasty part of town, a crappy neighborhood where the Little Mermaid spent her lonely eternity perched on a rock watching lowlifes pursue baser pleasures. The waterfront district was devoid of legitimate business; it was where you went to buy sex or drugs or cheap, untaxed tobacco. I was terrified and exhilarated because, being in the market for another illegal commodity, I fit right in. I forced myself to take slower, deeper breaths. How far was the reach of the *Staatssicherheit*? Could they somehow be linked up with Interpol in some secret, behind-the-scenes alliance? I hadn't a clue, as Simon would say. Was I being overly suspicious? I didn't know that, either. There was a lot I didn't know. Never in the accumulated nineteen years of my long life had I had so many questions without answers. What an indelible impression East Berlin had left on me.

Purposely, I walked several times past the address I was seeking, glancing up surreptitiously at the number, before I stopped. I had already scouted out this decrepit building from the other side of the canal. How odd, I thought: We'd taken similar precautions when we visited Johann's apartment in East Berlin. Here I was, in Copenhagen, the bastion of freedom in Scandinavia, where 'anything goes' was the rule, scared shitless. I felt very alive. I was doing something, perhaps for the first time in my life, which had purpose, maybe even meaning.

In the evening light, I could barely make out the numbers from across the water. I had memorized the address, 4376, because I didn't dare to carry a scrap of paper with that number on it. In fact, I didn't even have my passport with me, my work visa, now expired, or any other document that could identify me. Since I'd left Denmark in the spring without paying any income taxes on my winter's earnings, I'd taken a chance just crossing the border. The Danish tax collectors were insidious, in their own way, and as much a threat to my freedom as the *Vopos* had been. All my papers were safely back in my hotel room. Maybe I was just being paranoid, but if we really were going to help Johann Klaus Volker and Liesl Schmidt flee from East Germany to Greece, some paranoia was justified, even useful.

The only things in my pockets were two envelopes: One had five pictures of Ben Franklin and the other had photographs of Johann and Liesl. I had gone to four different banks that afternoon to exchange traveler's checks for American dollars. Smaller transactions would be less suspicious than one single request for five hundred dollars in American currency at one bank. I carried these two envelopes close to my heart.

Why was I doing this? It was a question I asked myself more and more often, and I still had no answer. Maybe because all of us were doing this together, one step at a time, Louisa back in the States, Simon somewhere down on the Greek border, me in Copenhagen, it didn't seem so preposterous. The best justification I'd been able to come up with was that it was an honorable and worthwhile thing to do, if not particularly intelligent. But I was naive and idealistic and the purity of purpose, if you will, was appealing. Or so I believed.

There were no names on the door at 4376 Christianshavn, not unusual for such a run down part of town. Most of Copenhagen's neighborhoods were nicer than this slummy one, which was made up largely of cheap hotels, basic one-room rentals, seedy bars, and not much else. The neighborhood was too rough even for a youth hostel. Few of the four and five story walk-up apartments had the occupants' names on the letterboxes outside, only numbers. The two places I passed which could claim any legitimacy of purpose were a maritime museum and the Danish Longshoreman's Union hall. Both were closed. The sole business open at this hour was a kiosk displaying *Politiken*, a variety of football and soccer magazines, and lots of hard-core pornography. Nearly all of the people wandering the streets and drinking in the open-air bars were sailors, dockworkers, and women dressed in short, shiny skirts and tight, skimpy tube-tops. Simon's kind of girls.

I stood on a corner at a red light, waiting for the traffic to clear. A taxi with a couple in the back stopped at the crosswalk. From the other side, a woman emerged, spit several times and hurried away. You should be *here*, Mick.

A tall, fleshy blonde girl with a tight, black vinyl mini-skirt materialized from behind the newsstand. Her miniscule red blouse was unbuttoned and loosely knotted across her belly, barely concealing her pendulous breasts. She lingered a few feet away from me, looking up and down the street. She took a cigarette from an oversized purse and put it between her brightly painted lips.

As she struck a match on the bottom of her shoe and brought it to her face, I could see her cheeks cratered with deep pockmarks. The unlit cigarette fell to the sidewalk. She made eye contact with me for the only the briefest of moments and then turned and bent over for the cigarette, allowing her black skirt to ride halfway up her creamy buttocks. She was not wearing underwear. As she stood up, she turned toward me and recovered her loose, rouged nipples. The light changed just in time and I crossed the street. She returned to her post by the kiosk. This part of Copenhagen was not the *Strøget* or *Rådhuspladsen*. The pedestrian street and the main square, only a few blocks away, were safe and clean; here the thick air smelled of salt and diesel and urine, a fetid climate favorable to unsavory deeds done in cash transactions. I had been down to this canal just once before, in the daylight, to find the building.

Lars had given me the address after he stopped laughing.

"*Du vil vide hvor man kan købe forfalskede tyske pas?*" Lars had asked. "*Hvad skal du med dem?*"

"*Det er sådan,*" I answered. "*Vi har mødt nogle mennesker i øst Berlin, et par som gerne vil til vesten.*"

Lars held up his hand and looked around. "Perhaps," he said in English, "we should speak in English."

At first I thought it odd that Lars should be nervous talking about counterfeit passports in a Danish student bar, but, then, most of his income derived from illegal activities and maybe he was just being cautious on general principal. Who was I to question someone else's paranoia? We switched to English.

"They're kids, Lars, just like us, and we want to help them. We have a plan."

I was surprised that I still remembered enough Danish to keep up the semblance of a conversation. It'd been several countries and even more months since I was last in Denmark.

Lars took a long drink from his bottle of Tuborg. "I think there are many in the east who would like to come to the west. Why these two? For what reason do you choose to make such a dangerous plan?"

I thought for a while before answering. "I don't really know, Lars. They just happen to be the two we met. Something about them was, I don't know how to say it in Danish. In America, we would say 'simpatico'. There must be a Danish word."

"I do not know this word," Lars said. "German?"

"Sorry, I only know it in English."

"It does not matter."

"You know, I left the States partly because I didn't like the government. I came here for something better. But seeing how things are there, in East Berlin, I don't know."

Lars pulled closer to the table, smashing the stub of his cigarette into the full ashtray. Tobacco was expensive in Denmark, in all of Scandinavia, and his fingers were stained from smoking cigarettes down to the very end. Even though he now supported himself by smuggling untaxed cigarettes into the country, he still retained his old habits acquired when he had to buy them in tobacco stores like everyone else.

Lars lowered his voice. "Such a thing is possible. I have met such a person some times. He will be found on the canal and only in the evening." This was the old Lars I remembered from last winter—hushed tones, furtive glances—who on occasion had asked me to help him deliver cigarettes.

He paused while the waiter came to the table to see if we wanted more beer. I said yes, and Lars told him to empty the ashtray. He gave Lars a funny grin, dumped the ashes and butts on the floor, and wiped the table with his towel.

"I figured if anybody had the connections I need, you would be that person," I said, once the waiter had disappeared.

"I don't know if I must be grateful for this confidence." Lars locked his fingers behind his neck and stared up at the ceiling for a moment, on the verge of laughing.

"Can you help me?"

Lars' pale green eyes bored into me from behind overgrown blond bangs. "Yes, but only if you trust in me and do exactly as I will say to you."

I took a deep breath. "OK."

"You know Christianshavn? *Langeline*? The area on the canal by *den Lille Havfrue*?" Lars wasn't laughing any more.

I nodded. I had visited Copenhagen's most famous landmark many times and I was familiar with the waterfront area around her. Ships to and from Sweden, Finland, and Germany passed several times a day. Transients and assorted riffraff lived and worked in the area. Other than the famous brass sculpture of the Little Mermaid, who lived coiled on a rock a few feet offshore when pranksters weren't stealing her, there was not much else to attract tourists and few ventured there. The atmosphere was harsh; an ideal location for a document forger to set up shop.

"Here is the number and the street. You must go after sundown, but before midnight." Lars was speaking very quietly now, almost whispering, and I had to lean over the table to hear him. As quietly as possible, that is, considering the boisterous din around us. *Pilegaarden* was a student pub and most of the clientele were young, noisy, and in various stages of in- ebriation. It was doubtful anyone would have cared one way or the other about Lars and me discussing fake passports and east European intrigue. Beer and cigarettes were of more importance to this crowd. *Pilegaarden* would have been a good place for Lars to conduct some business, if he'd wanted to, and I was flattered that he was devoting his full attention to me. Lars' English was better than my Danish, and although nearly every- one in Denmark spoke English, we guessed that our conversation might be more opaque in English. The waiter returned with two more Tuborgs and waited until I paid him.

"And what then?" I asked. "When I get to this address, who do I ask for?"

Lars grimaced. "You will not ask for any person. You cannot use real names." He went on to describe exactly how I was to get to the building, and into the room with the counterfeiter. Finally, Lars gave me a code name.

"You must be very careful. What you are doing is not allowed. You could go to prison. The person you will see also is in great danger if your purpose is discovered. You must talk as little as possible and give no in- formation not needed. He will expect this and will be the same with you. Do not ask any questions. This man is not your friend. You will be making business with him, not friendship, and it is a black business."

"I know that." In great detail, I told Lars about our arrest at Checkpoint Charlie and the humiliating strip search we had been sub- jected to before we were finally released.

"Not much could be worse than that, Lars, do you not agree?"

A couple of girls approached the table and one of them leaned over and whispered something to Lars. I couldn't tell what they wanted; they were somewhat drunk and I thought maybe they were trying to pick us up. They were both pretty, and I waited to see what Lars would do. He smiled, shook his head, and waved them away.

"What did they want?"

"They are customers of me. I have nothing for them." Lars grinned and tried to change the subject. "Tell me about this girl, this Mara."

"She won't go along on this trip. Perhaps she will meet us in Greece. I don't know."

"She is the smart one." Lars took a long drink of his beer, tipped the bottle back until the last drops had dripped into his mouth, and then lit another cigarette before he continued. "You must remember, in Berlin they are like Nazis. They treated you badly, frightened you as only Germans know to do, but in the end you were set free. Here is Denmark. The police will be quite kind and polite, and then they will send you to prison, perhaps for a very great time. It will be pleasant until the iron door shuts."

We sat long enough for me to finish my Tuborg and then we left. Lars led the way, winding his way through the throng, past the table where the two girls were sitting with some friends. Without so much as a glance, a word, or even a break in stride, he dropped his almost-full pack of Marlboros on the table and we went out the door. Again I thought of Mara, probably sitting at a bar somewhere in Amsterdam, with some other kids, her pack of Marlboros safely in her shirt pocket, one in her hand. I was doing my best to pine for her. Louisa was far away—across the pond, as Simon would say—asking her father for money. Why was it so much easier to miss Lou than Mara?

Stopping finally at 4376, I glanced around to be sure I hadn't been followed, and then climbed the steps. The door squeaked as I latched it behind me. Broken glass, beer-bottle green, glittered in the faint light. The walls had peeling paint and stains. The pungent stench of fermenting urine was nauseating. I stood in the dimly-lit hallway, trying to get my bearings as I looked down the two rows of identical doors. I figured the building was once a maritime boarding house for sailors temporarily adrift on land. It had that transient feel to it. Or possibly the place had been a brothel and maybe sometimes still was. Now 4376 was little more than an abandoned flophouse. A bare bulb cast a faint light over the third door on the right hand side. I passed it and stopped in front of the last door, almost invisible in the dark.

I knocked on the door in the prearranged sequence of knocks Lars had given me: Three raps, pause, two more, pause, and then three more and finally, after a long pause, one definitive bang with my fist. I waited a full five seconds before that final thump. It was too dim to see my watch but not dark enough for the phosphorescent hands to be clear, so I remembered my old method of counting time when I played hide-and-seek as a kid: One Mississippi, two Mississippi, three Mississippi and so on until five seconds passed. I felt the envelope in my inner jacket pocket.

My eyes flitted back and forth between the doorway and the exit to the street. I shivered in the heat.

Suddenly, with a metallic groan, the door opened and a tall, thin man stood in the doorway. A wide-brimmed hat hid his face. With the light behind him, I knew he could see me clearly while I could only make out his silhouette. He turned his head slightly and the light glinted on his wire-rimmed glasses.

"*Hej. Kan jeg haelpe dig?*" The skinny guy's voice was flat and not inviting.

"We have a mutual friend," I said, in English.

"Yes. I understand. And the name of the person we both know?"

"Peter Anders Lindstrom." I carefully pronounced the fictitious code name Lars had given me.

The wide brim bobbed down and up once. "Please come in." He quickly shut the door behind us. We were in a bare room with nothing but a table for furniture. On one wall was a counter with a dirty sink and a dripping faucet. The only window had a soiled olive-drab blanket nailed over it. A door at the other end of the room sagged on its hinges. I assumed it led to a back alley behind the row of buildings.

"What do you require?"

"I need two passports. Two West German passports."

"The price is five hundred dollars. You must pay in American dollars, not kroner. I must have passport photographs." Lars had been right. The counterfeiter didn't ask whom the passports are for, why I needed them, or anything else. It was a straight business deal, no frills, no unnecessary discussion or exchange of information.

"Clearly." I removed the envelope with the five one-hundred-dollar bills. From another pocket, in another envelope, I took out the photos of Johann and Liesl. I'd been careful not to put the photos in the same envelope with the cash and the thought had crossed my mind that maybe I was being apprehensive beyond reason. Then again, I was trying to buy two false West German passports for the purpose of spiriting two East German dissidents out of East Berlin. How could I be *too* careful?

The thin man counted the bills and slipped them into an inside pocket of his jacket. He examined the photos of Johann and Liesl, first under the light and then holding them up to the light. His face, still shadowed by the hat, was expressionless.

"You wish the names to be the same?"

"Only their first names, Johann and Liesl. One new last name. They are married."

"Please, you will come here again after one weeks' time. You will remember the signal, yes?"

"Yes. *Mange tak.*"

"You are welcome. *Farvel så laenge.*" The thin man didn't wait for me to say good-bye but disappeared through the rear door, leaving me alone in the room. I felt the hairs at the small of my back curl as I tiptoed down the hallway to the street.

For the next week, I hung around Copenhagen, visiting familiar haunts from the previous winter, sometimes bumping into old friends. It was a surreal state of mind to be in; I was trying to enjoy myself as a tourist while waiting for some shadowy criminal to manufacture two bogus passports. More than once, I found myself looking over my shoulder, expecting what? To see a platoon of East German border police following me? Perhaps some Interpol cops or *Stasi* thugs? The days passed more quickly when I filled them up.

On July 2, that sad anniversary, I searched out a bar that had a bottle of Absinthe and enjoyed a solitary toast to Papa Hemmingway. When that seemed inadequate for the occasion, I followed it with a second and then a third, and after that I lost count. Late that afternoon I returned to my hotel and immediately fell into a deep, dreamless stupor.

I spent an entire day at the Louisiana Museum, which housed an eclectic collection of art. The Louisiana was just outside the city, and I'd discovered it soon after I arrived in Copenhagen the first time. It was one of my favorite places, smaller and more accessible than some of the larger art museums in Copenhagen proper. The paintings and sculptures at the Louisiana were mostly by second-tier artists I had never heard of. I thought Mara would like the Louisiana and I wondered if I would ever have the chance to show it to her. Would Johann's paintings one day hang on these walls? Would his work stand on it's own, or only attract casual curiosity associated with his dramatic escape? It occurred to me that I hadn't seen a single art gallery east of the Wall.

Nights alone were the worst; my doubts and fears bloomed in the dark hours. Some nights I hardly dared to leave my hotel room and on others I had to force myself to return. Every time I passed the desk clerk, I searched his face for some hint, some warning that *they* were waiting in my room. I wasn't expecting any messages and there were none. Without the comforting camaraderie of Simon and Louisa and deprived of the physical pleasures of being with Mara, I felt more vulnerable to my own insecurities. I couldn't get over the eerie feeling that I was being watched and followed, that furtive, shadowy men were lurking around every corner, waiting to arrest me.

One evening I cruised for hours around Tivoli, reasoning that it was safer to immerse myself in a crowd than to hide out alone in my hotel room. Tivoli was a colorful blend of carnival, circus, amusement park, and county fair, and was much better explored at night. Once, the previous winter, I'd been at Tivoli with some Danish friends and a newcomer to the crowd, after hearing me speak Danish, asked what part of Norway I came from. That I'd taken as a compliment, since Danish and Norwegian are essentially the same language, with about as much difference as English and American. It had been a long summer and I'd crossed many borders and had forgotten most of what I had learned, a fact which only added to my overall feeling of inadequacy.

I stayed until closing, snacking on *Pölser*, open-faced sandwiches, *smørrebrød*, and Tuborg. Several Tuborgs. I thought that maybe the Danes had something to teach the East Germans about beer. Very late that night, or perhaps it was early the next morning, I walked back to my hotel. I lingered for a moment outside, long enough to roll a Drum, scanning the street before I entered.

"Has anyone come to see me or ask about me?" I asked the desk clerk.

"No, there has been no one." He gave me a funny look. "You are perhaps expecting a visitor?"

Yes, I am here in Denmark to buy counterfeit passports so that I can smuggle two East Berliners out of their run-down, police state of a country to freedom in the west. I'm sure that at any moment I'll be discovered and thrown into jail. If Interpol is waiting upstairs in my room, you wouldn't tell me, would you? Johann and Liesl are already in an East German prison being interrogated and tortured into revealing our names, aren't they?

"No," I said. "Just an American habit."

One day I took a tourist bus up to Elsinore, and walked around Kronborg castle. How was it that Shakespeare set his most blood-soaked tragedy in tranquil Denmark, of all places? I never would have anticipated, seeing Hamlet live in Oregon just before my senior year, that I would one day visit the actual location the Bard had in mind for his greatest play or that the setting would look so innocent. It was easy to let my imagination loose: Was this the hallway where Hamlet had skewered Rosencranz and Guilderstern with so little provocation? Could this be the garden where Ophelia had offered herself to the Prince, only to be spurned and ordered to spend the rest of her life in a nunnery? Could that be the bedroom where Polonius had spilled his guts, quite literally, on Hamlet's blade? Alas, it was all conjecture and fantasy; in the past four hundred years, the white stone castle had been scrubbed clean. There was not a bloodstain to be found anywhere. The walls of Kronborg castle were as free of evidence of carnage as the ground near the Wall where Peter Fechter had fallen.

I also went on an overnight sojourn to the middle island of Odense, birthplace of Hans Christian Andersen. His stories had been the first I'd heard as a child, read to me by my father. Before Uncle Remus, before Disney, before any other nursery rhymes, I had been given the gift of 'The Little Mermaid' and 'The Ugly Duckling'. That I could be walking on the same floor…. I was just as moved this time, as I had been the first time I visited his tiny, plain cottage with its wooden bed, desk, and chair.

It had been a kind of pilgrimage for me when I'd first arrived in Denmark the previous fall, still innocent and naïve, not yet involved with Lars and his associates. That was before I had learned to exchange money on the black market. Before I'd hidden magazines under my clothing and walked through Checkpoint Charlie. Before a fat, blonde, *Vopo* bitch had shoved two fingers up my ass, lifted me off the floor, and in one searing instant of pain, changed forever my view of the world. How many visas would Johann need from the visa office to be permitted to visit Hanau, the birthplace of Jacob and Wilhelm Grimm?

Nothing, it seemed, could distract me from the course of events I had initiated and was now immersed in. The innocence with which I had enjoyed Denmark less than a year earlier was gone; every place I went, everything I did was now viewed through a darker prism. I felt like I was floating down a river that was becoming frothier and frothier as it approached the falls, or like I was riding on a galloping stallion, clutching handfuls of mane as the reins bounced in the dirt between the horse's hooves. I tried to set it aside, to forget about East Berlin, Johann and Liesl, and what we were planning, but I could not. I could not do it. Every waking minute and, I would be willing to bet my dreams as well, were consumed.

A week later, I returned to the decrepit Christianshavn neighborhood, again waiting until well past dusk. I walked down the opposite side of the canal, pausing directly across from 4376 to twist up a cigarette, but nothing alerted me. I crossed the bridge.

If anything, the stench of the hallway was even worse. As I began the sequence of knocks, the door, which was not shut tightly, swung open, the squeak of its hinges sending a shiver down my back. Cautiously, I peered into the room and then stepped inside. There was no sign of the skinny man in the broad hat and the wire-rimmed glasses. Except for the table in the middle of the room, the place was empty. A single dim light bulb barely illuminated the gloom; the walls disappeared in shadows. On the table lay a copy of *Politiken.* I jumped at the sound of the door swinging shut behind me. I was alone.

I knew immediately I had been cheated; the so-called counterfeiter had absconded with my five hundred dollars, never to be seen again. What a fool I had been to hand over all that cash! I should have insisted on paying only half up front and the rest upon delivery. Maybe Lars could help me track the double-crossing bastard down. Lars, at least, would be easy to find. Unless he was in on the swindle, too. What a dope I was; *of course* Lars was in on it. Why should I assume that a fleeting friendship with an American expat would stand between him and a quick buck? After all, since I'd left Denmark; I was no longer of any use to him. Lars was probably laughing at me already, gloating over his windfall.

I turned to leave the room, disgusted with myself and my trusting gullibility. I was out five hundred bucks with nothing to show for it. Ready to slam the door on my own stupidity, I took one last look around. Something didn't look right. The paper didn't lie flat on the table; there was a slight bulge in the middle. I flashed back briefly to the elevation of France on the map in Johann's flat. Hidden underneath the newspaper, I found two shiny new West German Passports. One had the name and photograph of Johann Müeller, the other of Liesl Müeller. I closed my eyes and took a deep breath.

I stuffed the passports into my inside jacket pocket and slunk out of the building, checking the street while I was still safe in the shadows. I heard a siren in the distance, getting louder, and a black patrol car raced by and turned down a side street. Startled, I realized I'd been holding my breath.

My furtiveness once again reminded me of our visits to Johann's apartment. Anyone walking down the street could be a cop ready to bust me; everybody was suspicious. Each step I took only reminded me of how unsuited I was for what I was trying to do. My hands shook so badly I didn't even bother trying to build a cigarette. I took several deep breaths, as if a few lungfuls of foul air could restore my spirit.

This part of the plan was now finished. Before I left Christianshavn, I walked down to *Langeline* and, for luck, said 'farewell until later' to the Little Mermaid, as sailors had done for years. I wondered if Mara would ever sketch her, if she and I would ever come to Copenhagen together.

Would *den Lille Havfrue* be the image that would cause Miriam Liebowitz to once again put pencil to paper? As I stood gazing at the little bronze statue, half girl and half fish, curled on her rock, I closed my eyes and saw Liesl, standing naked in the Spree River.

As I sauntered back down the canal toward the center of town, I hoped that Simon and Louisa were having similar success with their tasks. Simon, by now, should have been at or near the Greek/Yugoslav border. He'd left, as planned, on the back of a BMW R60 motorcycle headed south, with my Yashika and several rolls of film. I didn't envy him the long ride on the rumble seat; it hadn't been all that long since our detention at the Wall.

Louisa was in Chevy Chase, laying out the whole plan for her father but finessing the details to her mom. She had decided to fly home for a couple of days to discuss the matter with them in person. What she felt she couldn't discuss in a letter or even over the phone was the possibility of failure, with all the horrible consequences that would follow. Being on the loose in Europe, bumming around from place to place with no fixed return date was quite a bit different than being locked up in some jail behind the Iron Curtain with no fixed release date. Louisa said like the whole idea of getting Johann and Liesl out of East Berlin would be better discussed face to face.

Hopefully, he would come through with some money, since the cost of the passports had left me damned near broke. Louisa had some money of her own in a savings account, and she promised she would return, help from her dad or no help from her dad, with cash.

I had no way of knowing, of course, how Johann and Liesl were making out with the East German visa bureaucracy. They had to get permission from two different agencies; one had to approve their in-country request to go from Berlin to Dresden, the other to leave the DDR for Czechoslovakia. And both visas would have to be granted in spite of Johann's status as a dissident and troublemaker. It seemed impossible that such a feat could be accomplished without the ever-present secret police intervening.

The desk clerk looked up as I entered the lobby and, without waiting for my question, smiled and shook his head.

In the locked privacy of my room at Hotel Terminus, next to the railroad station, I examined the two passports and compared them to my American passport. To my inexperienced eye, they looked perfect, but then, how would I know the difference? A trained border guard might spot some irregularities in the documents I held in my hand, but even though I looked them over front to back, and held them up to the light, nothing leapt off the pale green pages screaming: FAKE! I was eager to compare them to a genuine West German passport. I couldn't, of course, come right and ask anyone if they looked real; even the friendly concierge downstairs would be too risky.

These passports looked genuine to me, and I could only hope all the border guards and police and hotel clerks between Karlovy Vary and Greece would also be fooled.

9 July —

Amsterdam

✦✦✦✦✦✦✦✦✦✦✦✦

I'm just not gonna go through with this, and I wish you wouldn't, either," Mara pushed her hair back from her forehead with the flat of her hand, dislodging a few ashes from her Marlboro which settled like dandruff into her curls. "What you're talking about scares the hell out me. I don't want to go to prison or get shot. You're fucking crazy. We could all get killed." Then, after a moment's consideration, "No, *you* could all get killed. Not me, because I'm done with it. You can do what you want, be knights in shining armor, whatever suits your fancy. I'm finished."

"Quite right," Simon said. "We are all free to make our own decisions. At least on this side of the Wall. Nobody is forcing anybody to do anything they don't want to."

Mara turned her attention to Louisa. Her tone of voice now was plaintive. "What about you? I can't believe you want to hook up with this dumb-assed idea. Can't you see where it's gonna lead?"

Louisa thought for a moment, but when she started to answer, Mara interrupted her.

"How was your trip home, anyway? You can't tell me your father goes along with this shit."

At first, Louisa didn't say anything, but pulled her neck wallet out from under her blouse and unzipped it. She fanned a large stack of one-hundred dollar bills. Louisa stared at Mara without flinching until Mara lowered her eyes.

"He goes along." Louisa returned the money to her wallet.

"But, my God, why? Why on earth—?"

Louisa cut her off. Flecks of gold flared in her eyes. "You know, I'm German by birth. Hate to see Germany sliced in half. What the Russians have done to Berlin is horrible. Done to Germany, for that matter. Of course, Hitler was bad, terrible, and so on. Goes without saying. But in spite of this damned cold war, the Nazis, everything, Berlin is a beautiful city. Once was, anyhow. And the people are all Germans, whether they live in the east or the west. For me, if I could help get Johann and Liesl out, it would be a way of fighting back. Can't explain it any better than that." Lou turned toward me and waited a long time before she continued. "Somebody with some common sense has to be along to keep these guys in line. Out of trouble." Although she said 'guys', her attention focused on me, as if I were a wayward traveler in need of a personal guardian angel. Which, in a way, I guess I was.

Mara looked at Louisa for a moment and then shook her head and refocused her attention on her fingernails. Whatever battle was being fought here, she was losing and Louisa was winning. I could feel Mara shrinking away, receding into some other place; lonelier, perhaps, but safer.

"Besides, somebody needs to be along to translate."

"Translate?" Mara was incredulous; maybe she wasn't going to concede this war without a fight. "You're gonna risk your life for a couple of strangers because you speak their language? That's it?"

Louisa opened her mouth to answer her, but stopped without saying another word.

Lou was stronger and more daring than Mara. What would have happened if I'd met her before I hooked up with Mara? She and I had a lot more in common, more psychologically attuned to each other. But in the summer of 1966, I was nineteen years old, had a full tank of testosterone and knew everything I needed to know.

I looked back at Louisa and had the distinct feeling that my mind had been read. I felt my face getting warm and I fumbled for my pack of tobacco, unable to remember exactly which pocket I'd left it in.

Louisa interrupted my thoughts. "Had a long talk with my dad. Several, in fact. Didn't go into too much with my mom, but I told Father everything." There was that dancing sparkle in her eyes, those divots in her cheeks. I felt busted for what I was thinking; what, for Lou, was *everything*?

"So, what did he say?" I struggled to regain my composure, grateful that the subject had been changed.

"At first, he was completely against the idea. Tried to talk me out of it. Told me what would happen to us if we were caught."

"Exactly," Mara had found an opening, a chink she could exploit. She bored right in. "And what did he say would happen to you? Did he describe German prisons? *East* German prisons?"

"Forget it," I said. "We're not going to get caught."

"Told him we were going to try to help Johann and Liesl regardless. One way or another."

"Yeah, and…."

I glared at Mara wishing she would shut up.

"He said to be careful and he is worried. Gave me two thousand dollars. There's more if we need it."

"Jeez, Lou, that's great," I said. "We'll need you if this whole scheme is going to work. It'll be important to have someone who speaks German. I'm really glad you're not chickening out."

"*Chickening out*? Not wanting to get shot or go to some fucking Nazi gulag prison is chickening out?" Mara was puffed up with indignation. "Don't believe in leaving much middle ground, do you, Slick?"

I turned to Simon. So far, he hadn't opened his mouth, except to suck on a Players. I was pretty sure he hadn't changed his mind since his return from southern Yugoslavia, but I needed to be certain and I wanted to give him a last chance to bail out if he had any qualms. Mara had provided him an exit if he wanted one.

"What about you, mate? You sure?"

"Well, you know, I like an adventure as much as the next bloke. And don't forget, I come from a country full of fools willing to take foolish risks. It's in our character, daring-do and all that rubbish. Part of being English. It's odd, indeed, but the further I stray from Liverpool, the more English I feel. I reckon you couldn't keep me away at this point."

"I do believe I know exactly what you're talking about."

"Besides, I still haven't forgotten that damned strip search up my bum. That was pretty bleeding cheeky of them."

"So to speak," Lou said.

"So to speak." Simon grimaced. "Not to mention the need for somebody to look after you."

Did everybody except Mara feel the need to look after me?

"That's enough about your bum," Mara said. "We all had that same fun, remember? I'm still fucking sore."

I allowed her juxtaposition of words to pass without comment. No sense in roiling the waters any further; Mara was plenty volatile enough as it was, once again mixing up Nazis and *Vopos,* and even throwing in Siberian prison camps for good measure. Mara locked up all the bad guys and bad things into one dark, ominous place, where she could keep a wary, frightened eye on them. But did keeping them straight, as I did, make them any less dangerous?

"Yes, well, it makes me want to stick it to those buggers." Simon lit another Navy Cut and left the open pack on the bench, an odd invitation, since I rolled my own, Mara smoked Marlboros, and Louisa didn't smoke at all. It was like he expected somebody else to join our circle. I loaded a paper and started rolling a thick Drum.

"Funny," Mara said, without a trace of laughter in her voice, "it makes me want to never go back. Ever."

"I guess it affected us all in different ways," I said.

"You can have Berlin and Czechoslovakia and any other place run by those fucking Commies. I can do just fine without any more *Vopos* or Bolsheviks or whatever screwing up my life." Mara frowned and lit a Marlboro. The red and white box disappeared into her backpack.

"I don't know why we can't all just stay here in Holland and France and Denmark and not get mixed up with all that political crap." Mara took a deep drag on her cigarette, her ample breasts straining the cotton fabric of her flowered shirt. I fantasized for a moment and imagined unbuttoning those buttons and peeling back the petals of those huge embroidered red roses to find Mara's thick pink nipples underneath.... Maybe tonight would be a night to search out a cheap hotel or pension instead of the youth hostel. Even if she stayed behind, things could still be patched up between us. There it was, the old dichotomy my father had once warned me about: The yearning of the flesh undermined by a drifting apart of the souls. Why couldn't Mara just....

Just what? Go along for the ride? Risk spending the rest of her life starving in some godforsaken, freezing Nazi, *Vopo*, Commie, Bolshevik gulag prison because she wanted to be with me? I didn't have the energy—or the heart—to try to talk her into that. She had to come voluntarily or not at all. As I watched the ebb and flow of people around us, I wondered if Mara saw this freedom of movement the same way I did.

Amsterdam was a little cooler than Berlin, and not so muggy, a welcome change. We were sitting in Dam Square, where we'd all agreed to meet. It was here, on this exact same bench, that Lou had first proposed the trip to Berlin a few weeks ago. Now, as then, with the lunch hour nearing, the Square was jam-packed.

A scruffy man in dirty jeans, no shirt, and a backpack passed behind us. Without stopping, he muttered, "Hash, Ganja, good shit, cheap." As quickly as he had appeared, he was gone, melded into the throbbing mass of people in the Square. Just like a moneychanger.

I was relieved that Mara was going to drop out of the plan, at least the Germany-to-Yugoslavia part of it. Which would be almost the whole trip. For one thing, we couldn't afford to have anyone involved who might give us away by crumbling in a tight situation. Here we were in Amsterdam just talking and already Mara was chain smoking and pulling her hair out. Miriam Liebowitz completely decomposing at some unfriendly, armed frontier crossing wasn't a comforting image.

Not that any of us had track records with helping people slip illegally across borders. But I knew in my gut that having Mara along would be a big mistake. Also, I didn't fancy the idea of arriving in Greece cold, without a welcoming face of some sort. I found Mara attractive and appealing most of the time and, being teenagers, I liked our nights alone together. At nineteen, sex was strong glue in a shaky relationship. But Mara was beginning to get on my nerves with her negativity and crappy attitude. Staying in youth hostels with segregated sleeping dorms meant that we didn't get to smooth over our spats with a good roll in the sack as often as I might have liked. Some time apart might be a good thing for us.

I was beginning to realize with each passing day and with each unfolding event that we were playing a grown-up game. I had the ominous image of us careening down a dark and dangerous tunnel, and that by the time we came to our senses and tried to turn back, it would be too late. Simon traveling to Greece on a reconnaissance mission, Louisa flying to Washington to hit her dad up for operating cash, me buying passports on the black market in Copenhagen were all a lot different than sitting around some youth hostel casually deciding what city we wanted to hitchhike to next. A month ago, we would not even have been thinking with words like *'reconnaissance mission', 'operating cash',* and *'black market passports'.* Helping people escape from East Germany was big-league, 'the Majors', as my dad would have said, and the consequences for a single misstep would be catastrophic. Maybe it was time for *me* to grow up.

Dam Square was the central meeting spot in Amsterdam, where those of us on the road got together. Every major city in Europe had the equivalent of Dam Square: The Zoo in Berlin, the area around the Blue Mosque in Istanbul, American Express in Paris were all metaphysical magnets for us expat nomads. If you were in Paris, say, and planned to meet someone in A'dam, only the date and time had to be set. Everybody understood the place would be Dam Square.

On the ground a few feet from our bench, someone had drawn a near-perfect rendition of Van Gogh's 'Sunflowers'. I'd never seen the original, but Mara had and she said we were looking at a pretty good copy, considering the Dutch master used oil and canvas and this copycat had only colored chalk and rough concrete to work with. Next to the drawing was written, in big red letters, NEED MONEY FOR TRAIN TO LONDON, and next to that, a Greek fisherman's cap weighted down with a rock. I saw some German marks among the mostly Dutch coins. No paper money to blow away. Mara searched her pockets and dropped a few francs into the hat. Without thinking, I contributed a handful of *Ostmark* to the collection.

"You know, those are pretty worthless here." Louisa opened her purse and found a five-dollar bill and tucked it under the rock.

At each end of the Square was a vendor selling cups of French fries with sweet mayonnaise. Tourists with shorts and cameras mingled with Dutch office workers, students with book bags, dealers, the occasional hooker, and other dropouts like us. On another bench a few yards away, sat a kid with a knapsack on his lap. Every so often, someone came up, exchanged a few words, handed him some money, and quickly walked away with a packet. Amsterdam had a well-deserved reputation as a city even more wide open than Copenhagen, where you could get anything you wanted. I probably could have bought the passports here, if I'd known where to look. But I didn't know Amsterdam like I knew Copenhagen, and my buddy Lars had been a sure bet. *How could I have doubted him?* I was suspicious of everyone, though; it was as if I were wearing tinted glasses that colored everything sinister and I couldn't take them off.

"Listen," I took Mara's hand, as if this small gesture, this touch, could somehow bridge the widening chasm between us. "You can take a train down through Italy and cross into Greece on a ferry at Brindisi or somewhere else close by. That way, you won't have to go through east Europe at all. In fact, you could go all the way down to Athens to the West German Embassy there and tell them what we're up to."

Mara pulled her hand away. "Don't count on it," she hissed.

"Good idea," Louisa said, as if she hadn't heard her. "You'd still be helping out quite a bit, and you wouldn't be putting yourself in any danger. Better if the embassy knew about this in advance, anyway."

"Like I said, don't count on it." This time, Mara nearly spat the words out.

"Don't worry." I watched as the dealer suddenly closed up his backpack and darted across the street between lines of taxicabs. A few seconds later, a pair of bicycle cops pedaled into the Square. "I'm not counting on you for anything."

OK, girl, if that's the way you want it, that's the way you got it. I couldn't quite figure out if Mara was my girlfriend, my traveling companion, or just a thorn in my side. Miriam Liebowitz was all of that and more. And yet, something was missing, some element of a relationship which just wasn't there. Maybe it never had been, or maybe I was just beginning to notice. When things were going well and she was happy, she was affectionate and I was very fond of her. We'd spent long hours pleasuring each other. But things weren't always like that, and she could be a royal pain in the ass. Like she was now. Like she'd been that day in Paris.

She'd wanted to go to the Louvre to see the da Vincis, the Raphaels, the Michelangelos and of course the Mona Lisa. All the stuff she'd missed on her first pass through the City of Light. I planned to spend my hours in the Louvre with the Impressionists and Surrealists. My lack of interest in seeing da Vinci's masterpiece annoyed her.

"It's only the most famous painting in the world," she said. "Of course I want to see it."

"It's only the most famous painting in the world because someone decided there *has* to be a 'most famous painting' and some goofy broad with a grin that could mean anything might as well be that painting."

"*Goofy broad with a grin*? Jesus fucking Christ. Just because you want to look at a bunch of really dopey pictures of people with oranges for heads and clocks dripping off logs—"

"I don't think that picture is even in the Louvre," I said.

"Maybe not, but the Mona Lisa is."

"You're quite sure about that?" I asked.

"Fuck off."

That spat had set the tone for the day, and Mara had bitched and moaned from the moment we left the hostel. She didn't like the Paris Metro system to begin with, and then to make matters even worse, since we didn't speak French, we got off at the wrong station and had to walk back to the museum.

"Jeez, Miriam, we're in *Paris*," I said. "Don't think of it as a screw up, think of it as a chance to see some streets and neighborhoods we might've missed otherwise."

"Fine," she said, jamming her sketchbook into her armpit. "Let's just get there." And then, almost as an afterthought, "And it's *Mara*. Don't push me."

Mara wasn't a risk taker, if you didn't take into consideration her being in Europe, alone, not yet twenty. At least, not the kind of risks the rest of us were going to be taking by traveling through three East Block countries with two runaway East Berliners holding counterfeit West German passports. I had never met Mara's parents, but she talked about them often enough and I'd read a few of their letters. I could imagine what their reaction would be if they thought their precious Miriam, their only child, was involved in a hair-brained scheme to help dissidents escape from East Berlin. Although they were Jewish, they had viewed the Holocaust from the relative safety of Provincetown and preferred to fight the evils of the current world with their money rather than with their daughter. Louisa had a good point as well; when we made the final crossing from Yugoslavia into Greece, it might be good to have someone waiting for us. I had no idea what problems we might confront on our journey, but the possibility of Mara waiting for us in Greece, with open arms and maybe even some money, was comforting in a vague way. I had no way of knowing if she'd be there. Maybe it was just the thought of her waiting for me that was exciting. Given her current churlish attitude, I doubted Mara would go to Greece. It was too much to think about.

"So, Simon. How was your trip?" I wanted to change the subject, get back to the topic at hand.

"My arse is sore, mate, if you must have God's truth about it."

"Yes, well…." I answered, unsure what to say. The long trip on the back seat of a motorcycle must have been torture. "What did you find out at the border? Is it still a mess, construction going on and all like I remember it?"

"'Ere, have a look." Simon passed out an envelope of photographs he'd taken at the border. Where had he had a chance to get film developed in such a short time? How long had he been in Amsterdam before I got back from Copenhagen?

"Damn. These are great. How did you manage it?"

Simon ignored my question. "Well, it's pretty much as you said it was. The frontier area around Bitola's a bloody mess. They're building roads and watchtowers and what not. There're detours everywhere. Lots of earth moving and road-building equipment, trucks, and the like, mucking about in the dust. I reckon we should stay away from the main highway and cross over on some back road or another."

"Just as I thought," I said. "You got any ideas about where a likely route might be?" I unfolded a map I'd picked up at a bookstore, more localized than the worn out whole-of-Europe map I'd been marking my travels on for nearly two years.

"We drove around the place for a bit; damned dusty on that motorcycle. There's another border crossing up near Kukis, closer to Bulgaria. I can't fathom if that would be better or not. The whole area seems about the same—confusion, dust, noise and so on. Everything looks temporary. The barriers are wooden, not concrete. It's a dirt and gravel road there as well. Quite disorderly, I should think." Simon pointed to a thin grey line that crossed the solid red boundary between Yugoslavia and Greece. "Here. This spot is as bad, or should I say good, as any."

"How about border guards and soldiers?"

"Of course, there were some, but it didn't look unusual. Border patrol and officials, in the main. I don't reckon I saw any army soldiers, but then you can't always tell one from the other. I didn't see any more uniforms than you'd expect at a border. Less, if anything, considering I was in Yugoslavia and the next country was Greece."

"How carefully were they searching people?" Louisa asked. "Think they will be very suspicious? You see anything that would help us?"

"Depends. I dallied around a bit and kept my eyes open. What the bobbies do is, they check and search as much as they have time for. During slow periods, when there isn't much traffic, they're apt to be more diligent. But when a mob goes through, they slacken off. And they spend an enormous amount of time on the Gypsies."

"Gypsies?" Mara asked. "What have they got to do with anything anyway?"

"Haven't a clue. All I can tell you is that I saw the guards completely unpack a car full of them. Got photos of it somewhere here." Simon shuffled through the rest of his pictures. "There were pots and pans and clothing and kids and stuff all over the ground. I can't say what they were after, but whatever it was seemed to take all the coppers to look for it. They were involved with those Gypsies for over an hour."

"Good," I said. "Maybe we'll get lucky."

"Here. Have a look." Simon found the images he was searching for.

"You're going to need a shitload of luck," Mara said. "I still think you're fucking nuts."

Simon ignored her. "They didn't spend as much time on the western tourists. Or, should I say, on anyone in a Mercedes or an Audi or a BMW. Westerners have an easier go of it."

"So, maybe we should rent a classier car. Might help us get through the borders," I said.

In one of the photos, several uniformed men were searching a Czech-plated car, probably a Tatra. The black sedan was covered with grime and sagged in the back. A family of Gypsies stood to one side, watching the border guards strew all their worldly possessions on the dusty ground next to the car. Two of the women held babies. The guards hadn't been careful; suitcases with clothes spilling out, cooking utensils, boxes of food lay where they'd been flung.

Gypsies, or Romanies, were known to travel without documents thorough most of east Europe and were subject to more scrutiny, harassment really, than any other travelers. Once we'd seen some Gypsies in a campground near the German/Dutch border, but how they had managed to slip through the Iron Curtain remained a mystery to me. Although

Gypsies were originally from Romania, they were considered stateless and usually didn't have passports or identity papers. We considered ourselves gypsies of a sort, floating around Europe from place to place, rootless, free to come and go as we pleased. But we all had passports which were carefully checked everywhere we went. The Gypsies in Simon's snapshot didn't look all that happy, however.

Another photo showed a table set up with several rubber stamps, an antiquated-looking telephone, piles of papers, and a bottle of slivovitz. The image of plum brandy in the middle of all that other official paraphernalia was encouraging.

"That's about how I remember it being," I said.

"How did you make out in Copenhagen?" Louisa asked. "Almost afraid to ask."

This was my moment to shine. With a big grin, I unzipped the side pocket of my backpack and produced the two fake West German passports embossed with the names of Johann and Liesl Müeller and passed them around. Mara looked at them over Simon's arm, but refused to touch them. Since none of us had West German passports, we didn't have anything to compare them to.

"Cor, mate, these look bloody perfect."

"Well, they'd better look bloody perfect. They're not worth jack shit if they don't."

"Find out soon enough," Lou said. "We apply for visas tomorrow, right?"

Mara slid down the bench away from us.

"I wish there were some way we could test them ahead of time, like at a border or a bank or something," I said. "But since we don't look like Liesl or Johann, and they're not here, I don't see a way."

"Hey," Louisa said. "Next time we hear someone speaking German, I'll ask. See how they stack up against some real ones."

"I rather expect they will be looked over quite carefully when we go around for the visas," Simon held one up to the light. "If they pass at the embassies, consulates, they'll do at the borders as well, I should think."

"Let's wait 'till we get back to the hostel tonight, Lou," I said. I wouldn't trust just anyone. There are bound to be some German kids there. I think we should be on the lookout, even here."

"You got that right," Mara said. She ground her cigarette out on the cobblestones.

"Christ, Miriam, lighten up a little bit, OK? It wouldn't kill you to be a little more positive."

Mara stood up. "I'll show you positive, Slick. And it's *Mara*."

"See you back at the hostel?" I tried to suck in my gut, making a silent resolution to cut down on the French fries and mayonnaise.

Mara didn't answer. She shouldered her backpack and started across the Square. I hurried after her.

"Sweetheart, let's skip the hostel and find ourselves a hotel room tonight."

"You think a good fuck can fix every problem you create? You should be so lucky." And with that, she turned and crossed the street, just in front of a trolley car. When the car had passed, she had disappeared into the crowd.

Nobody said anything. I watched the spot where Mara had vanished, part of me relieved that she was gone, the rest wanting to run after her and bring her back. There was an awkward silence. When I turned around, Simon was fumbling for a match. Louisa had an intense, unsmiling look on her face. Her blue eyes bored into me.

Finally Simon said, "She can be a bit of a twit, can't she?"

"Indeed." I might have used a stronger word, but 'twit' would do. How could I have missed her so much while I was in Copenhagen, and now find her so annoying? I sat down and began twisting a cigarette, trying not to tear the thin paper.

Louisa stood up and stretched, first on her tiptoes with her hands clasped up over her head, and then in a backbend with her fingers laced together across the small of her back. When she'd finished her gymnastics, she stood directly in front of me with her hands on her hips.

"So, what comes next?" There was barely the hint of a dimple in her left cheek.

"Do you suppose we'll see her back at the hostel tonight?" Simon asked.

"I dunno, your guess is as good as mine. Right now, I don't much care."

Louisa sat next to me and put her hand on my arm. "I'm sorry, David. Got to feel terrible, I know. But, you don't deserve to be treated that way."

We sat and watched the pot dealer, who had reappeared on his bench, make a few more sales. The weight of her hand felt more comradely than intimate.

"And don't pretend you don't care," she added. "You're better than that."

The palace bells began to chime. It was noon, and the somber tones reverberated across the Square.

"By the way, let me give you some of this money." Louisa gave my arm an almost imperceptible squeeze before she turned it loose. She unbuttoned the top of her shirt, reached down inside and pulled out her neck wallet and handed me a thousand dollars. "Here's half of it. Don't think I should carry it all."

"Wow! Thanks." I fondled the money and then stuffed it in my pocket. "What I laid out for the passports just about cleaned me out. I can't believe he really gave you two grand."

"Yes, hard to believe. At first, he said no, that he wasn't going to help me throw my life away. Mother just about fainted when she overheard us. Finally, Father saw that we were determined to try to help Johann and Liesl one way or the other, and he caved in. Didn't ever really argue with the idea itself. Even offered to send more money if we needed it. I told him we would end up in Athens. Can't count how many times he tried to talk me out of it and begged me to be careful."

"Careful, I should say so," Simon said. "We're really going to do this, aren't we?"

"We're really going to plan to do it, anyway," I said. "I feel an obligation to Johann and Liesl. We've gotten their hopes up and all." I turned to Lou. "I feel like we've already come too far to quit. I want to go all the way."

"And you're willing to lose your bird in the bargain?" Simon asked. His eyes shifted between us like he couldn't decide who he should be looking at.

"I don't know why I have to make that choice. She's the one who's splitting." I realized with a quiet little inner click that I wouldn't really miss Mara as much as I would miss getting laid so often. *That* was a big deal. Or was it?

"You're *both* making that choice, mate," Simon said.

I looked at Louisa. "What do you think, Lou?"

"Don't get me involved in this. I'll go along with helping get our friends out of East Berlin. I speak German—"

"And you have the money," Simon interrupted.

"—and I can help with the money. But I'm not a marriage counselor. You and Mara have to figure out your own problems." Louisa gave me a hard stare. There was no hint of dimples now. I wished her hand were still on my arm.

"Thanks for the moral support, friend."

"Don't mention it. By the way, Father gave me the name of an old friend in Frankfurt. Suggested we rent the car there rather than here. What do you think?"

"Fine with me." I tried to feel relief at the change of subject. "We can hitchhike down there or take the train."

"Right. Well, that's settled." Simon stretched his arms over his head. "What's next?"

I didn't feel like anything was settled. Mara's abrupt departure was just too fresh for me to move on.

"Tomorrow," I said, "we'll go to the embassies and see about getting all our visas. We've gotta get everyone's passport stamped, including Johann and Liesl's."

"Hope we can do that without them here," Lou said.

"Once we get all the visas collected, I think I should go back to Berlin to let them know we're ready, that we have the passports and visas." I looked down the street where I had last seen Mara, remembering the time I had grabbed her hand and pulled her back onto the sidewalk. "You guys can come with me or stay here."

"Think I'll come with you, if you don't mind," Lou said. "Somebody's got to keep you on the straight and narrow." Her voice was still hard, but she couldn't prevent the tiny golden flecks in her eyes from glittering in the mid-day sun.

"If that's your aim, you've got your bloody work ahead of you." Simon looked back and forth between Lou and me and slowly a mischievous grin formed on his thin face. "I reckon I'll just stay here. You two run along to Berlin and hurry back. And try to stay out of mischief."

I thought back to the evening we'd spent wandering the de Wallen section of town. "*You're* the one who should try to stay out of mischief."

We sat for a while longer talking and smoking. We agreed that we should rent a Mercedes for the trip, no matter how much it cost. I wanted to put as much contrast between us and the Gypsies as possible. From what Simon had seen at the border, if we rolled up in a Mercedes, we'd be less likely to arouse suspicion. It would be counterproductive to ignore his observations and not act on his impressions.

We also decided to take the train from A'dam to Frankfurt since we were no longer cash poor.

"Any chance we could divert a spot of that capital for some dinner?" Simon asked. "After all, an army travels on its stomach."

"'One for all and all for one' eh, mate?" I said.

"I'm not flat; I can chip in. Me mum sent me fifty quid."

"Well, *you* certainly travel on *your* stomach," Louisa grinned. "You're like a Komodo Dragon, lurching along, devouring everything in its path."

I chuckled, enjoying Lou's sense of humor.

"Make up your minds, dear friends of mine, am I to be an Asian lizard or a bleeding French musketeer?"

"Depends," answered Lou. "Which one eats more?"

★ ★ ★ ★

10 July —
Amsterdam

＊━＊━＊━＊━＊━＊━＊━＊━＊━＊━＊

S imon, Louisa, and I spent most of the day in downtown Amsterdam getting photographs, visiting various embassies and consulates for visas. We'd mapped out a route the night before at dinner; every place we needed to go was within walking distance for us. Mara had gone her own way for the day. Even though we got an early start, she had already disappeared by the time the three of us met in the common room. Perhaps she intended to give me a preview of what life without Mara would be like; I flattered myself that longing could work both ways.

Although Den Haag was the capitol of Holland, most people applied for visas at the consulates and embassies in A'dam. While bumming around west Europe was relatively easy, involving nothing more than the presentation of your passport at the borders, travel behind the Iron Curtain was a different story. Most east European countries had twenty-four hour waiting periods for tourist visas; lengthy applications, accompanied by two photographs and fees payable in hard, western currency were usually approved overnight.

Our intended itinerary required entrance and exit (transit/tourist) visas for Czechoslovakia, Hungary, and Yugoslavia, and entrance visas for Greece. Except for Greece, these were Iron Curtain countries and I was prepared for lots of bureaucratic red tape.

Liesl and Johann were responsible for getting themselves out of the *Deutsche Democratic Republik*. Our plan was for them to enter Czechoslovakia with their real names, Johann Klaus Volker and Liesl Schmidt, using their East German passports. Once we were all reunited in Karlovy Vary, they would become Johann and Liesl Müeller, just an ordinary West German couple on holiday. Depending on how long their visas were valid for, we would have a few days' head start on anyone who might be tracking us down.

The first real test, a field test, of the bogus passports would come when all five of us crossed from Czechoslovakia into Hungary. In fact, every time our papers had to be produced, whether for border crossings, hotel registrations, exchanges of currency, routine police inspections, or any other reason, we would be at considerable risk. All we'd need would be for one over-zealous cop, alert border guard, bank teller, or even a hotel clerk to be suspicious and we'd be in serious trouble. Deep shit, as Mara would say.

We hadn't seen Mara since she left us in Dam Square. I thought we might cross paths with her as we made our way from consulate to consulate, all of which were in downtown Amsterdam, but we didn't. Louisa reported that she hadn't returned to the hostel before curfew. I wasn't worried. Yet.

We encountered an obstacle at the Hungarian consulate that threatened to derail the entire plan. We were informed that only an applicant, *in person*, could apply for a tourist visa. In addition, visas were not issued on a 'while-you-wait' basis. Our applications, which would have to be sent to the Hungarian Embassy in Den Haag, would take one to two weeks to process. I explained that the Müellers were friends of ours, traveling companions, but, as they were sick in bed at the hotel, would be unable to comply with this 'in-person' regulation. Their doctor had recommended that they have as little contact with other people as possible, due to the contagious nature of their illness. I even offered to bring a letter from the 'attending physician', which brought a startled look followed by a fit of coughing from Simon.

Louisa, cool and calm as always, didn't even raise an eyebrow. She made sure the clerk saw her wallet full of cash. I was relieved, as I would be many times in the days ahead, that Louisa was there instead of Mara.

Claiming contagious illness was a lame explanation, like Huck Finn waving off the slave catchers on the Mississippi to protect Jim, but I couldn't think of anything else at the moment. I pointed out to the clerk that our Czechoslovakian and Yugoslavian visas were dated, and in order for our trip to take place as we planned, we couldn't wait two or three weeks for Hungarian permission. That part was true; we had copies of our applications, stamped with the relevant dates, to back up our story. (How curious, I thought, the order in which we visited the consulates had been random, determined solely by their locations on the street map. Now it made a difference.) I hoped the documentation regarding the

Czechoslovakian and Yugoslavian visa applications would spill over and lend credence to the fictitious 'doctor's orders' part of my story.

The desk clerk retreated into a back room, together with the passports, the required photographs, and enough cash to cover the steep application fees, ostensibly to confer with a superior. During the lengthy interlude, I reflected that I was as nervous about getting these visas, which should have been more or less routine, as I was when I'd purchased the counterfeit passports in Copenhagen to begin with.

About fifteen minutes later, she returned with the passports, extracted more cash from Louisa to pay for what we understood was expedited handling, and told us we could return in the morning for our visas.

✦✦✦✦

11 July —
Amsterdam

M ara was in the common room the next morning, smoking a Marlboro and nursing a cup of coffee. Lots of people were up making breakfast, smoking, chatting in several languages. The babble sounded like a kind of hippie United Nations.

I slid into a chair next to her.

"Who invited you to sit down?"

"Well, it's a table for two and it's that time of day."

"Very funny, Slick."

"So, where've you been?"

"I stayed at a hotel. I'm sick of this place."

"I missed you yesterday, sweetheart."

"You're going to miss me a lot more if you go back to Berlin."

"How's that?" I asked.

"You know what I'm talking about."

"I was hoping you'd be in Greece in a few weeks waiting for us."

"I don't know about that. Right now, I kinda doubt it."

I reached across the table and tried to take her hand, but she jerked it into her lap. "So, this is it for us? We're done?"

"Look. I don't want to be hanging around somewhere wondering if I am ever going to see you again. Wondering if you're in some godforsaken prison in some fucking Communist police state. You want to risk your life for some strangers, you go right ahead. Just count me out. That's all."

"Sweetheart—" I said.

"Quit sweethearting me, David. You know how I feel about this shit."

We sat quietly for a while, listening to the clatter of knives and forks and spoons on plates and the swish of dishwater, the rhythm and hum of words we didn't understand. Gradually, the dining room thinned out.

"So, are you telling me you're leaving me?"

"I'm not the one who's leaving, remember?"

"Come on, Mara, don't play word games with me."

"I don't know what I'm telling you. It's just not that goddam easy."

"Well, I hope you're going to meet me in Greece. Us, I mean."

"Maybe. I already miss you, and you're not even dead yet. Don't count on it, though. Shit, I don't fucking know." Mara lit a fresh Marlboro from the stub of her old one.

"OK. I won't." I stood up. "Lou and Simon are waiting for me."

"I see. So it's Lou now?" She blew a stream of smoke toward the sidewalk. "No more Louisa?"

"Just like it's Mara, no more Miriam."

"Oh, sure, I get it."

"It's not like that."

"Isn't it?" Mara tucked a stray ringlet behind her ear, dropping Marlboro ashes onto her shirt. Taking a deep breath, she brushed them away with cupped hands.

"I gotta go." I forced myself to look away.

"So, go already." Mara's eyes were shiny.

"See you in Thessaloniki." I needed to leave before real tears began to flow. "I mean that. I hope you're there."

"Ciao," Mara said. And that was it, just like that. No kiss, no hug, nothing. Which was fortunate; I don't know what I would have done if she had stood up, wrapped her arms around me, crushed her all-too-familiar soft body into mine, and begged me to give up this insane fantasy and stay with her.

I walked back upstairs to the men's dorm to look for Simon. By the time I found him, the stinging in my own eyes had nearly stopped.

"Let's get Louisa and go collect our visas." I fumbled for my handkerchief, blew my nose hard, and furtively daubed my eyes. Simon wasn't fooled.

"Did you see Mara?"

"Mara who."

"Right."

Louisa was sitting on a bench outside. I slipped on my dark glasses.

"What say we get a spot of breakfast before we make the rounds?" Simon asked.

"I can eat," Louisa said. "No Mara, huh?"

"I guess not," I said.

"Think she's gone for good?"

"Haven't a clue," I said, with a definitiveness I wasn't sure I felt. It was one of Simon's favorite phrases, but I didn't mind borrowing it. "I really don't want to talk about it."

The three of us ate a big Dutch breakfast consisting of several kinds of bread, cold cuts, jams, fruits, pastries, tiny bits of chocolate, and coffee. We left food on the table, which didn't happen often when you dined with Simon.

"Enough to eat?" Louisa asked.

"Reckon I'll be fine 'till supper." Simon stuffed the remaining rolls into his rucksack.

"How about you, David? Had enough, yet?"

I was about to answer when it dawned on me that she wasn't talking about food.

"Sure," I said. "You bet. Let's get the hell out of here."

After we'd revisited the Czechoslovakian, Hungarian, and Yugoslavian embassies and gotten our passports stamped with tourist visas that would get us into and out of each country, we returned to the youth hostel. I'd been pretty apprehensive the day before, especially at the Hungarian embassy, presenting our genuine passports along with the bogus ones at the consulates; if anything about the freshly minted Copenhagen forgeries aroused their suspicions, the Hungarians would have confiscated the whole batch, leaving Louisa, Simon and me without even our own documents. At this point, there was nothing to connect Johann and Liesl with the fake passports but the three of us would have had some explaining to do at our own embassies.

Making the rounds of the various consulates and presenting our passports, including the bogus West German ones, had been the first test of the Danish counterfeiter's skill. They had been carefully scrutinized, (we hoped!) by officials of the Czechoslovakian, Hungarian, Yugoslavian, and Greek governments trained in such matters. All had passed their inspections; we literally held the proof in our hands. Professional bureaucrats had looked them over and given them their official blessings, in the form of rubber stamps and glued-in stickers.

By the time we had reclaimed all the passports it was mid-afternoon. I felt strangely free and light, as if everything heavy I normally lugged around with me had been left behind on a table somewhere. Nobody had mentioned Mara since breakfast.

"Let's find some café so we can get a bite to eat and figure out where we're at with money. Someplace a little more private." I knew Simon would be ready for 'high tea', which for him meant lunch and a beer.

"Good on you, mate. I know just the spot." Simon led us several blocks away in the direction of *de Wallen.* Down a narrow side street, we saw a Heineken sign hanging over an open doorway. I wondered how Simon had discovered such a peculiarly named tavern, but decided to wait and ask him sometime later. *Wijnand Fockink* was almost empty at this hour; besides us there was only one waitress and one bartender. It felt oddly familiar to the *gaststätte* in Berlin where we'd first gotten to know Johann. We ordered food at the counter and took our schooners of beer to a table in the dimly-lit rear end of the bar.

All told, the visas in all five passports had cost us over two hundred dollars. We all dug into our backpacks, neck wallets, and pockets and arranged our cash on the table in front of us like poker players. Including the money Louisa's father had given her, we pooled over three thousand American dollars, along with a few hundred more in kroner, guilders, marks, and francs. Simon had about a hundred pounds plus the uncashed wire transfer his mother had sent him. The East German marks I didn't even bother to include. In a zipper pocket in the back of my passport wallet, I found a few hundred Czech koruny that I'd forgotten about, left over from my brief trip to Czechoslovakia with Mara. I wondered if she had any koruny left, and if she did, whether it would remind her of me.

"I think money will be the least of our worries, especially if we exchange on the black market."

"So, what exactly *are* your worries, mate?"

"Two Americans, two Germans, and one limey traveling together, for starters."

"I wouldn't worry about that at all. You've been here long enough to see how things are. They'll look at the passports and the visas and the cash."

"Still." I hoped we wouldn't arouse any suspicions as we crossed through the Iron Curtain countries on our way to Greece, but I wasn't under any illusions that we would have a trouble-free romp through three Communist police states. Somewhere, sometime, we were likely to get caught. I had no idea what we'd do when that happened, although bribing our way to freedom seemed like an option. Three grand was more money than I'd come over to Europe with in the first place and it felt like a fortune. I remembered from the Museum at Checkpoint Charlie that for the right amount of hard currency, passage out of East Berlin could be purchased. Would similar arrangements be possible elsewhere? Could, say, a Yugoslavian border cop be bribed? From that perspective, three thousand dollars didn't look like so much.

12 July —
On the Road to Berlin

‐‐‐‐‐‐‐‐‐‐‐‐‐‐‐‐‐‐‐‐

Well, this is it for the time being, friend." I was standing with Simon at the edge of Dam Square waiting for Louisa to get back with a rental car. "We'll see you here in a few days."

"I reckon I can keep myself occupied." Simon turned and looked in the direction of *de wallen*.

"Ah, yes, there's always that Irish pastry."

"Crumpet, mate, haven't I taught you a bloody thing?"

"You stay out of trouble," I said.

"I should think you're the one needing that advice. *You* be careful."

"Here, you hang on to these." I took the new passports out of my backpack and handed them to him. "I don't see any reason to take them back into Berlin. Safer here with you."

"Good thinking, that." Simon slipped the passports into his own rucksack. "Pass along my regards to Johann and Liesl and for God's sake, don't try to sneak anything in. No more smuggling magazines. Keep your wits about you at the Wall."

"I just hope we don't run into Blondie. Or that other prick."

"You be careful, mate."

"Thanks, I will." I muttered and wrapped Simon in a bear hug.

"You bloody Americans are never satisfied with a simple handshake." I could hear the chuckle in his voice as he disengaged himself from my awkward embrace. Simon held me by my shoulders at arms length for a long moment, his face losing its trace of mirth, as if he were considering for the first time the wisdom of entrusting his future to me. "I mean it, mate, you take care."

"Hey, we Californians are just a touchy-feely kind of people."

A crescendo of car horns, streetcar bells, and yelling voices squelched any further conversation.

"DAVID!" Louisa yelled at me from the street. "Can't park here. Let's go!"

I hoisted my backpack and sprinted toward the curb. Lou was sitting in the driver's seat of a huge Audi, traffic backed up behind her. I tossed my gear through the open window of the rear door and then hopped into the front seat just as the light turned from green to red.

"Good timing," she said with a grin.

"Runs in the family. You know, Lou, when you smile like that, you've got dimples other chicks would kill for."

"You mean like this?" Louisa exaggerated her smile until I could see most of her white teeth.

"Yeah, like that." The horns started up again. "Light's green; let's go."

Louisa and I made our way through the mid-morning traffic to the edge of town where, at almost exactly the same place on the road we ourselves had stood waiting for a ride to Berlin just a few weeks earlier, we stopped to pick up two girls lugging suitcases. One of their bags had a cardboard sign taped to it that said: BERLIN. How much had changed in that short span of time. For me, the word 'Berlin', without East or West preceding it, no longer existed. I opened the trunk and arranged their suitcases, along with my backpack, next to Louisa's gear.

"Thanks for the lift," the shorter girl said. "Those friggin' suitcases are heavy."

"You should dump them and get backpacks," I said.

"No shit, Sherlock. Next thing on the list."

We got back into the Audi and Lou accelerated into traffic.

I turned in my seat. "I'm David and this is Louisa."

"She's Maggie and I'm Sarah," the taller girl said. "We just got here."

"Where from?" Lou asked.

"New York. The Big Apple. Only been here a day." Sarah's hair was cut in a pageboy and she wore a western-style shirt with mother-of-pearl buttons down the front and sequins spattered on both collars. She didn't look like the New York I remembered.

Maggie ran her hands over the leather seats as she inspected the interior of the Audi. Most of her fingers and both thumbs carried rings and she had on a red bandana that forced a mass of tight, black curls out the back like an exhaust pipe.

"Cool short," she said.

I looked at Lou with a blank expression, but she just shrugged her shoulders.

"Cool short?" I asked.

"Yeah, cool short. You know, nice car. How long've you been here, anyway?"

"Little over a year." Not even two years away from home and already people my age were speaking a different language.

"Wow, that's outta sight," Sarah said. "Where've you been so far?"

"Everywhere. Far south as Paris and as far north as Copenhagen."

Louisa looked at Maggie in the rear view mirror. "Here only one day and you're already going to Berlin?"

"We heard Berlin's a pretty groovy trip," Maggie said.

"That it is." I turned back around and tried to remember which pocket I'd stuffed my pouch of Drum in. "That it certainly is."

We arrived in Berlin well after dark and went straight to the Charlottenburg youth hostel. The city was wide-awake, as always, but it had been a long day on the autobahn and I was ready for a beer, some dinner, and a good night's sleep, in that order. Sarah and Maggie had dozed off most of the way, oblivious to the sinister East German guard towers spaced every few kilometers along the corridor, so they were well rested and ready for a night on the town. West Berlin would be perfect for them.

"So, clue me in," Maggie asked, "where do you score good eats around here?"

It took me a few seconds to translate. "Well, there's an OK Italian joint around the corner. Guido's Authentic Italian Bistro."

"Good pasta bar," Louisa added.

"Fergetaboutit." It came out of her mouth as one long word. "Me and Sarah didn't come all this way to Berlin to scarf down spaghetti. We can get that in Little Italy."

"Well," I said, "you can get sauerkraut and bratwurst or currywurst in just about any bar you find. Plenty of places to eat here in Big Germany."

"Hey, it'd be far out if you guys, like, hooked up with us." Maggie's face was pasted against the window. "We're gonna go check out the action."

Louisa shook her head, more of a twitch, really, just enough for me to get the message.

"Thanks, but no thanks. You chicks had a nice nap. We'll catch up with you in the morning, maybe."

"OK, well, stay cool," Sarah said. "Color us gone." She took Maggie's hand. "Come on, Mags, let's split."

And just like that, they did.

13 July —
Berlin

✦✦✦✦✦✦✦✦✦✦✦✦

Louisa was waiting in the common room when I trudged downstairs from the men's dorm the next morning. I couldn't remember my head hitting the pillow.

"So, what time did those hippie chicks get in last night?" I asked.

"No idea. Fell sound asleep right away."

"I don't doubt it. You were half dozing off into your linguini."

"Rare luxury. Don't dare sleep with food on your plate when Simon's around."

"Aw, come on, Lou. He's not all that bad."

"I know." Full grin, dimple to dimple. "Fun to tease about him, though."

"So, what's our plan?"

"Guy who runs the place said we can leave the Audi in the alley behind the hostel long as we leave him a key in case he has to move it. Thought I'd give him five bucks."

"Cool," I said. "That's far out. Let's lay the keys to the short on him and split."

"Groovy." Lou looked at me and winked. "I can dig it."

"Tell you the truth, I couldn't understand half of what they were saying."

"Been away too long," Lou said.

"Yeah, maybe you're right."

"Ever think about going back?"

What kind of a question was that?

"Sometimes. But then, there's the war and the draft."

"Yeah, those are big. But there's other things to consider, too."

"Like what?"

Lou cocked her head to one side and gave me the half-smile-with-a-hint-of-dimples look. "You're a smart boy. You'll figure it out." She flagged down a cab and we were on our way.

By ten o'clock we were at Checkpoint Charlie. The *Vopos* passed us through, ignoring the collection of East Berlin stamps already in our passports. They either didn't notice or didn't care about the visas for Czechoslovakia, Hungary, Yugoslavia, or Greece. Neither the fat blonde *Vopo* nor the slender *Kommandant* were on duty. Without Mara along, our hike through East Berlin was much faster.

When we got to Johann's apartment, my stomach clenched into a knot. In the middle of the street were the charred remains of a fire. Neither of us said a word.

As before, Johann's neighborhood was deserted. Liesl answered the door and whisked us inside. We followed her upstairs.

"Where is Johann?" I saw all the art had been removed.

Liesl's eyes were pink and moist. "He is now working."

"And, this...." I swept my hand around the apartment at the bare walls.

Liesl shook her head. "Did you not see the ashes in the street?"

"Jesus Christ. When did this happen?"

"From one week now." Liesl turned toward the window, unable to stop the tears flowing down her cheeks.

Lou put her arms around Liesl and smoothed back her hair. "Good news, *Meine Freundin*," she whispered. "We have the passports and the visas."

"Yes? This is true?" Liesl stood back, holding Lou's hands. She looked at me. "Yes?"

"Yes. Everything is ready."

Liesl dropped her arms to her sides and again turned to the window. She said a few words in German, very softly, which I couldn't understand. Louisa looked at me and zipped her lips shut and shook her head. A full minute slid by.

The silence was broken by the sounds of a door slamming and then heavy footsteps coming up the stairs.

Suddenly, there was a loud knock at the door, followed by a single shouted word: "*Polizei!*"

We all froze. Liesl put two fingers in front of her lips, her face pale and her eyes wide.

"*Ja? Wer ist da?*"

"*Polizei! Öffnen Sie die Tür!*"

"*Einen Moment bitte. Ich bin unbekleidet.*"

Liesl beckoned us into the sleeping alcove and drew the curtains shut. Peeking through a slit in the gauzy fabric, I watched her quickly strip naked and then walk to the door with a towel. Lou and I held our breaths. I reached out and found her hand.

Liesl clutched the towel across her chest with one hand and opened the door a couple of inches with the other. A breeze coming up from the stairwell fluttered the flimsy terrycloth between her knees. Although I couldn't hear their muffled exchange, we soon heard cloggy boot steps retreating back down the hall.

Liesl locked the door and then dressed. Her motions were efficient and without artifice; she slipped into her shirt, panties, and shorts as easily as she had out of them. Motioning us to stay hidden, she crossed to the window and looked down at the street. I opened my mouth and breathed as quietly as I could.

"They are gone." Liesl stepped back from the window. "But please, we must speak softly. I have told them I am here alone." She switched on the radio.

"What did they want?" I asked.

"They ask after Johann. It is nothing about you."

"Pretty clever how you got rid of them," I said.

Liesl blushed. "Do you wish a beer? Johann do keep many beers here for your return."

"Yes, I'd drink a beer, thanks." I fished out my pack of Drum and rolled a cigarette. Liesl watched, fascinated, as the tiny rectangle of paper and the stringy tobacco transformed into an approximation of a real cigarette. "Can I make you one, too?"

"Yes, *bitte*." I handed her mine and built another.

"Tell me, Liesl, was Johann able to get the visas for you to travel to Karlovy Vary?" I dreaded asking the question.

Liesl inhaled deeply and blew the smoke out her mouth into her nostrils and coughed. "We have now the papers for making travel from DDR to Czechoslovakia, but not at this time from Berlin to Dresden. For this we are having great hope, but not success. It is very difficult, the visa officials."

"Is it even possible they will grant you travel visas at the same time they are burning Johann's pictures in the street and sending police to your door in the middle of the day?"

Liesl laughed softly. "You do not understand East German government. There are so many departments and officials they do not always know what the other one is doing."

"We have a saying in English: 'The left hand doesn't know what the right hand is doing.'"

Lou translated this into German for Liesl, who smiled and nodded. *"Die linke Hand weiss nicht was die rechte Hand tut,"* she repeated. "It is the same, English and German, I think."

I looked around. The room, which had had a sort of 'artist's loft' ambience to it the last time we were there, now felt barren and lifeless. No art, no artist. "I wish there were more we could do. We will be in Karlovy Vary waiting for you in one week."

"By the baths," Lou added. "We will wait by the baths each day at noon."

"We are having a hope. Johann have talked to his mother on telephone from two days ago. She is much more sick than before. A terrible thing, but it can perhaps make some difference with the permission."

"So, the worse Johann's mother is, the better your chances are."

"Yes, this is true," Liesl said, then added in a whisper, "I do not understand the workings of God."

"Well, Hitler gave us that lesson already, right?"

Liesl began crying again. Louisa glared at me and pulled the zipper back across her lips.

"Always know the right thing to say, don't you?" She hissed.

"I'm sorry."

"Go make yourself scarce for a while."

"OK, but I think we should head back to Checkpoint Charlie pretty soon."

"Just leave us alone for a few minutes. Meet you downstairs."

Almost a whole smoke later, Louisa met me in the ground floor foyer. Furtively, we checked the street, and then we slipped out and headed for the Wall. There was no sign of the police who had interrupted our visit. I reached down and pinched a bit of ash and folded it into an East German ten-mark note and slid it into my pocket.

"Did you manage to get Liesl calmed down a little bit?"

"No thanks to you."

"I'm sorry. I didn't mean to upset her."

"I know. It's OK. You couldn't help it."

We walked a few blocks without talking. I wondered how long it would take Lou to get over being pissed off at me.

"I wish I knew for sure that they were going to make it to Dresden." I looked back over my shoulder.

"Not going to know that ahead of time, David. Just have to go to Carlsbad and see if they turn up. While we're waiting, you can take some lessons in tact."

"I know. I'm sorry. Believe me." I couldn't look her in the eyes.

"It's OK." She forced a smile. "Fergetaboutit."

"It's a fucked up way to run an operation, if you want my opinion."

"Think it gets any better than this?"

"No, probably not." I shook my head and fingered the lumpy, folded banknote. I still had enough *Ostmark* to surrender that I doubted the *Vopos* would search my clothing.

If luck wasn't running in Johann's favor, it was in ours; neither the fat blonde guard nor her boss were in the bunker and we passed uneventfully back into the West Sector.

"What do you think about staying here in Berlin for a few more days and to see if Johann gets their exit visas?" I asked, once we were in the relative privacy of a cab.

"Not a good idea. Too dangerous. We're taking a big risk every time we go in there. Making it harder for them, too, if anybody's keeping an eye on them."

As we waited at a red light, I watched the rotating East German searchlights illuminate the Wall and, every few seconds, the red, white, and blue fluttering over American Army Headquarters.

"I sure hope we know what we're doing," I said, with more hope than conviction in my voice. All those stars, all those stripes.

"Little late for doubts now. Come on, got a green. Let's go." Lou encircled my wrist with her thumb and forefinger and pulled me into the crosswalk.

When we reached the opposite curb, she didn't let go.

━✦━✦━✦━✦━

14 July —
Amsterdam

———————————

Lou and I left the Charlottenburg youth hostel about eight o'clock in the morning for the long drive back to Amsterdam. We'd done all we could; Lou was right, we wouldn't accomplish anything more by staying in Berlin. After taking a final WC stop and filling the gas tank, we hit the autobahn headed due west.

We arrived in Amsterdam late that afternoon. It didn't take long to track down Simon. I wanted to find out what he'd been up to the two days we'd been away, and if he had seen anything of Mara.

"Saw her yesterday, mate. She was dressed for the road and said she was going south."

"South? South *where*? South could mean Belgium or France or Italy."

"Can't help you there. All she said was south."

"Or Greece," I added.

"Haven't a clue, mate. Could be Johannesburg for all my guesses."

We were sitting at an outdoor café a block off the Square. Lou had gone to return the Audi to the rental company. I rolled a Drum and offered the pouch to Simon, who shook his head and lit up a Navy Cut. "Not that bloody desperate, yet."

"And what about you, friend, did you take a riding tour of Dublin?" I nodded toward *de wallen*. "Did you manage to make contact with the IRA?"

"You know a bloke never kisses and tells." Simon arched his eyebrows. "Why don't you tell me how it went with Johann and Liesl."

"We never did get to see Johann. Only Liesl."

"He hadn't been—"

"No, no, he was actually working, according to Liesl."

"Begin at the top, mate."

"Well, to start with, we picked up two chicks, two *birds* that is, on the 'bahn and gave them a lift all the way in."

"They were from Britain?"

"No, New York. Good Karma, at any rate, picking them up."

"'Tis that."

"Couldn't understand half their slang."

"Maybe you've been abroad too long. But get on with it."

I paused for a minute before I continued. "Like I said, Johann wasn't there." I related the details of our trip, including the visit from the police and Liesl's clever ruse to keep the cops out of the apartment.

"And there was this." I fished the folded packet of charred paper out of my pocket and carefully opened it on the tabletop.

"What's this?"

"I scraped it off the street in front of Johann's door."

Simon looked at the tiny pile of ashes smudged across the face of Friedrich von Schiller, then at me, realization hardening his eyes. "Bloody fucking bastards."

I carefully refolded the banknote and put it away.

"So, you and Lou stayed at the hostel?" Simon tilted his head back and peered at me over his lower eyelids.

"Of course, why not? Why wouldn't we stay at the hostel?"

"Nothing, mate. Not to worry. Get on with the tale."

"That's about it."

"How does it look, though, for the visas?"

"I think he has a fighting chance. His mom is worse; her condition is more deteriorated, according to Liesl."

"So, if his mum kicks the bucket, he gets a travel visa, right?"

"It's a shitty situation, no doubt about it."

"A sticky wicket, that." Simon signaled the waiter. "Another beer?"

"No more for me." I stood up and put a couple of guilders on the table. "I'm ready to call it a day. Berlin's a long drive."

"Oughten'd we wait for Louisa?" Simon asked.

"Don't need to. She said she'd meet us in the morning in the common room."

We made our way back to the youth hostel. I was sound asleep before Simon even got out of the shower.

15 July —

On the Road to Frankfurt

I woke up the next morning drowsy from too much sleep. After a shower, though, I felt refreshed and ready for the day. Lou and Simon were waiting in the common room when I came downstairs.

"About time you got up, you lazy sot," Simon said. "Close to lunch-time already."

"Got you a few rolls at the bakery," Louisa said. "There's still coffee here."

"That'll be plenty. Let's get a move on; I've already made us late."

Mara had disappeared, at least for the time being. I scribbled a note to her:

> Mara, we left for Frankfurt. July 14. See you in Greece in a
> few weeks. Take care and be safe.
> Love, David & Simon & Louisa

I pinned it to the bulletin board among a dozen similar scraps of paper.

The two thousand dollars from Louisa's father, with the promise of more if we needed it, had made hitchhiking unnecessary, so we buckled up our backpacks and headed for the railway station

Had the totality of our relationship disintegrated to that? A few impersonal lines written on a half-size piece of notepaper and hung from a thumbtack in the common room of a youth hostel? When was the last time we'd slept together and had sex? When had we last spent any time alone together? *Why couldn't I remember?*

Louisa's father's contact in Frankfurt was an old friend from the time before her family had immigrated to the States. He met us at the station and drove us to a car rental agency. How much information Louisa's dad gave him regarding our current intrigue I couldn't tell. He didn't speak very much English, so his conversation was limited to chatting with Louisa, who didn't bother translating much of it. Later, she told us that he offered his help, if we needed it. It wasn't clear to her if this was a generic overture made simply because we are kids on the road loosely connected to an old friend, or an offer specifically related to our escape plan.

At the rental agency, a woman with hair coiled so tightly that it pulled at the sides of her face and who spoke flawless, if accented English, presented us with a stack of forms to fill out. Renting a car was going to involve more paperwork than getting our visas had.

"Where do you intend to drive this automobile?"

"We plan to take a trip through Czechoslovakia and Hungary and then down the Dalmatian Coast to Greece," I said.

She tilted her head back and peered at me through gold-rimmed glasses perched halfway down her nose. "For what reason will you go to such places?"

I looked at Louisa and Simon and then leaned into the counter. "We want to see for ourselves the countries of east Europe."

"I am sorry. It is forbidden to operate our automobiles in the countries you wish to see." She slid the rental forms off the counter back onto her desk.

"What? Forbidden? How can this be?" I exploded. This was a big problem; without a car, our whole plan was dead. I had never considered the possibility that we might not be able to rent a car; it had been a detail too small to worry about. And now it was a potential roadblock. What would happen to Johann and Liesl if *they* got to Karlovy Vary and *we* weren't there to meet them? All because we couldn't rent a car.

"Let me handle this." Lou and the agency woman began a heated discussion in German. I was too agitated to understand what they were saying.

The haughty agent retreated to an inner office and slammed the door behind her.

"What did you say, anyway?" I asked.

"I told her to ask her supervisor."

We waited for a few minutes until the woman reemerged from the office with an older man behind her. The woman stood to one side out of deference to her boss, but still glared at us.

"You will please explain your travel plans to me," the supervisor said.

I told him that we had a strong desire to visit the countries behind the Iron Curtain, that we had traveled throughout west Europe and wanted to see the other part.

The supervisor shook his head. "It can be as you wish. For this, however, you must pay additional insurance. The normal insurance will not be sufficient for travel to these countries."

The cost of insurance coverage for east Europe was almost twice what coverage limited to the west would have been, but we had no choice, since we would have to present not only our passports and International Driver's Licenses but also proof of insurance at each border crossing.

"Use your head," Louisa said. "Last thing we want is anything wrong with our papers when we cross borders. Just costs what it costs."

Lou was right, of course. Already I was thankful she was there.

Louisa began extracting twenties and fifties from her neck wallet. "Do you accept American money, or should we go to a bank?"

"Yes, American dollars, naturally. Helga will telephone the bank for the exchange rate. Please enjoy your holiday." He smiled wearily and returned to his office. We finished the transaction and Lou folded the paperwork into her passport.

After arranging our backpacks in the spacious trunk, we took off, Louisa sitting next to me in the front and Simon sprawled across the wide rear seat.

The Mercedes had a heavy, solid feel to it and I was amazed at how quickly it accelerated when I floored the gas pedal. I wondered if we would need all that power since the roads of east Europe as I knew them were backwater, country lanes, not autobahns.

After an hour of driving around town, we arrived at the youth hostel. We were probably the first kids to arrive at the Frankfurt youth hostel in a shiny, brand new Mercedes Benz 280SE luxury sedan. I heard more than a few snickers as we unloaded our packs.

I could hear Simon's stomach grumbling as well; we hadn't eaten since breakfast in Amsterdam and I knew that if *I* were hungry, which I was, he must have been ravenous.

In our haste, we'd neglected to bring anything to eat with us on the train, which being an express commuter run, didn't have a dining car, or even a strolling vendor. The excitement of our impending adventure must have been catching up with Simon, who usually planned or at least thought ahead, for his meals. We didn't want to bother shopping for food and then cooking it in the hostel, and we had plenty of money anyway, so we found an Italian restaurant. I ordered fettuccine Alfredo, which reminded me of Mara, who loved pasta as much as Simon did. I imagined she'd be eating lots of it on her trip through Italy. *If* she'd gone to Italy.

I was looking forward to my upcoming separation from her. In spite of the fact that we had known each other for more than a year, had a great time in the sack, as my father would say, and had taken a few trips together, Mara had plenty of annoying habits that got on my nerves. More than once, I was happy that youth hostels had segregated dorms. Our lovemaking, which had started out as a furtive quickie by the side of the road in Germany, had matured into unadulterated lust by the time we got back to Holland. Since then, sex had become faceted and taken on additional nuances as we learned each other's secrets. I was looking forward to meeting her in Greece and at the same time hoping she wouldn't show up. Mara Liebowitz was a mixed blessing. Or, was it Miriam?

16 July —

On the Road to Karlovy Vary

———※—※—※—※—※—※—※———

Th…is is it, you know," Louisa said. "Today we go into Czechoslovakia. Tomorrow we meet Johann and Liesl in Karlovy Vary. No going back. You sure you want to go through with it?"

For once, Simon didn't look like he wanted a beer or a cigarette or a sandwich. He cocked his head to the side, waiting for me to answer. We were at a figurative crossroads this morning, and within a couple of hours, we would be at a literal one as well. When we crossed that Iron Curtain border we would be on enemy terrain. I thought about the Wall, about our numerous crossings through Checkpoint Charlie, and about the blonde *Vopo* who had tried to rip me in half. A shudder went down my spine and I realized I was clenching my jaws so tightly my teeth were grinding. I thought of Liesl standing naked in the Spree River with a vacant expression on her face, and the residue of black ash in the street in front of Johann's apartment.

"Well," I said, "it is the most bone-headed thing I've ever done. It doesn't make any sense. Mara's right—we could get into some very serious trouble." If I was trying to talk myself out of it, I was failing. Completely. I fingered the packet in my pocket.

"So, in other words," Simon's face was more serious than I had ever seen it, "it's all systems go."

"I guess so."

"Better be sure," Lou said. "'I guess so' doesn't sound convincing."

"I'm sure. I want to do this. Remember the look on Liesl's face the last time we were there?"

"Yes, she was bloody crying, as I recall," Simon said.

"So was Mara when we got busted." I felt my jaw stiffen again as a cold tingle shot back up my spine. "You're damn right I want to go."

We sat in silence for a minute, watching the activities around us in the great room. The youth hostel in Frankfurt was one where breakfast was included with the nominal lodging fee, and we were just finishing our bockwurst and fried potatoes. We were scrubbed and our clothes were freshly laundered. Even though Simon had given up on his scraggly beard and shaved, he still had a disheveled look about him. How had I ever pictured him in East India?

"This will be our last German food for a while, mates. Our next food will be Czechoslovakian."

I could imagine Miriam: *I still think you are out of your minds to be doing this, Slick. Lots of shit could go wrong. All it will take is one border guard with a hair up his ass to look at those passports closely, make a phone call, and you'd be fucked. Plain and simple. FUCKED!*

"I reckon this is our last chance to bail out," Simon said. I was accustomed to his accent and English phrases and whenever he used an American expression I chuckled inside.

"No can do," I said. "I mean, if they manage to get as far as Dresden and then into Czechoslovakia, I don't see how we can stand them up. Liesl said they already had permission to go from Dresden to Karlovy Vary. Suppose they showed up there and we weren't there? I wouldn't want to live with that for the rest of my life. I feel like we have to go at least as far as Karlovy Vary."

"And if they don't show up? What if we get to Karlovy Vary and … no Johann and Liesl?" Simon asked. "What then?"

"Just tourists," I said. "We will just be tourists enjoying the baths."

"'Taking the waters' is the way they say it, I believe," Louisa said.

"Dear Mums, I shall be taking the waters at Karlovy Vary. Love, Simon." Simon tilted his head back, squinted down his nose and pantomimed writing a letter.

Dear Mums, I thought to myself, *I shall be spending the rest of my life in prison.*

Simon, Lou, and I left the hostel around nine o'clock, early by our standards, under a sunless, gunmetal-grey sky. We calculated that the drive to Karlovy Vary would take us all day, even though we would be on the autobahn most of the way. German freeways did not have speed limits, arguably the only positive legacy from Adolph Hitler, who believed that automobile speed should not be regulated by the government. The journey from Frankfurt to Karlovy Vary was about five hundred kilometers and would take us through Nuremburg, the site of the Nazi War Crimes trials. We would also be in the area of Flossenbuerg, where Liesl's parents had been murdered. Unlike Dachau and some of the other Nazi concentration camps, this one didn't appear on our map.

Late that afternoon, we crossed the border into Czechoslovakia at Cheb, just as a few raindrops spattered the windshield.

We passed the same side road Mara and I had hiked down on our trip into Czechoslovakia only a few months earlier. The weather was the same, but it felt like years.

"You know—" I mused, looking out the window at the rutted dirt road leading into the thicket.

"'Fess up, mate, was this the spot—"

"Never mind. It's in the past. Forget about it."

If Louisa wondered what Simon and I were alluding to, she didn't indicate it.

Geographically, Cheb was the westernmost point of east Europe and jutted into the belly of West Germany like a blunt weapon. As such, it was a main portal through the Iron Curtain. The spattering on the windshield had developed into a light rain.

We stopped behind a line of at least twenty cars. There were several lanes but only one manned border kiosk and it took us thirty minutes for our turn to come. I rolled down the window as we drove under the canopy.

"*Die Pässe, bitte.*"

I handed our passports to the guard, who stared at each of us briefly but intensely, matching our faces to our photos. I thought of the two counterfeit passports hidden under the floor carpeting beneath my feet and hoped he wouldn't search the car. Finally, satisfied that we were who our passports claimed we were, the guard stamped them, wrote in the date, and handed them back to me through the open window. The whole process had lasted about five minutes.

"Please to enjoy visit to Peoples Republic of Czechoslovakia!" He saluted as we drove through the heavy steel gate into the border plaza. From huge sentry minarets, soldiers armed with AK-47s watched everything. There was not one single car in the westbound lane. As we drove slowly away from the booth, tall towers topped with large lights reminded us that we were once again behind the Iron Curtain.

"Blimey, mate, not half bad, that. What's that make it? One down and how many to go?"

"Three. Hungary, Yugoslavia, and Greece." I ticked off the names. He knew very well how many borders we had to pass.

"Hope they're all that easy," Louisa said softly, her face turned toward the rain.

Czechoslovakia, like the rest of east Europe, was plagued by chronic electricity shortages. However, there seemed to be plenty of power to keep the lights on at the borders. It was as if the Commies were saying this: *Even if you have to live your lives in the dark and move at half speed, we are going to make absolutely certain you never get out.*

The roadway changed from the smooth, nicely paved autobahn to a two-lane road with ragged edges and many potholes. The westbound lane had clumps of thick grass growing out of the cracks, a telling testament to its disuse. Once we were a few kilometers away from the clear-cut area around the border, a thick forest grew almost to the edge of the broken blacktop. We were frequently obliged to slow down behind horse-drawn farm wagons, old farmers on bicycles, and the ubiquitous *Trabbies* trailing their telltale plumes of black smoke, waiting for an opportunity to pass. With the border and West Germany receding far behind us, we were interlopers in a medieval world. The steady hum of the Mercedes and the swish of the windshield wipers sounded out of place next to the sounds of horse hooves clopping and steel wheels scraping against cobblestones. Our headlights shone too brightly into the fading day.

Two hours later, we descended into a canyon at the bottom of which lay Karlovy Vary. Soon we located a hotel near the center of town. The concierge, a large, middle-aged woman in a black dress and steel-rimmed glasses, dutifully wrote down our names, passport numbers, and auto registration information in a ledger so wide that everything fit on one line.

"Do you speak English?" I asked.

"*Na.*" She shook her head.

"German? Deutsche?"

Again she shook her head. "*Kein Deutsch,*" she muttered.

"Guess that answers that," I said.

The concierge held up three fingers. I nodded and drew a circle in the air and held up a single finger. One room would be enough until we exchanged money. I forgot about the few koruny I had. The woman resumed writing in her ledger.

"Should make it a point to spend only one night in any one hotel," Lou suggested. "Might make it harder for anyone trying to track us."

"You're going to turn us into vagabonds yet," Simon said.

"Won't be hard with what I've got to work with," Louisa fired back, a grin in the sound of her voice as well as on her lips.

Since we hadn't yet had a chance to exchange any dollars for Czech koruny, we had to pay for our room at the official exchange rate, in West German marks. I laid a selection of paper money on the counter. The concierge selected several bills and pushed the remainder back toward me. I calculated we were paying about fifteen dollars for the night.

"We need to find a moneychanger as soon as possible," I said.

"Do you really think that's smart?" Lou asked. "Changing money like that? We're not just tourists here, you know. Don't know if you want to tempt fate that way."

"It's a tough call. I wonder about it myself. Like Johann painting apartments. Does he suddenly start turning up at work and risk getting noticed for doing his job right or keep dodging? Which arouses less suspicion?"

"You've got a point, mate," Simon said. "It's your show—you decide."

"My show? I thought we were in this together."

Our room was furnished with three narrow beds, not much wider than cots, and a single table that had a mosaic of cigarette burns. In one corner was a water stained sink with a single dripping faucet. Next to that was a towel bar with three tiny towels. The room had a musty smell to it. Lou tried to open the window but too many coats of paint and too many years of disuse had sealed it shut forever.

"I like your idea of only staying one night in each hotel," I said. "They can't all be as bleak as this one."

Later that night, as we walked back to the hotel, a stocky man wearing a black leather sports jacket, white shirt, and skinny tie approached us. Almost in a whisper, he asked, "Czech crowns? I give ten to one, dollars."

"*Deutsche* mark?" I asked.

"*Deutsche* mark three to one."

I glanced around to make sure we were alone on the dark street.

"*Zweihundert* mark." I handed him two one hundred mark notes. He counted out six hundred crowns and stuffed the West German cash into his pocket. The entire exchange had taken less than twenty seconds and he was gone, invisible in the night.

The communist countries were so desperate for hard, western currency, that black market money changing was largely ignored. Illegal, but tolerated, like so many of the laws in the States which are not enforced but still on the books, waiting for some rare occasion, some obscure need, to be dredged up by some cop.

"It's bloody amazing how much more money you get under the table," Simon said. "What do you figure? Three, four times the official rate?"

"Something like that. I know it freaked Mara out when we were here last year. She was positive we'd get caught."

"You gave him, what, two hundred marks? What did you get?"

"Six hundred crowns."

"Should be enough for the rest of the time we are in Czechoslovakia," Simon said.

"I'm sure there's more where that came from, if we run out," I said.

"Still think it's pretty risky," Lou said.

"You're beginning to sound like Mara," I said.

"Mara?" Simon said. "Mara who?"

Louisa glared at him. "You know Mara who."

✦ ✦ ✦ ✦

17 July —

Karlovy Vary

* * * * * * * * * * * * * * *

A t noon, the twenty-foot tall statue of Yuri Gagarin, the first Russian cosmonaut, cast almost no shadow across the plaza in front of the mineral water baths. In spite of his stony presence, the ancient town of Karlovy Vary felt as distant from the Union of Soviet Socialist Republics as it did from the United States of America. For over five hundred years, since they were discovered in the mid-fourteenth century, the magic waters of this narrow valley had soaked royalty, serfs, fascists, communists, and capitalists. Black, brown, yellow, and white humans had made pilgrimages here in search of cures for maladies both real and imagined. I wondered idly if Yuri Gagarin had ever soaked in these baths, perhaps to sooth the cramps of being cooped up in his tiny space ship.

Simon, Louisa and I wandered around the colonnade, fascinated. The Ohře River flowed close enough for us to hear its gurgle behind the polyglot of languages surrounding us. The air smelled of sulfur and sweat. I picked up a brochure from the ground.

"Says here that Goethe, Schiller, Chopin, Beethoven, Karl Marx, and dozens of other famous people have drunk these mineral waters and soaked in these steaming baths." We were looking for only two not-so-well known people; escaped comrades Johann Klaus Volker and Liesl Schmidt, soon to be known as the Müellers.

"So, this is what they mean when they say 'taking the waters for a cure'." Simon was holding his nose.

"Been doing it for centuries," Lou said. "You're the one who likes to eat and drink. Should try some."

"Not this laddie."

"Suppose not." She grinned. "Doesn't smell much like beer."

I cupped my hands under one of the fountains and splashed some of the elixir into my mouth. "Well, I'm here to tell you it doesn't taste much like beer, either."

"Speaking of which—" Simon said.

"Speaking of which, we're here to meet Liesl and Johann," Lou said. "Time for beer later."

The waters at Karlovy Vary had been a cure for Europeans suffering their various ailments for much longer than the continent had been divided by the Iron Curtain. Anyone wishing to avail himself of the foul-tasting and foul-smelling hot water could do so in a number of ways. You could breathe the vapors by inhaling from steaming, pungent pipes sticking out of the masonry. You could fill (and refill as often as you wanted) small intricately decorated pitchers and drink the water. Called *poharek*, these were for sale in shops and kiosks all around Karlovy Vary. Louisa bought one on a string as a souvenir for her mother and hung it around her neck. We watched people dressed in suits, jeans-and-tee-shirts, skirts and blouses, caftans, robes, and about any other kind of clothing you could imagine, wander aimlessly around the pavilion with these little spouted drinkers suspended by strings and chains from their necks, sipping mineral water and stopping to top up when the pitcher was empty or the water was cold. If breathing the pungent vapors and drinking the hot mineral water was an inadequate cure for whatever ailed you, there remained one final avenue to health: You could cook yourself in large, immersion baths that sealed around your neck, sauna-like, until you were cured. Indeed, we saw several soakers, wearing only bathing suits or towels and looking like lobsters, mixed in with the drinkers and inhalers. Here and there a glistening head protruded from a steaming canister.

As we searched through the crowd, we heard fragments of many languages. A few, German, Danish, Dutch, French, Italian, we recognized. Many more, we did not, although we made some educated guesses. (Matching physiognomy with language to deduce country of origin was kind of a game; people watching taken to a higher level.)

There were all manner of people here: Some, like us, were kids living on the road, youth hostellers, passing through. Others, looking considerably more somber, appeared to take the purported medicinal potential of the water seriously and likely had made Karlovy Vary a destination in hopes of curing some health problem. Johann had told us that in Germany a doctor could advise a patient to take the waters at Carlsbad, and I wondered how many of the people we saw in this huge open-air bath house were filling such prescriptions. The cosmopolitan ambiance was well suited for the next phase of our plan. Karlovy Vary did not have the look or feel of a Communist city. It was the perfect atmosphere for a rendezvous.

There was only one problem: Liesl and Johann were nowhere to be seen.

"Any sign of them?" I asked. We were standing next to Yuri's space boots. The three of us had split up and taken different sections of the vast area to search. Although only about fifty meters wide, the colonnade was very long, paralleling the river for almost a mile through the center of town. We had scoured the entire area, combing back and forth without success.

"Not a trace," Simon said. Lou shook her head.

"Its still early, let's just keep looking," I said.

A few yards away, partially hidden by the wide columns, two men in black leather coats surveyed the scene. They were more concerned with their surroundings than each other and looked out of place among the bathers. At first, I took them to be moneychangers; they had that shifty furtiveness about them, but they were not approaching anybody. They didn't show much interest in the mineral water, which was everyone else's focus, and this lack of attention made them stand out. Neither had a *poharek* hanging around his neck or was dressed for a bath. One was tall and thin and had a pasty white complexion and wispy blond or gray hair. The other was slightly shorter, and powerfully built. The guy had a swarthy face highlighted by a thick black mustache, bushy eyebrows that almost connected above his flat nose, and matching hair. Every time I looked their way, he shifted his head. I had the creepy feeling that when I was looking anywhere else, *he* was staring at *me*. They were too far away for me to hear what language they were speaking.

"Look at those two guys," I said. "What do you make of them?"

"They look like they would do better with a spot of water," Simon said.

Lou didn't say anything.

Simon studied them a little longer. "Why do you ask? Do you recognize them?"

"Not really. I thought at first they were moneychangers."

"What makes you think they're not?"

"I don't know, really. I just haven't seen them make those kind of moves."

Simon cocked his head and grinned. "Reckon the water here is a good cure for paranoia?"

"OK, forget it." I tried to put the two guys in leather out of my mind.

The plan we'd worked out earlier in Berlin was for the five of us to meet up at this bathhouse on this day, as close to noon as possible. Johann and Liesl were to make their way down from Berlin to Dresden, and then from Dresden to Karlovy Vary. If we didn't find them, we were to come back the next day at noon, and keep returning until they appeared. None of us had been to Karlovy Vary before, though, and the Yuri Gagarin Colonnade was much larger than we'd anticipated. It would be easy to miss them.

"This is like trying to meet somebody on Sloan Square," Simon said. "And we don't even know if they're here."

"They'll be here," I said, with conviction I wished I could justify. I wondered if the pretext of Johann's mother's illness had been sufficient cause to earn them exit visas, and if so, how they would get from Berlin to here. Lots more could go wrong with their part of the plan than with than ours; we had money and freedom on our side.

Our drive in from Frankfurt the day before had been uneventful and we were right on schedule. Cruising down the autobahn in such luxury was a new way for us to travel; hitchhiking usually got us rides in Volkswagens, Fiats, Peugeots, and other 'blue-collar' cars. (Once Mara and I had been picked up in Hannover by some Russians in a Volga and been dropped off, drunk on Vodka, in front of the American Embassy in Bonn. Why the driver thought we needed an embassy more than a youth hostel, I couldn't figure out.) Seldom, however, did a Mercedes stop for us.

We hadn't stopped for any hitchhikers on our way in. We most likely would have picked people up if we hadn't been involved with this bizarre escape plan. One of the rules of the road was that if your circumstances changed, if you somehow had the wherewithal to have your own car, you were obligated to remember those still on foot. But then again, if we weren't helping Johann and Liesl leave East Berlin, we would not have been in a Mercedes Benz 280SE in the first place.

As the afternoon dragged on, we separated and regrouped without success. Johann and Liesl were not in Karlovy Vary.

"Look, mates, its about three-thirty. What say we go find some place to get a meal?"

Reluctantly, I agreed. We drifted away from the bathhouse plaza in search of a restaurant. Down one of the side alleys, we found a tiny café with three outside tables.

"Sit outside," Louisa said, "on the off chance—"

"I'll go order." I went inside and found the waitress. There were several diners, mostly working-class types. One guy was tucking into a big plate of boiled potatoes and slices of roasted meat. I pointed at his plate, held up three fingers, and pointed to the outside table.

"*Da*," said the waitress. "*Pivo?*"

I nodded and again held up three fingers. Soon the waitress appeared with three tall glasses of beer, and shortly thereafter three plates of food.

"What do you reckon happened?" Simon asked, his mouth full of potatoes and gravy.

"I don't know," I answered. "Maybe they got stopped at the border. Maybe the *Stasi* revoked their travel visas. Maybe they got cold feet. Who knows?"

"We come back tomorrow, right?" Lou said. "Stick with the plan we made."

We didn't talk much as we returned to our hotel room, forgetting that we were going to stay each night in a different place. This was to have been the big day, the day Johann and Liesl should have been in town. They hadn't shown up, and I was worried. I lay awake in my bed wondering what could have gone wrong. Deep into the night, I heard a match strike and turned over to see Simon's shadowed profile, his face barely illuminated by a glowing Player's Navy Cut sticking straight up.

✦✦✦✦

18 July —

Karlovy Vary

L ook! Over there!" Lou grabbed my arm and pointed across the plaza. Sure enough, Johann and Liesl were standing at a stoplight waiting to cross. The light changed from red to green and we met them in the middle of the intersection. I shook Johann's hand and then gave Liesl a big hug. She embraced me back, strongly, and then pulled away to look at me with clear, grey/blue eyes.

"Where is Mara?" she asked. I thought I heard Lou snicker, but it could have been some street noise. It was late in the afternoon and we were in the midst of what must have been end-of-the-day commuter traffic. For a second day, we thought we'd searched in vain; by late afternoon, we had almost given up on meeting Johann and Liesl.

"I'm not exactly sure," I answered. "I believe she is going to meet us in Greece."

"Need to get out of the street," Lou said, taking Liesl's hand.

"How was the trip down?" I asked.

"It was, how do you say it, with a chance," Johann said.

"Chancy," Simon said. "Or dicey."

Honking horns alerted us to the traffic light change and we ran to the sidewalk. If we wanted to be inconspicuous, if our intention was to cross unobtrusively over several international borders, we were making a piss-poor beginning. A policeman shouted something at us that I didn't understand and I thought I saw someone taking a photograph in our direction. I just smiled and shrugged and we hurried to lose ourselves in the crowd.

"*Ya*, chancy. Leaving from East Berlin into East Germany was the most difficult. The *Vopos* in Berlin keep us waiting for greater time than one hour. They telephone the *Stasi*. They did not do the same for every person, just for some. But we had the correct papers from the internal visa office, the proper exit visas to make this travel to Dresden. At the end, they permitted us to depart."

"How did you get from Berlin to Dresden?" Louisa asked. That part of the plan had not been worked out in advance.

"Liesl she have a friend who make deliveries in this region. He did carry us to Dresden in his truck."

"I did not want to ask him this favor," Liesl said. "I was afraid for him for what might happen if it is discovered he help us escape."

"But we did not tell him we are flying to the west," Johann said. "Only that we were visiting my mother in Dresden. Perhaps he was suspecting, but we did not tell him this."

"*Und deine Mutter?*" Lou asked.

Johann paused, looking first out the window and then down at the unlit cigarette in his hand. Finally, he spoke. "My mother she is very old. She is not well since my father died in the war. The bombing of the city killed my father and my mother say many times it will be better for her to die the same."

Lou handed Johann a book of matches, which brought only a faint smile to his lips.

"What is Dresden like?" I asked. I wanted to take his mind away from the death of his father, but asking about Dresden was likely the wrong tack to take. "Is it anything like Berlin?"

"No, not like Berlin. Dresden was not much important in the war like Berlin. It was once a fantastic beautiful city with many gardens and old palaces. Much famous pieces of art did stay in Dresden in museums. Beautiful old churches. No warplanes or tanks or bombs were made there; Krupp had not a factory in Dresden. But the firebombing in 1945 have killed greater than 135,000 people."

"Bloody hell," Simon said. "That's more than you Yanks killed in Hiroshima or Nagasaki with your damned A-bomb."

"Can't be true," Lou said.

"It bloody well is true," Simon replied. "Seventy-two thousand in Hiroshima and more than that in Nagasaki."

"So, you're a military historian in addition to everything else?" I said.

"Rubbish, mate. One shouldn't have to be a military historian to know how many people have been incinerated by atomic bombs."

"The bombing of Dresden had not military importance," Johann continued. "I believe it was coming from Winston Churchill as, how do you say it … *sich rächen.*"

"To revenge," Lou translated.

"Yes. To revenge Hitler for the Blitzkrieg of London. One very famous old church, *Frauenkirch*, remains yet now only a big pile of rocks."

"The Blitzkrieg was terrible, from what they say. I'm glad my family lived in Liverpool."

"And what thing is the most wrong?" Up to now, Liesl had been following the conversation without comment. "More people have died in Dresden from the old bombs but the Atomic bomb must be very much bad. In school, we have seen photographs of people with eyes melted."

"Well, I've seen pictures of London in 1943 and it wasn't pretty, either," Simon said.

"And, so, your mother?" I asked. I had to put it to rest, once and for all.

"It is better she stay in Dresden. When she will die, she want to be buried by my father. For her, the waters of Carlsbad can do no good."

We were all silent for a while, letting the enormity of the situation sink in. If we were successful in reaching Greece, Johann would never see his mother again, at least until the Iron Curtain rusted away and east and west Europe were reunited. And that, we all knew, would never happen.

The original plan was to bring her to this ancient resort town for the waters, at least that was the pretext by which Joann and Liesl had obtained their exit visas from East Berlin. Maybe Johann had known all along that his final goodbye to his mother would take place in Dresden rather than Karlovy Vary, but as blunt and forward as I was, that I couldn't bring myself to ask. I thought of my own mother, and my father, and my tangled relationships with them, and I wondered if it was the same all over the world. How had Johann come to be living in Berlin, anyway, when his mother was old and ill in Dresden? Had Liesl been the only reason he stayed in Berlin? And what of Liesl? She'd told us nothing of her family other than that her parents had been murdered by the Nazis.

And what had all our parents been doing twenty years ago, during the war? Only two decades earlier, this part of the world had been the epicenter of the Second World War. Simon's, Mara's and my parents were on one side, Johann's on the other. Liesl's mother and father had died in Hitler's death camp at Flossenbuerg. That we three were even in Germany at all was a little strange, when you stopped to think about it. How long would it be before Americans strolled the streets of Hanoi? The idea was inconceivable, just as it must have been impossible for a U.S. Army GI in 1943 to imagine American tourists shopping along the Kurfürstendamm. And who could possibly have imagined a three-meter high concrete wall dividing Berlin?

So now we were risking our lives to help two German teenagers escape, one of whose fathers might very well have been shooting at one of our fathers about the time we were all born. How Louisa, a German/American émigré, fit into this odd social equation was anybody's guess. I still knew very little about her. Had her father made his fortune *before* or *after* the war? Or *during*? Maybe he had been a part of the German war machine or a member of the Third Reich. Or worse, maybe he had been in the military. Would he have helped us if he knew Liesl was Jewish and had been made an orphan by the Nazis at Flossenbuerg? On the other hand, maybe Louisa had told him Liesl's story and that was why he had given her the money. Maybe someday I'd know Lou well enough to seek some answers.

Part of the code of the time was that you didn't pry into someone else's family history beneath what they were willing to reveal. Everybody had a past. It was prudent to remember that nobody was responsible for the acts of their parents. Some day in the future, if the five of us ended up safely in the west, we could ask each other questions. We had more immediate problems to deal with.

"Coming here to Carlsbad from Dresden was not so difficult." Johann broke the silence. "We passed through quickly. Maybe they did not know from the visa office in Berlin we are bringing my mother here. It did not say such on our passports, and so there was no suspicion put upon us at the border."

"We have take the autobus," Liesl said. "It is not good to stand by the road and ask for a ride from strangers. How you say it, Louisa, *trampen....*"

"Hitchhike," Lou said.

"Or thumb a ride." I stuck out my thumb in the universal gesture of those on foot seeking help from those with wheels.

"Where is this, this Mercedes?" Johann asked.

"Just up the street." I tilted my head. "We can walk; we don't need to *trampen.*"

To say that Johann and Liesl were impressed with the Mercedes Benz would be an understatement. Their motoring experience was likely limited to the stinking little Trabants, which were the pride of the *Deutsche Demokratische Republik,* if not the East Germans themselves. For a society that prided itself on engineering triumphs and technological achievements, and whose coins and flag were embossed with a hammer and compass, the fiberglass *Trabbie* had to be a national embarrassment.

"From where did you get this fine car?" Johann asked.

"We rented it in Frankfurt," Lou said.

"I cannot believe it. We must wait for months or even years to have a Trabant. And even a new *Trabbie* is not grand like this."

"Think upon your friend Gunter." Liesl had apparently decided that conversation, at least when the five of us were together, would be in English, even when she was speaking directly to Johann. This had the effect of binding our little family more tightly together, and at the same time it reinforced our 'us' versus 'them' mentality.

Johann laughed. "Ah, yes, Gunter. He is having one Trabant sometimes working and another he keep for the parts!"

"Gunter is having luck to have two Trabants. He have to wait many years for one more," Liesl said.

"It takes that long to get a new car?" I asked.

Johann laughed. "It is almost a, what can man say, a humor for us. The wait is quite long. We say that if you have a baby, you must the same day the baby is born order a new Trabant and perhaps it will arrive when the child is old enough to drive!"

"Amazing," I said. "In America, you go to a car dealership and pick out the one you like. They have many so you can choose what color it is, what size engine it has, and so on. If they don't have exactly what you want, you go somewhere else."

"And the cost?" Johann asked. "You must pay much for a new auto?"

"Well, every car has the official price written in the window. If you don't like that price, you offer another amount you would be willing to pay. If you cannot agree with the dealer, you simply go to another one."

"Fantastic!" Johann said. "Here, they tell you 'this is your car.' If you don't like the color, you may decline but then you must wait many years for another chance."

I doubted if either Johann or Liesl had seen anything as fancy as the white 280SE we were all sitting in now. I pressed the buttons to open the electric windows and sunroof. Sunlight and fresh air flooded into the car, carrying a hint of the malodorous mineral baths nearby.

"Let me see your passports. You won't need them anymore." I looked up and down the street and then I took the envelope out from under the carpeting and handed it to Johann and Liesl. "*Achtung! Achtung!* You are now Liesl and Johann Müeller."

They opened their new West German passports to the photo pages. They stared at the pictures I'd taken just a few weeks before, which were now affixed to what appeared to be genuine *Bundesrepublik* passports. Liesl's eyes began to glisten. If I'd handed them bars of pure gold, I don't think they could have been more moved. I slid their East

German passports under the carpet where the counterfeits had been hidden.

"*Meine Güte.*" Liesl now had tears running down her face. "Until this moment, I must not believe such thing can happen."

Johann was silent. Lou smiled. Simon looked embarrassed and stared out the window. I felt giddy. Liesl made no effort to stop crying and Lou rummaged in her backpack for a box of tissues. Johann just stared at his new passport and shook his head.

Finally, Liesl spoke. "I could not think such a thing is possible. These passports are looking so real. Tell me again one time how you did get them."

Simon passed around his pack of expensive English cigarettes. Johann took one, but Liesl shook her head; she was too engrossed in my answer.

I related the story of my trip to Copenhagen, my meeting with Lars and then my going to the seedy building on Christianshavn. I described the counterfeiter as best I could, and pointed out how he had been careful to not let me see his face. I tried to leave out the part about the five hundred dollars, but Liesl insisted on knowing how much the passports had cost.

"It is so much money, what you have paid," she said, once she'd done the calculations from American dollars to East German marks. "How can we pay this money?" There were still tears on her cheeks, in spite of the Kleenex. Her fingers were white from clutching her new passport.

"We don't have to worry about that now," I said. "Lou's father has lots of money and he was happy to help us do this. He sent enough cash with her for us to rent this car, too."

"You must remember, my mother and father come from München and I was born there, too. My father does not like the East German government."

"And he was not worried about you doing this thing for us?" Johann asked.

"Of course he was worried, but the chance to help someone escape from the DDR was too great for him to ignore. Besides, he knows me well enough to know I would have done it anyway, whether he sent the money or not. I am his daughter, after all, and he did leave Germany. So, he just made it easier and perhaps safer as well."

"You must tell your father how thankful we are for his money to help us." Johann pointedly avoided asking the obvious question: *Where was he and what was he doing twenty years ago?*

"Yes, but maybe someday you can tell him yourself," Lou answered.

That comment quieted us right down. Up to that point, we hadn't discussed what would happen after we were safely out of east Europe. I hadn't given much thought about what our plans might be once we arrived in Greece, assuming we got that far. In fact, up to that moment, I'd never really considered the possibility that we might get caught, either. Being arrested, spending my life in prison, or even getting shot were outcomes I connected in my mind with Mara, whom I was trying not to think about. Furthermore, it seemed to me that if I had let myself dwell on failure, we wouldn't have even started. The planning of this escape had extended only to the Greek border, so neither eventuality had concerned me much. Sneaking Liesl and Johann out of East Berlin had been my sole focus. Now that we were actually doing what we had only talked about before, I realized that we would, sooner or later, have to confront the future. Whichever future it turned out to be.

For the present, however, I was preoccupied, suspicious of everyone and everything. Every soldier walking down the street with a gun, and there were plenty of them, was poised to arrest us. Every tourist with a camera was a secret agent of the DDR following us. Every whispering moneychanger was an undercover cop whose assignment was to entrap us. Navigating through this army of enemies was enough; I certainly hadn't given any thought to what might happen once we got to Greece.

Maybe Mara was the smart one, after all. It was the first time all day I had thought about her. Where was she at that moment? I could only speculate. If she were planning to meet us, she would have be somewhere in northern Italy. That was a big 'if'. I was glad she wasn't with us, but I was starting to miss her. Just a little.

"Right, then," said Simon. "What do you say we have a beer and something to eat? It's a bit past lunchtime, don't you think?"

"More than a bit, I'd say," I said. "We might as well call it dinner at this point."

"Call it whatever you bloody well want as long as it's a meal of some variety or another."

Lou helped Liesl recompose herself and then we got out of the car and went in search of a café or pub: Johann and Liesl Müeller, in possession of their new West German passports, Simon, Louisa, and I.

Our meal was watery soup made of beets, cabbage, and potatoes, only marginally nudged toward flavor by the addition of salt and pepper. We sopped it up with slabs of thick dark bread and washed the whole thing down with beer. Like many meals we'd had, what was lacking in quality and flavor was compensated by abundance. Even Simon didn't leave the table hungry. I didn't care for the beer and was reminded of the tasteless ale we had had on our first visit to East Berlin.

"It's pilsner, mate," Simon said. "It's supposed to be light. Look at the map and you'll see how close we are to Pilsen."

"Well, I've enjoyed as much as I can stand. It's getting late. Let's find a place to spend the night. I'd like to get an early start in the morning."

I decided to leave the car where it was since the side streets were too narrow to park. We'd seen enough soldiers and police patrolling the place that I wasn't worried about anybody breaking into it or stealing it. It didn't occur to me to remove the old DDR passports hidden under the carpet.

We walked through the colonnade to the other side of town and on a little side street we found a rooming house of sorts. Johann and Liesl waited outside and down the block a few meters while Simon, Lou, and I went in to register. I sensed that the 'Müellers' didn't quite trust that their new documents would survive the scrutiny of a hotel clerk. I handed the desk clerk all five passports.

"*Máte pit pasù.*" The clerk looked at the photos in the passports, and then at us. "*Jste jenom tøi. Kde jsou tí ostatní, tí Muellerovci?*" He held up the West German passports.

Shit, I thought, just what we need, a fucking Commie hero. The only word I recognized was 'Müellers'.

Somehow, Lou understood the question; the desk clerk wanted to know why there were five passports and only three of us.

"They are in the baths, *die baden,*" Lou pointed in the general direction of the colonnade. "We are here to take the waters." She held her recently purchased tiny blue porcelain *poharek* up to her lips and mimed drinking.

The clerk seemed satisfied with that explanation and continued filling out the register. I mouthed a silent 'thank you' to Lou, who smiled back.

"*Kolik izeb chcete?*" The clerk looked up from his paperwork.

I didn't understand what he was saying so I looked at Lou and Simon and shrugged my shoulders. They both looked back at me blankly.

The desk clerk stood up, allowing his ancient wooden chair to emit a series of squeaks and groans, and laid several keys on the counter. He shrugged his shoulders and began counting with his fingers.

"Oh," I said. "He wants to know how many rooms we need."

Lou looked at me with a faint smile at the edges of her mouth—not quite enough to make dimples—and held up three fingers to the clerk.

I felt myself blushing slightly, sure that Simon, who didn't miss much in such matters, had caught the small vignette.

When the whole procedure was finished, I handed the desk clerk the equivalent of about ten American dollars in Czech crowns, and was amazed when he gave me some change along with three keys.

We walked outside and retrieved the Müellers from down the street.

"Everything went fine. *Alles ist gut.*" I was fracturing their language, but so what? At least I was making the effort.

"You say in America, 'super duper', ya?" Johann said.

"Ya, super duper," I grinned. "I think we should go to bed now so we can get an early start in the morning."

Once upstairs, we found we had three adjacent rooms each with two beds. At the end of the hall, next to the third room, was a communal shower room, and beyond that, its doorway facing the hall, was a tiny closet with a single toilet. A rusty chain hung from the overhead tank. I gave a key to Johann and Liesl, who quickly disappeared into the first room. I heard a click as they locked the door from the inside. I offered the second key to Lou, but Simon snatched it out of my hand.

"Do you mind awfully? I rather fancy a night alone, mate. Could you two share a room tonight?"

I flustered and fumbled; Mara would never approve of this arrangement. "Well, sure. If it's OK with you, Lou. There are two beds—"

"Of course it's OK with me." There was no mistaking the upturned corners of her mouth now; she was in full-dimple mode.

Simon went into the middle room and closed the door with a definitive clunk. Lou unlocked the third door and I carried our backpacks in and dumped one on each bed.

"Think I'm going to wash up before I turn in." Lou unpacked her dop kit, took a towel and washcloth from the bedside table and walked down the hall barefoot. As I watched the sway of her hips in her loose shorts, I remembered a phrase my father had once used to describe a waitress in a drive-in restaurant he found attractive. She had 'a well-turned ankle'. I had not thought of that term for years and I felt myself thickening.

I took my shirt off, rolled a halfway decent Drum, and opened the map to refamiliarize myself with the next leg of our journey. From somewhere, I thought I heard the faint sound of a woman's voice. Pilsen was the next big city, and after that Bratislava, which would be a good day's drive on the back roads. The cigarette smoke drifted out the window into the muggy evening air. An occasional breeze reversed the current, bringing in a vaguely sulphurous odor from the mineral baths a few blocks away. Not sweet but also not unpleasant.

Through the thin wall, I could hear humming mixed in with the sound of the water. I tried to concentrate on the roadmap and calculate the kilometers. After a few minutes, the water stopped. Lou was definitely humming or singing. I folded the map to the appropriate section for the upcoming day, quickly finished undressing and climbed into bed.

Lou opened the door and came in carrying her clothes and wearing only the bath towel wrapped around her. Water dripped onto her shoulders. A little rivulet disappeared between her breasts into the thin cloth.

"Mind if I use the other towel?"

"No, go ahead. I'll shower in the morning."

As she began drying her long blonde hair, the towel she was wearing hiked up exposing the bottom of her firm buttocks. Lou bent over to pull back the covers of her bed, and I tried, unsuccessfully, to turn my head away. The map slipped into the narrow crack between the two beds.

"If you're done reading, I'll turn the light out." Lou's bare feet made faint squishy noises as she walked over to the light switch by the door.

"Don't worry about it; it's on a timer and it'll go off by itself in a minute."

The words were no sooner out of my mouth when the single overhead bulb clicked off. The only illumination came from the full moon outside. I watched Lou carefully drape both towels over the two chairs and scoot them next to the open window and then pad naked back across the room to our beds. She turned toward me and shook her head playfully, splattering me with water. I could see a few droplets of moisture in her thick golden triangle, sparkling in the moonlight.

"*Gute Nacht,*" she said quietly before turning her back to me and lying down in her bed.

"*Schlaf gut,*" I answered. The last thing I remember wondering before I drifted off was if I would be able to sleep at all, as aroused as I was.

I awoke in the middle of the night. A soft breeze had joined the light coming through the window, billowing the curtains. Still in a slumber, I felt myself rolling to the middle of the mattress where I collided with a naked body. Was this really happening or was I in the middle of a very pleasant erotic dream? I started to say something and felt fingertips brush my lips.

"Shhh...." Lou was lying on her side with her head on my chest, her still-damp hair across my face. The sweet scent of shampoo filled my nostrils. Her uphill leg was draped casually across my thighs. Her soft breathing gradually became heavier and heavier, and eventually she was in a deep sleep.

Lou's fingers slid off my chin and her hand came to rest on my chest. I wasn't dreaming; she was in my bed, cuddled up with me, completely unaware that I had turned our sheet into an ersatz tent. I had an overwhelming urge to roll on top, slide myself into her, and smother her face with kisses. Where was Mara? In Italy, en route to Greece? Back in Amsterdam on to some gloomy new adventure with someone else? Wherever her physical location was at that moment, I felt a million miles away from her in my heart.

I moved my hand down Lou's body, past the dip of her belly button, until I felt her damp, velvet crotch.

Lou covered the back of my hand with hers, pressing it against her, neither letting me withdraw it nor move it further. I stilled my trapped fingers. Her breathing didn't change.

I woke up about seven o'clock in the morning, alone in my bed. Louisa was already up and dressed, brushing her hair.

"About time you woke up, you slug-a-bed."

I rubbed my eyes and squinted at the bright sunlight flooding into the room.

"Lou, about last night—"

But Louisa was already out the door with her toothbrush and toothpaste in her hand. She'd made no mention at all of the previous night. I was certain now that it had all been a dream, a wonderful, erotic fantasy. I looked at her bed, which was not badly ruffled up but also not unmade. I must have been missing Mara, or at least missing sex, more than I realized. That had to be the explanation: I was fantasizing that Liesl was flirting with me, dreaming of making love to Lou, all because my nineteen-year-old libido was running wild. It was time to get hold of myself, leave lala land and get back to reality.

And then, there on my pillow, I saw a single, long strand of the most golden hair I had ever seen.

--*-*

19 July —

On the Road to Bratislava

✦✦✦✦✦✦✦✦✦✦✦✦✦

We left Karlovy Vary about nine o'clock in the morning, after a simple breakfast of coffee and rolls. Simon grumbled some, but I wanted to get on the road. Although we could make a plausible case that were just 'students on holiday' and had no real proof that we were being followed, there would still be less danger if we kept moving rather than hung around in one place too long. As we headed south out of town toward Pilsen, I noticed a long, black car, probably a Tatra or a Skoda, behind us. Like our Mercedes, it stood out in the traffic of smaller Trabants and Fiats and a few VWs. I pointed out the black sedan to Johann, who was riding right behind me.

"I can tell you that the Communist Party people do not travel in *Trabbies*." Johann squinted into the rear view mirror.

"Maybe I'm just being paranoid, but I'm sure that car is following us."

In the rearview mirror, I could see Liesl slumped down against Louisa in her seat, her eyes already a little shiny. Simon jabbed me sharply in the ribs.

"On second thought, they're probably just tourists or businessmen." I made a mental note to keep my eyes open.

Johann and Liesl were very nervous about their new identities and didn't want to risk exposure in a large city where they believed the police might be better trained and their new West German passports more carefully inspected. We chose to take the southern route along narrow back roads through Czechoslovakia, avoiding Prague altogether. Our Mercedes did not blend in as well with farm wagons and bicycles as it might have with Skodas and Ladas and even Trabants on the main highway, however.

"It bothers me," I said, "that this part of our plan seems to be so disorganized. Too haphazard."

"Think it's actually a plus," Lou said. "If we don't know what we are doing, where exactly we are going, harder for anyone to follow us."

It does make it much more interesting if we don't know where we're going or what we're doing, I thought to myself, remembering the previous night.

"If they care in the first place," Simon said.

"I'm sure they care," I said. "Remember that museum? People have been shot for trying to do what we're doing. I just wish we had more of a plan."

"Safer having loose plans," Lou said. Maybe she was right. I was beginning to trust her judgment more, even though I felt I understood her less. Especially after that golden hair on the pillow.

The bogus passports had passed their first test. The concierge had given all five documents a perfunctory glance and then matched three of them to our faces. The photographs on the visas were more important than the passports themselves. Liesl and Johann resembled their passport photos closely; their photos had been the most recently taken. I probably looked the most different. I'd grown a beard and my hair was much longer since I'd left California. At least my visa pictures reflected how I now looked. If the innkeeper found anything odd about two Americans, an Englishman, and two Germans traveling together, he didn't indicate it. He seemed more interested in the Czech visas than in the passports themselves. Potentially, this could have been a glitch in our escape plan: While the German passports looked authentic enough, and we all had the correct visas for travel *through* Czechoslovakia, only Lou, Simon, and I had actual *entrance dates* stamped in next to the visas themselves. Johann and Liesl had crossed the border from Dresden still using their old, East German passports, and consequently didn't have entrance dates in their new West German passports. Technically, as the Müellers, they were in Czechoslovakia illegally; Johann Klaus Volker and Liesl Schmidt's names would never again be entered on a hotel guest ledger.

The desk clerk's concern, if he had any, had dissipated when Lou made it clear that we were paying in American dollars, hard, western currency. The concierge dutifully wrote down our names, nationalities, and passport numbers in his ledger, preceded by the date, as required by law. He never did actually see Johann and Liesl in person.

Travel behind the iron curtain was carefully monitored. Innkeepers at every level, from youth hostels to the grandest hotels, were required to keep a log of all overnight guests, particularly those from the west. This ledger had to be available for on-the-spot inspection by the police, immigration authorities, and, presumably any other law enforcement agencies that might have a reason to look. Periodically, the whole guest register was submitted to the central state police. This system made it possible for the state police apparatus to determine the exact whereabouts within their borders of any foreign traveler at any time. At least, in terms of where he spent the night. Although the details varied from country to country, every Communist regime had such a registration system.

I looked over the bald head of the concierge at the page in the ledger. The well-worn collar of his black suit was dusted with dandruff from the fringe of dark hair above his neck. The first date on the ledger was 1 July, 1966. Our names were toward the bottom of the sheet. All the handwriting was similar, written by the same person. This timeworn pension was a one-man operation.

I didn't see any turned pages, which would have implied entries made before the first of July. Could it be that here the register was turned over to the police on a monthly basis? And how often was the paperwork from the border sent in? If all the records were tallied up monthly, then we had at least a two week head start before some overzealous bureaucrat in Prague put two and two together and discovered that a West German couple, Johann and Liesl Müeller, had spent the night in Karlovy Vary but had no entrance stamps from Cheb and therefore couldn't have legally entered the country in the first place. Maybe I was being overly suspicious, but after all that I had already heard and seen of how the authorities in east Europe operated, I didn't think we could be too careful. Our miserable experience with Blondie and the *Vopos* at Checkpoint Charlie was still fresh in my mind. I'd read Franz Kafka and Albert Camus at an impressionable age and I felt as threatened by bureaucrats with files as I did by soldiers with Kalashnikovs. If all went according to plan, we would be in Greece by the first of August. Maybe Mara would be there to greet me, tan and happy, and all would be right with our world. I forced a smile to my lips.

"There are two possibilities for those selected to be *Volkspolizei* or border guards," Johann said. The countryside of southwest Czechoslovakia was a beautiful landscape of rolling hills and forests. I'd asked him how it was that the *Vopos* didn't try to escape.

"A few of them, maybe like the fat one with the yellow hair who searched you, are true believers. She was most likely a Communist, a member of the Party. She will not want to escape as she is thinking the DDR is a fine place. She will be earning some more money and have other privileges most do not get. Perhaps extra meat. Such persons are not many. Most *Vopos* are married and have children. If they do cross over to the west, they will not see their families again. Maybe even their wives will go to prison and another family will take away their children. It is a strong binding. Very few leave a wife and child behind, even for freedom in the west. No young person who is not married can be *Vopo*."

"That would help explain why the other *Vopos* who searched us and the ones in the subway stations looked so young." I was still puzzled, though. "But why would they take such jobs, anyway?"

Johann continued to describe life behind the Iron Curtain. "There is much, how do you say it in English, *die Arbeitslosgkeit*...."

"Unemployment," Lou translated.

"And why is there so much unemployment here?" I asked.

"There must be electricity to have jobs. We have not so much electricity, as you already know, and so we are having not so much employment. The electricity comes from coal and coal comes from Slovakia." Johann grinned. "The miners do not work so hard."

East Germany, in Johann's view, was an Orwellian world of pervasive intrusion by the *Staatssicherheit* and the *Volkspolizei*. By his account, the *Deutsche Demokratische Republik* was the most repressive of the East Block countries. After having been arrested by the *Vopos* at the border, I was inclined to agree with him. Even though we were no longer in East Germany, I was still glad we'd decided to stay off the main highways as much as possible until we got to Greece: Crossing a frontier from a very repressive regime to one less so did not mean we were free.

It was particularly pleasing to Simon and Johann, who were eager to try the namesake beer from Pilsen, that we would be detouring through that city. I interpreted it as a good thing that an everyday, normal interest such as experiencing a particular beer from its source was beginning to displace our all-consuming obsession with police, border guards, false passports, and so on. We needed something to relieve the tension; beer was as good as anything.

"I have to piss," Simon said. "Too much coffee at breakfast."

"Or, just making room for beer when we stop to eat," Lou said.

"That, too. I'm ready for lunch. Have been since breakfast."

"Not surprising." Lou rummaged in our food basket and handed him an apple.

I pulled over to the side of the road into the first wide spot I saw. We all needed a break and a chance to stretch. A black Tatra zoomed past on the two-lane road and disappeared into the distance ahead of us. Soon, we were back on the road.

Finding a restaurant was not easy. One of the idiosyncrasies of traveling in East Block countries, where the government theoretically owned everything, was an almost total lack of advertising. Why would there be a need for competitive advertising if one company, the State, owned everything? Back home, some sales pitch was always being crammed down my throat. Here, though, some direction toward a café would have been helpful. It was pleasing to drive down the road and see scenery without billboards, but when you wanted to locate a bistro or a hotel, some signage would have helped. There were always trade-offs.

Eventually, we found a small roadside café. I circled around the back and parked between a hedge and a delivery truck with two flat tires. The dining room was cool and not a well-lighted place. We chose the table furthest to the rear; I sat where I could keep an eye on the door.

Instead of bringing us menus, a young waitress brought five one-liter steins of beer. She said something in Czech, which none of us understood. I rubbed my stomach with one hand and swept my other hand around the table. Soon the girl returned with a large kettle of stew and a basket of hard, black rolls.

"Must be the luncheon special," Lou said.

"No, it's just lunch," Simon said. "Its not very special." I had to agree with him that the stew, which was more like soup, was thin, watery, and almost flavorless. I shook my hand over the pot and the waitress returned with shakers of salt and pepper, the addition of which didn't help much. I didn't care for the beer, either, although Simon and Johann thought it was fine. I couldn't relax enough to give it a fair chance.

Every once in a while, when he was complaining about something, Simon reminded me of Mara. I wondered how she was doing. Was she traveling through Italy? Would she be waiting for us in Greece? I'd made a decision to not think about her, but she kept popping into my head anyway. Maybe I missed her more than I cared to admit, even to myself. But then, there had been that mysterious night with Lou in Karlovy Vary. I wished I had saved that strand of hair; without it, what I remembered could easily have been only a dream.

It was a good thing Mara wasn't with us now; every minute we were behind the Iron Curtain, every kilometer we drove, we were in grave danger. I was constantly looking over my shoulder, checking the rear view mirror, alert to whoever might be sitting at the next table. Although we had no hard evidence that we were being followed, the mere fact of what we were doing kept me on edge.

There was one additional benefit of not having Mara along: As luxurious as the Mercedes Benz was, it wasn't a limousine and was designed for five people. If she'd been with us, we would have been unbearably cramped.

✦✦✦✦

20 July —

Bratislava

✱━✱━✱━✱━✱━✱━✱━✱━✱━✱━✱━✱━✱

The sun disappeared into a haze of smoke and pollution as we arrived in the gritty industrial city of Bratislava. After the long day of
driving narrow country lanes, we were all tired, sweaty, and hungry,
especially Simon, who could usually eat, even after finishing a meal. The
road conditions and the pace, set by the underpowered Trabants, hay
wagons, bicycles, and even a herd of goats, had reduced our average speed
to about fifty kilometers per hour. We decided to forgo finding our usual
cheap hotel in favor of something fancier. We could easily afford a posh
hotel. The black-market exchange rate being what it was, we'd paid only
about five dollars a night for our three rooms in Karlovy Vary.

The multi-storied Intercontinental Hotel overlooked a large terrace,
beyond which the Danube River flowed quietly in the moonlight. The
Intercontinental catered to western tourists with hard currency. At the
same time we were checking in, a tour bus full of Swiss and Austrians arrived. Just as we'd mingled into the crowd at Checkpoint Charlie, again
we sought safety in numbers. In the flood of travel documents, West
German marks, Swiss francs, and our American dollars crossing his desk,
the harried clerk didn't seem to notice or care that the Müeller's passports lacked the required entrance date stamps. We settled into three
adjoining rooms on the fifteenth floor.

We ate dinner on the veranda. The entire deck between the hotel
and the river was brightly lit by curved lampposts, an oddity considering
where we were. I ordered a bottle of Zubrówka to go with the beer and
the meal. Zubrówka was good, Polish potato vodka flavored with a single
blade of buffalo grass in the bottle, much smoother and more flavorful
than any vodka I'd ever tasted in the west. It didn't take long to finish
most of the bottle while we demolished a platter of braised pig's knuckles

and fried potatoes and cabbage. Several times, Liesl switched her full jigger with Johann's empty one. Johann apparently had a capacity for alcohol to rival Simon's.

A warm summer breeze blew off the Danube. Couples strolled along, arm in arm, stopping to stare out over the river. Occasionally, a black marketer paused, wanting to exchange Czech crowns for dollars or marks, and then disappeared just as silently. Several other diners appeared to be residents of the hotel; they had that unmistakable local, bland proletariat look about them.

At one long table, a noisy party of tourists toasted one another in German and Italian. More and more people emerged from the lobby and joined them, and finally the waiter added another table. Soon all the seats were occupied and latecomers had to stand on the fringes. The waitress made trip after trip from the bar with fistfuls of beer steins. The maroon carpet runway into the hotel was wet with spilled pilsner.

An old woman, stooped by age and the weight of a large tray full of flowers, made her way through the crowd selling bouquets. The atmosphere in Bratislava was even more cosmopolitan than it had been in Karlovy Vary. I ordered two more bottles of Zubrówka, adding another dollar to our tab. Our escape scheme was working so successfully, we could not help but feel relaxed.

"Hope you don't plan to drink all that tonight," Lou said.

"No, we'll take it with us. This stuff is damned good. It can't hurt to have a bottle or two in the car."

Liesl stared across the river, mesmerized by the lights of Austria, which twinkled in her large, grey eyes. The west. It must have been both excruciating and tantalizing for the Müellers, as we were training ourselves to call them, knowing that soon they might be free, that their lives behind the Iron Curtain could be ending. As we gazed across the water at those flickering lights of freedom, I watched Johann and Liesl stare into the gloom, the sparkles now in his eyes as well.

"Sometimes, people escape by swimming the Danube." Johann's soft words snapped me back to the present. "It cannot be so difficult, with a small boat, to come to Vienna. This have I heard."

The Danube River, like the Berlin subway, existed long before the division of Europe and did not respect the postwar political boundaries. It flowed slowly east from the Black Forest in West Germany through Austria and Hungary on its way to the Black Sea and therefore offered yet another avenue of escape for dissident east European refugees. Johann was transfixed by the moonlit water, flowing slowly past us from Vienna, unable to return his attention to the table. How good a swimmer would you have to be to swim upstream to the other bank?

We sat for a while, feeling the gentle wind wash over us in soft waves. From the other side of the hotel, behind the boisterous noise from the veranda, I heard a clock strike eleven sonorous notes. The busload of Swiss partiers showed no signs of slowing down.

Johann stood up unsteadily and lurched toward the railing by the edge of the terrace. The seductive flow of the Danube was only a few feet below. He stretched his arms over his head and flexed his fingers and then he slowly peeled off his light windbreaker. All of a sudden, I realized what was going through his mind. Immobilized by fear, I willed myself to stand up. My legs felt like rubber and I grasped the edge of the table.

Liesl was way ahead of me. She jumped up and ran to his side, clutching at his shirt. Whatever she whispered into his ear was inaudible to the rest of us, quiet words meant for him alone. I started to follow her, but Louisa shook her head and put her hand on my arm, holding me back. An agonizing minute passed until at last, taking him by the arm, Liesl led Johann back to our table. I took a deep breath and exhaled a sigh of relief. My trembling fingers were unable to form a cigarette. Simon lit two.

Lou leaned over and surprised me with a kiss on the cheek before she whispered, "Leave it alone, David." Her eyes were hard and flinty in the glare from the white light overhead. "You don't need to say a word."

I recalled my own nighttime departure from New York two years earlier. As the *Aqua Serene* had churned past the Statue of Liberty, the lights of New Jersey had faded into the distance, and, finally, the tall lady's glittering crown disappeared into the mist. The powerful diesel engines, rumbling below deck, had transported me through the dark water away from Amerika, (my preferred spelling), toward a world free of the draft, racial strife, conspicuous consumption and conformity and all the rest of the things I hated.

So much had changed from that night in July when I stood at the stern of that tramp steamer and all I could think of was: 'Good riddance'. Once again it was a night in July and once again I was looking over dark water lit by blinking lights and the moon. Another escape. We were sneaking through east Europe with two refugees from Berlin for whom the meaning of that tall, green lady in the harbor holding the torch would be entirely different. Would we get that far? Would Liesl and Johann, two people our own age who yearned to be free from their own oppressive society, ever land on our teeming shore?

"I don't see any guns or *Vopos* anywhere." Simon interrupted my thoughts. "Maybe swimming the river *is* easier than climbing the bloody Wall."

At the mention of the *Volkspolizei*, I thought briefly of the oddly familiar dark-skinned man with the mustache and the monobrow lurking around at the baths in Karlovy Vary and tried to remember the faces of the East Germans from Checkpoint Charlie. Nothing matched and I chalked up my suspicions to paranoia. But then, I remembered the old adage 'even paranoids have real enemies'.

"Won't have to swim or climb either," Lou said. "Less than a week, we should be in Greece."

"That is, if everything goes along like we want it to," Simon said.

"That is, if we don't have to stop and eat and drink beer too often," Lou answered, looking at Simon with that faint grin on her face. She was clearly trying to lighten the mood at our table, clouded as it was by Johann's stagger to the river and Liesl's rescue.

"Blimey, a bloke's got to eat, I reckon."

"Yes, and drink." I was lightheaded from the Zubrówka and thankful that Lou was still on her first glass.

The flower peddler stopped at our table. She looked like she might be in her seventies, or possibly even older. She wore an old, shapeless black dress, which dragged as she walked, and a faded, timeworn black shawl around her head. Only her creased white face and hands were exposed. She reminded me of the Carmelite nuns who had a convent just down the coast from my home in California.

"*Kolik kvetin by ste chteli?*" She muttered in a thick, Slavic monotone, thrusting her tray of flowers at me. She stared at me with black eyes. A photograph of this crone taken in color would look no different than one taken in black and white.

I took a Dutch guilder and a West German one-mark coin out of my pocket and put them on her tray. She said something else and I reasoned that she wanted to know how many flowers I would like. I picked up the coins and handed them to her, indicating as best I could by shaking my head and holding my palms up, that I didn't want any change. She tipped the tray and scraped it with a wrinkled hand until flowers filled all the available space on the table. A river of purple flowed over everything, filling the low-lying areas between the plates and glasses and cutlery with blossoms. What there wasn't room for on the table fell to the ground. The old woman smiled a toothless smile, dropped the mark and the guilder into some hidden pocket of her dress, and shambled off with the empty tray tucked under her arm.

At a table a few yards away sat two men who had watched me buy the flowers. One of the men stopped the old woman with a hand on her arm and asked her something in what sounded like German. She shook his hand off and muttered, "*Da, da*," and then shuffled off. My purchase had been her big sale of the night.

The perfumed sea of flowers was extravagant and Mara would have loved it. At heart, Miriam Liebowitz was a romantic, an aspect of her personality I often lost sight of when she was being negative. She loved flowers, claimed to like drawing them, smelling them, having them in her life. Maybe, I thought, I could save some of these delicate, fragrant purple blooms for her and present them to her as a bouquet when we arrived in Thessaloniki in a week or so. That was exactly the kind of gesture Mara would have loved. She'd probably know what variety they were. I missed her more than I had thought I would when we went our separate ways in Amsterdam. I wished now that I had said more than 'See you in Thessaloniki'. I wasn't even sure she'd be in Greece. Her last word to me had been 'Ciao', which could have meant either 'See you later' or 'Good bye'. The vodka and beer were outpacing the food in my system and it wasn't the first time I envied Simon's uncanny ability to think clearly and function with coordination when he was drunk.

"We must become friendly with habits from the west," Liesl said. "One mark here is much money."

"Yes." I picked up one of the purple blooms and tucked it behind her ear. "But flowers are flowers everywhere. Even here."

I was awakened from a deep, Zubrówka-soaked sleep later that night by a knocking at the door. I wrapped a sheet around myself and lurched across the room in the dark, nearly falling as I tripped over my shoes. Could the police have caught up with us already?

"Who is it?" I asked without opening the door.

"Me. Louisa. Open up."

The dim hall light silhouetted Lou as she slipped into the room past me. She was dressed in a white tube top and a pair of white Capri's I couldn't remember having seen before. How odd, I thought, that we could have traveled so far together and she could still have a brand new—to me, anyway—outfit. Her hair was pulled back into a thick ponytail.

"What's the matter? What's wrong?"

"Nothing's wrong. Beautiful night. Let's go for a walk."

"A walk?" I was still groggy, awakening slowly while I waited for the room to come into focus. I glanced over at Simon, still clothed, snoring loudly on the other bed. "OK, but I gotta get dressed." I switched on a light. My clothes were scattered around the floor where they had dropped earlier when I'd stumbled in and fallen into bed.

Lou sat in a chair and watched while I tossed the sheet back onto the mattress and wandered around the room, pulling on my Levi's and denim shirt. She neither leered at my nakedness nor averted her eyes. Lou only watched, with her head tilted just enough for her ponytail to drape over her shoulder. I stopped in front of the sink, rinsed my mouth out, and combed my fingers through my hair.

"Come on," she said.

"OK, I'm ready." I locked the door and we took the elevator to the lobby and walked out onto the veranda. Most of the crowd had disappeared. A kid in a white tee shirt was sweeping the night's debris off the edge of the cement down into the Danube.

Soon we were alone, walking along the concrete path beside the river. A narrow layer of fog had settled a few feet above the water, partially obscuring the opposite bank. Lou slipped her arm through mine. I glanced at my watch: 2:30. What the hell was she up to, anyway?

"So, where do you suppose Mara is right now?" Lou asked after a long silence.

"Mara? I have no idea. Probably still in Amsterdam. Maybe somewhere else."

Lou didn't say anything, but tilted her head and looked up at me. She wanted more of an answer than that.

"Simon said when he last saw her she was headed south."

"Where do you *want* her to be?" Lou persisted.

I thought for a while before I answered.

"I don't honestly know. Sometimes, I hope she is waiting for us in Greece. Other times, I'm not so sure. I guess I should miss her, but I don't really and she would have hated this anyway."

We strolled along quietly for a few minutes, accompanied only by the sound of the Danube. Beneath the fog, the lights from Austria bounced off the water like fireflies. Finally, out of earshot of the hotel, we stopped walking and stood looking into the glittery darkness. Lou was luminous in white in the moonlight.

"Think he would have made it?" Lou asked.

"Beats me. What do you suppose Liesl said to him, anyway?"

"Doesn't matter. Whatever she said was the right thing. He's still here. We're all still together."

"Yes," I said. "But I was glad to see him walk to the edge and think about it."

"Why's that?" The edge of Lou's hand brushed against mine on the railing.

"Well, sometimes I wonder how much of this is my own ego working overtime and how much is really for them."

"How can you ask that? Look into her eyes and see her tears."

"I know, but I'm not always sure what they mean."

Louisa whirled around in front of me. "Bullshit! You know *exactly* what those tears mean. She's in love with Johann. She's scared to death, but she would never leave him. They want this as much as you do."

I was stunned by the vehemence of her outbreak. "I know that now, or rather I *feel* that now. I wasn't so sure until tonight."

"You're so dense sometimes." Lou said gently and turned her face back to the Danube, her ponytail coming to rest in the hollow between her shoulder blades. "You don't know much about love, do you, David?"

"Sensitivity's never been my strong suit. I've never been much good at insight, either."

"Maybe this time, but don't sell yourself short. You can be plenty sensitive when you want to be."

"I just tend to put my head down and charge ahead."

"Well, raise your head up and look around you." Lou turned back and faced me.

The clouds slowly slid away and the moon etched a hole through the fog and a soft light fell across the river and then onto us. Louisa stood in front of me, her hands hanging loosely by her sides. My god, I thought, what had I gotten us into? Simon was a big boy and he could take care of himself, come what may. Johann and Liesl knew better than anyone the risks they were taking. Mara was somewhere else, far away and safe, following her own dream. Her decision to leave me and stay in the west had been a smart choice. That left Louisa, vulnerable, in need of protection and depending on me, *on me*, for safe passage through this treacherous landscape. I wrapped my arms around her, pulled her to me and kissed her on the lips. I wanted to envelop her inside me so I could in some way shield her from whatever terrors I had so foolishly led her into. For a few precious seconds, I felt her fingers pressing into my neck and the small of my back as she returned the kiss, the tip of her tongue dancing with mine. Then, just as suddenly as I had embraced her, she pulled her face away from mine and pushed me away.

"No, please don't. Not yet." Lou turned and ran back along the cement walkway toward the deserted hotel veranda, her golden ponytail bouncing from side to side.

"Lou," I called out to her, "wait—"

But she was already in the hotel and the sound of my voice, after the faintest of echoes, fell uselessly into the dark Danube River.

✸✸✸✸

21 July —

On the Road
(Czechoslovakia/Hungary)

I awakened in the morning with a throbbing headache, a dry mouth, and a queasy sense of foreboding. The Hungarian border promised to be the first real test of the Müeller's counterfeit passports. Although they looked very authentic to all of us and so far had aroused no suspicions, the fake documents would have to undergo a more rigorous inspection by Czech and Hungarian border guards. So far, the only people who had been fooled had been hotel desk clerks. The Müellers were visibly nervous; Liesl fidgeted with her Mogen David and Johann was sullen, humorless and quiet. He looked like I felt.

Simon packed two unopened bottles of Vodka that I couldn't even remember buying into the trunk with our backpacks. As far as I was concerned, I never wanted to see another bottle of Zubrówka again in this lifetime. I wondered what the word for aspirin was in Czech. In any language, for that matter. I was happy to let Louisa drive.

Sometime during the previous evening, we had revised our thinking and we now believed that travel on the main highways would be less conspicuous than on secondary roads. In fact, we'd seen very few western cars on the narrow, country lanes we'd been on so far. The details of that discussion were still fuzzy, but even in the daylight the logic seemed reasonable, so we got onto what passed for a freeway in east Europe and headed for Budapest.

An hour into our day, Lou noticed a black sedan in the rear view mirror.

"Look at that car behind us," she said. "Same one that was following us yesterday?"

"I reckon I don't know." Simon turned his head, squinting. "There are lots of those, whatever they are, here."

"I think it's a Tatra. See if you can get a license plate number."

She slowed down and the black car closed the distance between us. There were two people inside. The driver had a broad, swarthy face framed with bangs and a mustache and several days of beard stubble. He looked vaguely familiar, but I couldn't determine where, or even if, I'd seen him before. The other man looked thinner and was balding. With her attention focused on the rear view mirror, Lou nearly ran over a horse-drawn hay wagon. The road twisted through the trees and I wondered if we'd ever get a straight stretch long enough for us to pass the farmer. Finally, she floored the gas pedal and accelerated around the farmer and two decrepit, slow-moving cars packed with people. The powerful Mercedes quickly left the traffic behind.

"Did you get the number?" Lou asked. It didn't seem rational that we were being followed, since Johann and Liesl had departed the DDR with the proper documents and now were no longer traveling as East German nationals. They had left Berlin legally and wouldn't be missed, at least for a while. I made a mental note to ask Johann later if their visas had a return date.

"No front plate," Simon said. By now, the black sedan was out of sight. "Whoever they are will be stuck behind those Gypsies for a while."

Around noon, we arrived at Komarna, the border crossing into the Peoples' Republic of Hungary.

"As soon as we get through customs, I think we should find a nice flat spot off the road and pull over for a while. I feel like I'm going to puke." Even before the words left my mouth, I could hear Mara admonishing me to keep my queasiness to myself.

Since Lou was the one who officially rented the Mercedes in Frankfurt, we thought it would be best if she drove whenever we crossed a border. She handed all five passports to the uniformed man, together with her International Driver's License and the insurance certificate.

"*Vystúpte si z auta, prosím,*" the guard demanded in what sounded to me like a German dialect.

"Think he wants us all to get out of the car," Lou guessed. Johann's face was even paler than usual. Liesl was quiet and trembling. We all followed the border agent into the customs office. I struggled to suppress my nausea.

"*Kolko dní ste boli v Èeskoslovensku?*" He asked.

Although I couldn't understand exactly what he was asking, I gambled that he wanted to know how long we'd been in Czechoslovakia.

"Three days here," I said, holding up three fingers. "*Drei Tage in Czechoslovakia.*" I wanted to divert his attention away from Liesl and

Johann, toward me. "We stayed two nights in Karlovy Vary and one night in Bratislava. You have a beautiful country. *Sehr Schön*, Czechoslovakia."

The guard looked at me with an expression somewhere between quizzical and disbelieving. "*Mozno Karlové Vary. Bratislava asi nie.Vraciate sa k ludom z Èeskoslovensku?*"

I shrugged my shoulders and held my palms up.

The guard smiled, clenched his fist, stuck his thumb up, and said, "Karlovy Vary." Then he reversed his hand position, lowered his head, muttered, "Bratislava" and made a spitting sound.

"OK," I said.

"Come more Czechoslovakia?" The guard asked.

"Perhaps," I said. "You will please stamp our passports correctly so that we may come back?" I smacked my fist firmly on an imaginary ink-pad and then my passport and my throbbing head immediately regretted the sudden movement.

The guard didn't answer. One at a time, he inspected each passport, matched it to a face, located the appropriate Czech visa, and then added another imprint. Lastly, he wrote a date in each passport. Inexplicably, the official didn't comment on the absence of entrance stamps in the two Müeller passports.

"*Máte èeské koruny?*" He asked.

I understood the word 'koruny' meant crowns, Czech currency. I recalled how the *Volkspolizei* had confiscated our East German marks every time we returned to West Berlin and reached for my wallet.

"Yes," I said, nodding.

"*Nechajte si peniaze na vás návrat do Èeskoslovensku.*" With a wide smile, he pushed my wallet away and slapped our passports on the counter. "Koruny for come more Czechoslovakia!" Already a little difference, maybe a little loosening. I couldn't remember a single Volkspolizei smiling; certainly not Blondie or the *Kommandant* who'd ordered us not to return to the DDR. Nobody at Checkpoint Charlie had invited us to save our money for another visit. We got back in the car.

The guard shouted something to another soldier who raised a red and white gate and saluted us as we drove through. Just past the barricade, the road turned right for a few yards then entered the Hungarian customs area. Three or four cars back in the queue, I saw a long black sedan. Was it the same one? A stoutly built man stood outside the car and waved his arms in exasperation. Behind it were the Gypsies, waiting patiently for their turn.

Entering Hungary was effortless. I reasoned that getting *into* a country would be much easier than getting *out*. Screening tourists ahead of time was the job of the embassy or consulate that issued the tourist visa; leaving was always with the permission of the border guards.

"Well, so far, so good. You have passed inspection at two hotels and one genuine border frontier now. I think those passports are going to work just fine." I didn't mention the dark Skoda or Tatra or whatever it was that I suspected was shadowing us.

The drive from the Hungarian border toward Budapest was quiet; Liesl and Simon dozed off in the back seat while I did the same up front. My headache had faded away, but I was still drowsy and glad Lou was behind the wheel. She and Johann occasionally exchanged comments in German.

In the first real town we come to, Tatabanya, we parked by the village square and were immediately approached by a black market currency vendor. Since we weren't planning to return to Czechoslovakia, I tried to exchange what was left of our Czech money for Hungarian cash. That didn't interest him and he disappeared back into the crowd. At the southern edge of the plaza we found a bank, and next to it an alley with a farmer's market. We exchanged our remaining koruny for Hungarian forint. From the row of makeshift stalls, we purchased bread, cheese, cured meat of some kind, and several bottles of beer and juice. Within an hour, we were back on the road.

"So," I said, turning around in my seat to face Liesl, "you are a teacher?"

"Yes. I teach in the *kinderschule*. Little children. How do you say it in English?"

"Elementary school," Lou said, not taking her eyes off the road.

"Yes, that is exactly right. And did you go to university in America?"

"No," I answered. "I graduated from high school and came here, to Europe, a few days later."

"So fast." Liesl fixed a clear, gray-eyed stare at me.

"As quickly as I could. I did not even wait for the official graduation ceremony."

"You wanted so much to go out from America?" Johann joined the conversation.

"I had to leave before I turned eighteen. At eighteen, you can be drafted into the army and shipped off to Viet Nam."

"This, this draft cannot fall upon you here?" Liesl asked.

"No. Here I am safe." What irony, I thought, to think of myself as 'safer' in east Europe than in the United States.

"I am understanding better now why you want so much to escape from America," Johann said.

"Yes, probably as much as you wanted to leave Berlin."

"I do not understand." Liesl shook her head, her fingers tapping Johann's forearm. "In America, you have everything."

"Yes, we have everything. Racial inequality, a war in Viet Nam, a corrupt political system, you name it." I knew my voice sounded bitter, but, then, I *was* bitter. Why shouldn't I be?

"You also have freedom to speak against such evil things. Here we have not such freedom."

"What does it matter if speaking out doesn't change anything? Many, many people organize and demonstrate for racial justice and against the war, but it makes no difference. They still ship us off to die. Black people are still treated as second class citizens."

"It is a difference that you are permitted stand and speak against such things."

"I can't argue with you. Everything just seems so hopeless."

"You don't honestly believe that," Lou said. "If you did, we wouldn't be here doing what we are doing."

"Enough of this blather," Simon said. "Let's find a place to have our lunch."

"Good idea." I was relieved to change the subject. "I'm getting hungry myself."

"Hungry in Hungary," Lou turned toward Simon, dimples in her cheeks.

"Quite."

A light rain had begun to fall, washing the dust out of the air and leaving the pavement slick. The wipers made a muddy mess on the windshield, but somehow Lou spotted an unpaved, winding lane off the main road. We drove downhill for about a hundred meters until we came to a shallow stream. Soon all of us, except for Simon, were scrunching our toes in the cool, clear water. Simon's operating temperature was several degrees lower than any of the rest of ours, and he usually wore shoes and socks and sweaters, even when the heat of the day invited sandals and tee shirts.

I needed to cool off; the discussion in the car had upset me more than I realized.

The grassy bank was still a little damp from the warm summer rain. Leafy trees in full foliage filtered the sunlight. The smell of newly mown hay drifted over from a field across the creek. Women in dark clothing raked the hay into huge piles that were then pitch forked into long wagons by men in dark pants, white shirts, and suspenders. The sound of water splashing over rocks masked the road noise. The cold water numbed my feet, carrying away the residue of anger I'd felt a few moments before. At that particular moment, I felt much closer to paradise than to the *Deutsche Demokratische Republik*. Or to Amerika, for that matter. Why did I have to travel six thousand miles from the richest nation on earth to one of the poorest to find such peace and beauty? *Why couldn't it be like this at home?*

We lunched on the picnic food we'd purchased earlier. The delicious meat turned out to be smoked boar, which we deduced as much from the image of a laughing pig jumping over a campfire on the label as from the flavor of the sausage itself. Simon, unfazed by our partying the night before, opened several bottles of beer and passed them around. I decided to stick with water from the stream. I didn't feel like drinking anything with alcohol. I tried hard to unwind, to imagine that we were having a normal picnic somewhere else. Anywhere else.

"What is like in America?" Liesl's question surprised me because she was normally so quiet. I could tell she was listening by the surreptitious taps on Johann's wrist, but Johann did most of the talking.

"Where I come from, northern California, it is very beautiful. My town is on the coast of the Pacific Ocean. It is foggy most of the time, and in the winter, we have great storms. Many artists live there as well. In fact, the town started out as an artist colony."

At the mention of an artist's colony, Johann spoke up. "Perhaps someday we can visit there. I wish to see what American art looks like."

"I think art is the same everywhere," I said. "Some is good, some is bad. Some you like, some you don't like."

"What do it look like, your California?" Liesl asked. "Are you living near the Disneyland?"

"No, Disneyland is in the south part of California. I come from the north. The ocean is too cold for swimming. The wind twists the Cypress trees into shapes. The coast just south of Carmel is wild and not many people live there. We still have mountain lions and wild pigs. Like this." I pointed my knife at the sausage casing. "It is an untamed part of America." I did a quick mental calculation, converting miles into kilometers.

Liesl tapped Johann on the wrist, who in turn looked at Louisa.

"*Ungezähmt.*" Lou translated 'untamed' for them.

"It is about seventeen hundred kilometers from the northern border of the state to Mexico at the south end," I said.

For the next few minutes, we all sat just listening to the burble of the water, smelling the summer scent of freshly cut hay. Simon lit up a Players and passed the pack around and then lay back on the grass with his hands under his head and the cigarette sticking straight up like the smokestack on a river barge.

"Why is it your president, this Johnson, makes a war in Viet Nam?" Liesl asked.

"That's a damned good question," I answered. I couldn't think of a good answer. Wasn't that why I was here in the first place, in Europe, on the run, trying to leave as little a trail as possible? "The official reason is to stop Communism."

"Why is Johnson not stopping Communism in East Germany?"

"Bingo!" Simon neither opened his eyes nor removed his cigarette.

"I can't answer that. Lots of the people in northern California are political radicals who do not like the war in Viet Nam." I described the huge demonstrations in Golden Gate Park in San Francisco.

"It is allowed for so many thousands of citizens to march against the government?"

"Yes, of course," I answered. "We may demonstrate any way we wish."

"What means 'of course'?" Liesl asked.

I turned to Lou for help.

"You're on your own here, David. You got into this." A breath of wind fluffed Lou's hair and I thought back to the hotel room we'd shared in Karlovy Vary.

"We have such freedom in America," I said. "It is promised in our Constitution."

"I would like to go to this place, this Carmel," Liesl said. "By your words it is beautiful."

I stood up and waded back into the stream. My feet still tingled a little from the cold water the first time. I'd never thought of Carmel as particularly beautiful, and here I was, making it sound that way. Maybe it was because I'd grown up there that I had such a lousy attitude about the place. Carmel was a tourist town and thousands of visitors clogged the streets and sidewalks and beaches all summer, making it almost impossible to move around. For example, every year we had a sandcastle-building contest on the main beach that was supposed to be just a local village event. People would start forming damp sand into elaborate, if temporary works of art at dawn. Over the years, as the event became 'discovered', the crowds on the beach became swollen with out-of-towners until there was no longer enough room for the sculptures. Eventually, the Carmel Pine Cone, our local weekly newspaper, had to quit announcing the contest months in advance and we Carmelites learned the date only by word of mouth.

I dropped to my knees and splashed cold water onto my face. When that wasn't enough, I dipped my head into the shallow water until my nose bumped against the pebbly streambed.

As I'd passed through high school, I could hardly wait for the day when I would leave. I hadn't liked the town of Carmel-by-the-Sea nor the people who lived there. I felt no ties to my hometown, to California, or anywhere else in America for that matter. Now, after being gone so long, my description of where I had grown up made it sound inviting. I could see why people might want to vacation there. After nearly two years on the road in Europe, my perspective was evolving. It was odd how you could develop different ways of looking at something, change your perceptions so gradually that you were not even aware of such subtle transformations until someone or something brought them to your attention. Liesl had done that for me. Back in June of 1964, the eastern seaboard of New York disappearing in the wake of the *Aqua Serene*, my portrayal of my own home turf had been much different. 'Beautiful' would have been far down the list.

All these thoughts were sloshing around in my mind, trying to obscure the obvious irony: Here I was in Europe, avoiding the draft because I did not want to fight in a war in Southeast Asia for a corrupt government which claimed to be waging that war to fight Communism, and at the same time risking my life and the lives of two friends to help two East German dissidents escape from their own totalitarian socialist government. And furthermore, it looked like I had probably lost Mara, someone who I was sure I had been in love with.

My face was cold and my feet were completely numb and I almost lost my balance turning on the slippery rocks. At least my headache was gone.

"Have to get out of Hungary, first. And Yugoslavia," Lou said.

"We can always count on you, Lou, to bring us back to earth." I toweled off my face with my tee shirt.

"Somebody's got to do it," Lou answered.

"And you're bloody well equipped for the job."

The sun had disappeared behind the overcast sky again and the temperature had dropped several degrees, so we packed up the remains of our picnic and loaded ourselves back into the Mercedes. Since Lou had been driving all morning, I offered to take over.

Within a few minutes, tiny raindrops began to sprinkle onto the windshield. Not a heavy deluge like a winter storm, but the same light summer drizzle we'd had earlier in the day. We had timed our picnic perfectly.

Cresting a hill, we nearly ran into a large flock of sheep that was meandering around, blocking the road. Further down the hill, a shepherd urged them across the pavement, prodding their woolly backsides with a stick. As we got closer, we heard him shout at the stragglers. I slowed almost to a full stop and waited for a path to clear through the livestock. Once the flock had divided itself with most of the sheep on one side and just a half dozen or so on the other, the road looked clearer and I sped up.

"Keep a sharp look out," Simon said. "They're not half stupid."

Suddenly, without warning, one of the sheep decided that she had to recross the highway to be with her friends. She turned and ran directly in front of us. I stomped on the brakes but it was hopeless; gravity took over and our heavy sedan slid downhill on the slippery pavement. The ewe collided with the front of the car on the right side and we felt two quick bumps as the Mercedes rolled over her.

I pulled off the pavement onto the narrow dirt shoulder. We all jumped out of the car. The shepherd ran up hill toward us, screaming and waving his stick, a black and white dog yipping at his side.

The bloody carcass of the dying sheep quivered in a pool of blood. Bits of wool and a red smear on the right front corner of the car made the shattered headlight look like a gouged eye socket. King Lear in the third act.

The ewe emitted horrible retching sounds. Blood drained out of her nose and mouth and discolored the rainwater. As we stood staring, unable to conceive of any remedy, her frightened eyes glazed over, her hooves stopped scraping the wet pavement, and finally she lay still. The air stank of sheep blood.

The dog got there first, excitedly barking and running in circles around the dead sheep. I could almost feel the little shepherd's anguish; her sole purpose in life was to guard this flock and keep them from harm, and she had failed. It made no difference that the rest of the sheep were grazing safely on both sides of the road. Her duty had been to guard the entire flock, and now the blood drained out of her failure and stained her little white paws.

The sheepherder arrived at the scene, breathless from running uphill, gasping and yelling at the same time. He beat the front of the Mercedes until the staff broke off in his hands. He kicked the headlight a couple of times, knocking out the remaining bits of glass. Since he was wearing sandals, his toes began to bleed. Finally, exhausted from the exertion of running and screaming, the shepherd stopped to catch his breath. He looked grotesque, wet with sweat and rain, his wounded foot adding his own blood to the ever-enlarging pool of gory water in which he stood. Fumbling in his filthy, baggy pants, he found a pack of cigarettes and lit one. The discarded match sizzled in the pink rainwater.

Another car pulled up next to us and the driver rolled his window down to see what the commotion was all about. The shepherd, once again shouting and gesturing, explained what had happened. The driver of the other car turned around and sped off back in the direction from which we'd come.

It didn't take long for the local police to arrive. After he heard the whole story from the shepherd, whose rage hadn't subsided much in the interim, the cop with the most stripes on his sleeve turned to us and spoke in Hungarian.

"*Mi tortenik itt?*" He asked.

"*Sprechen Sie Deutsch?*" Lou asked.

"*Ich spreche Deutsch,*" A tall, skinny officer with a single stripe on his sleeve came forward and spoke with Lou. With my limited German and the bloody scene in front of us, it wasn't difficult to figure out what was being said.

"He says we killed his sheep, which was doing no one any harm. It was a valuable sheep and we must pay," Lou said.

"Tell him his sheep ran in front of our car and there was no way we could stop."

Lou translated to the cop, who translated to the shepherd. The shepherd screamed something at the cop and waved what remained of his staff at us.

"He says we were driving too fast."

"The road is slick from the rain," I said.

More translations followed.

"He wants to be compensated for his dead sheep," Lou said.

"Tell him we want to be compensated for the damage to our car."

Lou frowned and then translated to the German-speaking policeman, who translated to the shepherd.

When he heard this, the shepherd began screaming again and threw the stub of wood at the Mercedes. The cops, like cops everywhere, made it a point to stay between us.

"*Vám ellenorzés! Útlevél kontrol!*" One of the other officers held out his hand. I recognized the word 'kontrol' and deduced that he wanted to see our passports, so I gathered them up from everybody and handed them over.

While he examined them, our negotiations with the shepherd continued.

"He says he was peacefully minding his flock and we raced through and killed one."

"Lou, tell him that we were not racing. Tell him that if he had been doing his job, he would not have let the sheep cross the road."

"I don't know, David, if I want to tell him that."

"Go ahead," I said. "Tell him what I said."

When this translation was done, the shepherd became apoplectic. His face was deep red and saliva began to drip from the corners of his mouth. One of the cops spoke sharply, grabbed the shepherd's shoulders, and moved him even further away from us.

"Tell him that the sheep belong in the pasture, the car belongs on the road." I sensed that we were gaining the upper hand. I could feel anger building in my neck. My ears were getting warm. "We don't drive in the grass and the sheep can't graze on the pavement."

Lou looked at me and shook her head, but continued talking to the cop in German.

"Point out to him that the car is still on the highway. There are no tire marks in the pasture."

Lou just looked at me with an exasperated expression. She shook her head and didn't translate.

"Bloody hell, David, I reckon you're going about this all wrong. Remember who we are and what we're doing," Simon said. " For God's sake, we don't want any more problems than we already have."

Simon was right. I must have been nuts to aggravate the situation. We weren't in Kansas any more.

"Lou, forget what I said before. Tell this asshole we're sorry about his sheep and find out how much money he thinks it was worth."

More German-Hungarian-Hungarian-German-English.

"He wants about 2000 florint, which is less than twenty bucks. I think we should give it to him and get on our way. We really don't want any trouble, right?"

I took my wallet out and gave the policeman two American twenty-dollar bills. He gave one to the shepherd and put the other one in his pocket. For good measure, I handed each of the other cops a ten-dollar bill. The cash appeased the shepherd, who carefully inspected the bill and then folded it and shoved it deep into his pocket. He dragged the dead sheep carcass off the road and launched it into the pasture. By now there were several cars lined up in both directions and some of the more impatient drivers were blowing their horns.

"If we have satisfied the shepherd, perhaps we may have our passports and be going," I said to the police officer who was holding our passports. I gestured to the lined up cars. Lou translated.

The officer who spoke German said something to the other cop who'd been reading our passports. After looking at each of our faces, the other cop handed them to me. The German-speaking officer turned back to Lou and said something more. I sensed that the head policeman was annoyed that a junior officer was taking charge of the situation by virtue of his language advantage.

"*Figyelmesebben kénne vezetned és vigyáz a tehenekre és a birkákra,*" he said.

I hadn't the slightest idea what he was saying, but I assumed he was telling us to drive safely. The incident was over and that would be the logical thing for a cop to say.

"Tell him that the proper place for the sheep is in the pasture and the proper place for the car is on the road. We will not drive in the pasture and he should try to keep his sheep off the highway."

"*Danke vielmals!*" Lou thanked the officer and shook his hand.

Johann and Liesl had not uttered a single word in any language during this entire episode.

As we drove away from the bloody scene, I heard a faint scraping sound from under the car. As far as I could tell, it was coming from the front of the car where we had hit the sheep. I hoped it wasn't anything serious.

We drove about five miles through the forest deeper into Hungary, listening to the grinding noise from under the car get louder and louder. My hope that we hadn't suffered any major damage evaporated as it was obvious to me that we'd broken something.

"I think we better have a look underneath and see what's going on," I said.

At the next side road we came to, I turned off, following a rutted, dirt path deep into the woods. As I cranked the steering wheel to the right, the noise from under the front intensified to the point where we could not only hear it but feel it as well. Soon we were completely out of sight, hidden from the highway by the trees. That was fine with me; if there *was* someone following us, I didn't want anyone catching up with us with a wrecked car.

I slid under the front of the Mercedes. The noxious odor of burnt rubber assailed my nose; I could smell as well as see that something was rubbing against the tire. There was a gouge almost a quarter of an inch deep on the inside sidewall. I knew we had a spare tire in the trunk, but even if we changed tires we wouldn't make it to Greece.

"There's something hitting the inside of the tire," I reported from underneath. A bar of bent metal was jammed between the frame and the tire. Maybe, I thought, I could bend it out of the way.

"Yeow!" The steel shaft was hot to the touch. I scootched back out and stood up. "We're going to have to figure out a way to move it back away from the tire."

"I'll have a look at it myself," Simon said, inching himself under the car. "It's the fender support, mate. We'll have to get a long lever of some sort."

"A lever? Where are we going to get one?"

"Haven't a clue, mate, but that's what we must have. We're lucky the bloody tire's held up this far."

I had no idea what we were going to do. Here we were, stuck inside the People's Republic of Hungary with a broken car, two runaway East German refugees, and most likely somebody chasing us. Our collision with the sheep and the resulting damage to the car convinced me that things were rapidly falling apart around us.

"This is farm land here," Johann said. "It is possible we will find the handle from a broken tool or wagon."

"Good idea," Lou said. "Let's start hunting."

We all set off in different directions, eyes to the ground, searching for anything we could use. Simon walked back down the road toward the highway and I went ahead further into the woods. Liesl, Lou, and Johann explored the clearing. After fifteen minutes or so, we reassembled at the Mercedes. Nobody had found anything useful, but Simon was still not back. I slid back under the car and grabbed the fender support, which had cooled off, and pulled with both hands. It moved about an inch, but sprang back against the tire as soon as I let go.

"This is hopeless." I wiggled back out and stood up. "I don't know what the hell we're going to do." I reached for my tobacco and began rolling a cigarette. I made it thin, since I probably never again would I be in a place where Drum was sold. Lou and Liesl disappeared into the woods somewhere to pee.

The silence of the forest was interrupted by the sound of a car, gradually getting louder, coming from the highway. I hadn't thought things couldn't get any worse, but now whoever had been following us was coming down this deserted country lane.

"You hear that?" I said. "We'd better get ready for more trouble."

Around the last curve a dirty white car rolled into sight, followed by a second. Both cars were stuffed with people and sitting on the hood of the first one was Simon.

"Hey, mate, look who I found!" The car came to an abrupt stop and Simon slid down the hood, his butt leaving a wide swath in the damp dust. In a few moments, we were surrounded by at least a dozen shabbily dressed men and women. "It's the Gypsies we passed a while back."

"That's just great. Do any of them speak English?" I asked.

"Don't need to speak English. Just show them what's wrong. These blokes can fix anything."

I held out my hand and a large man who looked to be in his mid-twenties stepped forward with a big smile.

"Hello, my name is David."

"Drago." He stabbed himself in the chest with a tobacco-stained forefinger. "Drago," he repeated.

I winced as my fingers disappeared painfully into his huge fist. "David," I repeated and I pointed at myself with my other hand and then at my friends. "Louisa. Simon. Johann. Liesl."

I motioned him over and showed him the inside of the tire and the jagged support which had worn the deep groove in it.

Drago stood up and said something to one of the men in the group, who nodded his head and opened the trunk of the second car. From underneath a mass of blankets, tarps, cooking gear and so on, the man took a bumper jack, a long heavy steel crowbar and a flashlight and handed them to Drago, who worked his way under the car with his hands over his head. When he emerged from his inspection, he said something to the other men who were standing around. While Drago jacked up the front of our Mercedes, two of the other Gypsy men rolled a log into position under the doorjamb. Once the car was stable, he jammed the pry bar between the wheel and the fender support and pried them apart. We heard the sound of bending metal and watched as the muscles in Drago's neck and arms bulged and the fender distorted back into something approximating its original shape. The screech from under the car matched the cadence of the fender popping in and out until there was a loud THWANG and the fender support landed about ten feet in front of the car in the weeds. As he extricated himself, all the Gypsy men began clapping and shouting and slapping the new hero on the back and we gladly joined in. Still smiling, Drago shook my hand, then Simon's, and finally Johann's.

I extracted my neck wallet and pulled out a twenty-dollar bill, which I offered to him. To my surprise, he shook his head and put up his hands.

"Simon," Lou said, "look in the trunk and see if you can find a bottle of that Zubrówka we saved the other night."

Simon rummaged around until he found the Vodka and I handed it the big guy who'd just put us back on the road. He took it with a smile and soon the bottle was being passed from man to man, accompanied by lip smacking and other appreciative sounds. By the time it got back to me, there was less than an inch of the potent liquor left. I was still feeling a little nauseous, but I tipped the bottle back and took a sip anyway. The blade of grass slid down into my throat and I coughed. Was this the Polish equivalent of eating the worm at the bottom of a bottle of Mescal? No sense in offending our new friends, and it was our Vodka to begin with. I chewed up the blade of buffalo grass and swallowed it.

"We should change the tire and keep the damaged one for the spare," Lou said.

"Good thinking, that." Simon unloaded the spare from the trunk and soon we had it on the car and the deeply grooved one packed away.

During this whole process, the Gypsy women had set up a makeshift kitchen at the edge of the clearing and begun cooking in two huge black kettles. The smell of boiling meat and onions and garlic permeated the clearing.

"Think we should be going," Lou said. "Still got a long way to go."

"We could just camp out here," I said. "Its getting pretty late in the day."

"This we cannot do," Johann said. "You will remember that every night must be accounted for when you give your passport for inspection."

"He's right," Lou said. "Without a hotel entry for tonight, we'd have a lot of explaining to do."

One of the Gypsy men motioned us over to the table where the women were ladling up bowls of gamey-smelling stew. For several days we'd lived mainly on bread and cheese and salami and I was ready for a good meal.

"Let's at least stay for dinner," I said. "We've still got plenty of daylight left."

"No worries here, mate." Simon accepted a bowl and began spooning the pungent food into his mouth. "Not half bad. Mutton goulash, I think."

"Jesus," I said, looking into my bowl. "You don't suppose—"

"Quite enough," Lou said. "Imagination's running amok."

Simon and I finished our stew, mopping the gravy out with chunks of bread. A broad-bodied, middle-aged woman with a big smile and gaps in her teeth ladled our bowls full again. For me, it was a welcome change from our typical cold cut picnics. Johann and Liesl were less than enthusiastic; the possibility that we could be eating our own road kill had destroyed their appetites. They were unimpressed with the irony of the situation and contented themselves with fruit and bread.

The sound of another automobile weaving its way toward us through the trees interrupted our impromptu meal. Conversation dwindled to a halt as our attention focused on the narrow lane leading up to the highway. An all too familiar-looking black sedan rolled to a stop in the clearing and two men got out. One of the guys was a heavy-set man, perhaps six feet tall, with dark hair and features. A thick monobrow extended across almost the full width of his face. The other man was pale and skinny, and a few inches taller. Both wore black leather trench coats. Words were exchanged between the Gypsies and these two newcomers. Although it sounded vaguely like German, or perhaps some German dialect, I couldn't understand a word of it. I glanced at Lou, but she just shook her head. The dark guy looked uncomfortably familiar.

Johann and Liesl had disappeared into the woods out of sight.

I was fairly certain I had seen the big bruiser somewhere, but where? I couldn't connect him with a specific place or time. Once again I tried to remember every face I had seen during our multiple crossings at Checkpoint Charlie, but other than the fat blonde *Vopo* and the skinny *Kommandant*, no faces came to mind.

I was just as sure I had never seen his buddy before, but I didn't like the looks of him, either. I recognized the car as the one that had been following us, at least since the accident with the sheep. Maybe before that, for all I knew. There was no front plate on the bumper.

"Keep your guard up, mate. These blokes look like trouble."

"They look familiar, at least the big guy does, but I can't place them."

"Right, but from where?" Simon was as puzzled as I.

The black haired guy said something to his cohort and began to push his way through the line of Gypsy men toward us. Lou walked around behind the Mercedes.

One of the Gypsies shouted something. Drago emerged from the crowd, still armed with the crowbar, and blocked his way. The goon tried to push him aside, but Drago swung the heavy steel bar like a club and landed a solid blow on his bicep, knocking him down. Screaming in pain, the swarthy man writhed in the grass, clutching his arm. As Drago cocked his arm back for another swing, he staggered to his feet and backed away, shouting and shaking his fist at us. The two of them jumped into their long, black car, gunned the engine, spun around and headed back toward the highway. Holding the crowbar like a javelin, Drago hurled it at the receding Tatra. It clanked off the bumper into the tall grass, much to the amusement of the Gypsies. The car was soon out of sight.

More than at any time I could remember, I wished I had spoken a foreign language. I wanted to ask the Gypsies who those guys were and what language they were speaking. I felt helpless because of my ignorance.

"Thank you, thank you very much! *Danke vielmals.*" I said.

One of the Gypsy men said something to me, but I barely recognized only one word, which sounded like "faschisti."

"*Deutsche*? German fascists?" I asked.

"*Da, da! Deutsch faschisti,*" the Gypsy said, nodding his head vigorously.

"He says they're German fascists. Probably means East Germans."

"They are appearing so." Johann had his arm around Liesl, who was clinging to him, her grey eyes wide with fear. At some point, the two of them had come out of the woods and were crouching behind the Mercedes with Louisa.

"Must be a bit of a comfort, that, knowing you're not paranoid; we are being followed." Simon tapped out a Players and offered one to Drago, who took the pack and passed it around. By the time the box made the circuit, it was empty. How exactly Simon took comfort in knowing that our suspicions had been confirmed escaped me.

"I guess so," I said. "But you'd think if they were on to what we're doing, they'd have just arrested us at the border. Why all this chasing after us stuff?"

"Their *old* names. Not looking for Johann and Liesl Müeller." Lou's explanation was so simple, I wondered why I hadn't figured it out. The East Germans had no idea who we (Simon, Lou, and I) were, so all they had to go on were the names 'Johann Klaus Volker' and 'Liesl Schmidt'. Nobody but us knew that Johann and Liesl were traveling with *new* passports and identities. There was most likely a search for only two people, not five, and Johann Volker and Liesl Schmidt would have been the names the border guards had. No one would be looking for a typical young German couple named Müeller on a summer vacation with friends. At least, not yet. I felt like I was trapped in a time warp; behind us, snapping at our heels, were East German agents tracking two Berlin runaways, and ahead of us were border guards who saw only five students on a holiday! Even if all the pieces didn't quite fit together, one thing was certain: We had to keep moving.

After several minutes of smiles, hand shaking, including another good-hearted bone-crushing grip from Drago, and futile attempts to understand any more of their language, we loaded up and drove back up the lane to the main road. The scraping sound was gone; the Mercedes handled as if nothing had happened. There was no sign of the thugs who had attacked us or of the black Tatra. The crowbar lay in the weeds.

"The Danube River bisects Budapest, a lively city of over one million residents. The Pesh section is flat. The Buda side of the river is hilly and wooded. A long castle/fortress stretches along the hilltop, dominating the skyline." I read from the back of the map.

"Hungary is very like the *Deutsche Democratic Republik*," Johann said. "We can maybe have some troubles here. It is not like Czechoslovakia."

"How do you mean?" I asked.

"Ten years ago, some peoples here thought to have more freedom and they make some laws and have some newspapers and other ideas which the Russians can not allow. The Russians brought tanks and stopped the revolution."

The budding rebellion in 1960 had been brutally crushed by Moscow. Images of Soviet tanks rumbling through Budapest had flashed across TV screens around the world. I remembered the events vaguely, but neither the Hungarian revolution nor the Russian response to it had deterred me from wanting to go to Europe.

If we could make it past the Hungarian border into Yugoslavia, I theorized the rest of the trip would be a cinch. That is, if we didn't slaughter any more livestock and could stay a step or two ahead of the black leather jackets. The unlucky sheep had caused mostly cosmetic damage to the Mercedes. Other than having a fender that flapped in the breeze and no right headlight, the car ran fine. I doubted we would be stopped because of a bent fender since many of the vehicles we saw were damaged in some way or another. In this part of the world, anything which was still capable of moving under it's own power did so. East Europeans were forced by necessity to wring every last drop of usefulness out of everything. It wasn't like West Germany, where every vehicle looked like it was in perfect condition.

The East Germans chasing us were another matter. How long would it be before they put two and two together and figured out that Johann and Liesl had forged documents and were traveling under different names? At some point, they would surely telephone ahead with a license plate number and a description of our car and, likely, us. Although they could logically conclude that we were headed toward freedom in the west, they had no idea of exactly what route we had planned for ourselves. By altering our route to both avoid and pass through big cities by using main highways as well as country back roads, we figured we had some advantage. Lou was probably right that lack of a plan made us less predictable. What I didn't know, and didn't want to ask Johann, was whether there was a European equivalent of a police All Points Bulletin.

My attention drifted back to the damaged Mercedes. Would insurance cover the repairs once we get to Greece? Was collision with livestock a covered event? Damage to the car was surely the least of our problems. With Lou driving, I dozed off reading the tiny print on the insurance policy.

We arrived in Budapest mid afternoon, and spent the rest of the day and early evening wandering around before we eventually located a small pension for the night. Our close call with the cops over the dead sheep and the furious shepherd was still with us; how easily our plans could have been derailed by a minor traffic incident. Fortunately, Lou and Simon had buffered my hot-headedness. That none of the policemen spoke English had been a rare blessing. My shortsighted anger could have landed us all in some Hungarian jail where the counterfeit passports would have been discovered. I'd have made a terrible spy.

By now we were accustomed to the procedures of paperwork at hotels, so I didn't pay much attention as the concierge dutifully wrote down our names, nationalities, and passport numbers. The picnic by the stream that afternoon, the relative ease with which we'd bribed our way out of the collision with the sheep, the fortuitous appearance of the Gypsies in the forest, the cosmopolitan nature of Budapest, and the uneventfulness with which we had crossed several borders in the past couple of days had made me lower my guard. Otherwise, I might have observed that there was no guest ledger, just a single sheet of paper, which the clerk folded and sealed in an envelope.

22 – 24 July —

The Dalmatian Coast (Yugoslavia)

We left Budapest early in the afternoon and drove almost without stopping for two days. I wondered if we would be called upon to explain a night for which we had no hotel receipt. Would a simple explanation that we had slept in the car be believable?

Johann had been particularly nervous as we approached the Hungarian/Yugoslav border. We had decided to cross at Barcs, a medium-sized town that lay on the direct route from Budapest to the Dalmatian Coast.

"It is now exactly ten years from the Hungarian rebellion," Johann reminded us. "We can be looked upon with special interest."

When we were close to the border area, I turned down a deeply rutted dirt road into the forest and we bounced along until we got to a spot wide enough in which to turn around. We all got out of the car, stretched and smoked and peed, and once again I checked our passports, visas, automobile documents, and maps. Other than Czechoslovakian entrance stamps missing from Johann and Liesl's counterfeit passports, and no overnight documentation for the previous night we'd spent driving, I could see nothing amiss. We packed ourselves back into the Mercedes and continued southbound on the main road.

At the Hungarian border, Johann and Liesl pretended to be asleep in the back seat while Simon, Lou, and I got out. I froze for a moment as the guard finished examining our passports and then shined a flashlight into the car. Just when I was sure we were in trouble, Lou gently pushed the flashlight aside, put her finger to her lips and made a 'shushing' sound, which, to my amazement, satisfied the guard. After stamping each passport and handwriting in the date, he handed them back to us without a word. I nodded my thanks.

A sleepy guard at the Yugoslav border gave only a cursory glance at our passports and waved us through. We took a route more or less directly south, which bypassed the large city of Zagreb by a safe margin. I was still leery of big cities and, with the exception of Budapest, we'd stayed out of them. On the rare occasions I allowed myself the luxury of thinking that the authorities couldn't possibly be interested in five young people on an innocent summer holiday, all I had to do was remember the brutal encounter in the forest to jolt me back to reality.

After leaving Drago and the Gypsy band in the woods, we stayed in one place overnight only once, in Budapest, figuring it was safer to keep moving, even though it meant we wouldn't have the proper lodging stamps in our passports. We stopped only for gas, food and cigarettes, switching off driving and sleeping. Although that incident had ended up more or less OK, (we were still a step ahead of whoever was pursuing us), the violent confrontation had served as a chilling reminder of just how dangerous our situation really was. The narrow, back roads south from Budapest through southern Hungary into the thick forests of northern Yugoslavia made me claustrophobic; I imagined roadblocks waiting for us around every twist and bend. Each slow-moving farm wagon we caught up with loomed as a barricade, trapping us, sometimes for miles, before the roadway was wide enough for us to pass. Time and time again, I felt boxed in by impenetrable trees that grew to the very edge of the pavement and horse-drawn wagons blocking our way. At any moment, I expected to see the black sedan materialize in the rear view mirror, blocking us in.

But no Tatra. So far, we had not been arrested and Mara's direst predictions had not come true. As we drove the last few kilometers to the coast, I took a deep breath, and reminded myself for the hundredth time that Liesl and Johann had legally exited from Berlin, not furtively escaped. I counted every kilometer we traveled further away from the *Deutsche Demokratische Republic* as a small success. Link them all together, and we'd be free. According to the map, the port city of Split was less than an hour away.

And then, in front and far below us, was the vast expanse of the Adriatic, complete with tankers, freighters, and fishing boats. As we descended down the impossibly engineered road, around tight hairpin switchbacks and through unlit tunnels toward sea level, the intimidating darkness of the mountains gave way to softly clouded blue skies. In a strange way, it was a relief to worry about nothing more than sheer, unfenced cliffs.

Split, laid out below us, could have been a coastal town anywhere. Besides, we were in Yugoslavia, the most open, the most western, of the

East Block countries. Even though we still had hundreds of kilometers to go before we got to Greece, I felt freer. Liesl's mood seemed to have improved, too. Her eyes were wide as she looked out over the water.

"I have not seen such thing before. Only in photographia books."

"Just wait until you see the Pacific," I said.

I would have liked to stay and explore; how could you *not* be curious about a city named 'Split'? As it was, we stopped only long enough to fill the tank with gas and buy food. I had to remind myself that we were not enjoying a leisurely vacation, but on the run. I was still haunted by the confrontation in the clearing with the thugs in the black Tatra.

Eventually, we did stop for the night in a little coastal town a few kilometers south of Split. We were exhausted from the endless hours of non-stop driving. We found an inn with a café and, most importantly, a parking area around back hidden from the main highway. After a huge dinner of fried fish, tomatoes and cucumbers, a welcome change from the sandwich diet we had been on for the past few days, we turned in for a long overdue night of sleep in real beds.

✶✶✶✶

25 July —

Southern Yugoslavia

━━━━━━━━━━━━━━━━━

"Tell to us a little more about America," Johann said. We were driving down the narrow road along the southern coast of Yugoslavia, nearing the Albanian border. On our right, far below us, the Adriatic Sea glistened under a cloudless sky. The shoulder dropped abruptly away from the road without so much as a guardrail or even a fog line to mark the edge. There was pavement and then—nothing but air. I drove at about fifty kilometers per hour, and slowed even more to pass horse-drawn farm wagons, bicycles, and the occasional cow or pig. A light wind frothed the water into inviting whitecaps and flooded the Mercedes with the smell of fresh, salt air. On our left the mountains of Montenegro disappeared into a gray fog. Soon we would be forced to leave the sunny coastal highway and head up through those mountains to skirt Albania. I was reminded of the wild south coast terrain around Big Sur. Many times in high school, even before I had my driver's license, I had driven down Highway One to explore, and sometimes camp out in, the arroyos of Garapata Creek and Mal Paso Canyon.

The most direct route from Yugoslavia into Greece would have been through Albania, short but impossible. Nobody got into or out of Albania; it was the only East Block country more closed than East Germany. The roads weren't blocked; there *were* no roads. Looking at a map of Europe, the paucity of information about Albania brought to mind ancient maritime maps wherein uncharted regions were simply marked: 'HERE BE DRAGONS'.

"There's a lot about America I don't like," I said, finally answering Johann. "We're fighting a war in Viet Nam which is completely wrong. Many people are dying, Americans, Vietnamese, Cambodians, Laotians, others. For no reason. To stop Communism, they say."

"I do not like Communism," Johann said. "You can see all what terrible thing it is when you came to East Berlin. You can see how the people live, what hardship there is."

"I agree with you completely, Johann," I said. "But I do not think Communism is a threat to America."

"And it is so that you must go to this war?" Liesl asked.

"Yes. As I told you yesterday, we have laws that say every man must register for the draft when he turns eighteen. Most get drafted into the Army and are sent to Viet Nam."

"Most of the soldiers are black," Lou said. "That is part of why we have such terrible race riots."

"White men are sending black boys to kill yellow boys," I said, paraphrasing Huey Newton, the Black Panther leader.

For a while, nobody said anything.

Then Liesl said, "And you? How is it you do not go to fight in this war?"

I couldn't answer right away. Finally I said, "I am against the war. One of the reasons I am here is that I refused to go into the army. I am what we call a conscientious objector."

"*Bitte?*" Johann asked. Lou explained in German what was meant by the term 'conscientious objector'.

"And you have the freedom to be this, this one which objects?"

"Well, yes and no." It was getting a little complicated. I did my best to explain how the Selective Service System worked, how some were granted CO status, some went to jail, some slipped across the border to Canada or Mexico, some disappeared underground, and a few, like me, escaped to Europe. This required much help from Lou.

"In the DDR, we do not have such a freedom. If it is decided that you will be a *Vopo*, as example, then you must become so."

"You can have no choice," Liesl said.

"What about you?" I asked. "How did you get out of it?"

Johann laughed. It was the first time he had laughed since we left Bratislava. "If I marry Liesl, then perhaps I must go in the army. Or *Volkspolizei*. If I do not marry, then I am a big risk for escape. There can be nothing to hold me. Also, it is still needed for housepainters."

"Not sure I understand," said Lou, wrinkling her forehead.

"The government think if you are married, you will not jump the wall and leave behind a family."

"We like to be married," Liesl said, "but it is too dangerous for Johann."

"If a man will escape from the DDR, the *Stasi* make it very hard for the family he leave behind."

"From what I saw, you need more than just housepainters," Simon said. "You need house builders as well."

"It is true. Much has not been repaired from the war. But what is not fallen down must still be painted!" Johann laughed again. It was good to see him relaxing slightly, becoming more like the Johann we remembered from Berlin.

"I'm sure you won't be missed," Simon said.

"I am hoping they do not miss me before we get to Greece."

Liesl said nothing.

At Kotor, we stopped at an outdoor market. The town itself lay along the edge of the ocean, protected by an ancient Roman fortress on the cliffs above. Lou went off with Johann and Liesl in search of the staples of our diet; cheese, bread, salami, and whatever else they might find suitable for a picnic lunch. I wanted a few minutes alone with Simon so the two of us started hiking up the trail that led to the castle.

"It's going too damned easy," I said. We'd found a little store that sold beer and wine. "I keep waiting for the other shoe to drop, or the sword to fall, or whatever you want to call it."

"You're going to bring a bloody curse upon us, mate. You mustn't think about such things."

"I can't help it, Simon."

"Worry about Mara. Worry about if we run short of money before we get to Greece. Worry about what's likely to happen when we *do* get there."

"I haven't even thought about her lately." I looked out at the Adriatic, now far below us, so that Simon couldn't see my eyes.

"So, think about her and the rest will fall into place. Let Louisa and me carry some of the load. You keep a stiff upper lip, as we say."

"I'll try to keep a stiff *something*," I said, trying to inject a little levity into it.

"That's the tic, mate. You worry about *that*."

We started back down the trail to the market.

"Do you fancy Louisa, then?" Simon's question caught me off-guard.

"Lou? I don't know. I don't want to get in your way, if that's what you're asking."

"Not a chance." Simon chuckled out loud. "You know me, mate. I prefer a more, shall we say, *commercial* approach to matters concerning the fairer sex."

"Can't we at least call it straightforward?"

"As you like it," he said, winking to make sure I got the reference, and that closed the discussion.

We were far enough south now that oranges were coming into season so we bought a crumpled paper sack of those as well. At one makeshift roadside fruit stand, an old man in overalls offered several varieties of apples, which must have been harvested the previous fall. When I shook my head and started to walk away, the farmer grasped my sleeve and pulled me back. He cut one of the apples in half and handed Simon and me each a piece. To my surprise, the pulp was crisp and sweet. I bought a dozen for about twenty-five cents.

We wandered back the way we had come until we found our friends. Together, we had plenty of food and drink for a good lunch. We loaded everything into the trunk and were on our way.

"How about a swim before we leave the beach?" I asked, once we were out of town. The highway was no longer half way up the side of the mountain as it had been for most of the coast drive, but had descended to sea level. We'd been driving with the windows down and the sunroof open and the air conditioning off. I felt a trickle of sweat run down my neck into the leather seat. "Might not get another chance for a while." A very long while, I thought.

"Will you think such an idea is good?" Johann asked. "Picnicking and swimming and so playing?"

"Sure, why not?" Lou answered. "Remember, we're students on holiday. Less suspicious to act the part."

We were nearing the end of our flight south. The last border would be the most dangerous; the borders we had crossed so far were all still within east Europe. The last barrier would be at the Iron Curtain itself, but there was no going back now, even if any of us had wanted to. What had begun almost as a fantasy in a stuffy Berlin apartment a few weeks ago now loomed as an ominous mistake. Before I was sent to prison for life, or shot at some godforsaken totalitarian outpost, I wanted to swim one more time in an ocean in the sun.

There were murmurs of agreement so I began looking for a place to pull off the main road. Eventually, the pavement dipped and widened. To the right, almost hidden by the thick foliage, a narrow trail disappeared in the direction of the ocean. We came upon it so abruptly that I had to back up several feet.

"Well, guys, what do you think?" I asked.

"I say we give it a go," Simon said. "Maybe we'll find a spot for a picnic."

"May have to back out," Louisa said. "Might not have any place to turn around down there."

"I'd rather take that chance than leave the car in full view of the road." I thought about the black sedan I now knew was trailing us. "I wish we still had that palooka with the crowbar around."

In the rearview mirror, I could see Liesl looking at Johann, who just shook his head. Lou did her best to translate 'palooka' into German.

Branches scraped the sides of the Mercedes as I navigated the grassy, two-track path through the brambles. What the hell, I figured they were going to have to repair and paint the fender anyway. A few more scratches wouldn't make the condition of the car any worse. The bushes opened into a wide, sandy parking area that even had a weathered wooden table. We could hear traffic but we were hidden from the road.

"This is perfect!" I said. "Let's go for a swim and then have some lunch."

"I rather fancy eating and then having a splash," Simon said.

"Mother never warned you about going in the water right after you eat?" Lou asked. She began to arrange the food on the table.

"Rubbish. Absolute rubbish. If I'd listened to me mum, I wouldn't be here with you now." Simon stuffed his mouth with a handful of olives.

As we stripped to our underwear, I was startled to see Liesl's bare breasts emerge from her blouse. Without pretense or ceremony, this quiet, East German girl was as naked as she had been the day Johann sketched her in the Spree River, the day she had deflected the police at her door. Her pale buttocks bounced as she trotted toward the water. At first, Lou kept her underpants on, but as she neared the surf, she threw those aside as well. If Mara were here, would she swim, naked, with the rest of us? I couldn't imagine her being so unreserved. I had seen her completely undressed so seldom that I remembered her soft, plump body more by touch than sight. *Where exactly was she right now?*

The Adriatic was as intoxicating as any liquor I had ever drunk. The midday heat opened the pores of my skin so that the salt water had a mild, pleasant, invigorating sting when I plunged in. For the next hour we cavorted like children, splashing, diving through the waves, trying to forget where we were and what we were doing. Global politics disappeared beneath the sensuality of the moment. For a short interlude, we were simply teenagers on vacation. We might just as easily have been on a beach in California. I kept a wary eye on the bank, nonetheless.

The hot sun, the buoyant ocean, the temporary relief from the stress of the past few days and the proximity of so much exposed flesh aroused me. As I floated on my back, naked and nearly weightless in the salt water, I soon felt myself swelling. A few waves away, I could hear Lou and Liesl giggling and chatting in German. From nowhere, Simon appeared by my side.

"Blimey, mate, looks like you have a periscope!"

"Just shut up, OK?" My reverie changed abruptly to embarrassment and I turned over and began swimming to shore.

"Bloody clever nautical invention, that; doubles as a keel!" Simon laughed.

"Aye, matey, if some damn limey had invented it, maybe Britannia would still rule the waves."

Whatever Simon shouted back was lost as a frothy wave swamped me. When I came up, the girls were swimming toward shore. Panicked, I looked to the beach, expecting to see a black sedan parked next to our Mercedes. We were still alone, but the carefree mood had disappeared.

Lou was the first one out. As I watched her squeegee the water from her body, I resisted an urge to offer my help. Still wet, she wiggled into her underwear.

"Better get a move on," she said, turning to us. As I came out of the water, trying to stay sideways, a full smirk filled her face. I imagined Lou so happy that if she floated on her back long enough, her dimples would fill with seawater and float like tiny tidepools in her sand-colored face below her sky-blue eyes. Her sheer wet panties barely hid her dark pubic hair. I thought back to the night we shared a room in Karlovy Vary, the warmth of her firm flesh against my own. Much to my embarrassment and against my will, my erection, which had begun to deflate, came back with a vengeance.

"Appears you're beginning to miss Mara," Lou said with a grin. "Missing something, anyway, by the looks of things."

I couldn't take my eyes off her body. Her nipples were erect from the cool water. The sunlight reflected off her smooth, tan skin. She was staring at my crotch.

"Blimey, mate," Simon snickered, "what are you planning to do with that weapon you're carrying?"

"What do you expect with everybody bare-ass naked, anyway?" I asked, turning away.

I felt my sun-warmed face turn even redder as I struggled into my jeans. I couldn't seem to stuff myself in. Finally, I just buckled my belt around my waist, unable to button my fly. Maybe a good, long piss in the bushes would help matters.

The girls were giggling, doing their best to ignore me. I jogged down the beach toward Johann, who was himself taking a leak into the weeds. I wished I'd stayed a little longer in the ocean.

We left the beach and continued south on the two-lane road, which became increasingly bumpy and filled with potholes. Within a few kilometers, the road ended at a concrete barricade topped with barbed wire and huge signs lettered in red. Although I couldn't read the language, the message was clear: This was the end of the line. Further ahead lay the TERRA INCOGNITA of Albania. Joseph Stalin might have departed the Russian political stage, but his ghost was alive and well in the person of Abner Hoxna, Albania's Communist dictator. There wasn't much of a road beyond the barricade. Ominous, dome-shaped concrete pillbox bunkers with slotted windows dotted the barren, rocky hillside. Here and there the sunlight glinted off a gun barrel. Our only choices were to go back or turn left. Back was not an option.

Within a couple of hours, we had gained several thousand feet of elevation. The sunny Adriatic was far behind us; the temperature had dropped at least twenty degrees and the blue sky had changed to a leaden gray. The open bag of oranges on the seat between us gave off a sweet, citrus scent, a fragrant reminder of the warmth and sunshine we had left behind. From summer to winter in only a few hours. Simon, already wearing a sweater, added a jacket.

With the windows rolled up against the chill, even the Mercedes' ventilation system couldn't keep up with the cigarette smoke, which hung in the air like smoggy haze. Louisa, our only non-smoker, didn't complain.

It was getting late in the day so we decided to find a hotel or inn for the night. There was not much to choose from in the way of hostelry, but finally in Pristina, a small town high in the Albanian Alps, we found a roadhouse of sorts. Several rusting vehicles, including a World War Two-era troop carrier, were partially submerged in aggressive shrubbery. Two skinny dogs appeared and ran circles around our car, barking. Soon a massive man with thick white hair and a brush-cut, tobacco-stained mustache opened the heavy wooden door. He barked something unintelligible at the dogs, waved to us, and without waiting for an answer, disappeared inside the inn.

"What have we got to lose?" I asked. "Not much else to choose from." Indeed, other than this stolid inn and a few small run-down huts, there were no other buildings to be seen.

"Right." Simon opened his door. "Let's you and me have a quick lookabout first."

"I'll go, too, maybe he speaks German," Lou said.

Once inside, our eyes gradually adjusted to the dim light, most of which came from a big cooking fire in the center of the room. To one side was a counter, barely illuminated in a golden glow by a smudged, oil lantern. As we crossed the wooden floor, the white-haired man reached up and turned the wick.

To my surprise, he waved away my hand when I offered him our passports.

"*Vecera I prenociste ce vas kostati 20 Florents po osobi,*" he said. His eyes bored into me from beneath bushy white eyebrows.

"*Sprechen Sie Deutsch?*" I asked.

"*Na,*" he said with an unmistakable tone of distaste, and bent over his desk, writing. He handed me a piece of paper, on which he had written: DM – 10.

"Lou," I asked, "do you have any West German money left? He wants ten marks for the five of us."

Louisa handed the white-haired man a ten-mark bill and he pointed to a stairway at the other end of the room.

"*Schlafzimmer,*" he said.

The inn offered dormitory-style sleeping quarters upstairs and a one-choice menu downstairs. Although it was quite a bit less swanky than the Intercontinental where we had been just a few nights before, it was not much different than the youth hostels we usually stayed in. We shared one large bunkroom with some Yugoslav road workers. At the end of the room was a short hallway leading to a single-stall toilet and a cold-water shower. The modesty we'd abandoned on the beach several hours ago returned; we took turns rinsing off the salty residue in the chilly trickle of water from the rusty spout. I stayed under the stream for less than a minute. My teeth chattered as I toweled off and dressed. I looked down and saw that I was shriveled from the cold, and I had to laugh to myself. Mere hours earlier....

At dinnertime, everyone at the inn assembled at a large round table downstairs. The scent of cooked meat and vegetables mixed with the harsh odor of Balkan tobacco. A gigantic boar's head mounted on the wall dominated the room. A pair of rifles on leather slings hung from its curved tusks. I had an eerie sense that the pig was watching every bite we took.

Everybody in the roadhouse ate together. After serving up large earthen bowls filled with thick, pungent goulash, the cook, a large woman with a blue kerchief on her head and hint of mustache on her lip, sat at the edge of the table nearest the kitchen. The Yugoslavs talked among themselves, occasionally glancing at Liesl and Louisa and then laughing. I could imagine what was going through their minds; I knew what *I* was thinking. Perhaps our fate was not to be arrested by East German agents but to be robbed and raped by burly Yugoslav highwaymen. In contrast to almost everywhere else we'd been in east Europe, we hadn't seen a single policeman or soldier all day. Just how safe would we all be, sleeping in one room?

"Do you reckon they have any beer here?" Simon asked.

"Can't hurt to ask," I said

"Pils? Beer? Pivo?" I asked the white-haired man. I made the drinking sign with my thumb and pinkie finger.

"*Ya.*" He grunted something to the cook, who stuffed her mouth with a slice of bread as she disappeared into the kitchen. She returned a moment later, still chewing, with the thumb and fingers of one hand inside five empty glasses and a dripping pitcher of beer in the other. With a frown, she set the glasses in front of us and clanked the pitcher next to them. As Simon poured the beer, the white-haired man held up one finger and said, "*Deutsch mark.*"

Fishing around in my pocket, I found a one-mark coin and slid it down the table to him.

"So," I said, "what bought us a whole tray-full of flowers in Bratislava now buys us just one pitcher of beer."

"If you think of it as a 'flagon'," Simon said, "it'll seem like a lot more."

"A flagon," I said. "Right. How much do you suppose a flagon is, anyway?"

"Enough. Still some left." Louisa looked down the table at the road workers, who were still making comments about us and laughing. "Buy them a pitcher too, David."

"What? Why should we—"

Lou gave me a hard look, and then smiled at the workers. "Just do what I say. *Now.*"

Sliding another mark toward the white-haired man, I waved my hand across the table at the road workers and said, "Pivo." The cook brought more glasses and another big pitcher of beer.

One of the men poured the pilsner and they raised their glasses to us and drank.

"*Tank. Tank. Danke.*" With a smile, the worker nearest us drained his glass and smacked it on the table.

"Not to worry," Simon answered, smiling. He drank the rest of the beer from our pitcher, which brought a round of applause from the workers and a growl of disapproval from the cook.

"You'll have to explain that to me later," I said to Lou.

"You're a clever lad; you'll figure it out."

"By the way, what do you suppose it is we are eating?" I asked.

"Haven't a clue, mate, you'll have to query the chef."

I skewered a chunk of meat on my fork, held it up and shrugged my shoulders. "*Was ist das?*"

The bushy-browed guy laughed out loud and pointed his knife over his head. The boar gazed down and didn't blink an eye.

After dinner, the five of us sat around the outdoor picnic table smoking and trying to relax. We were buttoned up against the chill of the high mountain air. The hot sun and warm beach felt years, not hours, away.

"You suppose they have any vodka here?" I asked.

"They'll have something," Simon said.

"None for me," Lou said. "You should take it easy yourself, after the other night."

I walked back into the dining room where the cook was clearing the last of the dishes from the table. There was no sign of the road workers. The white-haired man sat under the oil lamp reading a newspaper through thick, black-rimmed glasses. He had a glass of clear liquid in front of him and a bottle devoid of any label or markings.

"Vodka?" I pointed to the bottle.

He shook his head. "*Ne, vodka e rusa! Mi ovde piemo slibovitu!*" He removed his glasses and looked at me intently. The only word I recognized, besides vodka and rusa, was slivovitz. This guy wouldn't be caught dead drinking anything Russian.

"Slivovitz, then." I held up four fingers.

"*Lupa, donesi cetir case!*" the man shouted into the kitchen.

The cook waddled out with four small glasses. The white-haired man poured about an inch into each one from the bottle and slid them toward me with a grubby hand.

"Marks?" I asked. I fished into my pocket for some coins. "*Deutsche* marks?"

"*Americansi?*" He said to me. His eyebrows seemed to dance with each syllable.

"Yes, American," I slid my passport out of my neck wallet. He looked at the cover like he hadn't seen one before, and ran his fingers over the gold embossing as if he were reading Braille. Without opening it up, he handed it back to me and held up both hands in front of him and shook his head.

"Thanks," I said. I picked up the four glasses but the man put a hand on my arm. He drank what was left in his own glass and poured it full, replaced the cap and handed me the bottle. I cocked my head and shrugged.

"*Americansi.*" He smiled, exposing a collection of long, tobacco-stained teeth. "Kennedy good. America good." He held the glass up in the air and then threw the slivovitz deep into his throat.

"Yes," I said, smiling. "America good."

Such strange words to pass my lips. I thought back to the bitterness I had been filled with almost two years earlier standing on the rear deck of the *Aqua Serene* looking at New York harbor, then to the odd sense of security I felt watching the searchlights of East Berlin illuminate the red, white, and blue, and now this: 'America good'. Strange words, indeed.

With the bottle wedged under my arm, I walked back into the chilly garden carrying the glasses. I paused at the door and waited until Lou noticed me. I beckoned her over with my head.

"So," I said, "you've been chatting with Liesl. How do you think they're doing?"

"Can't say about Johann. She's scared to death. Has been the whole trip."

"It's probably just as well somebody is. You seem to be cool and calm as always."

"Just handle it differently. Should see me inside."

"And Johann?" I persisted.

"Don't know. Maybe a little more subdued. What do you think?"

"I think I'll be glad when we're finally in Greece."

"Think anybody will be there to greet us?"

"Like Mara anybody?"

"Like Mara anybody."

"I doubt it. Every day we're on the road—"

"Hope you mean that."

"Lou—" I tried to find her hand, but she had turned and started back to the table. A very light mist was beginning to bead up on my sleeve. I followed her down the path to where the others were waiting.

"Tomorrow's the big day, you know," I said. "Tomorrow night we'll be in Thessaloniki." I put the four glasses on the table and set the bottle in the middle.

"So we hope," Simon said, topping up the glasses until they were full. "'Ere's to a successful frontier crossing." He tilted his head back, raised his glass to his mouth and poured the clear, harsh plum brandy into his throat.

I offered a glass to Louisa, who shook her head. I sucked the slivovitz over my tongue and felt the inside of my head ignite. "Holy Christ on the Cross, Simon, I don't know how you did that."

"Practice, mate. That's all it is. Practice." Simon refilled his glass. Johann and Liesl hadn't touched theirs.

"Enough practicing for one night." Louisa smashed the cork into the bottle with the heel of her hand.

"Drink up, it'll help you sleep."

Johann took a sip of his slivovitz but Liesl shook her head.

For lack of anything else to do, I unfolded our map.

We found the spot where we hoped to cross from Yugoslavia to Greece, from east to west.

"This is the border, and here is Bitola, where we go into Greece." I indicated with a table knife where the thin red line of the road crossed the wider green band marking the international border. Suddenly, a drop of water splattered onto the map next to the pointed end of the blade. I looked up expecting to see the mist had turned into rain, but instead found only the moist, shining eyes of Liesl Müeller.

<hr />

26 July —

Bitola
(Yugoslav/Greek Border)

W ell, this is it. This is the day we go into Greece." I was stating the
obvious, talking more to break the silence. I wished someone
else would say something, but nobody did. In spite of the sound
of the strong, Mercedes 280SE engine and the road noise, the inside of
the car was eerily quiet; a quality of resigned calmness that I found inexplicably disturbing.

The cook had served us a breakfast of freshly baked bread, jams
and jellies, and strong, black tea. There was no sign of the Yugoslav road
crew.

The bushy-haired proprietor of the inn had given us advice, of sorts,
on which route would be best. Pointing at the map with his knife, he
had first touched the thin grey line near Kukis, frowned, shook his head
from side to side and given that choice a 'palms down' gesture. Then he
stabbed the end of his knife through the map into the table at Bitola and
nodded his head vigorously. Based on that, we decided that we would
take the Bitola route instead of going through Kukis. Bitola was only a
few kilometers from the border. It was still too early for the light morning
dew to have burned off. I flipped on the windshield wipers and realized
my mistake immediately; the residual dust mixed with the fresh mist to
make a pasty, muddy smear.

The Dragor River was close by, often visible through the clumps of
trees. We'd been on the road eight days since our rendezvous with Liesl
and Johann in Karlovy Vary, a month since we first entered Berlin. So
much had happened in that month: Our initial innocent visits to East
Berlin through the concrete maze at Checkpoint Charlie. Our meeting
with Johann and then Liesl. The concoction of this audacious escape
plan. My trip to Copenhagen to obtain the false passports and Simon's

reconnaissance visit to the same border we were headed for now. Lou's flight home and back for support from her father. The final details of the necessary visas and car rental in Frankfurt. My fight with Mara. In less than a month, I'd been in six countries; Germany, Denmark, Holland, Czechoslovakia, Hungary, and now Yugoslavia. Seven if you counted both Germanys. With any luck, today we would add Greece to the list. An American, a German/American, and an Englishman, helping two East Berliners escape the *Deutsche Democratic Republik* for a new life in the west. Today would be our last day on the run; the passports I bought for the Müellers in Copenhagen would face their closest examination.

The wipers smeared a blurry view through the mud on the windshield.

And no Mara. Where was she? What was she doing? I wondered if she were on her way to Greece, or headed in a completely different direction. Almost as if she could read my mind, Lou reached over and put her hand on my thigh. I looked over at her.

"Just keep your eyes on the road." There was a faint smile and those dimples.

"Are you nervous?" I asked, turning in my seat to Johann and Liesl behind me. In the distance, perhaps a kilometer behind us, I saw a black car. The suspicion that we were again being followed was unnerving and I wished I were just being paranoid. But I knew it was the same damned black car that had been there all along, with the same two thugs who had tried to attack us in the woods. I couldn't afford to give it much more thought than that. There were many black cars in this part of the world; why couldn't this car be one of them? What was it Henry Ford had said of his Model T? You could have any color, as long as it was black? In my heart of hearts, though, I knew. I sped up, taking curves a little too fast, but leaving the Tatra behind.

"It can be a lie to say no," Johann answered. "I cannot believe what we have done so far. It is like a dream. Sometimes a good dream, sometimes a not good dream. How do you say it in English?"

"Nightmare. A bad dream is a nightmare," Lou translated.

"Yes. That is it," Johann said. "We are close to our end, but we are not there."

"I never think to leave Berlin," Liesl said. "Before you come, we think, Johann and me, we make a life in Berlin, the best life we can make. Now, everything is different. All is changed."

"I am eager to be in the west, eager but afraid, also," Johann said.

"Things aren't perfect on the other side of the Iron Curtain," Simon said. "Just a bloody site better than they are here."

I reflected on this for a few minutes. "There are many things wrong on both sides. Nothing is perfect in the east or the west. Many things in America I do not like. But I can say what I want to about anything. I can protest and demonstrate. As I have told you, many Americans do not support the war in Viet Nam. There are huge demonstrations and marches against the war."

"And this is allowed?" Liesl still didn't quite believe me.

"Yes, it is allowed," I answered.

Suddenly, we rounded a turn in the road and came to a blockade. Wooden barriers fortified with leaking sandbags prevented us from continuing on the main highway. Within a few hundred feet, the roadway toward Albania disintegrated into a rocky, unpaved trail that led uphill to a series of squat, fortified machine gun nests. A small contingent of soldiers milled around, some sitting on the hoods of two dull green troop transports. We were directed by a lone uniformed traffic cop to take a detour.

As our Mercedes left the pavement and turned onto the dirt and gravel road, clouds of dust rose behind us. One of the dusty green carriers pulled into line behind us, followed by several more cars, and behind those, I could just make out the grill of the black *Tatra*. I didn't like the feel of it; silently, I repeated to myself the words 'many cars, few roads' over and over again until they became a kind of Mantra.

Nobody said anything. This was the border area I had visited months ago and Simon had scouted only a few weeks earlier. The major construction on the highway was still incomplete. An antiquated earthmover struggled against a giant boulder almost as large as it was. A dozen dust-covered workmen with picks and shovels labored under the watchful eyes of twice as many armed soldiers. I wondered if they were the same workers who had been at the inn the night before.

Just up the hill was an elevated platform that served as a watchtower. One machine gun was aimed at the immediate area where the construction was going on, the other was pointed at the road where we now waited in a queue of dust covered cars and trucks. We were very close to the frontier. On both sides of the road we saw more wooden towers with spotlights on top. Down a slight decline, through the dust, we could make out the buildings of the actual border and a red-and-white striped semaphore gate. A hundred yards separated the Yugoslavian guards from their Greek counterparts. A hundred yards of featureless landscape, a buffer zone between Communism and Capitalism, east and west. Midway across the barren strip, a single car moved slowly away from us, trailing a cloud of dust. A line of four or five cars and a truck waited in front of us. I was wide-awake. My heart pounded in my chest.

"What does it look like to you?" I asked Simon, who was sitting behind me in the back seat.

"About the same as when I was here before," he answered. "Too bad there aren't any Gypsies about. Would've made things easier, I reckon."

"I hope our luck isn't about to run out," I said.

I watched the procedure carefully. As each vehicle stopped, the driver handed documents and passports to the guard, who looked at the photo page of each one, looked at every person in the car, and then went into the shack. In a moment, he came out and handed the passports back to the driver, took a final look inside the car, and pointed toward Greece. Another sentry stood next to the semaphore gate. The gate itself looked flimsy, more like a safety gate at a county fair amusement park than the last barrier between east and west Europe. I would have expected something much more substantial, perhaps a maze like the one at Checkpoint Charlie. But maybe that was what the construction was all about. There was nothing inadequate about the machine guns or automatic rifles, however. Two more guards stood in the middle of the passage with Kalashnikovs pointed at each car as it waited its turn.

At the shouted command from the first guard, the others stepped aside, the gate was raised, and the car was permitted to pass. Once through, the gate was quickly lowered and the guards jumped back into position. Each driver then slowly crossed the bare ground, raising more dust, and stopped at the edge of Greece, perhaps a hundred meters away. I could not actually see the Greek border through the haze.

The truck, with its big enclosed cargo box, demanded a closer examination. While the head guard disappeared into the shack with the driver's passport and a fistful of other documents, the junior guards opened the rear doors and pointed their AK-47s inside. They inspected the cargo box with handheld searchlights powered by long extension cords that snaked through the dirt to the plywood customs shack. One of the guards leaned his machine gun against the side of the truck and climbed part way underneath with a flashlight. Satisfied, they closed the doors and waved the truck through. With a clash of gears and a belch of acrid black smoke, the truck rolled into the thin, barren strip of no man's land between Yugoslavia and Greece.

We were next.

The border guard impatiently waved us forward. My knuckles were white around the steering wheel. Sweat was beginning to form on my forehead. I felt a hand way inside my belly squeeze into a fist. At that moment, I knew with brutal clarity that our whole plan had been a huge mistake, a terrible idea that was now about to cost the five of us our freedom, if not our lives. I wished we had never gotten into this. Why hadn't anyone talked me out of it? Why hadn't I listened to Mara? Was Louisa's father nuts, too? This was insanity.

Because of the longer time the guards had taken with the truck, a line had formed behind us. A horn blew. Looking back, I saw the familiar black sedan. I couldn't think about them now. I had no idea what their plan was, why they were holding back. We had managed to stay ahead of them so far and there was plenty more to worry about in front of us.

We had deviated from our normal routine of Lou driving through the frontier crossings. This time, I was behind the wheel. Louisa was in the seat next to me, riding shotgun. *Riding shotgun*, what an image. As if a shotgun would be of any use whatsoever against the arsenal arranged around us. Liesl sat in the back, sandwiched between Johann and Simon. Lou reached back over the seat and squeezed Liesl's hand, and then rested it on my thigh. I covered her hand with my own and gave it a gentle squeeze.

Nobody said a word.

I shifted into low gear and slowly started driving down the hill toward the border shack. Sweat dripped off my chin. I felt the pounding of blood in my ears. I struggled to see through the dirty windshield in front and the dust behind. I stopped the Mercedes just a few feet from the gate. The single, red and white wooden gate was all that stood between us and freedom. A painted, four-by-six plank, balanced in the fork of a steel fulcrum, and what looked like the entire Yugoslav Army.

"Daitemi passport!" demanded the guard. He was holding a clipboard, something I hadn't noticed before. I handed him our five passports. After scrutinizing his clipboard and then us, he disappeared into the customs shack. He was gone for a very long time. Minutes passed, feeling like days. I thought about Mara. I was thankful that she wasn't here with us now but still I missed her very much. *Or did I?* For all the times I'd thought about getting caught and being sent away to a prison somewhere, I hadn't really considered what it would be like to never see Mara again. She'd almost exploded that day we smuggled Johann's artwork out of East Berlin; I couldn't imagine her visiting us in a Yugoslav penitentiary. And now there was Lou to think about, too. I looked at my watch, wishing I'd checked the time when I handed the passports to the guard, wishing I'd paid more attention to the duration of the previous passport checks. I looked back at Simon and then the Müellers. A patina of sweat glistened on Johann's forehead. Liesl was pale and her eyes were shiny with tears.

Her slender body was crushed against Johann, her hands in his. Simon lit a Navy Cut and passed the pack around. Johann took one but it slipped through his fingers to the floorboard. Louisa was the only one of us who appeared unperturbed. Her face was a sharp mask. I wanted with all my heart to be across the border, in Greece, not here. Anywhere but here. This didn't feel good. I was scared shitless.

"I'm sorry, you guys. I'm sorry I got us into this. Whatever happens—"

The guard reappeared at the car window. He did not have our passports or his clipboard.

"*Treba da se date dole iz masina!*" He barked. He gripped the windowsill with one hand and jerked his other thumb in the direction of the shack.

The other soldiers, who had been lounging on a bench in the shade since their inspection of the truck ten minutes earlier, began to stand up. The troops in the green troop carrier up the hill started to unload and scramble down the hill. The Tatra was still trapped behind the carrier on the narrow road.

"Is there some problem?" I asked. We had not seen the Yugoslavian police ask anyone else to get out of their cars. Even the truck driver had been allowed to remain in his cab while the guards searched his truck. I was afraid the steering wheel would break off in my hands.

"*Treba da se date dole iz masina!*" He repeated more forcefully. The head guard turned to the guards in front of the car and shouted, "*Voiska! Pazite vrata!*" His tone of voice was emphatic. He reached inside the car and tried to find the door handle.

"*Ne manite ovu masinu da prede!*" He shouted. Immediately, two helmeted soldiers kneeled into combat position in front of the lowered semaphore, bayonet mounted Kalashnikovs aimed at us. Other soldiers approached both sides of the Mercedes. This was all wrong. Had the East Germans finally caught on and somehow alerted these guards to watch for us and not let us pass? Was that the reason for so many more troops than we had seen at any border yet, even at the Wall?

Suddenly my eye caught a movement in the side view mirror. The black sedan pulled out of line from behind the army truck and began to speed up on the edge of the dirt road, raising fountains of dust behind it as it lurched along the uneven surface. The spinning wheels spattered gravel against the cars still waiting in line. Now everybody seemed to be blowing their horns. The Tatra slid to a halt about ten meters behind us. The driver leapt out. The tall, thin, balding guy got out of the passenger side. Even in the heat, they were both still wearing leather coats. The head guard, still grasping our doorsill, turned his head and looked at the commotion on the road behind us. As they ran toward us, I recognized, in one terrible instant, where I had first seen the heavy-set, black-haired guy.

"Son of a bitch," I shouted. "Look back there! Those are the bastards who have been following us!"

Johann turned around, an expression of recognition on his face. "*Mein Gott!* You are right! This man is from Berlin!"

The black haired driver was the bartender from the gloomy *gaststätte* Johann had taken us to in Berlin. They were the same two guys who'd stood at the nearby table on the veranda at Bratislava and shoed the old flower lady away. The same ones who were watching us at the mineral baths in Karlovy Vary. The wide, swarthy goon with the monobrow was the one the Gypsy kid had whacked with the tire iron. So, they *had* been following us all along in that damned black Tatra. I *wasn't* being paranoid.

Were they *Stasi*? Had they somehow been in on our plan from the very beginning? Were they following Johann and Liesl to find out what else they could learn? Or had Louisa been right? Were they following Johann Volker and Liesl Schmidt, and had we been keeping barely one step ahead with Johann and Liesl Müeller? The possibilities were endless and more than I could work through in the fury of the moment. Unreasonably, I wished for the strength of Drago, for the brawny protection he had provided us in the forest, knowing full well that he would have been about as useful as a shotgun.

All at once, the enormity of our predicament hit me in the face like the heat wave from a blast furnace. Our minutes were numbered, never mind our days. Our entire escape plan, which I'd thought was going to be successful due to careful planning and sheer good luck, was crumbling down on us. The plan was a failure and we were about to be sent to prison or shot.

It occurred to me that we'd gotten this far only because we had been allowed to. Of course, everything had been much too easy. Our luck wasn't running out, it had run out the afternoon Blondie had shoved her fat fingers up my ass, and now the *Staatssicherheit* was not about to let us go. Images of dead people, shot trying to escape, flooded into my head. Photos from the little museum across from Checkpoint Charlie flashed through my mind. I pictured photographs of our bullet-ridden corpses lying in the blood-soaked dust of southern Yugoslavia, on those walls next to the photo of Peter Fechter. Liesl started to cry quietly behind me. The head guard gripped the doorsill with both hands, his knuckles white, his face red. I thought he would rip the door off. He shouted again for us to get out of the car. The other guards were running toward us. The East German agents were back in their car. Everything was happening very fast, in slow motion.

We were dead.

"Hang on!" I shouted. I stomped the gas pedal to the floor and the powerful Mercedes Benz 280SE luxury sedan leaped forward. The head guard fell backwards, spun around by his grip on our door, still shouting orders. The rear tires spun, shooting dirt and pebbles everywhere. I almost hit the two soldiers in front of us who, at the last possible moment, jumped out of our way. We crashed through the wooden semaphore gate and sent it sliding and bouncing off to the side. A burst of machine gun fire shattered the rear window. Shards of glass blew into the car. The Mercedes quickly filled with debris and noise and the smell of gunpowder. I cranked the wheel to the left and then the right, trying to throw up dust. I could hardly see through the cloud around us.

"Get down!" I yelled. I pulled Lou toward me, crushing her head into the leather seat. I leaned over on top of her until I could barely peer over the dashboard. Behind us, I heard shouts and the deafening sound of gunfire from a dozen automatic guns. The Greek border lay ahead, the length of a football field away. I leaned on the horn and raised my head for a quick glance into the rear view mirror.

The chrome bumper of the black Tatra emerged from the brown haze.

"Motherfucker!" I shouted. "Stay down! Hang on to something!" I pressed against the seat and stomped on the brake pedal with both feet. We skidded. I braced, waiting for the Tatra to crash into us. We rocketed forward from the impact. I let off the brake and accelerated full-throttle toward the Greek border. I prayed that German engineering was better than Czech. I continued blasting away on the horn, not slowing down, not intending to stop until we were well inside Greece. There was no sign of the black sedan in the rearview mirror. I couldn't see anything in the dust behind us. The crackle of gunfire faded in the distance.

The noise and commotion alerted the Greeks, one of whom was positioned in the middle of the road flapping his arms. I waved him out of the way with my arm out the window. When he saw I wasn't going to stop, he dove off the road. I smashed the Mercedes through the second barricade in as many minutes and I didn't let up on the gas until we were at least a hundred meters past the Greek border. Finally, I coasted to a stop, forced myself to unwrap my fingers from the steering wheel, and turned the ignition switch off. My passengers slowly rose up and peeked out through the jagged glass.

"You're bleeding," Lou said. "Are you OK?" She groped in the glove box for some napkins.

"By God, I reckon we made it," Simon said. He fumbled a cigarette to his mouth.

In the back seat, Johann had his arms wrapped around Liesl, who was sobbing into his chest. All three of them were covered with dust and glass splinters.

My teeth chattered. My heart pounded and my ears rang painfully from the staccato sound of the Kalashnikov AK-47s. The acrid smell of cordite burned in my nose. I could feel adrenaline still flooding through my bloodstream. My neck was already beginning to stiffen from the impact of the Tatra. My hand came away bloody and I guessed that some of the shattered rear window had passed the headrest and cut me. The smell of urine mixed with the smell of cordite; someone had pissed in the car but I didn't know whom. I felt my crotch; it was dry. I got out of the Mercedes and saw three cars racing toward us out of the dust, red lights flashing and sirens wailing. I trembled so badly I could hardly stand up and grabbed at the door handle for support. I squinted at the onrushing cars and then put my arms in the air and smiled.

All three bore Greek license plates.

Epilogue

I August — Sifnos (Greece)

———✦✦✦✦✦✦✦✦✦✦———

In the late afternoon sun, Lou and I lay on the beach of Sifnos. Only twice a week did that tiny island have contact with the rest of the planet. We—unlikely heroes—had chosen this isolated dot on the map for exactly that reason: its remoteness.

Sifnos didn't have the panache of Crete or Nikonos or, for that matter, Ibiza or Mallorca. On most Tuesdays and Fridays, a tramp ferry arrived from the mainland with supplies for the residents, a couple of drums of gasoline for the island's sole car, a taxi, and occasionally stray tourists. That's what we were, stray tourists, just as we'd been before our sojourn to Berlin several weeks earlier. Deck passage being all that was available, that was how we'd arrived. It seemed appropriate that our mode of transportation was once again proletarian. There was no American Express on Sifnos and we didn't know how long we would be staying.

We'd been assured that the rented Mercedes Benz 280SE, currently in the custody of the police in Thessaloniki, would be returned to the office of the car rental agency in Athens. The insurance I'd thought was so over-priced when we were obliged to purchase it had turned out to be worthwhile. One sheep, two border gates, and more Kalashnikovs than I'd had time to count had totaled the car. In spite of how new and expensive it was, I doubted the Mercedes could be fixed. Besides some possible propaganda value, I couldn't imagine any further use for it.

"What do you reckon they'll do with the car?" Simon had asked that night at dinner.

"I dunno. Maybe ship it back to that museum in Berlin and put it next to the submarine and the hot air balloon. The *Haus am Checkpoint Charlie*."

"Rather fitting, I should think. What better symbol of the west could there be than a Mercedes Benz?"

"Yes," I answered. "I like the image of that big, strong car crashing through traffic jams of Trabants and sheep and bicycles to rescue Johann and Liesl."

The August sun hammered down, pinning us to the sand with a rain of hot nails. There weren't many other people on the beach. The afternoon heat had driven most sensible Greeks inside their whitewashed homes, which were cooler by virtue of their thick walls and slightly higher elevation from sea level. A soft breeze rippled over the Aegean surface and flowed through the glassless portals of the village houses, passing over the beach itself, leaving us to bake in almost complete stillness.

Simon had returned to England. The British Embassy in Athens would only issue him a short-term, temporary passport so he'd gone home to get a permanent replacement and also to have a long overdue visit with his family in Liverpool.

"I've been on the Continent for the best part of two years and I do miss me mum and me brothers and sisters. Whilst I'm waiting for my passport in any case, I expect I'll pop up to see them."

"I bet she'll be glad to see you're all in one piece," I said. The three of us were standing on the wharf in Piraeus, waiting for our boat to leave. My mind had been a couple of thousand miles away, on another beach, thinking of another mother. "Think you'll stay there or come back over?"

"I reckon I don't know, mate." There was a wry smile on his face. "Don't know if I'd tell you anyway. Traveling with you is a bit dicey."

"Never a dull moment," I said. "What was that famous line? 'All I can promise you is blood, sweat, toil, and tears'." We embraced, awkwardly, for a moment, and then Simon walked back up the dock. I watched until he vanished into the crowd.

"I'll miss him," I said to Lou. "He's a good traveling companion."

Lou didn't say anything, but laced her fingers through mine. The dockhands were beginning to cast off the lines holding our boat to the wharf. It was time to board.

Lou and I had come to this tiny Greek atoll on the Tuesday run from Piraeus. We'd been issued replacement passports from the American Embassy in Athens and there had been a wire transfer of money waiting for Lou at American Express. She had telephoned her father from Thessaloniki as quickly as she could once we'd settled in. After being questioned for hours by Greek, German, and American officials, we'd finally been turned loose.

When the news of our daring dash across east Europe reached the German Embassy, they'd immediately sent a car with diplomatic plates north to Thessaloniki to fetch us. We were, temporarily, stateless refugees, so the arrival of the long, black Mercedes 600 Limousine had been a welcome sight.

Johann and Liesl were still in the Greek capital, sorting out the details of their new life as refugees, political asylum seekers, or some as yet to be determined status. They were no longer in possession of their confiscated bogus West German passports but only their original East German ones, which I had neglected to destroy as I'd planned. They were telling the story of their unlikely escape through the flanks of the East Block to officials at the Embassy who, at least, spoke their native language.

The press reporters for the most part did not speak German, but our escapade still made the headlines. Photographs of the demolished Mercedes, including close-ups of bullet holes and the bloody fender, plastered the front page of every newspaper we saw, along side of pictures of Liesl and Johann. We managed to slip away just in time to avoid being caught up in the media excitement. It was doubtful we would have been recognized on the beach of Sifnos even if our pictures had been in the paper.

Now the Müellers would join the small, select collection of people who'd risked everything, including their lives, to swim, tunnel, float, buy their passage out of East Berlin, or crash borders in cars to be free. Our part in that adventure was finished.

None of us thought we could be of any further help to Johann and Liesl, who were navigating the bureaucracy. Indeed, being not just Germans, but East Germans, they'd had more experience with government officialdom and bureaucratic red tape than the rest of us combined. For Lou and me, it was a relief to escape the paparazzi, some of whom had seemingly been 'on' this story from the hundred-yard dash across no-man's-land between the Yugoslavian and Greek border to our arrival in Athens. The intensity of the past three weeks had left us all exhausted, depleted, and in need of psychic recharging. It was time to decompress.

We had somewhat vague plans to meet up with Johann and Liesl in a few weeks, either there on the island or back in Athens. They knew where we were. The total population of Sifnos was only about 300 people, so we wouldn't be too hard to find. Athens wasn't that large either, if you weren't Greek.

"Couldn't we have rented a bullet-proof car?" Simon's sense of humor had returned by the time we had dinner that first night; we were all getting back to normal, whatever that meant. He'd located a small Greek café and soon our table was covered with spanikopita, souvlaki, and lamb dolmas. The waiter brought several bottles of Retsina along with the food and hovered around the table, making a big deal of filling our glasses, and so on. We were not allowed to pay, so Louisa left a twenty-dollar bill as a tip.

The Greek immigration police had taken us from the border to Thessaloniki and towed the Mercedes along as well. The police had interrogated us for many hours, with the tone varying between official debriefing and joyful camaraderie. We had left the police station only after we promised not to leave town for a day or so.

We couldn't have slipped quietly into Thessaloniki if we'd wanted to. Our arrival in the main square caused quite a commotion. Within minutes curious onlookers, including several uniformed policemen, surrounded the bullet-riddled Mercedes.

Mara was not there. Somewhere along the way, my expectation that she would have made her way through Italy and be in Thessaloniki had gradually changed to hope that she had chosen another direction for herself. There'd been a postcard of the Mona Lisa waiting for me at the Post Office General Delivery.

Hey, Slick,

Hope you get this 'cause it'll mean you got to Athens without getting killed. We had some good times (remember hotel in A'dam?) got to see lots of neat shit together, but I couldn't do this trip with you. I'm on my way south, Spain??? You always said I should go to the Prado—maybe that's what I'll do. Maybe not. Hope you & Lou are well. Simon, too. Does he like Greek food, or has he found an Italian place there to get his pasta? Ha ha. Out of space.

Love, Mara

She'd gone her own way and although I had a stateside address for Miriam Liebowitz, I had no idea where on the Continent Mara might be. The card carried a French postage stamp, but the Paris postmark was almost two weeks old. She could be anywhere. I handed the card to Lou, who read it and gave it back without saying a word.

Louisa had rented us a room in a nice hotel on the beach in Thessaloniki with large windows facing the ocean. She'd insisted on inspecting the room before she paid, making sure we had one large bed instead of two smaller ones. Our room was on the corner of the building; the walls fell away out of view on both sides. I stood on the porch smoking a tightly-rolled Drum. In the dusk, a late returning fishing boat twinkled its way across the flat water toward port. Louisa stepped up behind me, wrapped her arms around my stomach and fumbled with my belt buckle.

"I want this to be perfect," she said to me. "Waited way too long for it to be anything else."

That first night we were together was wonderful and not nearly long enough to exhaust our pent up passion. In the single-digit hours before dawn, it became clear to me that Lou had never been ambivalent about us. She was waiting to see if my separation from Mara was permanent or only temporary. For her, I was all or nothing; she would never, she said, be satisfied with only part of me.

As I stood on our balcony in the warm breeze, I basked in that sweet glow, hoping that our future together would have many pillows in many rooms decorated with long, golden hairs. Perhaps, someday, maybe only one pillow in one room....

And who could have anticipated that our purposeful meandering down the Dalmatian Coast would climax in a fusillade of gunfire from a dozen AK-47s and a harrowing dash from the edge of Communism across a hundred yards of no man's land to freedom in the west? We'd passed the tighter borders from East Germany into Czechoslovakia, from Czechoslovakia into Hungary, and from Hungary into Yugoslavia. We'd skirted around Stalinist Albania because we had to. It was strangely ironic that the guards at the least restrictive national boundary, the supposedly open border of southern Yugoslavia, should be the ones to detect the counterfeit passports. That we had crashed the border *and* avoided capture by the East German agents was a miracle.

"I reckon it's bloody fortunate we were only five," Simon had said, mouth full of dolmas. "T'would have been rather snug in that car with six."

"Lucky Mara wasn't along," Louisa said. She gazed directly into my eyes, her serious expression betrayed only by that faint upturning at the corners of her mouth.

"Mara?" I asked. "Mara who?"

"That's the tic, mate. Mara who." Simon stood up and scanned the room for the waiter.

Louisa grabbed my wrist under the table. "Don't you *dare* do it that way," she hissed, just as Simon sat back down.

"Good thing we rented that Mercedes, too. I don't think we would have made it in a Trabant, or even a Volkswagen," I said. Lou was right, as she was about almost everything. Mara deserved more than 'Mara who?'

I wanted to change the subject. "Nobody even got hurt bad." As it was, none of us had needed to spend so much as a single night in the hospital. After being treated for various bruises and bumps and some cuts from flying glass, we'd been released into the glare of the hot Greek sun, the flashbulbs of the paparazzi, and the police.

Basking had become roasting in the searing sunshine, each of us with our own thoughts, not talking much, and turning often as if we were on spits. Every once in a while, one of us slowly rose up and waded into the surf to cool off. The sting of the salt in the wounds on my neck was a small price to pay for the welcome chill of the water. In between swims, I rested, oozing sweat into the sand, reflecting on the previous two years of my life, on the run in Europe.

"Are you happy?" Lou interrupted my meditation.

"Happy? I guess so. How do you mean?"

"Here. Now. Are you happy?"

"The sun is plenty hot and the water is cool. The sand isn't as nice as home, though. You can't build sandcastles with these pebbles." I thought of surfers in wetsuits in Carmel Bay and the clean white beach. It wasn't the right answer, and I knew it.

"D'you miss Carmel? Never been there, you know."

I raised myself on one elbow and visored my eyes with my other hand. I made a show of scanning the beach. We were alone. I looked down at the long, tan woman with straight, golden hair lying beside me. A month ago, I had not believed in miracles, but now they were beginning to pile up all around me.

"Just between you and me, I guess I do." There was a long pause. A fishing boat bobbed into view from around the rocky point, nets hanging from its spires. I lay back on the towel and shut my eyes. The bare sun was a dull red haze through my eyelids. I could have been back in Monterey.

"I'd like to show it to you."

Louisa snuggled up next to me with her lips so close to my ear that I felt more than heard her say, "I'd like that, David."

Lou lay next to me on the beach, dozing, her fingers laced through mine. That first night in Thessaloniki when we were truly together, she told me that she never for a single minute considered not coming with us. I wanted more than anything to believe her, to trust that from the moment Mara left me in Dam Square, Lou had every intention of going all the way to Greece, whatever the risk. Although I knew attempting to smuggle Johann and Liesl out of East Berlin was a crazy and dangerous idea, it had never really seemed real to me, still invincible at nineteen, that we might have gotten ourselves arrested or worse along the way.

I shuddered as a chill shivered along my back, and I realized I cared more about having exposed this woman to such danger with this fool-hardy adventure than I cared about my own safety. And that, for me, in the summer of 1966, was as good a definition of being in love as any I'd ever heard.

Lou's body was much too red from the sun. The olive oil we'd slath-ered ourselves in didn't offer much protection, but, lacking real suntan oil, it's all we had.

"This is fine," Lou had said with a grin. "We'll smell like dolmas."

Slowly freeing my fingers from hers, I stood up and shook the sand out of my towel. I bent over and gently covered her up. As my shadow crossed her face, she opened her eyes and stretched her arms and legs. When I stood again, sunlight ignited the flecks of fire in her blue pupils and Lou looked into me as deeply as anyone ever had.

"Nothing in my life will ever be as pure as this moment, right here, right now."

"Lou," I said, "I feel exactly the same way. I, I...." There were no more words I could add.

I paused for a moment and watched as she touched her pursed lips with her finger and then her faint smile became full, turning up the cor-ners of her mouth and forming dimples in both cheeks. I smiled back, waited until her eyes closed, and then I walked into the clear, blue Aegean Sea.

✦✦✦✦

What Were They Saying?

BERLIN

Was ist das hier?
What is this?

Achtung!
Attention!

Ich nicht sprechen Deutsch.
I don't speak German.

Bitte
Please

Ja, mein Kommandant.
Yes, Sir. (Yes, my Commander.)

Schnell! Schnell!
Quickly! Quickly!

Seid Still!
Be quiet! (Do not speak!)

Du hast es nicht gefunden.
You have not found anything.

Ich traue denen nicht!
I do not trust them!

Wir müssen sie gehen lassen. Wir dürfen keinen internationalen Zwischenfall riskieren.
We must release them. We cannot risk an international incident.

Jawohl, mein Kommandant.
Yes, Sir!

Auf Wiedersehen.
Good-bye.

Gaststätte
Restaurant or pub

Wieful cost eine Zimmer?
How much would a room cost?

Eine Zimmer mit Dusche.
A room with a shower.

ZIMMER FREI
VACANCY (ROOM FREE)

Ich bin ein Berliner.
I am a Berliner.

Die Mauer
The Wall

Das ist Berliner Weisse.
This is Berliner Weisse (a local beer).

ein Glas Wasser, bitte.
a glass of water, please.

Was möchtest du?
What do you want?

What Were They Saying?

Nichts
Nothing

Ich bin kein Künstler.
I am not an artist.

Warte! Warte, bitte!
Wait! Wait, please!

Ostmark? Haben Sie Ostmark?
East German marks? Have you (got any) East German marks?

Deutsche marks, bitte.
West German marks, please.

NEIN!
NO!

Guten Tag.
Hello. (Or, Good day).

Ich bin Johann.
My name is Johann.

Wir sahen dich gestern hier. Du bist weg gelaufen. Gestern Abend unterhielten wir uns darüber und wollten zurüch kommen um dich zu finden.
We saw you here yesterday. You ran away. Last evening, we talked about this and we wanted to come back and find you.

Ah, Sie sprechen Deutsch.
Oh, you speak German.

Ich bin in München geboren, bin aber nun ein amerikanischer Bürger.
I was born in Munich but I am an American citizen now.

Willst du meinen Ausweis sehen?
Would you like to see my passport?

Er kam vom Regen in die Traufe.
He came from the rain into the tub.

Polizei
Police

die Kindesannahme
Adoption Agency

Auf Wiedersehen
Goodbye

abspeichern
memorize

Danke vielmals.
Thanks a lot.

Mein Gott.
My God.

Druckerzeugnis.
Printed material.

Liebchen
Sweetheart

Kommen Sie mit mir.
Come with me.

Ausziehen!
Get undressed!

Was ist das hier?
What is this here?

COPENHAGEN

Du vil vide hvor man kan købe forfalskede tyske pas?
You want to know where you can buy two counterfeit German passports?

Hvad skal du med dem?
Why do you want them?

Det er sådan. Vi har mødt nogle mennesker i øst Berlin, et par som gerne vil til vesten.
It is for this reason. We met some people in East Berlin, a couple, who would like to come to the West.

Langeline. den Lille Havfrue?
The waterfront area of Copenhagen and the little mermaid?

Hej. Kan jeg haelpe dig?
Yes. Can I help you?

Mange tak.
Many thanks.

Farvel så laenge.
Good-bye until later.

Pölser.
A Danish variety of hot dog.

BERLIN

Meine Freundin
my friend

Ja? Wer ist da?
Yes? Who is there?

Polizei! Öffnen Sie die Tür!
Police! Open the door!

Einen Moment bitte. Ich bin unbekleidet.
Just a moment, please. I am undressed.

Die linke Hand weiss nicht was die rechte Hand tut.
The right hand doesn't know what the left hand is doing.

CZECHOSLOVAKIA

Die Pässe, bitte.
Passports, please.

Zweihundert marks.
Two hundred marks.

Da. Pivo?
Yes. Beer?

Und deine Mutter?
And your mother?

Trampen
Hitchhike

Meine Güte.
My goodness.

Máte pit pasù. Jste jenom tøi. Kde jsou tí ostatní, tí Muellerovci?
You have five passports. You are only three people. Where are these
others, these Müellers?

Kolik izeb chcete?
How many rooms do you want?

Alles ist gut.
Everything is good.

Gute Nacht
Good night

Schlaf gut.
Sleep well.

Kolik kvetin by ste chteli?
Would you like to buy some flowers?

Vystúpte si z auta, prosím.
Please get out of the car.

Kolko dní ste boli v Èeskoslovensku?
How many days were you in Czechoslovakia?

Drei Tagen in Czechoslovakia.
Three days in Czechoslovakia.

Sehr schön
Very beautiful

Mozno Karlové Vary. Bratislava asi nie. Vraciate sa k ludom z Èeskoslovensku?
Maybe Karlovy Vary. Bratislava maybe not. Are you returning to the
Peoples Republic of Czechoslovakia?

Máte èeské koruny?
Do you have any Czech crowns?

Nechajte si peniaze na vás návrat do Èeskoslovensku.
You will keep the money for a return to Czechoslovakia.

HUNGARY

Mi tortenik itt?
What is happening here?

Vám ellenorzés! Útlevél kontrol!
I demand to see your passports!

Figyelmesebben kénne vezetned és vigyáz a tehenekre és a birkákra.
You must drive more carefully and watch out for sheep and cows.

THE DALMATIAN COAST

Vecera I prenociste ce vas kostati 20 Florents po osobi.
Dinner and a bed will cost you 20 Florents each.

Ne
No

Schlafzimmer
Sleeping room (bedroom)

Ne, vodka e rusa! Mi ovde piemo slibovitu!
No, Vodka is Russian! Here, we drink Slivovitz!

Lupa, donesi cetir case.
Lupa, bring us four glasses.

Daitemi passport!
Give me your passports!

Treba da se date dole iz masina!
You must get out of the auto immediately!

Voiska! Pazite vrata!
Guards! Watch the gate!

Ne manite ovu masinu da prede!
Do not let this auto pass!